The

Pursuit

of

Other

Interests

ALSO BY JIM KOKORIS

The Rich Part of Life
Sister North

The Pursuit of Other Interests

JIM KOKORIS

ST. MARTIN'S PRESS 🐾 NEW YORK

THE PURSUIT OF OTHER INTERESTS. Copyright © 2009 by Jim Kokoris. All rights reserved. Printed in the United States of America. For information, address St. Martin's Press, 175 Fifth Avenue, New York, N. Y. 10010.

www.stmartins.com

Library of Congress Cataloging-in-Publication Data

Kokoris, Jim.
   The pursuit of other interests / Jim Kokoris. – 1st ed.
      p. cm.
   ISBN 978-0-312-36548-6
   1. Advertising executives–Fiction. 2. Corporate culture–Fiction. 3. Unemployed–Fiction. 4. Self-actualization (Psychology)–Fiction. I. Title.
   PS3611.O58P87 2009
   813'.6–dc22

2009019932

First Edition: November 2009

10 9 8 7 6 5 4 3 2 1

To Pat and George, without your

help this book wouldn't

have been possible.

The

Pursuit

of

Other

Interests

Chapter One

He was doing his breathing techniques when his heart stopped again. The purpose of the exercises was to lower his heart rate, but apparently he had mastered the technique so well, he was almost killing himself. Lying on his back in his bed, nothing beating inside of him, he waited for darkness and then the revealing white light. Instead he felt something kick in, felt life rush through him, an electric, hot current. He sat up gasping for air, his hands at his throat.

"Charlie?" Donna asked. Her eyes were closed and she seemed half asleep.

He coughed a little, and sucked in another deep breath. "I'm fine," he managed to whisper, although she hadn't asked how he was doing.

He had started the breathing exercises after returning from the agency's annual executive retreat for emerging thought-leaders held in a resort town in the Black Forest whose name he could never pronounce. The year before, the agency had been purchased by a German media conglomerate that firmly believed in training and career development for its key people.

One of the seminars was on "thought cleansing," and it was taught by a former monk who had written a book, *The Corporate Buddha*. The breathing exercises were a form of meditation and should ideally be performed while hooked up to an oxygen tank. Unfortunately, Donna wouldn't let him have an oxygen tank in bed, so he limited his routine to taking very deep breaths until he almost died.

He sat on the edge of the bed for a few minutes and waited for his heartbeat to return to what he felt was a normal pace, then went downstairs to the basement to do forty-five minutes on the treadmill. He ran ten-minute miles, an easier pace than usual. He was breaking in new orthotics for his feet and wanted to take it a bit slower. He also wanted to check his voice mail, which he couldn't do if he was running like a maniac.

While running, he reached for his headset, and carefully dialed his cell to check for messages. Surprisingly, there were only four. Three were inconsequential, but the last one was from Ursula in Berlin saying Helmut was coming to Chicago and wanted some time with him. Helmut was the chairman and founder of the media conglomerate, a complex man, both charming and abrupt, who did not suffer fools well.

Charlie considered calling her back, but decided to run another mile. He preferred to be at his desk with all his weapons handy when dealing with Berlin, not half naked on a treadmill. Besides, he had slept well, a rare occurrence, and wanted to keep going.

During his cool-down walk, he left several messages for his direct reports, reviewing the agenda for that day's staff huddle, prioritizing action items, and making recommendations for where to order in for lunch. He preferred the more human touch of voice mails over e-mails when communicating to his team. Besides, he couldn't use his BlackBerry while running on the treadmill. He had tried once and nearly fallen off.

After his run, he did some stomach crunches, then headed for the kitchen and breakfast: Cheerios with skim milk, topped with raisins, blueberries, flaxseed. Ten minutes later, he was upstairs in his home office checking e-mail. Not counting spam, he had only seventeen new messages, an unusually light number. He sent short responses, including one to Ursula about his schedule, then jumped into the shower, running the water as hot as possible.

Afterward, he stood dripping wet in front of the mirror, steam rising behind him, and took stock. Years ago, Charlie had the depressing revelation that it was impossible to look good naked after forty. Despite his best efforts, his body reinforced this conclusion. Though he was relieved to still have most of it, his once-black hair was more than a little sprinkled with salt. He also possessed a slight paunch, sagging shoulders, and only a hint of biceps. He comforted himself with the fact that he still looked fine with clothes on and, at fifty years old, he made a point of wearing as many clothes as possible.

While toweling off, he performed his morning mole check. He had detected a potential problem on his left shoulder (two weeks before he was pretty sure it was on his right shoulder) and had been carefully monitoring it. It was still in the pre-mole state, just a faint shadow, but he knew it was there and it worried him. Recently, a man in the creative department at the agency had been diagnosed with skin cancer on his foot and was forced to have a toe amputated. The specter of an amputation haunted Charlie, so he kept a close eye on this migrating mole. As soon as he felt the shadow was officially transitioning into something substantive, he would not hesitate; he would see a specialist.

When he finished in the bathroom, he walked over to his new humidifier and lowered his face into the rising jet of steam. The wet, moist air felt good and he took several deep, head-clearing breaths. While he had often slept with a humidifier on, he had recently become addicted to a new deluxe model, the Rain Forest Deuce, which offered twice the humidity. After only a few days, it seemed to be making a difference with his chronically aching sinuses, clearing out his cavities and generally making breathing easier. He deeply inhaled one last time, made a mental note to buy a smaller unit for business travel, then returned to the bathroom to dry his now-damp face.

When he reentered the room, he was startled to see Donna sitting up in bed, her arms folded in front of her, her eyes slightly open. Charlie could tell by the tilt of her head and the way she was breathing that she was still asleep. Throughout their marriage, she had been a turbulent sleeper. When they were younger, she frequently walked in her sleep. Once she had reached the alley behind the garage, and another time, wearing lingerie he had bought her, a neighbor's porch. Fortunately, her nocturnal activity had decreased over the years and was now limited to her sitting up in bed, or occasionally strolling about the room.

"Donna," he said soothingly, "go back to sleep." Sometimes this worked, sometimes it didn't.

This time it did. She gently lowered herself back down and onto her pillow.

He moved to the bed and looked down at his wife of thirty years. She was still pretty in a simple, natural way that other women probably envied, and that he probably took for granted. As he watched her sleep, her face calm, her eyes closed, he felt a sense of loss, and a sad shadow crept over him. He stood there and tried to make sense of it, but the feeling faded.

He pulled the sheet up and over her shoulder, then dressed quietly and went downstairs. As he waited for Angelo, his driver, he gazed out the window. The block was dark and quiet and still and he let the solitude wash over and hold him. He had been on the swim team in high school, a diver, and he likened this moment to standing on the board, arms at his side, while everything below him waited. He stood there wrapped in the stillness, until he heard Angelo pull up, the headlights of the town car straining against the dark. Then he picked up his briefcase and glanced down at his watch. For once, Angelo was right on time. It was four A.M.

Chapter Two

Charlie worked in advertising. It was what he had done for twenty-eight years. In his younger days he was in love with his chosen profession, thinking it inspiring, relevant, and even important. It was not a job, he thought, so much as it was a calling. It demanded his best efforts and he was happy to oblige. He came up on the creative side and spent long hours writing copy and later developing campaigns for mufflers, cookies, bagels, and cars. His work won awards, garnered praise, and for a long time that was enough.

While Charlie's love affair with advertising had cooled over the years—the hours, the client demands, and the competitiveness take a toll—he persevered, dutifully making his way up the ladder. Promotions came slowly, then quickly, and on the eve of his forty-ninth birthday Charlie found himself running one of the largest ad agencies in Chicago, an achievement that, at the time, he thought completed him.

His sense of satisfaction was tempered by the stress of the job. Heading up any large agency was a serious affair and the stakes were high; a loss of a key account could result in the loss of dozens of jobs, including his own. For the most part, however, Charlie felt he was up to the task, although there were moments he had his doubts.

After Angelo dropped him off, he took the elevator to the fortieth floor and allowed himself a brief stroll. It had been exactly one year since his promotion and he was feeling reflective. Despite mounting pressures, and the fact that business wasn't good and the economy was terrible, overall he thought he still enjoyed what he did. He certainly was a slave for the trappings of his job—the corner office with panoramic views of Lake Michigan, the overseas travel, the car service, the health club membership, and, of course, the pay. In particular, Charlie liked the agency's office: the sterile but elegant reception area with the marble floor and spiral staircase that led up to the creative department and down to accounting. He liked the artwork, German contemporary, with rivers and lakes and pastures, muted browns and greens, that lined the walls. And he liked the sense of order and purpose created by the row of cubicles that ran the length of the halls, the lunch area with the Ping-Pong table, the jukebox, the cappuccino bar, the Elvis Presley and James Dean wax figures, and the Idea Room, with its vaulted windows and solid oak circular table that he had personally selected.

Charlie particularly liked the way the office looked in the morning with the faint rays of orange light appearing over Lake Michigan, first a hint, then a burst, everything kissed in warmth and hopeful brightness. A new day dawning. A new day at work.

He had been recruited to the agency four years earlier and then been promoted to executive vice president, general manager, after Bob O'Malley left. Actually, Bob O'Malley died, leaving the company with dwindling revenues, poor morale—and Charlie temporarily in charge. (He was named interim general manager the day of O'Malley's funeral.) After what Charlie thought was a protracted five-month search, Helmut officially gave him the top job in a two-sentence e-mail: *We are removing interim from your title. Congratulations.* He printed the e-mail out and had it framed, even though he was disappointed that Helmet hadn't included an exclamation point after the word congratulations. He would have added the exclamation point. The occasion warranted one.

After he completed his lap around the floor, Charlie entered his own office, and took in the parquet floor, the Persian rug, the matching leather club chairs, the six-foot-tall gumball machine, and finally the framed portrait of Abraham Lincoln. He idolized Lincoln, drew strength from him. They both had had difficult if not impossible tasks: Lincoln's, to save the Union; Charlie, the Odor Eaters account.

He nodded once deferentially at the picture, and once again regretted his inability to finish one of the many Lincoln biographies he had bought. (Charlie had a short attention span and seldom, if ever, finished a book.) Then he slowly made his way to his desk and sat down. He had no desire to deal with Project Phoenix Rising . . . his plan for reorganizing the agency. He had been working halfheartedly on it for weeks, and dreaded what it involved. He was going to have to make some drastic changes, including realigning departments and cutting staff. Even though he knew these steps were necessary if the agency had any hope of returning to profitability, Charlie had been dragging his feet on finishing, much less implementing, the plan. He had no stomach for layoffs.

Before he plunged into Project Phoenix Rising, he decided to take another quick look at his now-infamous "fat" memo. Over the past year, Charlie had become increasingly concerned with the weight of his staff. He felt the agency employed a high number of obese or borderline obese people. During the last month, on two separate occasions, staffers had shattered chairs in client meetings, falling like loads of bricks onto the floor, scattering papers and files. In addition, a senior vice president who headed the largest account had taken to flying first-class (big seats) whenever she traveled because of her enormous size . . . a cost the firm had to absorb. In part, Charlie blamed their key clients—a fast-food fried chicken company, an international baker, and a cheese manufacturer, all of whom provided free samples or coupons to the agency on a regular basis. He primarily blamed O'Malley, though, who had made a point of hiring people as fat as, or fatter than, himself at every opportunity.

The "fat" memo (actually it was called Project Shape Up), which he had distributed more than two weeks prior, conveyed his growing concern over everyone's growing size. Among other things, it encouraged a collective effort to slim down through a series of 5K fun-runs, low-carb lunches, and nutritional seminars in which Charlie was not only willing to participate, but also to organize and underwrite. He knew he was dealing with a sensitive issue, but he also believed that the agency's fatness was hurting productivity and contributing to rising health insurance costs. Besides, he was sick of sitting in meetings where three out of four people were breathing heavily out of their mouths.

The memo had been poorly received by the staff. Julie, from human resources, reported that Aiesha, Margie, and Patty—longtime administrative assistants (and the fattest of the fat)—were considering legal action, claiming discrimination and harassment. Most everyone was insulted, even the skinny ones, by what they felt was the condescending nature of the memo. Julie thought Charlie should write a retraction and host a fried chicken lunch to make amends. Charlie refused to do either.

In the end, he chose to ignore the backlash but dropped the initiative. He would have to pick his battles. He would eventually get back to it, and hopefully address the issue more effectively before one of the floors collapsed.

He read the "fat" memo one last time, thinking it had been straightforward and, with the exception of one sentence, which was intended as a joke (*Elevator rides are getting downright dangerous!*), tactfully written. He then called up the Project Phoenix Rising document, looked it over, clicked it off, and called up the Summer Outing file.

The agency had been internally debating where to have their annual summer outing. The locations for the past outings had included a baseball park and an upscale horse racetrack.

The summer before the agency had hosted a picnic in a North Shore botanical garden and had invited families. This year—his first as head of the company—he was eager to make his mark and wanted to host the event at a local zoo. He thought this was an inspired, fun, and economical choice. Unfortunately, his decision was met with indifference, if not outright resistance, from the Summer Outing Committee, a group of aging, disgruntled administrative assistants who were lobbying for an elaborate dinner at an upscale restaurant with presumably steel-reinforced chairs. The ensuing stalemate had resulted in the passing of summer without an outing.

Since he had promised everyone the best summer outing in the history of the agency, he knew he had to take action. Consequently, he drafted a no-nonsense memo to the committee demanding that a date and a zoo (Chicago had two) be selected by the end of the week.

Charlie carefully read over the draft, fiddling with it here and there, adding lines about the agency's unique culture and the role the summer outing played in fostering it, before clicking back to the Project Phoenix Rising file. After staring at it helplessly, and feeling very much like a turtle on its back, legs hopelessly waving, he opened his Charlie's Book Club file.

A few months earlier, in an effort to improve morale, Charlie had started an agency book club. He thought this would be a unique way to bring all the departments together and build needed camaraderie. His first book, *The Corporate Buddha*, had been the wrong choice. No one read it and no one showed up for the discussion. For reasons he no longer remembered, he let Andre, their moronic associate creative director, pick the second book—*Rock You!*—which Charlie never got around to reading. It was about the life of a female rock band groupie. (Charlie learned, during the book club meeting, that if you took out all the sex scenes, nothing was left but punctuation.) Virtually the entire agency read this book, and was disgusted and outraged. The book discussion turned into a near riot and ended with Aiesha, Margie, and Patty walking out after threatening sexual harassment and legal action.

Charlie had decided to once again choose a book and, after starting with a list of thirty, had narrowed his choices down to either *Beloved,* by Toni Morrison, which had been an Oprah's Book Club selection, or *The Adventures of Huckleberry Finn,* which he thought an equally safe bet.

He was leaning toward Huck Finn, so he spent a half hour researching the book online, even taking a brief virtual tour of the Mississippi River. He then decided to table his final choice until the next day. He didn't want to rush his decision; he knew that the future of Charlie's Book Club hung in the balance. Besides, he had bigger issues to deal with. Heroically resisting the urge to sigh, he returned to the Project Phoenix Rising file.

Analytically speaking, the agency was in deep shit. They were hemorrhaging clients, costs were way out of control, and they had recently begun losing key people to competitors. The first page of the Project Phoenix Rising document included a list of issues (creative, staff, new business) that Helmut had identified as critical to the future of the agency, matters that needed immediate attention. Charlie studied the list, his eyes first burning, then blurring.

Staring at the computer screen, he was suddenly overwhelmed with the task at hand. "Fat" memos, book clubs, and summer outings were clearly not main concerns. Not for the first time, he felt over his head in his position and longed to be back on the creative side of things. He reread the list of critical issues, realized he could easily add another ten to it, then checked his watch. It was five forty-five in the morning. Then he put his head on his desk and closed his eyes.

He fell instantly into a dream about Huckleberry Finn. He was short and freckled and was pushing a raft made of logs into a fast-flowing brown river.

"Storm a-comin'," Huck said.

"Take me with you, Huckleberry," Charlie said. He glanced over his shoulder. The landscape was rocky and barren. He knew something terrible was out there, though. Something was coming just over the hill.

"Take me with you down the river," Charlie said. The wind was picking up. "I want to leave. I need to go."

He peered over his shoulder again and this time saw Aiesha, Margie, and Patty trotting down the hill toward him, waving pieces of fried chicken threateningly over their heads.

"I have to go now!" Charlie shouted at Huckleberry, but Huck had pushed off from the shore and was already drifting away. He pointed an oar past Charlie, at the approaching, thundering women.

"Wait! Please!"

"They'll swamp the raft," Huckleberry yelled as he disappeared into a mist Charlie had not seen coming.

"Please," Charlie yelled over and over. "Please." But Huck was gone and the mist was everywhere.

Georgia, Charlie's assistant, was frantic.

"Charlie Baker, you wake up now. You get up!"

"What? What are you doing?"

She heaved him upright in his chair. "You can't be doing this!"

"I'm not doing anything. Can we please ratchet down the emotions?"

"You sleeping on the job, Charlie! People see you like that, sleeping, what they going to think?"

Georgia was a short, stout black woman of indeterminate age. She had been Charlie's assistant at the old agency and had followed him to the new agency after his promotion.

"You get in to work too early," Georgia said. She dusted off his shoulders for some reason with her hand.

"What time is it?" Charlie rubbed his face.

"Nine o'clock."

"Nine o'clock?" This shocked him. He had been asleep for three hours.

"Helmut was looking for you. He's here."

"What do you mean? What are you talking about?"

"Helmut was here!"

Charlie stopped breathing. "Helmut? Helmut is here, in Chicago? Already? When?"

"About one minute ago. About sixty seconds ago."

"What do you mean, here? Where was he?" Charlie's voice was rising.

Georgia's eyes grew wider. "Here, Charlie. He was right here in your office." She whispered this last sentence.

"My *office*? You mean, here?"

"He just walked past me and opened the door."

The image of Helmut marching into his office like it was the Sudetenland and watching him sleep was too much for Charlie. He felt one of his arms tingle, a precursor to numbness. "You mean he just came in here? Did he see me?"

"Well, he was right here, standing right here." She pointed to the floor.

"But did he see me sleeping?"

Georgia nodded frantically and began wringing her hands. "There was no way he could miss you. He just walked in. I couldn't stop him."

"Why didn't you wake me?"

"I tried. I said your name, I said, Charlie, Charlie, you know, to wake you, but you kept right on sleeping. I didn't want to yell. I didn't think that would be appropriate."

Charlie clutched his heart, then pounded his desk with a fist. "This is unbelievable. Just. Unbelievable!" He pounded again. "What was his reaction? Did he say anything?"

"No, he just, you know, watched you sleep for a while."

"A while?"

"Then he took a picture of you, you know, with his cell phone, and left."

"What?"

"He said that he would call you after you woke up. He told me to tell you to wait here for him."

"Wait here for him." Charlie felt an unexpected and sudden flash of anger and indignity. He had nothing to hide from Helmut, had nothing to be ashamed of. "Does he know how hard I work? Does he know I get four hours of sleep a night? Does he?"

Georgia was confused. She continued to wring her hands. "I'm not sure. Well, I don't know. That didn't really come up."

"Does he know that I haven't had a weekend off in six months, that I haven't had a vacation since I came to this place? Does he know that . . . that I'm getting . . . a mole? Does he know that?"

"A mole?"

"Yes. A mole!"

"You have a mole?"

"Yes!"

"Where?"

Charlie paused. He wasn't sure where the mole was. "It's . . . it's migrating. Moving."

"You have a mole that moves?"

"It's a . . . just forget it, I don't want to get into it now. It's too serious." He took another deep breath, and tried to remember if Lincoln, in his years as President, had ever been caught sleeping at his desk, and if so, what his response had been. "Why do you think he took a picture?"

"I don't know, Charlie, he said something, I think it was in German, I couldn't be sure. Plus you were snoring, so I couldn't hear that well."

"Snoring! Jesus!" Charlie grabbed at his heart and took more deep breaths. "Listen, where is he now? Helmut? Just where did he go?"

"Helmut? He's down with Mr. Marken."

"Marken!" Charlie hissed this name. Marken was the chief financial officer, a rigid man with yellow teeth who was constantly harping over the dwindling revenue and spiraling costs. After O'Malley died, he had been Charlie's rival for the top spot and had made a point of making his life miserable every one of the past twelve months by plotting and conspiring against him. This was a worst-case scenario.

"Georgia, close the door," he whispered. By this point, Charlie had lost total feeling in his arm.

"It is closed."

"Georgia, I think I'm having a heart attack."

13

"A heart attack?" Georgia's eyes suddenly encompassed most of her face. She wrung her hands some more. "Oh, my God, Charlie Baker."

"I can feel it in my arm."

She looked terrified. "Your *arm* is having a heart attack?"

"It starts in your arm and makes its way over."

"How much time before it gets to your heart?"

"Minutes, seconds, Jesus, God, I don't know!"

Georgia made a move for the door. "I'm calling an ambulance."

"Wait! Don't! Don't call an ambulance! Do not! I don't have time to go to the hospital. Please just don't."

Georgia stared at him and considered the situation. "You want me to sit with you again, Charlie?" She asked this quietly.

He feebly nodded. Georgia pulled up a chair and sat across from his desk.

They didn't say anything. Charlie looked out the window. "I don't want to end up like O'Malley," he said finally.

Georgia appeared confused. "What do you mean?"

"It killed him. The job. The stress killed him."

Georgia was quiet again. "But Mr. O'Malley was struck by lightning."

Charlie continued to rub his arm, then he said, "He was worn down by the stress. If he had been in better shape, if he hadn't been *beaten down*, he might have withstood the bolt."

"But Angelo said Mr. O'Malley blew up. One of his arms ended up in a tree."

"I don't give a shit what Angelo says, okay? What is he, a doctor? They teach medicine at the limo academy? And for the record, it didn't end up in a tree, okay? I'm sick of hearing that. That's a rumor. That's ... that's myth! Everything was still attached. I saw photos. He was just a little red, that's all. And bald."

"Bald?"

"Yes, bald. Big deal."

Georgia sat back and shook her head. "He didn't seem stressed. He was always happy, you know, positive-like."

"Yeah, well, he was drunk all the time. That's why he was positive-like. Anyone can be positive-like after a case of Jim Beam."

"He didn't drink that much. Didn't drink much at all. Besides, a stiff drink won't hurt you. Loosen you up a little. A drink once in a while can help you deal with things. Make you less tense, you know . . . less uptight."

Charlie stopped rubbing his arm. "You think I'm uptight? Is that what you're saying?"

Georgia shrugged and looked off to the side. "I didn't say that."

"You were implying that."

"I wasn't implying anything."

"Yes, you were. I know when things are being implied. I'm very good at that. You were implying that I'm uptight."

Georgia sighed. "I don't want to get started with you today, Charlie Baker. I just do not."

"Is that what everyone is saying about me? Are they saying I'm uptight?"

Georgia pretended to pick at something on her skirt, before smoothing it with one hand. "I don't listen to what people say. I'm too busy. I got things to do. I spend all day running around here."

Charlie swiveled in his chair and looked back out the window. Michigan Avenue had come to life with buses, cabs, cars, clusters of pedestrians waiting at corners. It was a sunny and warm fall morning. As he stared down at this scene, the world seemed an orderly and rational place.

"You know, Charlie, if you don't want to drink, maybe you should pray once in a while. That's what I do."

He looked at Georgia again.

"Just a little prayer. Can't hurt, Charlie. That's the thing about praying, it can never hurt."

"Pray."

"Just a small one."

Georgia's recommendation to both drink and pray was doing nothing for Charlie's mood. "Let me ask you something here," he said. "And I need you to be perfectly honest, perfectly open. Do people hate me?"

Georgia looked uncomfortable. She cleared her throat and looked down at the floor. "Everyone likes you."

"That's very nice of you to say that, but I suspect that's not true. People hate me here. I can feel it. No one ever talks to me, or says hello to me in the halls."

"That's not true. People say hello."

"Yeah, well, that's all they say. Listen, what I need to know is who specifically hates me. Who the primary haters are. Who is anti-Charlie? I need names."

Georgia looked up. She was thinking hard. "Most people like you some of the time," she said.

It was Charlie's turn to think hard. He tried to repeat what she said, but gave up. "I'm not sure what that means. What do you mean?"

"I'm just saying that sometimes you're nice, quiet Charlie, and other times . . . you know."

"No, I don't know. What—other times I'm not nice and quiet?" He shouted this.

"Other times, you know, you're like, well, you know . . . crazy. A little."

"Crazy? What do you mean, crazy?"

"Just crazy, you know . . . excitable-like."

"Excitable and crazy are two completely different things. They have completely different definitions. They're not even close to meaning the same thing. Which is it?" He slammed the top of his desk with his hand. "Crazy or excitable? It's important that I know this. It's critical."

"Well, then crazy. You know, one minute you're nice and calm and thoughtful and smart and say nice, you know, intelligent things, smart things, insightful things, quiet-like. And the next time, you're running around like, well, like your hair's on fire."

"Like my hair's on fire." He thoughtfully repeated this. "Interesting. Very interesting. Is that the perception of the office? Quiet Charlie, Crazy Charlie?"

"More like Nice Charlie, Crazy Charlie. You're never really quiet. I mean, that quiet."

"Well, that's very interesting," he said again. "Very interesting." He worked hard to control himself even though he wanted to scream that he wasn't crazy, that this goddamn job with all these goddamn fat asses was making him crazy. He swallowed, did some deep breathing, shook his numbing arm. He felt enraged and hopeless. Then he felt impossibly overwhelmed and slumped forward in his chair. "Things aren't going very good here, are they?" he asked. "Tell me the truth. Things are going to hell, aren't they?"

Georgia shrugged again.

"What am I doing wrong? What do you think it is? Am I a bad guy?"

"I wouldn't work with you if you were."

"Then why does everyone hate me? Why do all those secretaries hate me? Aiesha and Patty and all of them? They practically hiss every time I walk by."

"Don't worry about them. They just miss Mr. O'Malley, that's all. We all do."

"Well, I'm not him, okay? I'm sorry he blew up or whatever the hell happened to him. I'm sorry I didn't martyr myself by deciding to play golf in a hurricane. You know, people forget that I was supposed to be part of that foursome. Angelo took my place. I was supposed to be there! *In Bermuda!* My flight was canceled! That bolt could have hit me. Me! No one gives a shit about that. No one ever remembers that. All I hear about is O'Malley, O'Malley, O'Malley!" He sat back and shook his head. "You know, it's hard to do this job when everyone is against you."

"Everyone isn't against you, Charlie."

"I have no allies here, no support, no friends. Zero, nothing, nada. I'm flying alone here. Alone."

"That's not true," Georgia said. "You have me."

Charlie swallowed, then gazed out the window again, focusing on the top of a bus as it inched its way through traffic some forty stories below. Georgia's comment made him feel like crying.

"You just having a bad stretch, that's all," Georgia said. "You had them before. Remember when we lost the Nike account? At the old agency?"

"That was bad."

"But you came right back and got the bagel account."

"And it was bigger than the Nike account. Twice as big."

"Everyone else was giving up, but you kept your head and brought in new business and all those awards you won."

"Two Effies. And we almost won at Cannes, for the Bagel Man campaign."

"Those commercials were funny. I would see them and I would laugh and tell my kids, that's my boss's idea."

"Those were funny spots. I came up with that campaign one night by myself in a hotel bar in Pittsburgh."

"I know. The Westin William Penn. And you worked all night on them."

"I did."

"And no one could believe you could get President Clinton to do that."

"It was Bob Dole. He was a senator. I don't even know if he's still alive."

"And we got the business and you saved everyone's job."

"I did."

"You did."

They were both quiet. Charlie didn't feel like crying anymore.

"Those were some fun times. We had some fun back then," Georgia said.

"They were fun, I guess."

Georgia smiled, her face relaxing. "You feeling better now, Charlie?"

"A little, yes, thank you."

"Heart attack gone?"

"For now." He gave a short smile back and stared at his computer. "Well, I'm not going to wait around all day for Helmut. What time is the staff huddle again?" he asked, even though he already knew. The huddle was always ten o'clock on Monday morning.

"It's canceled."

He squinted with confusion at Georgia. "Canceled? Who canceled it? It's my meeting."

"Mr. Marken canceled it."

"Marken? He can't cancel it! It's my meeting. He can't cancel it. Marken reports to me."

"He sent everyone an e-mail this morning saying it was canceled."

Charlie quickly swung back to his computer and checked his e-mail.

"I didn't get any message."

Georgia squirmed in her chair. "Well, maybe he just forgot."

Charlie stood up. "He doesn't forget anything. Where is he?"

"Still in his office, I guess. With Helmut."

He sat down again. Then he stood back up. "Well, this is bullshit. What are they doing in there? I mean, just what the hell are they doing?" He pounded the desk for a third time that morning. Georgia stood up.

"Where are you going?" she asked.

Charlie was standing perfectly still when she asked this. He really hadn't planned on going anywhere. But he realized then that he had to go see Marken and Helmut. His heart raced.

"I'm going to go see them."

"You are?"

"Yes." He moved quickly around the desk and headed for the door. When he placed his hand on the doorknob, he turned one last time to Georgia. "Tell everyone our staff huddle is back to the original time." He said this authoritatively and in a deep voice.

Georgia, eyes wide, swallowed.

When he opened the door, a tall, thin man was standing there. He was wearing an ugly, off-white short-sleeve shirt and a narrow black tie. Charlie had never seen the man before, so he had no way of knowing that he was staring directly into the face of his future.

"Mr. Baker?" he asked. He had a soft voice tinted with a British accent.

"Who are you?"

"I'm Ned Meyers."

Charlie stood there looking at him. He assumed he was from the mailroom.

"I'm here to answer any questions you may have and to help you with the transition."

When Charlie didn't respond, he continued, "I'm from Rogers & Newman." He said this in a way that assumed some understanding.

"Who?" The name sounded vaguely familiar.

The man searched Charlie's face with intense brown eyes, then looked embarrassed, his cheeks splotching red. He quickly checked his watch, mumbled incoherently, and disappeared down the hall in a lope.

Charlie glanced back at Georgia, who was standing silently by his desk, eyes still huge in what looked like fear.

"Who was that?" he asked. But at that moment his phone rang, and she answered it.

"It's Helmut," she said, her voice just above a whisper. Her face looked resigned. "He's in Mr. Marken's office. He wants to see you, Charlie. He wants to see you right now."

Chapter Three

Helmut had a head like a bullet. He was completely bald in a dramatic way that conveyed defiance, arrogance, and possibly violence. His shiny scalp came to an amazing point so pronounced, so sharp, that Charlie was sure it could be used as a tool or weapon if properly applied. Charlie made it a point not to stare at his pointy head, though at times he couldn't help himself.

"Helmut," he said when he walked into the office.

Helmut ignored Charlie's extended hand. Instead, he nodded and motioned for him to sit. He then sat down behind Marken's desk and opened a file.

"How was your trip in?" Charlie asked. He had decided to take a casual approach, though both his arms were now growing numb. He jiggled them gently and glanced around the office. It was only then that he saw Marken sitting on the couch behind him, looking like Lee Harvey Oswald. Seated next to him was Julie from human resources. He jiggled his arms again.

"Are we having a meeting?" Charlie asked.

Helmut ignored him. He carefully placed small, rectangular reading glasses over the bridge of his nose and started reading the file. When he glanced at Charlie over the rims, Charlie noticed that his starched white shirt was monogrammed. This surprised him. He had never seen Helmut in a monogrammed shirt before and he couldn't take his eyes off the initials on the pocket: HJK.

"We are making a change," Helmut said in his accent, which sounded darkly foreign that morning.

He stopped and fixed his green eyes on Charlie. On one level Charlie comprehended what he had just said, but on another level he did not. It was clear, though, that a response was expected, so Charlie asked, "What?"

"This past year has been a disaster," Helmut continued. "On all accounts. We have no option. There is no leadership here. Things have gone from bad to worse." He said all this in a horribly matter-of-fact way that made Charlie feel more ashamed than angry.

"I don't think that's completely accurate," Charlie said. His voice was high and weightless. He looked back at Marken, who glared.

"It's not? Then please tell me one thing you've accomplished since heading this office." He held up a finger. "Please. One thing. I would be very interested to know this information."

Charlie looked at Helmut's solitary finger and felt defeated. At that moment, he couldn't think of anything other than Charlie's Book Club.

"I'm sorry about this morning," Charlie finally managed to say. "I've been working long hours and I'm running on empty."

"We all work long hours," Marken said.

Charlie glanced back at him again. "Excuse me, Frank, but what are you doing here?" He turned to Helmut. "What are those two doing here, may I ask? Are we having a meeting?"

Helmut returned to his file. "The Southwest campaign was a disaster. The creative that you assured me, that you promised me, would be fresh and edgy, was flat. Your idea of that woman and that rat was preposterous."

"It wasn't a rat," Charlie said.

Helmut was referring to a short and very ill-fated campaign for Southwest Airlines featuring Paula Abdul and a cool-looking hamster that talked. The campaign had become something of a laughingstock within the industry and even though it wasn't *exactly* Charlie's idea, the shrapnel from that bomb had hit him squarely in his vital organs.

"We couldn't get Beyoncé," he said. "She was too expensive."

"That's no excuse."

"I can't be creative director and run an agency." Charlie immediately regretted saying this.

Helmut's eyes flared. "You insisted on leading that pitch. *Insisted* on it. You should have deferred to your creative team and kept out of the way. That rodent was ridiculous. You should have trusted your people. You were the manager, I placed you in charge. Instead, you took over the creative and stifled everyone."

"I never stifled anyone. As I explained before, I thought I had a clearer grasp of the client. I knew them. I knew where they had to go and what they should be saying."

Helmut raised his hand. "Please, I don't want to discuss that anymore. I've heard all of your rationalizations." He cleared his throat. "Anyway, I could list a number of additional issues here, a number of things you have failed to deliver upon, but I would rather not. Unless you would like me to do so."

"I don't understand," Charlie said, though he was beginning to, and clearly.

"As I said, we're making a change." Charlie couldn't speak. "We have prepared a separation package for you. It is nonnegotiable. You were not general manager very long. Under the circumstances, it is the best we can do."

Charlie found his voice: "Separation package?"

Helmut set his jaw. "We're making a change. We are terminating your employment here."

"Terminating my employ..." Charlie stopped and swallowed, then said, "That's ridiculous, that's crazy. You can't fire me. That's just not possible. That's not an option."

Helmut stared at Charlie without expression. "Excuse me?"

"You can't fire me, Helmut. Come on. You can't. Let's be serious. You can't come in here and fire me ... like I was someone else. I mean, it makes no sense."

Helmut looked over at Marken and then back at Charlie. "Don't make this more difficult than it has to be." Rather than angry, he seemed embarrassed.

"Stop it right now, come on, let's just stop this!" Charlie stood. "You can't do this. I work too hard. Listen. I'm sorry about the Southwest pitch and that stupid hamster. And I'm sorry for some of the other things, the 'fat' memo. That was wrong, I realize that now. I made a mistake, a mistake. Everyone makes them. But I'll make it up."

"It's too late for apologies," Helmut said.

"Listen, I need more time. This place was a mess. You know that. Plus, the economy. No one has budgets. Everyone's scared to spend money. Besides, I was making headway. I think we're going to keep Odor Eaters."

"Please sit down. Please."

Charlie sat back down, his head ringing. The room, he noticed, was shrinking. All he could see was Helmut's monogram. He licked his lips and put his hand over his heart.

Helmut assessed him. "Are you all right? Do you need water?" He looked Julie's way. "He needs some water."

"I don't need water." Charlie closed his eyes and jiggled his arms again. "I just need to get back to work now," he said quietly. "I have work to do."

"You're through here, Charlie," Marken said. "We're firing you. You're done."

Charlie whirled to face him. "Shut up!" he sputtered. "You just shut up. You're nothing but overhead, you know that? Overhead! An expense. You cost me two hundred and seventy thousand dollars a year to do the job a twenty-five-year-old accountant out of Illinois State could do."

"Go to hell," Marken said.

"I'll have none of that!" Helmut slapped his desk and pointed at Marken. "We must remain professional and show due respect."

Charlie turned back to him. "Listen, Helmut, I need more time. I'm turning it around."

Helmut paused and touched his forehead with a couple of fingers, an unfamiliar look of concern in his eyes. When he spoke again, his voice had softened and held no trace of its usual metallic edge. "I am sorry this did not work out, Charlie. This was all a mistake. I know you tried. I know you did your best. I know that. I know we put you in a difficult situation, but things have gotten much, much worse under your leadership. We have no choice. Thank you, and I wish you well. I sincerely do."

"Helmut, please, come on!" Charlie's voice caught and they both looked away, Helmut down at the desk and Charlie out the window.

Behind him, he heard the rustling of paper. Out of the corner of his eye, he saw Julie approaching, a descending angel of death, coming to take him away. He didn't move, though. He kept staring out the window, into the sunlight and the air and into nothing.

"Charlie?" Julie said.

After they fired him and after Julie from human resources gave him an envelope with his separation package, and after she asked for his company BlackBerry and cell phone and American Express card and office passkey, and after she asked him where she should ship his telescope and globe and gumball machine, and after he took his little gold clock the old agency had given him when he left them, Charlie took a cab to the nearest zoo.

When he got there, he walked. He wasn't exactly sure why he chose to go to the zoo, though it was the one place where he was sure not to run into anyone from the agency. He walked for a long time, passing cages and fountains, the monkey house, and pockets of children clutching snow cones, lunch boxes, and balloons. He thought and felt nothing, other than wondering how long the shock would last and hoping that, with luck, it might last forever. If he were a drinker, he would have been in a bar; if he were a womanizer, he would be in someone's arms; if he were a fighter, he would be with attorneys; if he were happily married, he would be at home. Instead, he was approaching walrus island.

He wandered all over the zoo, oblivious to his surroundings, Helmut's words, "This was all a mistake," trailing him. He thought of things he should have said to him, made a list of reasons why he deserved more time. Alone, at the Lincoln Park Zoo, he made a passionate case.

He was making progress. They had new business prospects. The staff would have come around and accepted him as the boss. He was on the verge of hiring a few key people who would shore up their weaknesses. He was only on the job for twelve months. The place was a disaster when he took over.

His anger was tempered by equal doses of shame and self-reproach. He should have seen this coming. He knew he was failing, knew that while he fiddled with book clubs and "fat" memos, Rome was burning, and brightly. He suspected that he should have stayed at the old agency making Bagel Man commercials with Bob Dole. Maybe, by now, they'd be working with one of the Clintons.

His mind raced erratically—money, his reputation, his mole—before stopping, exhausted, at his family: Donna and Kyle. How would they react? How would he tell them? What would he tell them? He walked on, one foot before the other.

He lost track of time but eventually saw long shadows and got the sense it was late. Rather than check his watch, he pulled out his gold clock. It was small and circular and had a cover that slid off to reveal the time. He traced his engraved initials with a finger, then returned the clock to his pocket.

He finally found himself on a bench near the lion cage. The light was fading and the wind was blowing stronger. Dark clouds formed overhead, moving quickly into each other, thick, gray. He realized that what he had thought was evening was really an approaching storm. He looked around, noticed he was alone, saw the lions slipping into their caves, casually glancing over their shoulders one last time before disappearing. Still, he sat there and waited for the rain, and when it came, he let it wash over him, let it run down the sides of his face and mingle with his tears.

Chapter Four

The next morning, Donna walked into the kitchen, holding the newspaper in one hand and an empty coffee cup in the other. When she saw Charlie, sitting in an exhausted daze at the table by the bay windows, his hands folded on his lap, she stopped dead in her tracks and glanced at the clock on the wall, then back at Charlie. "What are you doing here?" she asked.

"Nothing." He gave her a slight wave, then folded his hands back together. He had risen early with the intention of making a healthy breakfast for himself but had gotten sidetracked into staring out at the yard. "I was going to make coffee," he vaguely said.

Donna put the paper and cup down on the island. "It's eight o'clock. I thought you were out of town." She set about making the coffee.

"No, I'm here."

"Did you sleep here last night?"

"I slept in the other room, the guest room. I got home late, I didn't want to wake you."

Donna shook her head. "Well, if you were in town, it would

have been nice if you could have made the school open house for once. It was last night. It might have been nice for his teachers to see that Kyle actually has a father. I waited for you. For an hour. You never called. I assumed you had gone out of town."

Charlie looked over at her and swallowed. He had, of course, forgotten about the open house. "I was busy. I'm sorry," he softly said.

"Busy." She unfolded the paper with a snap.

He looked down at the floor, then rubbed a hand over his face. He now regretted not leaving the house at his normal time. He could have avoided all of this.

He cleared his throat, then attempted to change the subject. "Are you going to that place today? That community place?" He was referring to a center for disabled people where she volunteered. He had little to no idea what she did there, where it was, or even the name of it, but he knew she went there.

"Yes, I'm going to that place, that community place." Her voice was flat, completely void of emotion or inflection. "That community place, by the way, whose annual report you said you would help write."

He cringed. Another land mine. "Annual report," Charlie repeated. He remembered making that offer a few months back after he had missed the grand opening of a new wing, or new room, or new something there. "I'm sorry," he said again.

"Wow, you're sorry a lot."

"Listen, I don't want to fight right now. I have a lot going on. So can you please quit with the attacks? I mean, I'm just sitting here."

Donna shook her head again, picked up a section of the paper, poured herself some coffee, and walked out. A few seconds later, Kyle, tall but stoop-shouldered, slunk into the room.

"Hi," Charlie said.

Kyle jumped. "What are you doing here?" he asked in a still-wobbly sixteen-year-old voice.

Charlie gave him a tight smile. "Good morning."

Kyle stared at him. "What?"

"I said good morning."

"Oh, yeah."

Charlie finally stood up and walked over to the counter and poured himself a cup of coffee. "It looks like it's going to be warm today." He had no idea what the weather was going to be like, but he thought this was normal family banter and he suddenly needed to have normal family banter.

Kyle nodded, then opened the refrigerator. It had been a while since Charlie had seen him in daylight, or really any light, and his condition concerned him. He was wearing baggy gray sweatpants that hung low over his rear and a black Chicago Bulls T-shirt so tight Charlie was sure he couldn't exhale. His dark hair was shaggy and much too long.

"How's school going?"

"What?"

"School, how's it going?"

"Oh. Good." Kyle poured himself some orange juice, drank it in one gulp, then disappeared into the adjacent mudroom and out the back door.

"Have a good day!" Charlie called after him as the door slammed shut.

Charlie walked back to the table and resumed staring out the window. It was a sunny day, the brightness an insult to his dark and increasingly desperate mood. He was feeling very disconnected, very isolated.

He sipped some coffee and studied the backyard. It was large. Very large. He tried to remember what they had paid for the house: $1.3 million or $1.4. Then he wondered who had run the staff huddle in his absence. Marken, of course, yellow-toothed, overpaid, off-the-rack-suit-wearing Marken. He was probably using Charlie's office too, putting his cheap Florsheim penny loafers up on his desk, giving his globe a whirl with one of his stubby fingers. His skin grew hot. He finished his coffee and marched over to the counter for another cup.

He was back at the table, brooding, when Donna returned.

"What's your schedule this week?" she asked. She kept her eyes on the paper. "What days are you here?"

Her question surprised him. "I'm in all week."

She looked up. "All week? You are? I thought you said you might be gone one night."

Charlie caught himself. "No, wait. Yeah, I might be gone one night. Wednesday, tomorrow."

She went back to the paper. "I'm going to visit my brother."

"Who?"

"Aaron."

Charlie nodded and stared at Donna. Over the years, her freckles had faded, and this morning her face looked washed out and pale. Like Kyle, she was wearing baggy sweatpants and a T-shirt. He had made more than $400,000 the year before, yet his family had no clothes.

"What's wrong?" Donna asked.

"What?"

"Are you sick or something?"

Charlie hesitated, considered telling her right then and there, but instead said, "Actually, I'm not feeling all that good."

"What is it now?"

"Don't start on that."

"I just want to know what emergency room you're going to call me from next."

"I haven't been to an emergency room in a long time."

"You were there last week."

She was referring to a brief stop Charlie had made at Wilton Memorial to check on a spot, another potential mole he had noticed on the left side of his face, a spot the attending physician dismissed because he couldn't see it. "I was barely there," Charlie said.

Donna shook her head. "What's it this time? Heart attack, cancer? That . . . that sleep thing, that apnea thing? Six months ago you thought you were going blind. You were hysterical. You called me in the middle of the night screaming that you couldn't see."

"First of all, I wasn't screaming. And if you remember I ended up being diagnosed with a pretty serious problem."

"You had pinkeye."

"You say that like it's nothing."

He stared down into his coffee cup.

Donna ruthlessly turned a page, almost ripping it. "You know this job is killing you," she said. "You're crazy now. Crazy. You never used to be this bad."

Charlie sighed. These were familiar accusations. He looked back out the window and watched as the tips of the oak tree swayed in the early morning wind, its yellow leaves shimmering in the sunlight. Once again, his mind went back to his work and he remembered how he used to watch the sunrise through the wall-sized windows in the conference room.

He then realized that he was in the wrong place. He shouldn't be in the kitchen passively drinking coffee with his wife on a Tuesday morning. No man should be home on a Tuesday morning. At least not a man like him, not someone who had been named 1998 Ad Man of the Year, not someone who once made a commercial, an award-winning commercial, of a kitten, a live, breathing kitten, parachuting out of a plane wearing tiny red boots. Much of his career had been marked by aggressive bold moves and actions. His boldness was what distinguished him and his work. It was the core of his essence. He finished the last of his coffee and stood.

"I'm going now," he said.

"Where, to the doctor?"

"No." He brushed past her and reached for his car keys, which were lying in a corner of the counter. "I'm going to work."

While driving downtown to the office, he began to list some of his most successful impulsive acts: shaving his head in college thinking it would make him look dangerous and edgy for his oral interpretation final (he was supposed to read parts of *Heart of Darkness* aloud in class); buying a red BMW 325i on the way home from work after spending all of five minutes admiring it in a car dealership window while standing at a bus stop; completely changing the creative for the $90 million Midas business less than seventy-two hours before the big pitch;

asking Donna to marry him after their third date in the third inning of a rain-delayed Chicago White Sox game. All of those moves, he remembered, had paid dividends: he got an A on the final, loved the car, won the pitch, and, before she decided to start hating him, was loved, he thought, by Donna.

He now planned on adding to this list of bold moves. He was going to get his job back. He was going to see Helmut, insist on seeing him without Marken, and rationally, calmly, politely ask for more time. He would pledge to have Project Phoenix Rising completely fleshed out within a week. Upon approval of the plan, he would immediately make the necessary staff reductions, develop a separate new business unit, and appoint a deputy general manager to handle all administrative issues. This would free up his time and allow him to focus on client relationships, which was what he did best. If, after six months, Helmut was not satisfied with the progress and direction of the agency, he would willingly step down, gladly leave the company. It was a long shot, he knew, but a reasonable proposal.

Traffic was predictably heavy and it was well after nine when he finally pulled into the parking garage of his building. Although his mind was racing, he felt strangely confident in his plan. His instincts usually proved right. He was counting on them one more time.

While making his way through the garage, he called Georgia.

"Hi. It's me."

"Who?"

"Me. I'm coming to the office."

"What?"

"Meet me in two minutes."

"Where?"

He closed the phone and took a deep breath. All systems go, he thought.

She was waiting for him in the lobby, furiously wringing her hands.

"Hello, Georgia," he said. He tried to sound crisp and cheerful, but the words were thick in his mouth. He glanced at the receptionist, who smiled at him. Charlie smiled eagerly back. "Why, hello, Vicky."

"Good morning, Mr. Baker." She said this as if it were merely another morning. Charlie thought that a good sign. If everyone could just act the same way, everything could go back to normal.

Georgia, however, wasn't playing along. She pulled him over by the spiral staircase and started whispering fast. "Charlie, what are you doing here?"

"I came to see Helmut."

"He's gone now. He went back to Germany."

"He did?" Charlie hadn't factored this possibility into the bold-move equation. "Why didn't you tell me on the phone?"

"You didn't give me a chance. Everything is happening so fast. I tried calling you last night. . . ."

Charlie tuned her out. His plan was dissolving. With Helmut gone, he wasn't sure who he should talk boldly to. "Is Marken here?"

She nodded and looked around the lobby. "He's back, you know, in a meeting or something." She pointed down the hall. "They're all meeting now. Charlie, maybe you should come back and call him on the phone. Go home, have a drink, then call."

"I'm not doing that."

"Then what are you going to do?"

Good question. Charlie had to think about this. Even if Marken were free, he had no use for him. Helmut was his only chance. "I'm going to my office," he said.

"Your office? Why do you want to go there for?"

"Because . . ." He paused. If he could just get to his office, everything would be all right. Back in his cocoon, protected by his things, he could determine his next steps, maybe contact Helmut. "Because it's my office."

Georgia grimaced and peered over his shoulder. "I can't stay here right now, Charlie. I have to go. You know I love you,

34

I tried calling you all last night, but I can't be here right now, out here like this with you. I just can't."

He gave Georgia a long look, and felt his heart breaking. He had worked with this woman for close to twenty years. They had eaten lunch and, on a few occasions, even dinner together. He knew her children, though he could never remember their names and at that particular moment wasn't really sure if they were boys or girls. He knew she had three of them, though. Or four. "I understand," he quietly said. "I'll just go to my office, then."

"Charlie, why don't you go home? Relax a little, then call back later."

He reached over and squeezed her wrist. "I'll be all right. I'm not going to act crazy. Nice Charlie is here."

"Yeah, well, Nice Charlie, he don't always stick around. Sometimes he leaves early."

"Well, this time he's staying." Charlie winked. "I promise."

He left her frozen at the foot of the staircase and strode quickly down the hallway, his head straight, jaw set. He smiled and nodded at a few people as he passed, not stopping long enough to gauge their reaction. Everything seemed to be going along as well as could be expected until he passed the desk of the oversized administrative assistant, Patty. She was lowering what looked to be a vanilla éclair the length of a Louisville Slugger into her mouth. When she saw him, her face lit up like a slot machine and she proceeded to cough, then choke. Within seconds, she was standing by her desk gagging, her hands clawing at the base of her throat.

"Good morning, Patty," Charlie said. He walked faster.

When he reached his office, he closed the door and leaned against it. His resolve had drained off him and was now a small, sad puddle around his feet. He was breathing heavily and his eyes felt blurry. He feared a pinkeye relapse.

He pushed himself off the door and walked slowly to his desk, gazing about the room. His office looked like a looted U.S. embassy. His Persian rug was gone, his wastebasket overflowing, his Bagel Man cape, worn by a number of celebrities including Joe Montana and Elton John, carelessly tossed in a heap on the floor. A handful of boxes were stacked in the center of the room and pens and paper clips littered the floor. All that was missing was anti-Charlie graffiti on the walls and the sound of distant gunfire and sirens.

It wasn't until he reached his desk that he noticed his chair was gone. *His* chair. The one he sat in twelve, thirteen, fourteen hours a day. It was leather, swiveled, and was ergonomically designed by Swedish engineers to ensure maximum lower back comfort. He had discovered the chair in one of those odd little ads in the back of *The New Yorker*. In its place was his gumball machine, or what was left of it. It had been mounted on a clear plastic base, but now it sat detached and alone on the floor, its head, the bubble with the gumballs, decapitated. He picked up the head, anger and sadness sweeping over him, then gently put it back down. It had come to this. It had come to this.

He was allowing himself to slip back into shock when Georgia entered. "You doing okay in here?" she asked. She shut the door and resumed the wringing of her hands.

"They took my chair," he said. "The Swedish chair. The one I used to sit in. The one from *The New Yorker*."

"I know, Charlie. You used to love that chair. Made by the same engineers who made the Saturn."

"Saab. They made the Saab." Charlie's voice cracked and he held up a finger. "I've been gone one day. One day."

"Charlie, you can't stay here. You got to go."

"Did Marken send you in here?"

"No. Julie did. She knows you're here. Everyone knows you're here. What did you say to Patty? She's coughing and acting crazy. She wants to go to the hospital."

He leaned against the wall and slipped all the way down to the floor. "I said good morning." He closed his eyes. A few seconds later, he felt Georgia's hand on his shoulder, and heard her sniffle.

"Oh, Charlie," she said. She sniffled some more and he grabbed for her hand. "How you feeling?"

"Like I died." He opened his eyes and she let go of him.

"You know, maybe this is a blessing," she said.

"What do you mean, blessing? What do you mean?"

"I mean, this job put a lot of stress on you. You were always sick and rushing off to the doctor and everything. You never used to be this way. Well, you were, but never like this. Maybe you needed to get out of here. Maybe this is for the best."

"It's not for the best, trust me, getting fired is never for the best, it's just not, especially now. Do you know how many people are out there looking?" He sighed. "Did they name a replacement?"

"Not yet. But someone told me that Mr. Marken is going to be named head of the office."

"Who told you that?"

"Mr. Marken."

Charlie let this sink in. "He took the Swedish chair, didn't he? Tell me the truth. It's important I know."

Georgia looked very sad. Her bottom lip trembled again and she looked down at the floor.

This piece of news, this final indignity, was a dagger in Charlie's heart; he no longer had a seat at the table. He was fired. "The Smart Chair," he whispered.

"I know, I know. I feel so bad for you, Charlie. So bad. I know you and Mr. Marken never got along. And now he's got your chair. Your special magazine chair."

"What's the reaction? What's everyone saying?"

She paused. "Oh, everyone feels real bad about what happened. Real bad. No one can believe you got fired for, you know, sleeping at your desk."

"What? How did that get out? How do people know about that?"

"Well, I don't know," she said quickly. "I'm not sure."

"That's not the reason I got fired. Jesus Christ, Georgia! Come on!"

"I know, I know, that's what I keep telling everyone. I keep telling everyone you got fired for lots of different reasons, lots of reasons."

He stared into her eyes, then shook his head again.

She was quiet. "Where do you want me to send your things? Your telescope and your globe and everything? Your gumball machine. Your picture of President Lincoln. You love that picture. Do you want me to drive it out to your home? I can do that. I can do that myself."

"I don't care."

"What about the telescope, then?"

Although he had never once used the telescope, he had a sudden desire to have it. It was white and sleek and stood impressively on a delicate wooden tripod. He had no idea how he had come to own it.

"Where is it?"

"Angelo has it. But I can get it back."

"Angelo? Jesus, did these people storm my office? Were they holding torches?"

"He just said he wanted to borrow it and look at some things."

"Send it to my house. Just ship it to me. Ship it out to Wilton. That's mine."

"What about the other things?"

"Keep what you want and throw everything else away. Shred it, I don't care. Shred the globe."

"What about the cape?" She pointed to the Bagel Man cape.

"What? Oh. Send that too. And the Lincoln picture. Be careful with that, though."

"What about the drawing of the Cocoa Puffs Bird? The big one? The original Cuckoo for Cocoa Puffs poster you bought at that auction? You paid a lot of money for it. You said it was a piece of history."

"I don't care about that Cuckoo for Cocoa Puffs poster, okay? I don't know what was on my mind when I bought that thing. I must have been drunk. Just throw it out or give it to charity or . . . or a museum."

"Are you sure?"

Charlie sighed. He actually did like the poster. The Cuckoo

Bird was colorful and happy, and it had, he remembered, a very expensive frame. "Where is it?"

Georgia pointed over to the door, where the picture sat propped up against the wall.

"I don't know, maybe." He sighed yet again. "Have they sent out a press release or something announcing the change yet?"

"They wrote one up," she whispered.

"What did it say about me? That I resigned? I was fired?"

"They said you resigned to pursue other interests."

Charlie actually laughed. "They always say that. You would think they could come up with something original. It's an ad agency. Something a little more creative. No wonder we're losing clients."

"I was supposed to send it out yesterday. Mr. Marken asked me to do it. I work for him now. I was supposed to do it yesterday, right after it happened. But I didn't do it."

"Why not?"

Georgia shrugged.

"Why not?" he asked again.

"Do you remember that time, during my divorce, how you helped me out? You remember when I was late all the time? I was doing everything just to keep from going underwater. The kids and everything. I missed a lot of work. You remember that?" Then she said, "I do."

Charlie swallowed. Her loyalty surprised him.

"Thank you, Georgia. But sooner or later, they're going to want to know why nothing ran."

"You being gone is your business, no one else's. Besides, newspapers are big places. Press releases get lost sometimes, sent to the wrong people."

"The papers, everyone is going to find out sooner or later."

"They can find out later." Georgia was quiet again and Charlie thought she might start crying.

"How did all this happen?" he asked. "You work all your life and you end up like this. I didn't steal anything, I didn't embezzle, I didn't screw anyone, I didn't break any laws. All I did was work hard. You know, that's all I did. That was my crime."

"I know, Charlie, I know." Georgia reached out and helped him to his feet.

"Well, this was a big mistake. My coming here."

"You going home now?"

"Someplace like that."

He straightened his jacket while she smoothed the lapels.

"Is there a big crowd out there? A mob? Are they going to hurt me?"

"No. Everyone's at a birthday party for Aiesha. They're having cake in the conference room."

"Cake in the morning. Perfect. All right. I'm out of here, I guess."

Georgia was in the process of giving him one last hug when Marken and Julie walked in.

"What do you think you're doing?" Marken asked.

Charlie buttoned his blazer, cleared his throat, and took Marken in. He was wearing a new dark Italian suit that Charlie didn't recognize, though he did recognize its implication. Meet the new boss.

"Hey, Frank, glad you could stop by," Charlie said. "Nice suit. I didn't know Walmart had suits. Hey, I was hoping to ask you how my chair was doing. Enjoying it? Are you here for the light fixtures now? Maybe the air vents?" Charlie opened up his mouth and pointed to his teeth. "How about my fillings, huh? I got a gold crown in here. You can probably yank it out if you want to. Come on, come on, yank, yank. Go on, help yourself." He opened his mouth again.

Marken snarled before turning to Julie. "Get him out of here."

Julie looked helplessly at the floor. "Mr. Baker, you really shouldn't be here," she said.

"Don't worry about it, Julie. I'm leaving, I'm leaving. It will be my pleasure to get out of this hellhole. This swamp. This fat farm."

"Mr. Baker, please," Julie said.

"He doesn't care what he says," Marken said. "He never has. He doesn't care about anything or anyone but himself." He took a step closer to Charlie and spoke in a low, even voice. "I've been here twenty-five years. I knew Mrs. DiSanto and Mr. Herr. I was here when they started this shop. This used to be a special place. You wrecked it. This is the worst shape we've ever been in. Ever. And it's all your fault."

"My fault? My fault?" Charlie's rage surged. He was not going to take this from this man, a man with a comb-over, a man who once suggested they meet at *Denny's* for lunch. "You know, Frank, this place was a mess when I got here, a mess. And maybe, if I had a different CFO, someone who could add three-digit numbers and not miss our budget by seven hundred and fifty thousand dollars, someone who could occasionally, maybe, possibly, work past five o'clock, maybe things would have been different."

Marken's eyes went wide and his face flushed. "Julie, get him out of here!"

Julie looked like she was about to cry. "Mr. Baker, if you don't leave, I'll have to call security."

"Security. Please. Just save the theatrics. I'm leaving. Security. I'm going to go home and celebrate my freedom, my liberation." It was then that his eye caught the gumball bubble on the floor. He picked it up, tucking it under his arm like a football. He would be *damned* if he would leave it for Marken and the other barbarians to feast on.

He was about make his exit when he caught Marken smirking at Julie. Obviously, he thought the taking of the gumball machine cute. This was the last straw, the final insult. Under no circumstances would he be smirked at by this man. Without thinking, Charlie reared back and threw the bubble at Marken, who, at the last moment, ducked. The bubble shattered against the wall, gumballs spraying everywhere. Both Georgia and Julie screamed and covered their faces with their hands.

Marken remained in a crouched position, his mouth agape, his arms out in front of him. "Look at you now," Charlie said. "Just look at you now." He glanced around his office one last time, nodded a farewell to a shocked and shaken Georgia, then quickly walked over to the door, picked up the Cuckoo for Cocoa Puffs poster, and briskly left.

Chapter Five

The Wilton Public Library was a surprisingly small building located on the edge of town. It had two levels: an adult floor and a children's floor, which, from what Charlie could see, was filled with broken toys and bulky, outdated computers. Considering what they paid in taxes, Charlie thought the library would be more spacious and modern, have several floors, possibly a coffee shop, or a cyber-café.

Most of the newspapers and publications in the periodicals section were weeks old and all of the librarians had an annoyed and lethargic Department of Motor Vehicles mentality about them. When he asked one of them, a short, stocky woman with uneven bangs, if they had any books on moles, she looked at him blankly and said she was on break.

After taking a quick tour, he found a cubicle tucked away in a corner, far from any window. He knew he was taking a chance on being seen by a neighbor, but he didn't really know any of his neighbors, so the risk felt minimal.

Once situated, he decided to finally analyze his separation package. It was, as Helmut had said, bare bones: three months' pay; six months' use of the outplacement center; health insurance for a year. As the cover note from Helmut explained, the agency was struggling financially and was not prepared to offer "enhanced benefits." He considered calling Sean, his sometime lawyer, to discuss it, but Sean was Donna's brother and Charlie wasn't ready to involve him just yet.

The pay was what concerned him the most. Three months was twelve weeks, which wasn't long. The money would run out around the holidays. He imagined a Bob Cratchit Christmas: Charlie coming home with a thin and sickly-looking goose; Donna sitting by a weak fire, mending whatever people mend; Kyle standing by the window, leaning on a homemade crutch; all of them wearing baggy, stretched-out sweatpants.

Faced with this looming reality, he decided to table his mole research and review their finances. He called the bank, the brokerage, and the mortgage company on his cell phone, punching in account codes and PIN numbers and listening to automated responses, trying to reacquaint himself with their money. He had no idea of where they stood.

Unfortunately, his research revealed they weren't doing very well.

Their situation was the result of a combination of poor management and bad luck. But mostly poor management. A few years earlier, Charlie had made an ill-advised and risky investment in real estate, entering into a limited partnership with some business acquaintances from the old agency. The proposed retirement community, El Rancho del Sol, was supposed to be based in a suburb of Houston. For reasons he never totally understood (something to do with the subprime mess), the proposed location was shifted to El Paso and later to Biloxi, Mississippi, before shifting into oblivion. It never got off the ground. While lawsuits were still pending, he wasn't sanguine about his chances of recovering any of the losses his accountant categorized as "staggering." In addition, he had lost big in the stock market bust, having bet heavily on financial companies.

As a result, in terms of net worth, the Baker family was at low tide. They had some cash, about $40,000, about $65,000 in mutual funds, and some, but not much, equity in their home. They also had a ton of worthless stock options in the agency.

These assets were no match for their monthly costs: a $5,000 mortgage; $2,000 in property taxes; $2,000 for the Wilton Country Club; $2,000 in car payments. There were other bills too, for things he was only vaguely aware of, like utilities, clothes, food, etc. Up until yesterday, none of this had mattered. Up until yesterday, he'd thought he was rich.

He stood up, did some stress-relieving deep knee bends, then walked quickly to the men's room to wash his face with hot water. On the way back, he saw the librarian with the bad bangs standing by a Soviet-era photocopy machine. She was trying to hang a poster announcing an upcoming travelogue on Florence, Italy, on a wall. The poster featured a map of Italy so crude it looked like it had been drawn with the left hand of a right-handed person. A tiny smiley face denoted where Florence apparently was located.

"Excuse me," he whispered, "but do you know where I can get a copy of today's *New York Times*?"

The woman didn't look his way. Instead, she continued to adjust the poster, which was nothing more than a large piece of blue construction paper. "Yeah," she whispered back, "New York."

Safely back in his cubicle, he considered risking a short walk down the street to Will's, the local coffee shop, when his cell phone vibrated. He answered tentatively.

"Yes?"

"Are you coming home tonight?" It was Donna.

"Donna?"

"Are you coming home tonight?"

He swallowed. "Yeah."

"You're going to make it back? I thought you said you were going to be out of town tonight."

Charlie paused, confused. "Yeah, I'm in New York. I probably won't make it back. It's pretty late. I'll be back tomorrow."

There was a pause. "Are you sure?"

"Yeah, why, do you have something going on?"

"I just wanted to know. I'm going to bed."

"Okay, well. I'm at a dinner here. Just finishing up." They both fell quiet. Charlie closed his eyes and took a deep breath. He considered telling her, end the charade, then decided tomorrow might be better. This was something he would have to do in person. "Maybe we can go out to dinner tomorrow."

"What?"

"Dinner, just you and me."

There was a long, painful silence. "I have a dinner at Bright Day tomorrow. The benefit."

Charlie quickly retreated. "That's right, never mind." There was another silence. "Oh, you know, I meant to tell you, you had one of your sleeping spells the other night," he said. "You were sitting up in bed in a trance. I told you to go back to sleep. You were staring at me. Are you exercising? Remember, the doctor said if you exercised, you could cut down on those episodes."

"I wasn't sleeping," Donna said.

"Yes, you were."

"No, I wasn't. I was watching you." She hung up.

"Hello?" He stared at the phone, flipped it shut, opened it, then closed it again and sighed.

Donna. Wife of almost thirty years. Miss South Side Irish, 1978. Daughter of a bar owner. Five large, older, football-playing brothers. The love, he remembered, of his life.

Telling her was going to be a problem. A big problem. He couldn't imagine it, couldn't conceive of the conversation. She had never wanted him to take this job, never wanted them to leave their old home. She had been comfortable with her life on the South Side. In fact, she had loved it.

They were married on her twentieth birthday, one year after they met. Five years later they bought a small colonial with high ceilings less than a mile from her father's home, and three blocks from two of her brothers, and for years life was fine. He kept her amused, made her laugh. She kept him grounded, balanced. He shopped on Saturday mornings, mowed the lawn on Sundays, cooked meals. The summer after Kyle was born, he actually built a swing set in the backyard, poring over the instructions like they were the invasion plans for D-day, fitting and pounding the joists together with his own hands. It took him close to a month to construct it and on the day he finished Donna hosted a neighborhood barbecue to celebrate. It remained the only thing he had ever built.

How he had gotten from that point to this point, he wasn't exactly sure. He wasn't sure of anything anymore. What he was doing, what was going to happen next. It felt like just yesterday he was building that swing set. Just yesterday everything seemed fine. How does a life jump the tracks like that? He needed an explanation.

He was mulling things over when his phone went off again. He quickly answered, hoping it was Donna, but it wasn't.

"Mr. Baker? Hello? This is Ned Meyers."

"Who?"

"Ned Meyers. From Rogers & Newman. The outplacement firm. I'm your transition consultant."

"Who?"

"We met very briefly yesterday. I knocked at your door. In the office. I had the wrong time. I came too early and I apologize for that. That was completely unprofessional. Completely. There's no excuse for that. None."

"What? Oh." Charlie remembered him now. The man in the short-sleeve shirt and tie. "How did you get this number?"

"Your assistant. I meant to come back and meet with you, but I had another appointment. I'm sorry I couldn't stay. Everything was a bit of a mess."

Charlie checked his watch and wondered how long the library stayed open.

Ned Meyers cleared his throat. "I know it's a bit unorthodox, me calling you this late, but I wanted to see how you were doing. How you were carrying on."

"Carrying on," Charlie repeated. "I'm fine. Terrific. I am carrying on splendidly."

Ned Meyers nervously chuckled. "Are you sure?"

"Yes. Positive."

"Well, I heard some reports."

Charlie sat up and glanced over his shoulder. "What do you mean? Reports about what?"

"Nothing. Only that you seemed a bit . . . upset."

Charlie assumed he was referring to his stunt with the gumball bubble. "I don't know what you heard, but I'm fine."

There was a pause before Ned Meyers said, "Yes, well, I was wondering if you planned on coming in soon. We should really get together. I'd like to show you our offices, our resources. We're part of your separation package and I want to make sure you know what is available to help you."

"I don't think I'm going to need to come in," Charlie said. "But thank you."

"Well, I really think you should."

"I'm fine. I have my own office at home and I'll be fine. I won't be out long."

Ned Meyers paused again. "I really think you should come by."

"I'm fine," Charlie repeated. He flipped the phone shut.

He decided to take a break from the finances, so spent the next hour reading back issues of health magazines. One article—"Are You One Day Away from a Heart Attack?"—had him particularly alarmed. At first he decided he didn't have any of the symptoms listed, but after a second, more thorough reading, he was pretty sure he had all of them. He beat back an urge to make another appearance in the ER, however, and continued to browse magazines until they turned the lights off. Then, since he had nowhere else to go, he walked down Main Street to Will's.

It was dark and the street was deserted, so he felt it was safe to move around. Though he really wasn't hungry, he thought he should eat something. Afterward, he would probably go to a hotel and spend the night, since he apparently was supposed to be out of town. He thought this probably was for the best. Though he would have liked to have been in his own room and in his own bed with his own humidifier, he decided he needed a night to himself to figure things out and determine the best approach to telling Donna.

As he was crossing the street, he realized he might not have much time. For there, sitting by the window at the restaurant, was Donna. He stopped in the middle of the street, then quickly backtracked to the other side. Even from this greater distance, he was sure it was her. She was talking on her cell phone and there was no mistaking her curly mane of hair.

He stood frozen. He had spoken with her not much more than an hour before "from New York"; how could he explain his presence? When he decided he couldn't, he beat a fast retreat to the library parking lot and jumped into the Navigator. He sat there for a full ten minutes considering the situation. He wondered if she had seen him, wondered what she would think he was doing in Wilton when he should have been in New York City. Then he began to wonder what *she* was doing out at this hour when she should have been at home. It was after nine and she had said she was going to bed early. Her presence in the restaurant seemed strange. Suddenly her calling to see when he was coming home seemed even stranger.

He left the Navigator and slowly walked back toward the restaurant for another look. He had some questions of his own.

When he turned the corner, he could immediately see that she was gone. The table by the window was empty. He quickly glanced up and down the quiet street, and then stepped into the shadows of the Wilton Penny Theater to wait for her to emerge from the front doors. When, after a few minutes, she didn't, he decided to take a chance and strode across the street and pressed his face close to the window, shielding his eyes against the streetlight's glare. He saw a man washing tabletops, a woman drinking a cup of coffee in a booth, and the cashier counting money at the register. He saw all these people, as well as his own sad reflection, in the low, wide mirror behind the counter, but as hard as he looked, he saw no sign of his wife.

Chapter Six

While Charlie had only skimmed the book *The Corporate Buddha*, he did read a chapter on "bottoming out"—a belief that when things were going bad, it was best to get out of the way and let them go bad, let things fall completely apart, until you've hit bottom.

According to the Buddha (who had been Burger King's human resource director before becoming a monk), bottoming out was an essential part of the natural ebb and flow of life, the cyclical, To Every Season rhythm of things. Rather than fighting the fall, the Buddha believed that you should endure it, then, afterward, accurately assess the damage, learn from your mistakes, and move on. The key, of course, was knowing when you'd hit bottom.

Charlie suspected the bottom was coming into plain view when he asked Rafael, a bellman at the Four Seasons Hotel in downtown Chicago, if he could send a prostitute up to his room. He had finished checking in and was standing by the elevators when he did this.

"I'm sorry, sir?"

He repeated his request.

"I'm sorry, sir, no," Rafael said. He was standing close to the elevators resplendent in a red and gold uniform, complete with an impressive tall black cap that had a tightly knotted gold braid dangling from it. He reminded Charlie of one of the witch's guards in *The Wizard of Oz*.

"O-E-O! O-YEEE-O!" Charlie shouted, and marched up and down. He was very drunk, and Rafael, to his credit, did his best to ignore him.

Charlie laughed insanely, then followed Rafael, who was pulling a baggage cart loaded with boxes, into the elevator.

"What floor, sir?"

"Oh." Charlie glanced down at the small envelope with his key card. "I don't know, I can't read this." He held it out for Rafael.

"Room 1624."

"Is that a good room?"

Rafael eagerly nodded. "Yes," he said. He had a thick Spanish accent.

"They'd be better if they had prostitutes in them," he said.

"Yes." Rafael pressed the button and the elevator began to move upward. Charlie stared at Rafael, who stared straight ahead at the door.

"Hey," Charlie said, "what time is it?"

Rafael glanced at his watch. "It is one o'clock, sir, yes."

"Jesus, one o'clock. Jesus. I've been drinking in the bar downstairs for almost three hours. Just like they do on *Mad Men*, I guess, the TV show. They're always drinking and screwing on that show. It's about advertising. Do you ever watch that? I watch it when I travel sometimes."

Rafael shook his head, then went back to memorizing the door.

"Drinking for three hours," Charlie said. "I must be shit-faced." He shook his head, stared at his shoes, then squinted at Rafael. "Hey," he said. "I probably should clarify something here. I don't really want a hooker. I don't know why I just said that. I'm loaded, that's why. That's something they would do on

Mad Men. I wish I worked back then. All we do now is drink Starbucks and stare at our BlackBerrys. You know, I've never been with a hooker in my life. Ever."

Rafael said nothing.

"I think you'd have to be crazy to get a hooker nowadays. Disease and everything."

"Yes. I understand."

"I can't understand people who get hookers. I couldn't enjoy it. I mean, I've thought about it, but I never would. I don't know how that would work. Do you pay them before, after? Do they give you change? I've never been unfaithful to my wife. Have you ever been unfaithful to your wife?"

"I'm no married, sir."

"Really? Not once? Well, good for you. Good for you. I thought everyone was married."

Charlie studied his own distorted reflection in the doors. He looked short and fat; a misshapen dwarf. "Could you do me a favor?" he asked. "Could you not tell anyone I asked you that? About the prostitute, I mean? I don't know why I said that. I just got fired, that's probably why I said that. From my job. Fired." He waved a hand. "You know, completely."

"Are you all right, sir?"

Charlie had started to cry. He wiped the tears from his cheeks with the back of his hand.

"I'm okay. I don't know what's wrong with me. I'm just, you know, it was unexpected and I haven't told my wife yet or anyone."

The elevator stopped on the sixteenth floor. He sniffled. "Hey, instead of a hooker, can you send up a humidifier?"

"What. Sir? A hum . . ."

"Humidifier. Yeah, you know, for the air. Like a vaporizer. I need one to help me breathe. That's got to be easier to find than a hooker."

Rafael looked worried. "I don't know if we have humidors, sir."

"No humidifier? Jesus. Marriott always has them. Well, how about some toothpaste and a toothbrush? I can't sleep unless I brush my teeth. I can't sleep with dirty teeth. I lie awake all night thinking about them, just sitting there, decaying."

"Yes," Rafael said.

"Really? Are you the same way? My wife thinks I'm compulsive. She thinks I'm obsessive-compulsive. She thinks I'm a lot of things. She doesn't like me anymore. Can you believe that? Even though I've never been unfaithful. She used to love me, though, before I became, you know"—he waved a hand in front of himself—"like this. She thinks I've changed, thinks I'm crazy. I don't think I've changed. Well, maybe I have." He shook his head. "I probably have."

Rafael studied Charlie with dark, sad eyes. He was holding the doors to the elevator open with one hand and clutching the side of the baggage cart with another.

"Are you sure you don't have a humidifier?" Charlie asked. "I'll pay extra for it. This is a big hotel."

"I will check, sir, but it is late."

"Well, thanks." Charlie stepped out of the elevator and into the hall. "What's your name again?" he asked, even though Rafael was wearing a large gold name tag.

"Rafael."

"I'm Charlie Baker." Charlie offered his hand, but the doors were shutting.

"Good night, Rafael," he shouted. "I mean it, good night!"

It took him a while to locate his room. He kept walking in circles, squinting at doors and announcing room numbers aloud: 1645, 1647, 1649. When he found 1624, he fumbled with the key card for such a long time that he considered lying on the floor and sleeping outside his door. Once he finally made it inside, he took a hot shower, put on a white terry-cloth hotel bathrobe, and sat on the bed and watched TV. He must have briefly dozed off, because the next thing he knew there was a knock on the door. He shuffled across the room, opened it, and found Rafael ceremoniously holding a silver tray with a travel-sized tube of toothpaste, a toothbrush, a can of shaving cream, and a shiny stainless steel pot of coffee.

"I'm sorry, I no find a humidor. They are all in use," he said. Then he said, "May I, please?"

Charlie looked at him, not sure, at first, who he was. "Oh, sure, sure," he finally said. He stepped aside to let him pass. Rafael walked briskly across the room and placed the tray on a table by the window. He was an older man with a graying mustache and had a hushed dignity about him that Charlie instinctively respected and appreciated.

"Hold on. Let me get my wallet." Charlie headed over to the chair where he had tossed his pants.

"No, sir. It is fine, sir." Rafael started toward the door.

"No, wait." Charlie retrieved his wallet and fumbled for some cash. He wanted to give him a big tip. Rafael, he realized, was the best friend he had ever had.

"Here you go." He held out three twenties.

"Oh, no, sir, too much."

"Please, please." Charlie thrust the bills closer to him. "Money means nothing to me. It means nothing. It can't buy you love, can it? No, not love. Here." He pinned the money against Rafael's chest with his hand.

"Thank you, sir," Rafael said. He took the money and folded up the bills. Then he considered Charlie with his deep-set eyes before reaching into his back pocket and pulling out a business card and handing it to him.

"It's the number. For a service," he said. "The woman escort." He looked embarrassed.

Charlie accepted the card, confused. "What? Oh, no, no, I don't want it. Thanks, though. I said I was kidding about that." Charlie handed the card back to him. "I'll just watch a porno movie, maybe."

Rafael nodded and put the card back into his pocket. Charlie gazed at him through blurry eyes. "You want some coffee?" he asked. He walked over to the table.

"No, thank you, sir."

"Want to shave?" Charlie held up the can of shaving cream and read the label. "It's extra foamy."

"No, thank you." Rafael appeared to be very uncomfortable.

He glanced down at the folded-up bills, then held the money back out to Charlie. "You keep. You keep the money." When he said this, Charlie started to cry a little.

"No, no, no. Please, you keep it, though that's very nice of you," Charlie said. He quickly wiped away a tear. "See, that's the difference between people like me and people like you, Rafael. See, I would never do something nice like that, never. I'm not a nice person. I'm only nice to clients. Everyone hated me at the agency. Except maybe Georgia. I don't know why. I wasn't that great to her either." Charlie collected himself and cleared his throat. "Listen, I don't need the money. I made four hundred and twenty-five thousand last year. I didn't get a bonus, though. Not even a token. Besides, I didn't really get fired. I quit my job to pursue other interests. I have lots of other interests. I brush my teeth, I shave. I'll probably just do that full-time now."

Poor Rafael was speechless.

"I'm bottoming out right now. I'll be hitting the bottom soon. After I do that, I'll be okay. Can I ask you a question, Rafael?"

"Yes."

"Have you ever bottomed out?"

Rafael looked down at the floor. "I don't think so," he said.

"Well, I'm about to do it now. Any minute. It looks like I'm standing here, but I'm actually falling."

Rafael swallowed and nodded. He slowly folded the bills up again and put them in his back pocket. "I am sorry, sir," he said.

"Don't worry about it. No biggie. I was in advertising. Did you ever hear of the Bagel Man commercials? Ever see them?"

Rafael just stared at him.

"They were very popular a while ago. I made them at another shop. The place I should have stayed. I never should have left that place. Never. My wife told me not to quit that job. I should have listened to her. She has excellent intuition. She wanted me, us, to go to counseling. Marriage counseling. She blames my career. She hates it. She's very down-to-earth. I met her when she was nineteen. Man, you should have seen what she looked like back then." Charlie shook his head in wonder. "Legs up to here. She's forty-eight and she still looks pretty good. Hasn't even gone gray yet. Everyone thinks she dyes her hair, but she doesn't. It's still black. It's that weird Irish thing. We never talk much anymore. I'm always gone. When she sees me, she just attacks me now anyway, so what's the point in talking to her, right, I mean, what's the point, right? I mean, am I right? I just try to avoid her. Except now I can't. I got nowhere to go. I got to face her now, maybe make things better."

Rafael nodded.

Charlie shook his head again. The room was starting to spin. "It's good I can talk about this with someone, I need to talk. Can I tell you something else?"

"*Sí.* Yes."

"I never told anyone this before, so can you keep this quiet? It's a secret, a very big secret, so I'm counting on you to be discreet, you know, secretive."

Rafael was expressionless.

"I have low sperm count."

"*Por qué?* What?"

Charlie clutched his groin and spoke loudly. "The sperm. Nada count. For making the babies, *los niños.*" He clutched his groin again.

Rafael looked at Charlie, confused. Then he said, "Oh, *sí, sí,*" and looked at the floor.

"Yeah, I know. We didn't think we could have kids. Kyle is a miracle. Low sperm count. You can't tell by looking at me, but I do. I mean, I look normal. Even when I'm naked, I look fine. Donna wanted kids, more kids. We should have adopted. That would have made her happy, kept her busy. She wanted to adopt, but I didn't."

Rafael now looked at the floor.

Charlie made his way over to the bed and sat down. "Anyway," he said.

"Are you all right, sir?"

"Fine. I'm fine. I just have low sperm count."

Rafael bowed and made his way to the door.

"Hey, wait, before you leave, can I ask you something? How many hours do you work a week? Can I ask you that?"

"Forty hours, sir. I work forty hours."

"Forty hours. See, I work about, I don't know, eighty hours a week. I'm nuts. I don't know what's wrong with me. I don't think I even really like my job anymore, but that's all I can do. That's not normal, is it? I mean, there's something wrong there, something's out of whack, but I can't stop. I can't. I didn't use to be this way, but I turned into this way."

Rafael just stared at the floor.

"Hell, I'm not making any sense." Charlie stood and approached Rafael. "Go home, get out of here. Listening to a loser like me. No job. Go on. Here." He held out another twenty. Rafael slowly reached for it and took the bill.

"Thank you, sir."

"No, thank *you*."

"God bless you, sir."

"No, God bless *you*."

After Rafael left, he brushed his teeth and, since he had shaving cream, shaved. It was about three in the morning, when he usually got up and was ready to start his day.

He got back into the bed, turned up the TV volume, and started a game with the remote. He let one person say something, and quickly changed the channel before another person could respond. He did this for some time and was getting good at it, when he suddenly grew bored and settled on a movie about a door to door salesman who had mild cerebral palsy and very large ears. The salesman limped from door to door selling household products. His customers loved him because, despite his challenges, he was very upbeat.

He watched the movie with great interest, believing it was on for a reason. He was destined to see this movie—based on a true story—about perseverance, determination, gigantic ears. Here was a man who could barely walk and talk, and look how he made out. He was loved and admired; they made a movie about him! Charlie thought about this and felt the faint electrical stirrings of hope and inspiration cruise through his body.

As the movie wore on, though, the sense of well-being faded and he began to feel wistful, then envious. He wanted mild cerebral palsy. He wanted gigantic ears. He wanted, needed, an obvious cross to bear. He wanted to be a refugee from a Third World nation, be a dwarf, have one leg shorter than the other, be the product of alcoholic parents, be an African-American woman. But he was white and male, came from a very stable household, and, migrating moles notwithstanding, was in good health. He had no excuse for his failure, no one to blame but himself.

He turned off the TV and then the lights and lay in bed. He feared he might die there, alone in a hotel wrapped in a strange bathrobe. He felt the tears coming again, fought them back, cursed out loud. Then he reached over for the phone and called home. He needed to talk to Donna. If he could just hear her voice one more time, one more time. He didn't want to be alone like this. He needed someone, and the someone he needed was his wife.

She didn't pick up, of course; it was three-thirty. Instead, he got their answering machine, and when he heard her recorded voice, he placed the phone over his heart and pressed it close before hanging up.

He lay in bed like a child, scared and wondering in the dark. He took deep breaths and swallowed. He curled his hands into fists. He lay there all night, just like that, thinking, and when the morning slowly made its way into his room, dirty and gray, he said a small prayer, his lips moving silently in the thin light.

Ned Meyers was a tall, slender man with a pale face and straight Julius Caesar bangs. His attire, cardigan sweater, woolen tie, well-worn corduroy pants, and Hush Puppies—*Hush Puppies!*—as well as his overly earnest face and sincere brown eyes, reminded Charlie of a high school guidance counselor. Because of all these things, mostly because he never liked his high school guidance counselor, but especially because he never trusted people with British accents, Charlie took an immediate disliking to him.

"I respect what you're saying, but I still think I should sue them," Charlie said.

"You have no grounds to sue anyone," Ned said. "None whatsoever."

"How about age discrimination? How about that? I just turned fifty. They waited for me to turn fifty, then"—Charlie snapped his fingers—"bam, they move on me, they attack."

"They compiled quite a file on you, Charlie." Ned opened a manila folder that was on his desk and scanned its contents. "They have many documented issues. The lack of business, that issue about everyone being fat, that obscene book club, that strange commercial with that rodent."

"Hey, for your information, that hamster tested great in the focus groups, okay? You know the Geico Gecko, that little green thing? We were trying to do the same thing. People love little creatures like that. Paula Abdul was the problem, okay? I don't know how the hell she ended up in the thing. It wasn't the talking hamster. The talking hamster was fine, believe me. He looked great with that little cowboy hat on and those boots."

"I'm just reporting what they have documented."

"Yeah, well, listen, I don't care what they say, I'm going to sue for a better package. What they gave me was ridiculous. Ridiculous."

"Also, there is that photo of you sleeping. At your desk," Ned said.

"Listen, he had no right to take that picture! No right at all! That's an invasion of my privacy, my civil liberties."

"But you were sleeping on the job. Literally."

"So what? I basically blacked out. Collapsed. I worked constantly."

"Well," Ned sighed.

Ned and Charlie were facing each other in an airless office at Rogers & Newman, a blank room, lifeless with the exception of a crooked potted tree in the corner, a wall calendar, and a clichéd inspirational poster showing a wizened old man (WHEN GOING GETS TOUGH, THE TOUGH GET GOING) running up a wooded hill at twilight. It was Friday, two days after Charlie had bottomed out at the Four Seasons. Outside, in the functioning real world, people were working, checking e-mail, attending meetings, heading to airports, making lunch plans. Charlie, however, was cloistered inside an interrogation room, the stench of failure everywhere.

While Ned attempted to once again review all the resources Rogers & Newman offered, Charlie looked at his watch. It was close to eleven o'clock and, other than attending a special birthday bash for Augie, the panda bear at the Brookfield Zoo (he had spent a good part of the day before watching the staff hang decorations in preparation for it), his schedule was fairly clear for the next thirty to forty years. Still, he wanted this meeting to be brief. He was ashamed to be in a transition office, ashamed to be sitting with a patronizing Hush Puppy-wearing man, talking about his career and his life.

He was also annoyed that Ned Meyers was working with him. Earlier, out in the hall, he had briefly met a couple of sharp transition consultants, Frank and Tom, two outgoing young men nattily dressed in appropriate business-casual Brooks Brothers attire. Whoever determined the assignments had made a mistake, Charlie thought. Either Frank or Tom, with their firm handshakes and excellent eye contact, should have been assigned to him.

He studied Ned again and, when he noticed a spot on his tie, said, "I have another appointment, so we're going to have to make this quick. I just stopped in because I wanted to know my rights."

"Rights?" Ned smiled. His long, skinny hands were folded on top of the now-closed manila folder, the indictment against Charlie.

"I mean, what I can do here," he said. "Your resources."

Ned cleared his throat. "Well, I've been trying to do just that. You have access to all of our office equipment: fax, phone, computer, e-mail. We can provide cell phones if you have to go out of town. We're open from seven-thirty A.M. to seven P.M., six days a week. Everything we do here is designed to get you out there again."

"Out where?"

"Out there in the workforce, of course. With a job." Ned smiled again. "We also have a daily networking meeting grouped by industry where we all get together and share information and progress reports. You, of course, will be part of the marketing group including advertising, public relations, sales promotion people. We currently have a super group of people in that group. They call themselves the refugees. They're a super group."

Charlie again glanced at his watch and said nothing.

Ned's smile grew. His cheerfulness was insincere, manufactured, and worst of all patronizing, Charlie thought. Charlie wanted to tell him how much money he used to make, tell him how many people he used to manage, and wipe that smile off his face.

"Would you like to meet them now?" Ned asked. "The refugees? Some of them are here. I know Bradley is in. Bradley Smith. He's a nice man. Very big in the marketing community. Very well connected."

Charlie ignored the invitation to meet Very Well Connected (though he had never heard of him) Bradley Smith. "Where do I work? Where's my office?" he asked.

Ned sat up rather officiously in his chair. "We assign you an office every morning when you come in."

"Well, is it a private office?"

"Yes. If you get in early enough, I mean."

"What do you mean?"

"I mean, you have to get in early enough sometimes to obtain a private office."

"What do you mean? What happens if I don't come in early? Do I stand up all day?"

"Ha! Very funny. No, no. You get a cubicle in the back, that's all."

"A what? A cubicle?" He reacted as if Ned had just told him

he was to spend his day in the men's room of a Greyhound station. It had been more than twenty years since Charlie had sat in a cubicle. He didn't even like walking past them.

"Yes. We have cubes in the back," Ned said.

"Well, that's unacceptable."

"I'm sorry?"

"Unacceptable. I'm not sitting in a cubicle."

"Then you should make sure to get in early."

Charlie was about to respond, but decided to drop it. He was usually at work by five A.M., so it was a moot point. He glanced at his watch. "What else do we have to go over? What else?"

Ned straightened some papers. "Well, other than first-come, first-served on the offices, we don't have many ground rules, but we do have a few. We ask that you attend the networking meetings. We also ask that you are self-sufficient with office equipment."

"What do you mean? Self-sufficient? What does that mean?"

"We won't help you with photocopying, collating, e-mailing, formatting things on your computer. This is intentional."

"Why? What do you mean, intentional?"

"We want you to be self-sufficient. We feel it's important for our clients to learn to take care of themselves in office settings. Most of our executives are accustomed to having assistants, secretaries, and others do all the work for them. Part of our transitional training involves learning to help yourself. We will not enable you. We had one client here not too long ago, a chief marketing officer of a huge corporation, who didn't even know how to use the mouse on his computer. He put it on the floor and stepped on it. He thought it was some kind of pump."

"I know how to use a computer," Charlie said. "Well, at least a BlackBerry."

"We don't issue BlackBerrys here. Just a regular computer."

"Is it a laptop?"

"No. It's a standard Mac. A little dated, I'm afraid, but still very usable. You can do Excel and Photoshop, PowerPoint, desktop publishing, and Mail Merge on it. Programs you might need."

"Oh, good," Charlie said. He had no clue how to use any of those programs. That had been Georgia's domain.

"Well," Ned said. "We should get started today. We have some basic paperwork we need to go over."

Charlie grimaced. The office had absolutely no ventilation and was getting altogether too warm. "I really have to be going."

Ned looked hurt. "But you just got here."

"I know, but I have an appointment."

"Are you sure?"

"Yes."

"Well, then, I guess I'll just give you these." Ned shuffled through some papers and handed Charlie a bulky brown envelope. "There's some background information in here as well as our workbook."

"Workbook?"

"Game plan."

"Game plan?"

"Strategy. Our strategy to get you back out there. Our strategy for success." He made a fist and shook it. "Our strategy to help you win."

Charlie took the envelope.

"I'm going to ask you to do a little homework before I see you again," Ned continued. "I'm going to ask you to make a list of everyone you know who has a job, absolutely everyone. Include phone numbers and e-mail addresses. You need to build a tree. A networking tree. Do you know what a networking tree is?"

"Yes."

"You do?"

"I can conceptualize it, yes."

Ned paused and regarded Charlie closely before speaking again. "It's a synergistic structure. Everyone feeding off each other. One contact leads to another." He clasped his hands together, his long fingers interlocked. He was trying hard to look wise and knowing.

"Listen," Charlie said. "I appreciate the advice, but I really don't need to make a tree, or whatever. I've been in advertising for a long time. It's a pretty tight community. I have a lot of contacts. Everyone knows who I am, and I know everyone. I won't be out long."

Ned unlocked his hands, disappointed. "Of course you have contacts," he said. "But it's best if you organize them in an efficient way." He locked his hands again and raised his eyebrows hopefully. "Besides, it's a very difficult marketplace right now."

"Fine." Charlie stood to leave. "I'll get working on my tree right away."

"Terrific. Now, before you go, I'd like to cover a few more things." Ned motioned for him to sit back down. "I'd like to offer you some rules to live by, if you will."

Charlie remained standing. "What?"

Ned motioned again for Charlie to sit. "Please. It will only take a moment. Please."

Charlie finally sat.

"Yes, rules to live by." Ned cleared his throat and looked at Charlie intensely. "First, stay above the fray. Don't say anything negative about your former employers. No matter what."

Charlie wondered if throwing a gumball machine qualified as staying above the fray. "Okay," he said. "Fine."

"Don't burn bridges. I know that's easier said than done. But please, we had one client who smashed the windows of his supervisor's car. He was arrested and now that shameful incident is on his record. He had to pay for lawyers, go to court. And when it was all settled, he went out and did it again. Smashed more windows. It was a mess, so don't do that. You must stay in control. Don't go back to your office, or leave rude voice mails, or . . ."—he paused, tilted his head, and inspected Charlie from the corner of one eye—"or throw things. At people."

Charlie looked at him blankly.

"Such as former coworkers."

Charlie continued to look at him without saying anything.

Ned readjusted his head. "Right. Second, it's important that you acknowledge your feelings. You're going to feel guilty, angry, frustrated, scared. You're going to experience wild mood swings, almost manic. One moment you'll be fine, happy and optimistic, the world is a wonderful place full of opportunity, and the next minute, well . . ." He softened his voice. "Well, the next minute, you'll be quite sad."

"I'll make sure to guard against that."

"Excellent. Now for number three." Ned held up three fingers here. "Take a close look at your finances and develop a workable family budget. Remember, the two most important things are food and shelter. Everything else is secondary. Food and shelter," he repeated.

"We have both."

"Excellent. Because food and shelter are important. They are essential."

"That's what I've heard."

Ned tilted his head again and regarded Charlie. "Yes. And finally . . ." He held up four fingers now. "Finally, Charlie, don't be afraid to lean on the support of your family. Don't be ashamed to reach out to them for encouragement. And don't be afraid to ask for help. Being fired is humiliating. Being told you're no longer needed, that you have failed, that you're expendable, is a tough, tough pill to swallow. Your family will help."

Charlie's lips tightened.

"May I ask, how did they, your family, take the news?"

"What?" He shifted positions in his chair.

"The news, your family."

"Actually, they took it very well."

"How did your life partner react?"

"Who? You mean my wife?"

"If that's who your life partner is, yes."

Charlie paused. He couldn't work with this guy, he would ask to be reassigned. "She's fine. My life partner was very understanding. Extremely supportive."

"She sounds like an amazing woman."

"Well, she *is* my life partner."

Ned stared at him. "Yes." He cleared his throat. "Does she work?"

"Yes. No. She used to be a nurse, for years, but when we moved, she quit. I was traveling so much, she had to stay at home to be with our son."

"Hmm," Ned said. "So you're both not working?"

"Yes."

"Hmm."

"What's wrong? What's the problem?"

"No problem, just digesting information." He jotted something down. "Anyway, telling your life partner, your wife, is without a doubt the most difficult thing you can do. People tend to forget that when one partner gets fired, the other one really is getting fired too. He or she suffers too. That's why I'm relieved to hear she took it so well. Many spouses have a very difficult time with it and problems arise."

"What do you mean? What do they do? Do they leave their husbands?"

Ned's face puckered up. "That happens. Unfortunately, yes."

"How often does that happen?"

"I'm not exactly sure."

"Give me a rough idea. What, one out of three, one out of four, what?"

"I don't know specifics. Enough times that it's a concern."

Charlie chewed on his bottom lip.

"But those marriages were probably in bad shape to begin with," Ned added.

Charlie chewed harder.

"Anyway, I can take you on a tour now."

"I can't now." Charlie tapped his watch. He simply had to get out of this office and away from this person. "I have to go." He stood again.

"Are you sure? I was hoping you could stay for lunch. We have a nice little deli downstairs, wonderful soups. We can talk there."

"Can't. Maybe next time."

"Well, when can we expect to see you again?"

"Soon. Very soon."

As Charlie was making his way back out, down the hall, he

shuddered at the office's blandness: battleship-gray carpet, egg-shell walls, painful fluorescent lights. Someone had managed to position a few potted plants in the corners of the hallways, all of which seemed to be in various stages of death. Overhead, he heard forced, stale air humming from the vents. His mind flashed back to his old office, the marble floor, the winding stair-case, the German art, and he walked faster.

By the elevators, he ran into a tall, silver-haired man hold-ing a briefcase. The man pushed the button twice and then turned toward Charlie.

"You the new guy?" His face was ruddy and intelligent and he had on a tailored blue suit. If Charlie were casting a com-mercial for a bank or brokerage house, he would have had him on the short list for the role of wise and benevolent chairman.

"I'm new here," Charlie said. He focused on the elevator doors.

"Who's assigned to you? Who's your caseworker, your babysitter?"

"Ned Meyers." He gestured with his head at the glass doors of the office behind them. "I just met him."

The man smirked. "Ned. He's mine too." He extended his hand. "I'm Bradley Smith."

"I'm Charlie Baker. Ned mentioned you."

"He did, did he?" Bradley chuckled for some reason, his smile a flashbulb. "What did he say?"

"We didn't talk long. He just mentioned you."

This seemed to disappoint Bradley Smith. He put a hand in his pants pocket and jingled some change. His smile disap-peared. A few seconds later the elevator doors slid open and they both got on.

"Actually, Ned said you were well connected."

This cheered Bradley. His smiled returned, brighter than before. "What line of work were you in?" he asked.

"I'm still in it. I'm in advertising. I was with DiSanto & Herr."

"Another marketing guy. We'll be in the same group, then." He jingled more change. "I headed up marketing at the Bank of the Midwest."

"Oh, sure. I know the place." Charlie was pretty sure Bank of the Midwest didn't exist anymore.

"What do you think of Rogers so far?" he asked.

Charlie shrugged. "I was only there for a minute. Everything seemed fine."

"It's not a bad place. Beats working." They both laughed too hard at this, then continued staring at the flashing floor numbers.

"How's the advertising business right now?" Bradley asked.

"Little tight."

"It will turn around."

"It will."

"How long have you been out?" Bradley asked.

"Just a week. Not even." The elevator was extremely slow. "How long have you been out?"

Bradley's smile faded again and Charlie thought he heard the air leave him, a wistful prairie wind.

"Two years," he said. "Two years next month."

The elevator bounced when they hit the ground floor.

Chapter Seven

In the daytime, their house was a still and fragile place. The kitchen was breathless, the living room apprehensive, the family room watchful and waiting. Drifting through the empty rooms, Charlie felt he was upsetting the natural order of things, disturbing the cosmos. He was an intruder, his presence illicit. It was early afternoon, the middle of a workday, and he should have been anywhere but home.

Rather than celebrate Augie's birthday at the zoo, he had decided to head back to Wilton. He remembered that Donna spent most Fridays volunteering at that community place. Frequently, she was out until eight or even nine o'clock, so he thought he'd take a chance. He also thought that if she was home, he would go ahead and tell her, and be done with it.

Making his way through their house, on his way upstairs to his office, he was struck by how spacious and aggressively furnished their home was. Their huge kitchen still managed to look crowded, with its granite-topped island, Sub-Zero refrigerator, separate wine refrigerator, and a small flat-screen TV that flipped down from one of the cabinets. All of this was surrounded by quarter-sawn oak cabinetry that he had picked out from a catalog because Donna couldn't make up her mind.

The kitchen flowed into an equally large family room that was dominated by a fifty-two-inch flat screen TV, an imposing leather chair and ottoman, two couches, and an area the Realtor referred to as a reading nook. This nook was lined on three sides by bookcases and overlooked their backyard, which, he realized, was the size of Tara.

He stood by the window and counted the trees; there were four fully grown and expensive-looking trees and a number of smaller, presumably cheaper ones. There was also an expansive deck that a Cessna could safely land on. He observed the trees, wondering if and how they affected his tax bill, then slowly made his way into the living room, where he stopped in front of a bookcase filled with photos: Kyle riding a bike on their old block; the three of them at Disney World, all wearing Mickey Mouse ears; the three of them standing on the front porch of their old house, Kyle in a black and white Little League White Sox uniform, Donna proudly beaming. Their wedding photo, Donna glowing, beautiful. There were no pictures of them in this house, he noticed. None. The picture-taking had evidently stopped a few years ago.

He wandered over to the black Steinway baby grand piano. Over Donna's protests, he had purchased the piano with the full intention of mastering it. Though he had never taken lessons or played an instrument of any kind, he believed that, being creative, he possessed innate musical talent and that this $20,000 piano would unleash it. He imagined entertaining guests and friends with Bach, show tunes, Beatles songs at lively parties and gatherings, everyone crowded around. Though Kyle had taken a few lessons, Charlie had never learned to play, losing interest in the piano soon after it arrived. He plunked one key and listened to its lonely, high sound, a lost note, reverberate throughout the room. He decided it was a metaphor for something, and moved on.

In the front hallway, he scooped up the mail that lay scattered on the floor by the door slot, then walked upstairs. For some reason, they had five bedrooms, including a master suite complete with a once-used fireplace and the requisite Jacuzzi in the bathroom; a warm and brightly painted sitting room, where he had never seen anyone stand, much less sit; and his office with a skylight, a definitely too-large desk, a new computer, and another once-used fireplace.

He sat down at the immense desk and attempted to check his e-mail at the agency. As expected, his access was denied. He next checked his voice mail and was surprised to discover that it was still connected. He had one message, from Nick Coston, a small manufacturing client based in Wisconsin, telling him he had heard the news and wished him well. I know you'll be fine, Nick said. Rather than heartened, this message opened a hole in him. Being an object of sympathy was a new experience for Charlie. He hung up the phone and began reading the mail.

There was a letter from Dr. Pamela Getty, family therapist. This was the marriage counselor Donna had wanted them to visit. She had scheduled a meeting a while ago, but Charlie had a last-minute conference call and had missed the appointment. He skimmed the letter, *we're still hoping to reschedule*, then placed it aside and addressed the bills.

There was one from the landscaping company for $2,000, an orthodontics bill for $700, an electric bill for $345, and a $2,800 bill from the John Byrnes Sleep Apnea Clinic, which he had attended two months prior in an effort to improve his sleep habits.

He dropped those bills in a pile, picked up another, and examined it. This one, for $1,213, was from Tony DeAngelo Plumbing. Other than a brief description, *ongoing work to correct water flow*, the bill was short on details. The amount didn't concern him as much as the ongoing part. To the best of his knowledge their water was, and always had been, flowing just fine. He got up, marched down to the hallway bathroom, flushed the toilet, and ran the water in the sink. Everything seemed in order. He repeated this process in all of their bathrooms before returning to the office, sitting back down, and staring out the window at their peaceful, expensive yard.

Money was going to be a problem. A big problem. Apparently, unlike their toilet water, it was steadily flowing out of their house like a turbulent river. The levee, his job, which had kept the whitecapped torrent in check for years, was gone. If they didn't economize, the floodplains would be swamped and lives lost.

He pulled out a yellow legal pad from a drawer and wrote *The New Frugality* across the top in dark, meaningful letters, which he then underlined to make even more meaningful. He next drew several columns for various cost centers and marked them accordingly: *Shelter, Food, Utilities, Insurance, Miscellaneous.* For the first time ever, the Baker family was going to have a budget that would be honored, followed, adhered to. This budget would not be optional.

He took Ned's advice and addressed the issue of food and shelter first. While their shelter costs were fixed—there was no negotiating their immense mortgage and preposterous taxes—he thought there might be some wiggle room in what they spent on food. He had no idea what they currently were paying for food, but he was sure they could spend less. They could clip coupons, buy generic items, stop ordering out, skip meals, get themselves invited to other people's homes. Donna would have to become more creative in the kitchen, make do with less costly cuts of meat, canned foods, Spam, generic things in white boxes.

Inspired, he wrote *$100 a week* in the food column. When he realized that this came to a little more $14 a day (less than half his daily parking costs on days he had driven to the office), he decided to increase it, first to $125 a week, then to $150, and finally to $200. Then he pushed the legal pad aside because he realized that he had no idea what he was doing and put his head down on the desk.

He felt a growing need to gather himself, regroup. As Ned had predicted, he was experiencing a mood swing, slipping from benignly despondent to psychotically angry. He was mad at Helmut, then Marken, and then his parents. They were both high school teachers and they never should have let him go into advertising, he thought. Never. They should have steered him into their profession. He had the potential to be a modern-day Mr. Chips, beloved, admired. He would have worn spectacles and turtlenecks. Schoolgirls would have had crushes on him, future authors would have dedicated books to him. Advertising was a horrible and shallow business, full of horrible and shallow people.

He once again turned his anger back at Helmut, then Marken, then Trainor, his client at Southwest who had fired them, then, finally, inevitably, himself. He was hardly blameless in all of this. He should have worked harder, used better judgment, finished at least one Lincoln biography and mastered diplomacy. Maybe Charlie could have learned something.

He stood up and walked over to the bookcase, looking for a book on Lincoln. He carefully searched all six shelves, found dozens of self-help books, three biographies of Elton John, another biography on the life and times of Vanna White, but not a single Lincoln tome. He wondered where they all were. Probably still at the office. Marken was probably poring over them now, committing speeches to memory. He sighed, picked up the book on Vanna White (he had made a mattress commercial with her years ago), then silently put it back.

He felt the room closing in. He did several deep knee bends. He did fifty of them, until the blood was roaring behind his ears and he was sweating. He sat back down and, still breathing heavily, dug into his briefcase for the materials Ned Meyers had given him.

Among other things, there was a workbook on building résumés that sell; a binder designed to organize your business contacts; and a thin paperback book, *Coping with Job Loss*, by Thomas J. Murphy, a former publishing executive who, according to the back flap, had been fired twelve times over the course of his successful career. He leafed through the book, pausing to skim a chapter on depression, then another on guilt. While looking for some words of advice on rage and revenge, he came across a chapter entitled "Informing Your Life Partner":

Informing your family and, in particular, your life partner can be an extremely emotional experience. Careful preparation should be taken to ensure it goes as painlessly as possible.

The book urged the use of "message points":

Before breaking the news, write down a few key message points—specific and concise things you want to convey to your life partner when you meet. Spend some time developing and rehearsing them. This will ensure that you say the right thing at the right time. Remember, keep them short and to the point and don't deviate!

Message points. Charlie leaned back and considered this concept. When and how to tell Donna had been weighing on him. He had envisioned taking her to a restaurant, having a nice, relaxed meal, and then, after nine or ten drinks, telling her about getting fired in an off-handed, casual by-the-way. Exactly what he was going to tell her, though, was a concern. He didn't want to alarm her about their finances or the fact that he was a fifty-year-old man looking for a job in a recession. He also didn't necessarily want to admit that he had failed. The book was right: how he handled the conversation was critical.

Inspired, he whirled around in his chair, turned the computer on, and began typing.

MESSAGE POINTS TO DONNA
(WHILE AT A NICE RESTAURANT)

1. I was let go, but it was a mutual decision.
2. Yes, fired. Whatever.
3. I got an excellent severance package, though.
4. We will be fine financially; we have plenty of money. Really.

5. This is for the best.
6. I will have a new job soon.
7. This is really for the best.
8. Everything will be fine.
9. Really.

He paused and reviewed the list. Then he added a few more.

10. I know you told me not to take that job. I know that.
11. I know you and Kyle have made a lot of sacrifices. I know that too.

He stopped. Then:

12. I hope this doesn't make you think less of me.
13. I'm still a decent husband.
14. On certain levels.
15. I don't drink, beat, or cheat.
16. I could have cheated.
17. Oh, sure I could have, sure.
18. I don't know. On five different occasions.
19. At least.
20. They came on to me.
21. I don't know, women I worked with. Clients. Women in hotels.
22. But I didn't.
23. It's not because I was afraid of herpes. I knew you would say that.
24. It's because I'm married.
25. To you.
26. Anyway.
27. What were you doing at that crappy restaurant by yourself late at night when you said you were going to bed early?
28. I think I have a right to know.
29. Every right.
30. I'm your husband.

31. Damn it!
32. I was too embarrassed to tell you that I got fired, so I was hiding.
33. Yes, hiding.
34. Across the street.
35. By the theater.
36. I'm not pathetic.
37. Now, what were you doing there?
38. Where did you go?

Then:

39. Do you want dessert?
40. Let's split something.

He read over the message points, put his head back down, and closed his eyes.

Later that day, after he had finished accomplishing absolutely nothing in his office, he made his way downstairs to the kitchen, opened the refrigerator, and studied its contents. With the exception of a bottle of mustard, some orange juice, and a small plastic container of cherry tomatoes, it was empty. He was wondering how he could somehow combine these ingredients to produce a hearty and tasty meal when he heard someone cough. He jumped, turned. Kyle was standing a few feet behind him, an outrageously overstuffed backpack slipping down his shoulders.

"Jesus! You scared me."

"Hi."

Charlie shut the refrigerator and walked over to the island. "What are you doing here?"

Kyle shrugged. "What are you doing here?" He had his hands in the front pockets of his jeans and was slouched over.

"What do you mean? I'm home, that's all."

"Why?"

"What do you mean, why? Because I live here, that's why. I

came home early. I was in a meeting and it ended, so I came home. Sometimes it works like that."

Kyle nodded. He seemed to accept this explanation as plausible. He opened the refrigerator and stared into it. Even leaning forward, he looked incredibly tall.

"How tall are you?" Charlie asked.

"What? I don't know." He continued to look into the refrigerator.

"About how tall?"

"Six-two."

"Six-two. That's tall. You get that from your mom's side. From your uncles."

Kyle shrugged again and pushed the orange juice carton to one side.

"Hungry?" Charlie asked.

"Yeah. But there's nothing to eat."

"What are you talking about? There's tomatoes in there."

Kyle didn't say anything.

"Do you know when your mother is coming home?"

"What? No."

"Where is she?"

"I don't know."

"Is she gone a lot?"

"Sometimes." Kyle closed the refrigerator. He looked tired and disheveled. Despite his size, he still had traces of little boy in him: oversized and innocent eyes, smooth soft skin. His thick black hair hung low over his eyes.

"You need a haircut," Charlie said.

Kyle didn't respond. Instead, he turned toward the dining room.

"Where are you going?"

"Nowhere. Upstairs."

"What are you going to do up there?"

"Nothing."

"I thought you said you were hungry."

"There's nothing to eat."

"Well, maybe I'll go shopping, then."

Kyle stopped and turned back to face his father. "What?"

"I'm going to the store."

"Mom always shops."

"Yeah, well, this time I am. What do we need?"

"I don't know, everything."

"Everything," Charlie said. "Can you be more specific? What do you want to eat?"

"I don't know. Chips and stuff."

"Anything else?"

"I don't know."

"What about for dinner?"

"Dinner?"

"Yes, you know, dinner. When we all sit down together and eat food at the end of the day. At night."

Kyle considered this concept. "When do we do that?"

"Never mind," Charlie said. He reached for his keys on the island. "I'll be back."

"Don't forget chips," Kyle said.

It was a mild Indian summer afternoon, and the wide, tree-lined streets of Wilton were, as usual, peaceful. No people, no cars. Driving through the town, on his way to DeVries, a local grocery store, he was reminded of why he had insisted on moving. It was a beautiful community, full of impressive, well-maintained older homes set on deep, well-appointed lawns. Imposing trees arched overhead, their leaves a canopy of colors. Fall was always Charlie's favorite time of year, and in Wilton it was on majestic display.

The grocery store was located near the town's historic district, a two-block "square" featuring cobblestone streets, gas lamps, and original storefronts from the early twentieth century. They had moved into their house on the Fourth of July weekend. Charlie remembered sitting with Donna at a picnic table and watching a flag-raising ceremony in the square and thinking that, for a while at least, they had nowhere higher to climb.

He parked and walked quickly into the store, his head down.

Even though it was after five P.M. and he had every right to be home from work and entering a grocery store, he nonetheless felt self-conscious and wanted to be discreet.

It had been years since Charlie had done any shopping, so he initially found the grocery store overwhelming. For starters, there were a number of aisles and an infinity of products and he had no idea where anything was located. Fearing he might draw attention to himself, he made a reconnaissance trip to get the lay of the land. Finally, after making a mental map, he doubled back to the front door, grabbed a cart, and began to shop.

He worked deliberately, checking prices, calculating costs, and evaluating needs. As he suspected, their usual brand of orange juice was pricey, so he bought two cans of frozen concentrate. He resisted the fresh strawberries ($4.95 a container) and instead loaded up on canned fruit cocktail. Then he bought a bag of baking potatoes, some iceberg lettuce, slightly bruised tomatoes which were half price, a can of lima beans, and some other cheap, but, he hoped, filling items. In the frozen food aisle, he stopped to get Donna a pint of Häagen-Dazs Rocky Road, her favorite, but upon seeing its price opted instead for a tub of Mr. Goody's Chocolate Ice Cream Experience. He worked in advertising and knew that consumers spent millions on brand names, convinced they were getting something they were not. At the end of the day, there was little difference between Häagen-Dazs and Mr. Goody's, other than maybe a thirty-second spot during *The Simpsons.*

There was also very little difference between Starbucks and Aunt Bula's French Roast Blend, Cheerios and Tasty O's, Nabisco Fig Newtons and a white box simply stamped FIG COOKIES.

On his way to the checkout, he stopped at the meat counter. There had been a line of customers there when he first entered the store, but no one was waiting now. A kindly-looking butcher with a ruddy complexion and carefully combed white hair eyed him as he approached.

"Can I help you?" he asked.

Charlie looked around, smiled. "I have a rather unusual question for you," he said.

The butcher took a small step back. "Okay."

Charlie chuckled nervously. "Well, it's not *that* unusual." He moved closer and tried to keep his voice down. "What is the cheapest kind of meat you have? The absolute cheapest, now."

"Cheapest?"

"Rock-bottom. The cheapest."

"Well . . ." the man looked a tad embarrassed. "I'd have to say the chicken necks." He pointed vaguely toward the glass meat case that separated them.

"Chicken necks. Really? What are they? I mean, are they actual, you know, chicken necks?"

"Yes. I think that's why they're called that."

"Boy, I didn't know chickens even had necks. I mean, I never thought about it."

"I don't know why you would," the butcher said.

Charlie paused. "Chicken necks. Absolute cheapest, now?"

"Yes."

"Absolute cheapest." Charlie considered this. "How do you prepare them? Do you eat them like chicken legs? I mean, I never see them at Kentucky Fried Chicken."

"People make soup out of them."

This intrigued Charlie. Soup was nutritious and they could make a lot of it, maybe enough to last for several years. "Oh, chicken neck soup. Is that what they call it?"

"I don't think they call it that."

"What do they call it, then?"

"I'm not sure." The butcher glanced over Charlie's shoulder and wet his lips. He kept smiling, though. "Would you like some necks?"

Charlie fell silent. He didn't think he was quite at that point yet. Buying chicken necks was a statement, an admission, that he wasn't ready to make. "No, not this time."

"Are you sure?" The man scanned Charlie's cart and saw all the cheap and barely FDA-approved items. "I can give them to you if you like."

"Give them to me? What do you mean? You mean for free? Free chicken necks?" This offer and the sincere, hopeful way it was presented greatly saddened him. Like Rafael, this man was a truly decent human. Charlie had had no idea there were so many decent human beings out there, just walking around, giving away free chicken necks. He had spent too much time in advertising, a soulless profession. "No, no. I couldn't do that. No, no. But thank you. You're a very kind, very decent person."

The butcher was embarrassed. He puffed his cheeks out and nodded.

"I don't want the chicken necks," Charlie said.

"Are you sure? Won't take me a minute."

Charlie waved at him. "No, no. I don't know how to make soup anyway. I'll take some pork chops instead."

"Pork chops?"

"Yeah. Some cheap ones. Thin ones. Doesn't matter. Just as long as they're safe to eat."

The butcher looked relieved. He snapped his fingers. "We have some on sale," he said, eagerly reaching for them.

Charlie paid for the groceries in cash, then quickly made his way back to the Navigator. Despite the depressing exchange over the chicken necks, he felt good about his shopping experience. It was a step in the right direction. A start. Even after he got a new job, he vowed to adhere to the spirit, if not the bottom line, of the New Frugality. There was no excuse for the way they had been living; no excuse for Cheerios when Tasty O's would do.

Since he was in no hurry to get back, he decided to take the long way home. He made his way down one side street and then another, drinking in the evening and enjoying the homes with their winding brick driveways and sweeping lawns. While driving, he experienced an unexpected sense of well-being. He had lived in Wilton for more than four years and had never simply driven around, enjoying the neighborhood, his neighborhood, the one he had worked so hard to join. He pledged to do this more often, promised himself that he would take time, make time, to enjoy simple things like sunsets, warm evenings, driving in his Lincoln Navigator and looking at two-million-dollar homes.

He drove for a few minutes in one direction, and then another, until he found himself in the parking lot of the Wilton train station. He occasionally took the train to work and was always impressed by this particular station, a quaint stone building with an arched entryway and inviting red wooden door. He cut the engine and watched the brightness of the door dull and fade into the darkness, listening to the singsong of crickets. Gradually, other cars pulled up alongside and soon he heard the rumble of an approaching train. When it came to a stop, Charlie slunk low in his seat and watched as its doors slid open and commuters jumped out. Some were in suits, but most were dressed casually, their raincoats and jackets open to the warm evening. They walked past Charlie holding their briefcases and newspapers, their eyes faraway, their thoughts transitioning from work to home. No one looked his way and, as they disappeared into waiting cars and humming SUVs, no one seemed to see him; Charlie was no longer of their world.

After the train pulled out and the people and cars had dispersed, he drove home. His sense of well-being was gone, replaced by a thin but deepening melancholy. Who was he without a job? What was he? He felt useless. Dead. A ghost haunting old spots. He drove slowly with the windows down, the sound of the crickets rising and falling.

When he reached the house, he found Donna playing basketball in the driveway. His depression vanished, replaced now by a sense of panic. He would have to explain his early arrival home, the groceries, everything. He turned off the Navigator and sat there, breathing and thinking.

She was wearing shorts and a white sleeveless T-shirt and was dribbling with her back to him. It had been a long time since he had seen her do this. Years ago, when Kyle was a boy, they all used to shoot around in the driveway. Donna had played in high school and was very good and Kyle, he remembered, was something of a prodigy, dribbling behind his back and running circles around Charlie.

He sat in silence for a moment longer, then slowly stepped out of the Navigator and stood in the driveway, his eyes on his wife.

Her form was smooth and fluid, and despite the darkness, she seldom missed as she worked her way around the basket, swishing the ball through, first from five feet, then from ten. He waited for her to acknowledge him, but she never did, so intent was she on her shooting. He was beginning to wonder if she was deliberately ignoring him when he saw her earpiece and then the iPod tucked into her side. He reached in and grabbed the two bags of groceries.

"Hello," he said loudly, walking past her.

Despite her new commitment to look as expressionless as possible anytime he was near, she was clearly confused when she saw Charlie with the bags. Her eyes grew wide.

"What's going on? What are you doing?" She pulled out the earpiece and followed him inside.

He opened the side door and walked into the kitchen, trying to act as normal as possible, trying to pretend that it hadn't been years since he had gone to the grocery store or even carried groceries. "I went shopping," he said.

"I shop on Saturdays," she said.

Charlie put the bags on a counter. "Yeah, well, we didn't have anything to eat tonight and you weren't home, so I went."

"I didn't know you were going to be home. What are you doing home?"

"I came home a little early, that's all."

She studied Charlie for a moment, then sat on a stool at the island.

"What were Kyle and you going to do for dinner?" he asked.

"We usually get a pizza on Fridays."

"We might want to cut back on ordering out so much." Charlie quickly began putting things away, turning his back in an effort to shield the groceries from her.

"What did you buy?" she asked.

"A few things."

"What's that?" She pointed at an immense jar of peanut butter: "Doc Nutty."

"Nothing. Just peanut butter." Charlie grabbed the jar and shoved it into a cabinet. It barely fit, it was so huge.

"What is all this stuff?" She was now standing and pulling things out of the bags. "Why did you get so many canned foods? What are these?"

"I don't know. Lima beans."

"*Lima* beans?"

"Yeah, lima beans." Charlie took the can away from her. "I'm just trying to economize." He was beginning to perspire, his forehead growing damp. Thank God he hadn't bought the chicken necks.

He proceeded to unpack the second bag. "I saw some of our bills. The one from the plumber. What's this ongoing water flow problem?"

"They're almost done with it."

"Almost done with it? It's costing us a fortune."

"Since when do you care about our bills?"

"I always care about our bills." He pretended to study the label on the can of lima beans. "What's that two-thousand-dollar landscaping bill?"

"We had to replace all those evergreens in the back. They were dead. It was your idea. I didn't even want the damn trees." She suddenly slammed down a can of stewed tomatoes on a countertop. "You know, you have a lot of nerve."

Charlie jumped. The ferocity of her attack surprised him. Up until now he would have categorized their relationship as a Cold War with quick border skirmishes. This full frontal assault indicated a worrisome escalation of tensions. "What's wrong now?" he asked.

"You have a lot of nerve to start asking about our bills. You're the one spending all the money! You're the one who wanted the piano, the . . . the big TV. That tank you drive, that car. The BMW wasn't good enough. You're the one who wanted to move here to the world's most expensive house in the world's most expensive suburb, so don't start counting pennies now!"

Charlie remained calm. "All I'm saying is that we have to watch our money, that's all. Just make a little effort."

"Since when?"

"It's the responsible thing to do. We are in a recession, for the record."

"Responsible? What do you know about that?" Donna was wound up, her face red, her freckles out in full force. "You're . . . you're never here, I have no idea where you are half the time. And when you are here, you're hovering over your computer or checking that stupid thing, your precious little BlackBerry. You have no interest in Kyle, no idea what's going on here. You couldn't care less."

Charlie resisted the urge to slam the can of lima beans down on the counter and instead said, "I care," very quietly.

"Yeah, right," Donna said. She stormed off.

He considered following her, but decided to let things be for the moment, let things bottom out. Obviously, this outburst had been building for some time, he thought. She had reasons to vent. He had been almost nonexistent on the home front the past two years, and when he was home, he was distant and irritable. Setting things right and winning her back would be a challenge. But he was confident he could do it. He needed to. With his job gone, he had no energy, no desire to fight with his wife. He needed things stable, peaceful at home, so he could concentrate on his future.

After he had finished with the groceries, he started in on dinner. He began broiling the pork chops, made a salad with the bruised tomatoes, and popped three baking potatoes into the oven. Despite his frequent absences, he was no stranger to the kitchen. Early in their marriage, he had done his share of the cooking and still knew the basics. Besides, he had worked on a number of food accounts over the years and consequently had been forced to know the inside of an oven.

Once he thought the chops were done, he poured himself a

glass of chardonnay, took a sip, and headed upstairs to their room. The door was shut and he knocked before opening it.

Donna was sitting in the middle of the bed reading. At first she didn't hear him and for a moment he saw her how he used to see her: relaxed, interested, slightly amused. He was both surprised and insulted that she could switch gears so quickly, moving from argument to being absorbed in a book in less time than it took for pork chops to broil. When she finally glanced up and saw him, the light in her face flickered out and she looked extinguished.

"Are you coming down to eat? I actually made dinner."

"You what?"

"I made dinner." He tried to say this very nonchalantly, as if cooking were something he did every week, as opposed to never.

She went back to her book. "By any outside chance are you going to be home for the next few days? I want to visit Aaron. He threw his back out again."

"Visit Aaron." Charlie was embarrassed at the flood of relief he felt over this news, knowing that she might be leaving. Aaron was one of her many ex-football-playing older brothers who used to harass him in high school. He lived in Minneapolis now, in between wives. He had chronic back problems, the result of twelve years of playing linebacker for the Minnesota Vikings. At the age of fifty-four, he could barely walk.

"Are you going to be in town for Kyle?" she asked. "Are you going to be traveling? Because if you are, I won't go."

"No, I'm not, actually. I'm here."

"You are?"

"Yes."

"Are you sure? You're not going to sleep in the office downtown getting ready for some big, important pitch?"

"I said I'd be here."

She went back to her book.

"What are you reading?"

She flipped the cover of the book and Charlie saw the title: *Dreams and What They Mean.*

"Is it good?"

She flipped the book back.

He watched her read. He needed to tell her now, he thought. He needed to say he had been fired, thrown out, tossed aside, and that he needed her help and support and love because he wasn't sure what he was going to do. But instead he said, "I made pork chops."

"Pork chops."

"I broiled them. Come on."

She seemed to be studying him with interest.

"What?" he asked.

"Nothing." She returned to her book.

"Come on, let's eat, then. I cooked and everything."

"I don't want to. I'm reading. I'll eat later. I just want to be alone. I had a bad day too. You're not the only one who has bad days."

"What happened? Are you getting sick?"

"I never get sick."

"Well, did you have a bad day at that place you go to, that community thing, that bright place?"

"It's called Bright Day. I've been going there for almost two years now. Why can't you remember the name of it? It's Bright Day, Bright Day, Bright Day!"

"Okay, Bright Day, whatever."

"Don't say whatever."

"Okay, all right, just calm down." He took a deep breath and tried to regain control of the conversation. "So are you going to come down or what? It's not like I cook every day."

She shut the book hard. "What is going on here, huh? Just what exactly is going on?"

He swallowed. "I made dinner."

"You shopped, you ... you cooked, you're ... you're reading our bills."

"So what are you so mad about? You're always saying I'm

never at home, so when I am home and when I do help out, you attack me." He shook his head and made a big point about sighing. "Anyway, are you coming or are you going to stay up here and read another dream book?"

She picked up the book again and Charlie could see she was making an effort to calm herself. "I'd like to be alone. So just leave me alone. Please."

He was about to answer when he heard a creak in the hallway. He turned and saw Kyle standing at the top of the stairs.

"Did you get that food?" he asked. "I'm hungry."

"Yeah. I even cooked it. Come on." Charlie looked at Donna one last time, then headed downstairs.

Kyle put his glass down. "This tastes kind of weird," he said. "What is this?"

"It's soda pop."

"What kind?"

"What difference does it make?"

Kyle reached for the huge plastic bottle and read the label. "Mountain *Dude*?" He pushed it away. "Do we have any Mountain Dew?"

"This is the same thing."

"Tastes kind of weird."

"It's the same thing. There's not much difference in products. There's just a difference in prices. It's all advertising."

They were sitting at the kitchen island, eating dinner and watching the flip-down TV. Up until this point they had both been quiet: Kyle absorbed in *Jeopardy*, and Charlie with Donna. He was debating when to tell her.

"Can I have more of that stuff?" Kyle asked.

"You mean the lima beans? Yeah, here." Charlie passed the serving bowl, then played with his own salad. In contrast to Kyle, he hadn't eaten much. What he really wanted to do was drink, and not Mountain Dude. He went to the wine refrigerator and pulled out the bottle of chardonnay. He would have preferred something harder, but he thought it best to stick with wine in front of Kyle.

"So, how was school? How's it going? You like it?" Kyle was a sophomore at Wilton Township, reputed to be one of the best public high schools in the state. Donna had been very apprehensive about sending him there, worried that it was too competitive, too large. She had wanted him to go to the smaller Catholic school back on the South Side where they used to live, an hour's bus ride away.

"It's going okay," he said.

"Are you going to do any sports? Go out for anything? I remember you said you were thinking of running cross-country." Charlie sipped his wine.

Kyle shrugged. "No, I'm not doing that."

"How about swimming? I used to swim."

He shrugged again. "I don't think so."

"You should give it a try. At least one of them. You're a good runner. I remember you won that race that one time."

"What race?"

"You know, that one time. In the park with the big hill out in Naperville."

"That was in seventh grade." Kyle ate some lima beans, his eyes on the TV. "I'm going to play basketball. Going to try out again."

Charlie sipped his wine. "You are?"

"Yeah."

"You didn't play last year."

"I was going to, but I broke my ankle."

"Oh, yeah, that's right. Yeah."

Kyle watched more TV. Charlie drank more wine. "What is the Bay of Pigs?" he said.

"What?" Kyle looked at him.

Charlie nodded to the TV. "It's the answer to the question."

"Oh."

"Who is Fidel Castro?"

"What?"

Charlie nodded again at the TV.

"Oh."

Charlie moved his salad around. "Do you know who Fidel Castro is?"

Kyle shrugged. "Yeah, I think so."

"Who is he?"

"I don't know."

"He's the leader of Cuba. Do you know where Cuba is?"

Another shrug.

"You don't know where Cuba is? Come on, Kyle. Don't tell me you don't know where Cuba is, don't tell me that."

Kyle picked up one last lima bean, pinched it between his thumb and his index finger, and examined it before popping it into his mouth.

"Guess," he said. "Take a guess. I know you know it."

"Asia."

"You're kidding me, right?"

"Asia Minor."

"Come on, Kyle! Jesus! Cuba is an island off the coast of Florida. You should know this stuff. I mean, come on, it's important. I know you don't think it is, but it is."

"Why is it important?"

"It just is. Knowing where Cuba is, is important."

Kyle mumbled something.

"What's that?"

"It's probably only important if you're on a game show."

"No, it's not."

"Why is it important, then?"

Charlie stopped here. He couldn't think of a single reason, in the grand scheme of things, why knowing the location of Cuba was important. "Do you want some ice cream?"

"Yeah. Okay."

Charlie got up and took out the enormous plastic tub of Mr. Goody's. He had to use both hands to pry open the lid. Kyle stared at the tub. "Did our old grocery store burn down or something?" he asked.

"No." Charlie started to scoop the ice cream.

"What kind of ice cream is that?"

"It's chocolate."

"It looks weird."

"It's all the same. It's frozen cream." He was having trouble scooping; Mr. Goody's had a different consistency than Häagen-Dazs and seemed to be much heavier, like it was waterlogged.

"I don't want any," Kyle said.

"What do you mean?"

"I'm full." He pushed his plate away and stood up.

"You know, you're going to have to lower your standards once in a while," Charlie said. "This ice cream is just as good as the other ice cream."

"Häagen-Dazs?"

"Yeah. You know, Häagen-Dazs is expensive."

"Do we have any?"

"No." Charlie stopped scooping and turned to face him. "I've got news for you, Kyle, you're not a kid anymore and it's time that maybe you understand how expensive things are. Things cost money. This house costs money. Ice cream costs money." He pointed his scooper at him. "Your braces cost money. How much do you think your braces cost?"

Kyle's hand went up to his mouth. "I don't know. How much?"

Charlie didn't really know this either. "A lot. And we all have to do our part, as a family, to make sure we economize. We have to be more frugal. Do you know what frugal means?" he asked.

"Yeah."

"What does it mean?"

"I don't know."

"It means we have to live cheaply. Not spend as much money."

Kyle didn't have any immediate response to Charlie's lecture on The New Frugality. Instead, he picked at his braces with his pinkie finger and started to leave the kitchen.

"Where are you going?"

"My room."

"What are you going to do there?"

"Nothing."

"You always say that, but you're not doing nothing. You can't be. No one does nothing."

Kyle thought about this. "You're doing nothing when you're sleeping." Rather than being combative or sarcastic, he looked quite profound when he said this, as if he had been wrestling with this notion for quite some time.

"Yes, you are, you're doing something when you're sleeping. You're sleeping," Charlie said. "Are you going to sleep?"

"No."

"What are you going to do, then?"

He shrugged. "Nothing."

"Nothing." Charlie studied Kyle, a lima bean stuck in the side of his braces and the fly of his jeans halfway down. He felt his heart break. He remembered him as a quiet little person who liked to hum, play Legos, draw pictures of the moon, the stars. He had no idea where that humming little drawing person had gone; he wondered what this tall, shaggy-haired, geography-challenged person, this man-child, had done with him.

"Well, do your homework, at least."

"It's Friday."

"Okay, well, go up to your room and do nothing."

"Okay."

"Brush your teeth, though. Your braces are full of crap," Charlie yelled after him, but he was gone and Charlie was alone. He looked at the TV. *Jeopardy* was still on.

"What is the Cuban Missile Crisis?" he said out loud, then went to find the bourbon.

Chapter Eight

’m Bradley Smith. For eighteen years I was the chief marketing officer of the Bank of the Midwest. I oversaw the marketing efforts of our sixty-four branches in a nine-state region. I initiated the development of an aggressive campaign that repositioned the bank as a relevant and dynamic institution that catered to start-ups and other companies in the high-tech industry. However, due to a merger between the Bank of Tokyo and the Bank of the Midwest, I was one of fifty employees released from the bank.”

“Excellent,” Ned Meyers said. “Succinct. And I like the use of the word released. Very nice. Now add some personal backstory.”

Bradley looked around the room and smiled. “I’m from Texas, West Texas, played football for the Longhorns, served in Vietnam. I have three kids, all grown and gone. I’m a grandpa, though I don’t feel like one.”

Everyone chuckled at this and Ned clapped his hands. “Excellent. In a few short seconds, we’ve learned a lot about Bradley. He sums up well.”

Ned turned to a pale man sitting next to Charlie. "Walter, your turn."

"Do I have to do this again?" the man asked.

"Yes."

The man gave his head a slight shake. "I'm still Walter Konkist. For eight years I was a director of marketing at Ellenbee, Asperger, and Powers, a nationwide insurance company. Due to a consolidation of our offices, I was fired."

"Walter," Ned wailed, his voice a siren.

"I was released."

"I think 'let go' works better for you," Ned said.

Walter let out a breath. "I was let go and am currently working as a consultant for a number of smaller, regional insurance companies. I am, however, interested in exploring full-time opportunities."

"Excellent. I like the fact that you include your consulting experience. I think that makes you relevant."

"Should I say I'm consulting too?" Bradley asked.

"Are you?"

"No. But neither is Walter."

Ned turned to Walter. "You're not?"

"No," Walter said.

"Well, I'm not sure you should say that, then."

"Why not?"

"They may ask you about your consulting jobs. They may want references."

Walter appeared unconcerned. He had a fleshy face with flat, glossy eyes spaced too far apart. "My problem," he said.

Ned persisted. "I would advise against doing that. Lying to a potential employer."

"My problem."

"Well. I'm afraid it's your decision." Ned looked down at his legal pad. "Any personal backstory?"

"I'm married and have two kids."

"Anything else to add?"

"We have a dog too."

"Fine." Ned next turned to an attractive blond woman sitting across the room from Charlie. She was wearing a short skirt, a blessed distraction from the dreariness of the room. Charlie had been admiring her legs for most of the meeting.

"I'm Karen Brisco. I was a director of communications for Shelter."

"Excuse me," Ned said. "*A* director of communications? *A* director? Was there more than one director of communications at Shelter?"

Karen uncrossed her legs and sat forward in her chair. "No."

"Then you were *the* director of communications." He looked proudly around the room.

"I was *the* director of communications for Shelter, a national company that owns assisted-care facilities. In my capacity as director of communications, I oversaw the company's publications and internal employee newsletters. I also oversaw crisis communications efforts, including the coordinating of media relations surrounding the tragic murders of nine residents by an orderly in Darien, Connecticut. Due to the economic downturn there was a major staff reduction. However, my experience at Shelter was invaluable and has prepared me for new, senior communications opportunities."

Ned Meyers tapped a fingertip lightly against his nose. "Karen, I know you want to get the killing incident in, but it's a bit awkward. I think you're forcing it. I don't think it should be part of your summary."

"But it's the most important thing I did at Shelter. It was on all the networks. I was the chief spokesperson. It got intensive coverage. I was on CNN."

"I know, I know, and it's very impressive. Maybe we should work on the wording a bit, then. Murder sounds so negative."

"Well, he did kill them." She looked around the room. "With a hammer."

"I know, I know." Ned seemed genuinely distressed. He kept tapping the tip of his index finger against the point of his nose.

"How about using the word *slaying*? The tragic slaying of nine of our residents?"

"I don't think that sounds right," Karen Brisco said. "Slaying. You don't slay someone with a hammer."

Ned thought about this, then asked, "What does everyone else think?"

Charlie avoided Ned's eyes and fiddled with his cell phone. He and about ten other refugees had been sequestered in a small, windowless conference room at Rogers & Newman for more than two hours, sitting in a circle and rehearsing their public statements out loud. These statements, according to Ned Meyers, were explanations used to summarize former jobs as well as the reasons for leaving them.

"Well, I think we can revisit that later, Karen," Ned said. "Before we move on, anything personal you'd like to add?"

"Yes. I'm single, love fiction and poetry, and am a big sports fan. I've also run in two marathons."

"Two marathons," Ned said, impressed. He stared at Karen a bit gooey-eyed, as faint red blotches formed on his neck.

Ned cleared his throat and turned to Charlie. "It's your turn, Charlie. I hope you're ready for this."

Charlie sat up. He hadn't prepared anything, of course. He thought the whole exercise beneath him, something better suited for middle managers rather than senior management. He let out a deep breath. "I'm Charlie Baker. For twenty-two years, I worked at Collins & Park. I started as a copywriter right out of Northwestern, where I was on partial academic scholarship, and worked my way up to creative director of the Midwest. My most notable campaigns were the Yacker's toilet tissue account, which was controversial because it involved throwing a live kitten, live cat, out of an airplane. It had a parachute on, made partially of toilet paper, so it survived. Of course, I also did the Bagel Man campaign that featured celebrities like Elton John, who agreed to change the lyrics to his song 'Rocket Man' to 'Bagel Man.' I actually wrote the line, 'I think it's going to be a long, long time until I taste a bagel quite as fine.' I don't know if you remember that campaign, but it ran a long time and won a significant number of awards for the agency. They almost made a sit-com out of it, but the pilot wasn't picked up."

"Thank you, Charlie," Ned said.

Charlie paused. "I'm not done yet."

Ned said, "Oh, well . . ."

Charlie continued. "I was heavily recruited to join DiSanto & Herr three years ago. Initially, I refused their offer, but they were very persistent and made me a very good, very generous offer to become creative director and deputy general manager there. I was promoted to general manager last year."

Charlie stopped again and wished for a glass of water. "Once I was named GM, I quickly realized that the agency was on the brink of, well, disaster, and began to implement a series of dramatic but needed changes. I was in the initial stages of phase one of my strategic turnaround plan—"

"Excuse me, Charlie?" Ned tapped his wristwatch. "I believe your statement is running long," he said.

"What?"

"Long, it should be under thirty seconds."

"Thirty seconds? I can't sum everything up that fast. I've been working in this business for a long time. Thirty seconds is impossible."

"But that's the whole point of the exercise. To be concise."

Charlie glanced around the room. Everyone looked blankly back at him, except for Walter, who was smirking. "Oh," he said. "Okay, well, let me try again, then."

"I'm afraid we're running out of time. Why don't you finish with a brief personal backstory?"

"Fine. All right, then." Charlie thought about this. "Well, I went to Northwestern University and was president of my fraternity, Phi Kappa Psi, which was a very good house—that was an elected position, by the way—and I was almost summa cum laude. I run a lot, no marathons—yet . . ." He pointed at Karen and smiled. "Though I run about four or five miles a day when I can, but it's tough with all the traveling I do. And, let's see, I enjoy reading, but once again, with my schedule, I don't have much time for leisure reading. I read mostly nonfiction—sorry, no short fiction ..." Once again he pointed at Karen. "And I have an extensive collection of works on Abraham Lincoln. I'm a big Lincoln fan. I've studied his lessons on leadership."

Ned tapped his watch. "Charlie ..."

"And I have a wife and son."

Ned stared at him and chewed on this upper lip. "That's fine, for now. We'll work on trimming it next time." Ned stood. "Thank you, everyone. I think we're about done for today."

Charlie gathered his things and checked his cell phone again.

"Charlie, may I have a word with you?" Ned asked.

Charlie looked up. He knew or realized that he had made a mess of his personal statement, and suddenly wanted to leave the office and be done with the refugee experience for the day. "Actually, I'm running late," he said. He continued to examine his cell phone for nonexistent messages. He missed his Black-Berry desperately. Over the years, it had saved him from numerous awkward encounters like this.

Ned's sad, wise eyes searched Charlie's face. "I was hoping we could chat. I already received the results of your self-evaluation tests. Are you interested in hearing what they had to say? They might surprise you. They offer some intriguing options to consider. Career options."

Ned was referring to a self-assessment test Charlie had taken the day before. Charlie had quickly completed the test, then nodded off to sleep in his office. According to Ned, the test could be used to help identify potential and exciting career paths.

"I'd like to hear what they have to say, but I have to go now."

"Really?"

"Yes, really." Charlie gave Ned a brief, snappy smile and headed for the door. He stopped when he felt Ned gently pull at his elbow.

"Charlie, may I say something?"

Charlie turned and frowned at the hand on his elbow, before slowly looking up at him. "Yes?"

Ned took a step back. "Charlie," he said, "I think it's important that you make a real effort here. The more you put into our seminars, the things we have to offer, the more you'll get out of it."

"I'm making an effort," Charlie said.

"If I can be honest, I don't think you are, at least, not yet. Though I know it's only been a week or so. But you did fall asleep during the assessment test, I peered in on you, and you didn't seem very prepared for today's session, even though we discussed it yesterday."

"Listen," Charlie said. He gave Ned another tight, short smile. "I appreciate your concern, but I'm not going to be here long. I just need an office and a phone. So you might want to focus on some of the others. They need your help more than, I think, I do."

Ned appraised him before saying, "I'm glad you're so confident."

"I've been in this business a long time. I think I know what I'm doing, so if you don't mind." With that, Charlie opened the door and walked out.

Chapter Nine

In addition to his being fired, Charlie had had three other traumatic experiences in his life, moments when he felt things were out of his control, when he was at the sole mercy of circumstance and fate.

The first was when Kyle was born. They had arrived at the hospital in plenty of time for the delivery, but had to wait almost an hour in a labor area for an available birthing room. By the time Donna was in a bed, she had been in labor for hours. The doctors and nurses, however, seemed unconcerned and warned him that it would be some time before anything happened. After Donna received an epidural, he briefly nodded off in a rocking chair. He woke a few minutes later to a room full of grim-faced doctors and nurses, all hovering over Donna, who lay silent and ashen-faced. When a nurse approached him, sitting paralyzed by fear in the rocking chair, he heard himself ask if Donna was dead.

"No. But we lost the baby's heartbeat."

He remembered fragments of what happened next: a whirl of doctors and equipment; a blue light flashing above the door;

a nurse holding his hand. He was a mere bystander, a witness to what was happening. Hours later, when the emergency C-section was over, and they let him briefly hold Kyle, a healthy baby, a miracle, his son, Charlie cried so loudly and shook so violently that they had to sedate him. He slept for eighteen straight hours and essentially missed the first day of his son's life.

The second traumatic moment happened the year he was in the Black Forest for the Thought Leaders Conference. He had gotten into a terrible fight with Donna over the phone about his constant travel and the lack of time he was spending with Kyle. The call was memorable because it was the very first time that Donna had ever hung up on him.

Rather than call her back, he decided to take a walk to let off steam. The resort didn't have much of an exercise room, so he set out on a hiking trail that wound uphill and through the woods. On the way back to the hotel, he took a shortcut and left the trail, heading into the forest. He eventually came to a train tunnel that he assumed was no longer in use; it looked ancient, its entrance overgrown with weeds. He walked into it, thinking the hotel was close by on the other side. Partway through, he heard a train whistle. He looked around to see which way the train was coming; he didn't see any lights, but heard the whistle again, this time louder and nearer. He also felt the ground tremble. The train was coming, and right at him. He started to run in the direction he had just come, staying as close to the wall as possible, but after a few seconds he realized it was hopeless; the train was on him. He threw himself off to one side of the tracks and crouched down, covering his head with his arms. The entire tunnel was vibrating, exploding with noise. He thought he was going to die.

He didn't, of course. The train passed overhead, on *top* of the tunnel, leaving him shaken but unharmed. After it was gone, he composed himself, went back to his room, and called Donna. He wanted to tell her he loved her, that he had always loved her and always would, but the phone just rang and rang.

The third time he was truly traumatized was the day the

paper ran a mention of his leaving the agency. The announcement in the business section was brief, dwarfed by the news that Sears was firing its agency: *Frank Marken named Managing Director of DiSanto & Herr, replacing Charlie Baker, who resigned to pursue other interests. The move didn't surprise insiders: reportedly Baker's frenetic style didn't mesh well with the new ownership.*

He read the item while sitting at his preferred cubicle in the Wilton Public Library. He had grabbed the paper off the front steps earlier that morning but hadn't gotten around to reading it until late in the afternoon. (He had spent most of the day reading the book *Beloved*, a Charlie Book Club selection finalist.) His head had kicked back when he saw his name in print. After a few stunned seconds, however, he made his way to the large dictionary by the ancient photocopy machine and looked up the word *frenetic.* Although he knew what it meant, he wanted to confirm that the word didn't have multiple or varying definitions that were, in fact, more insulting than he thought.

Unfortunately, there was an elderly man with a ripe smell using the dictionary and Charlie had to stand downwind from him and wait while the man looked up every word in the English language. When he finally finished, Charlie jumped on the book and found the word:

> *Frenetic: (1) wild and often compulsive behavior;*
> *(2) an anxiety-driven activity; (3) insane*

Charlie returned to his cubicle, sat down, and closed his eyes. It had come to this. *This.* His entire career, his entire life, was being dismissed, discarded, mocked. He had been diagnosed as frenetic. He was *insane.*

He took deep breaths, gulped them. It was one thing to be fired, it was quite another to be humiliated. No doubt the agency was behind this. Frenetic. Marken probably had the entire creative team working overtime to come up with the perfect word to publicly slander him. His fury overcame him. He clenched his fists, he cursed out loud, he pounded *Beloved* down onto the desk.

Then he called Ned Meyers because he really had no one else to call.

"I don't think you can sue someone over being called frenetic," Ned said.

"Then I think you're very naïve."

"I think you should move on."

"And I think I should talk to a lawyer."

Ned and Charlie were sitting in a large, sun-splashed conference room overlooking Lake Michigan, drinking coffee and discussing Charlie's pending slander case. It was the day after the mention in the newspaper and, while sympathetic, Ned was anything but helpful.

"Actually, I am a lawyer," Ned said.

"You are?" This threw Charlie. Ned was wearing a black turtleneck, a dusty brown blazer, along with his signature Hush Puppies, and looked like no lawyer he had seen before. "What do you mean, you're a lawyer? Like for the ACLU? That type of lawyer?"

Ned folded his hands in front of him on the table, delicate fingers intertwined. "I was a trial lawyer. Well, still am one, technically, though I don't practice anymore. I mean, I never introduce myself as a lawyer at parties. Not that I go to that many parties."

Charlie studied Ned a little longer before saying, "It's libel. It can hurt my career. Who's going to hire me? I'm frenetic? Would you hire someone who was frenetic? It's libel. It's like calling me a Nazi or something."

"Charlie, you're overreacting. You yourself said everyone in your industry, in advertising, already knows you, is that correct?"

"So?"

"So, what the newspaper says shouldn't have any bearing on your prospects. People all know you're a good adman. A damn good adman!" He slapped the top of the table, then sat back and crossed his legs, flaunting his Hush Puppies.

Charlie spoke slowly. "Thank you. That's very nice of you to say, but I don't know everyone everywhere. And that column won't help me. Do you know what frenetic means? It means insane."

Ned waved a hand. "It doesn't mean insane."

"It's in the dictionary. I looked it up! It's right there!"

"Please, calm down, please." Ned stood and clasped his hands behind his back. "Now, let's talk this through. Now, do you think you're frenetic?"

"What? No, of course not."

"Not at all? Maybe just a little?"

"You can't be a little frenetic!"

"You don't have to shout. Please."

Charlie took a very deep breath.

"Thank you," Ned said. He began to pace in front of the windows. It was still before eight in the morning and behind him the early fall sky was streaked pink. "Now, objectively speaking, how would you describe yourself, Charlie?"

"What do you mean?"

"How would you describe yourself to someone else? Someone who didn't know you."

"I don't know. I'm five-eleven and a hundred and seventy pounds."

"That's not what I mean. Would you describe yourself as a victim?"

Charlie seized on this word. "What? Yes, I'm a victim. Very much so."

Ned paced some more. "Interesting. A victim. Let me ask you another question here, if I may. Do you think there were any reasons, any legitimate reasons, for you being let go?"

"No."

"None whatsoever?"

"No. They needed a scapegoat."

"You're quite sure of that? You're being totally honest?"

Charlie was quiet.

"You're being quiet," Ned said.

"I don't know," Charlie said softly. He had managed maybe three hours of sleep the night before and was exhausted. He suddenly had no energy for Ned or any of this.

Ned reached a wall and stopped to examine one of the many inspirational posters that graced the halls and rooms of Rogers & Newman. This one was particularly clichéd: a canoe banked on the grassy shores of a river: SUCCESS IS A JOURNEY. "And what do you think some of those reasons are, may I ask?"

Charlie sighed. "Listen, I don't want to get into that now, okay? I want to know about my legal options. Who can I sue? The paper, the agency? That's all I want to know right now. You said you're a lawyer. Who can I sue?"

Ned removed his glasses, wiped the lenses with a white handkerchief, and resumed his serious pacing. "I'm sorry, as I said, I don't believe you can sue anyone." He put his glasses back on and slipped the handkerchief into his pants pocket. "Now I'd like to switch gears and talk about something else."

"What?"

"Grudman Simmons."

"What?"

"Grudman Simmons. Your evaluation test."

"Grudman, what? Oh, hey, listen, I don't want to talk about that test. Not now."

"I think we should. Now is as good a time as any." Ned cleared his throat. "As you know, Grudman Simmons reveals certain personality traits, certain characteristics that are important in the progression of your career. Would you like to know what your test said about you?"

"Not right now, no."

"It will only take a second. Now, according to your results, you're energetic and ambitious. But also impatient and, well, somewhat scattered in some areas."

This got Charlie's attention. He feared some kind of health risk associated with this condition. "Scattered. What does that mean?"

"It means you have a short attention span. You move from thing to thing to thing."

"So? I'm creative. I'm in a creative business."

"Well, yes. But that isn't always a characteristic needed in a manager."

"What are you saying? What's your point?"

"That you should consider getting back, possibly, on the creative side of things rather than pursuing another management position."

"I am a manager. I run things. You know, I wasn't even paying attention when I took that test."

"I know that." Ned sat down at the table again and opened a folder. "You shouldn't put too much stock in it, I agree. But still it is worth a look." He studied the contents of the folder and frowned like a schoolteacher examining a disturbing term paper. "The test showed that in addition to advertising, you might want to consider other professions. For example, according to the test, you have the same interests and traits as a musician."

"Musician," Charlie repeated.

"Yes. May I ask, do you play any instruments? The saxophone?"

Charlie thought of the Steinway, silently brooding in their living room, and ignored the question.

"To be honest, I didn't think that was very practical either," Ned said. He returned to his file. "According to the test, you might want to consider something in television."

This actually interested Charlie. In college he had briefly considered a career in TV. "What do you mean? Like a producer or writer?"

"Well, not exactly, no—but maybe as an on-air talent. Be involved in a talk show of some kind."

This took a moment to sink in. "You mean be a host of a talk show?"

"Cohost, actually."

"Cohost? Cohost of a talk show? You mean a sidekick?"

"Yes."

"Be a sidekick on a talk show. Like Ed McMahon? You know,

Ned, I don't know how long you've been in America, but there are like two jobs like that here."

"I realize that. I don't think we should take these tests too literally. We should view them more as suggestions, or guidelines. Find a position *like* a sidekick."

"Such as?"

"Well, a copilot, for example."

"A what? You mean like on an airplane?"

"Well, no. Once again, something like that. Something in a support role."

"Fine. I'll get on that right away." If Charlie had had somewhere else to go, he would have left immediately. But it was still early and neither the zoo nor the library were open yet.

Ned continued to study the file. "Now, the test also identifies your position in a tribe, or a tribal society. For example, it puts people into different categories such as tribal leader, medicine man, warrior, things like that."

"Where did I place? Head of marketing for the tribe?"

Ned laughed and pointed at Charlie. "Very good, very good." He quickly grew serious again. "You were—again, based on the test, which I know you didn't take that seriously because you were asleep—you were categorized as a warrior's aide."

"What's that? What do you mean?"

"Well, someone who sharpens the warrior's weapons, cleans animal hides, and clears the battlefield of dead bodies. You know, drags them off. Things like that."

Charlie paused. "A tribal janitor."

"Yes—well, no, I wouldn't go that far. But you were categorized, once again, in a support function."

Charlie fell silent and tried to imagine what, exactly, cleaning an animal hide involved.

Ned solemnly closed the file and folded his skinny hands on the table. "I think what we're hearing here is that maybe, just maybe, possibly, you aren't the right fit for leading an agency. That rather than head a company or a major division, you might be better off looking for second-in-command-type positions. Vice president, chief of staff. Those types of positions."

Charlie shook his head. He would have none of this. "Let me tell you something about my business, okay? I was head of an agency. Once you're the top man, once you're the boss, you can't take a secondary job. First of all, no one will give it to you, even if you want it. They'll think you'll take the job and then . . . then plot to take over. They're not going to trust you. Advertising is cutthroat. No one trusts anyone. It's a horrible profession. There's very little humanity."

"I understand that. But all I am saying is that you should at least consider what the test is telling us."

"Fine. I'll go clean animal hides. Now, can we talk about the column?"

Ned sat up straight. "Forget about the column, Charlie. You can't change what happened. It's wasted energy. It's such a small mention and no one reads the paper anymore. Besides, what do you expect to do about the paper?"

Other than demanding a retraction, *Charlie Baker Not Frenetic*, Charlie knew Ned was right. "Okay." He exhaled. "I'm still going to talk to a lawyer," he said, but not very convincingly.

"That's your prerogative. Now, what about that résumé? How's that coming along?"

"Do I really need one? I mean, come on, I've been working for close to thirty years. Everyone knows me."

"Everyone needs a résumé."

"I don't think I do."

"You do. Please, trust me. People are going to ask you for one. What are you going to say? 'I don't have one, because everyone knows me'?"

Charlie thought about this. "All right, okay. Maybe I'll get going on one."

"Today might be a good day." Ned raised his eyebrows. He had, Charlie noticed, a very square face.

"Okay, I'll get started."

"Today?"

"Today."

Ned acted like this was incredible news. He jumped up in his seat. "Really, right now?"

"Relax. Yes, right now."

Ned snapped his fingers. "Excellent! Now you're talking! I'll set up you right up." He started to rise from his chair.

Charlie didn't move. He was hesitant about what he was going to say next. "Hey, Ned. Do you have another minute? There's something else I think I need to talk about."

Ned seemed apprehensive. "Oh? Yes. Of course." He reseated himself and placed his hands flat on the table in anticipation. "I am at your service."

Charlie hesitated again, then decided to take the plunge. While Ned was annoying, he had to talk to *someone* about the situation with Donna. He started slowly. "I haven't really, officially, told my wife yet," he said. "My life partner."

Ned looked blank. "You haven't told her what yet?"

"You know, about me . . . my employment situation."

Ned's face remained expressionless, then all at once exploded—his eyes wide, his mouth open. "You mean you haven't told her about being fired?"

Charlie moved his coffee cup a little to the left.

"Oh, Charlie! I mean, she's going to read about it in the paper. Everyone's going to see that. Everyone reads the paper."

"She doesn't read the paper. At least not the marketing column."

"But still, the chances of someone else seeing it and telling her . . ."

"I know."

"This is very bad."

"I know."

"Very, very, bad."

"Can you stop saying that?"

"She has a right to know. How long has it been? Over two weeks?"

"I don't know. Something like that."

"I've heard about situations like this." Ned fell into thought, ransacking his memory for similar case histories. "Logistically, this doesn't seem possible. What are you telling her?"

"It's not as hard as you think. For us. We didn't . . . we don't see each other all that much." Charlie looked over Ned's shoulder at some thin, flat clouds that looked like paste against the still-pink sky. "I'm not sure how to approach it. I'm not sure what to do."

Ned chewed on his lip, then abruptly stood and hooked a hand in a side pocket of his blazer. "I know exactly what we have to do. And we have to do it now. Immediately."

Charlie stared at a framed poster on the back of the conference room door. This one featured yet another senior citizen, an old woman with a shock of gray hair, running downhill in a foggy mist, her body bent forward, her face a mask of determination. ACTIONS SPEAK LOUDER THAN WORDS! He wished that all he had to do was run down a hill. He picked up the phone, ignoring the pain in his chest, the numbness in his arm.

"Hello. Donna?" He cleared his throat. "It's me. Charlie."

"Who?"

"Charlie, your husband. We're married, remember?"

"Yes, dear?"

Dear. He paused and cleared his throat again. "I have some bad news."

"Before I forget, can you pick up some items from the market prior to coming home? We need some jam."

Charlie glanced at the receiver. Then he glanced down at a pad of paper with the message points Ned had developed. "I have some bad news. I was let go from my job. I was fired."

There was a silence on the other end of the line, then, "When were you terminated?"

"About two weeks ago."

"Two weeks ago? How very unfortunate! What are we going to do? How are we going to live? Why didn't you share this information with me, this news, sooner?"

"We'll be fine."

"Exactly why do you think it's going to be fine, dear?"

"Because it is."

"Well, what about our one child, our precious son, Clancy?"

"Clancy?"

"I mean Kyle. Of course I mean our son Kyle, dear."

"Stop calling me dear!" Charlie slammed down the phone. A few seconds later, there was a soft knock on the door, then Ned entered.

"Why did you hang up on me?" he asked.

"It's ridiculous. I can't do that."

"Role-playing is important. You need the practice. You need to rehearse this conversation. Keep to your message points."

"My wife never calls me dear."

"I was just trying to make it realistic, Charlie. You need to practice getting straight to the point. Not be sidetracked into mundane chitchat."

"My wife has never, *ever* asked me to pick up jam, okay? And we don't chitchat. We barely talk to each other."

"Oh," Ned said. He touched his mouth and looked at the floor. "I see."

"This is going to be tough. Complicated. More complicated than you think."

"Oh, I see," Ned said again. "Can I help in any way?"

"Yeah, why don't you tell her?"

Ned seemed to seriously consider this request. "No, I don't think that would be right, Charlie, I really don't."

"I was kidding. Do you know anything about sarcasm?"

"To be honest, I've never been good at detecting that."

Charlie shook his head. "Everything's falling apart," he suddenly said.

Ned studied him with sad, concerned eyes. "It just seems that way."

"No, it is. My job, my family. My wife. It's . . . it's bad. I just don't know how to . . ." his voice trailed off.

"Don't know how to do what?"

"Do anything. I got wrapped up in the bullshit, that's all. Just wrapped up. I lost balance. I just lost it." He exhaled. "Do you have anything to drink? I think I need one."

"You don't need to drink," Ned quietly said. "Just take it one day at a time, put one foot forward, one after the next. Before you know it, you'll be getting somewhere."

Charlie fell quiet, and briefly let despair fill him. He rubbed a hand over his face. He wasn't sure why he was telling Ned this. He was, after all, a stranger. He quickly caught himself and pointed at the poster with the running old woman. "You sound like one of those," he said.

Ned didn't bother to turn. "I hate those posters," he said. "They trivialize my work."

Charlie slowly stood. "I'm going to go work on my thing now." He waved a hand in the air. "My résumé."

"Are you sure you're okay?"

"I'm fine."

Ned looked at him a little longer. "Right," he said. "I'll get you set up in another office, then. Follow me."

Charlie spent the next three hours trying to compress his entire twenty-eight-year career onto two sheets of paper. According to the Rogers & Newman guidebook, *Transitions*, his résumé was not to surpass this page count if it was to prove effective. Anything longer would hurt "readability." *Potential employers regard long résumés as pompous and defensive. They are generally frowned upon. Remember: Less is more.* The guidebook also encouraged the use of words like *initiated, coordinated, led, launched, created,* and *established* to describe accomplishments. *Be dynamic,* the book urged. *Show pride and confidence!*

Despite this advice, Charlie's initial attempt at a résumé stretched to five pages. He was having difficulty choosing and prioritizing his many achievements. He couldn't decide which campaigns to showcase and which ones to drop. Bagel Man was an obvious inclusion. It had earned a permanent place in the consumers' consciousness. It was his masterpiece, his tour de force, his *Beloved.* Other choices weren't so clear-cut: the toilet tissue spot featuring the parachuting kitten in red boots, or the singing turtles for the beer company, for example, while not nearly as well known, still helped build awareness and consequently sales. As did the spoof of the *Godfather* films for the pizza company. While industry critics had dismissed that particular campaign as sophomoric and clichéd, it too had helped sales, particularly in the critical pizza-eating Northeast region. In the end, he decided to include all three, among others. He did manage to omit, however, the talking hamster. As far as Charlie was concerned, that never happened.

He also struggled with format; as hard as he tried, he couldn't get the margins right and, as a result, his sentences kept bleeding off into space. He repeatedly tried to make the margins consistent from page to page, but to no avail. The left margin was too large, the right nonexistent. He wished he had a secretary or an assistant to help him. It was ridiculous that they didn't provide anyone.

He was in the middle of trying to align things one more time when Bradley popped his head into his office. He looked unusually cheerful, his face a healthy pink, his eyes clear and excited. "Got an interview today," he announced. "My first one in a while. In four months, to be exact. We're having lunch."

Charlie sat back in his chair. "Hey, that's great. Who with?"

Bradley smiled and straightened his red tie. "Don't want to jinx it. Sounds good, though. It's here in Chicago too. That would make things easier. It just fell into my lap."

"That's great." Charlie tried hard not to feel jealous; Bradley's hell might be finishing, just as his was starting.

"How did you hear about it? A recruiter?"

"Naw, I'm done with recruiters. Actually, I guess they're more done with me. I'm off their radar, it's been so long. This thing just fell in my lap," he said again. "So, do I look young today?"

"You look eighteen."

He laughed, a Texas accent emerging. Then he turned serious. "Saw the paper yesterday," he said.

"Oh, that. Yeah."

"Funny, you don't seem frenetic."

"I'm heavily medicated now."

"That guy's a prick to have written that."

Charlie shrugged. "What are you going to do? Sue him?"

"Life's a bitch," Bradley said. "People pile it on when you're down. Man, I know that."

They both looked at each other for a moment, then Bradley slapped the side of the door. "Anyway, hang in there. Got to run."

"Good luck out there."

"I'm due." Bradley winked and was gone.

Charlie resumed his attack on the margins. He was considering calling Georgia, maybe she could help him over the phone, when Karen Brisco, the PR lady, and Walter, the fish-eyed man, appeared in his doorway.

"How you doing today?" Karen asked. She stared at him searchingly. Walter too looked at him intently.

"I'm fine," he said. Then he realized what was going on. "Oh, I mean, I'm pretty frenetic."

Karen laughed nervously. Walter's face, however, remained impassive.

"That was a cheap shot," Karen said.

"I've been called worse."

"I bet you have," Walter mumbled.

Charlie glanced at him, not sure he'd heard him right.

"Want to grab some lunch?" Karen asked. "We're running down to the deli."

"No, I'm fine."

"You sure?"

"You heard him, let's go," Walter said, turning. Before he left, he hitched his shoulder in a way that made him seem familiar. Charlie wondered if he knew him from the Ad Club.

"Come on," Karen said. "We're celebrating his anniversary. Walter's been out one year. It's a big day."

Charlie was stunned by this. One year. Twelve months, no work, no pay. "Congratulations," he said. "But I have to finish my résumé."

"Want us to bring something back?" Karen asked. "They have good soup."

"No. But thanks."

Karen smiled again and Charlie smiled back. She looked especially attractive this morning, with her shoulder-length blond hair and ski slope of a nose. She was wearing a short skirt again and her legs looked tanned and toned. "I'll get something later," he said.

"You sure?"

"Yep."

She smiled again and left.

A half hour later, having given up on the margins, he finally decided to put a call in to Preston Davis, the Wizard of Ads. Preston was a high-profile executive recruiter known for conducting the ad world's Alpha Dog searches. Charlie had been putting off the call; up until now, he wasn't sure he needed the Wizard. But Walter's and Bradley's situations had spooked him. He didn't want to be celebrating any anniversaries eating soup at the deli downstairs.

He had worked exclusively with the Wizard for years, retaining him for countless searches. Based on the amount of work he had thrown him in the past, Charlie knew Preston would take his call and wasn't surprised when Preston's assistant put him right through.

"Charlie Baker. Been trying to reach you," the Wizard said. His voice was deep and soothing, bordering on the breathless. Charlie always thought the Wizard sounded like a slightly more masculine version of Lauren Bacall.

"You weren't trying very hard. I got fired, not deported."

"I'm sorry. Please don't get all frenetic on me, now."

Charlie winced. "I'll try not to."

"How are you?"

"I'm doing all right."

"It's a shitty world, chief."

"Very."

"Where are you?"

"I'm at the outplacement place. Rogers & Newman."

"Shiver me timbers. I have a hard time picturing you there."

"I have a hard time picturing me here. Listen, I was hoping we might get together for lunch. Or breakfast."

There was a deep pause. Asking for a personal audience with the Wizard was a very forward move. Preston was an elusive target, somehow managing to be both high-profile and reclusive. During the course of their twenty-year relationship, Charlie had never seen, much less met, him. Rumor had it that he did not have an actual, physical form; he was simply a voice, or, at the most, a floating head.

"I'm jammed up, jelly-tight right now, but we can talk," Preston said. "Always happy to talk."

"Well, I think I need to get things moving. Get my name out there."

"Oh, your name is out there."

Charlie wasn't sure how to interpret that, so he chose not to try. "I think I want to move over to the client side. I mean, if the right agency thing came along I'd consider it, sure, but I want to try the other side. Give it a serious look."

"Client side? Charlie Baker work for a corporation? I find that hard to believe."

"I've been thinking about it. I'm sick of the agency life. All that bullshit. I'm getting too old for it."

"Speaking of bullshit, which I assume this is, which I hope this is, I heard a story about you," the Wizard said. "A tall tale."

"What are you talking about?"

"Something about a gumball machine and Frank Marken's head. Apparently, you have to work on your aim, chief."

"I don't know what you're talking about."

"Heard it from a good friend."

"You heard wrong, whatever the hell you heard." Charlie's anger flashed. "You know, that's just my point. That's why I want out of the agency thing. It's full of bullshit and slander. It's like high school."

The Wizard was quiet again. Charlie half expected him to say he had to go—conversations with him were nothing if not brief—but instead Preston said, "Are you really serious about going corporate?"

"Yes."

There was a pause.

"Preston? Are you still there?"

"Well, things are still on the tight side, but we'll make some calls, poke around a bit. Why don't you shoot me a résumé?"

"A résumé, come on, Preston! You're kidding me, right? Everyone knows me, knows my work."

"Sorry, Charlie, gotta have one. Think of it as your passport to exotic places. New lands."

Charlie sighed, and thought of the messy, rambling tome that was his first draft. "I'll get you one. Do you think you have anything? Anything come to mind?"

"We'll talk," Preston said. "Have to run."

"Give me a few names. What's out there?"

"We'll be in touch."

"All right," Charlie said. "Look forward to hearing back."

Chapter Ten

When Charlie got home, he found Kyle and a friend, an extremely tall boy with a crew cut, in the family room, spying at the house behind theirs with his telescope. The tall boy was wearing Charlie's red and green Bagel Man cape, which was seriously wrinkled.

"Hi," Kyle said.

"What are you doing?" Charlie asked.

Kyle shrugged, glanced sideways at the tall boy in the cape, and shrugged again. "Nothing."

"I can see that." Charlie walked over to the telescope and inspected it for damage. Despite the fact that he had never once looked out of it, Charlie was growing possessive of it.

"This stuff was by the front door," Kyle said. "In a box."

"And you opened the box?"

"Yeah."

"Without asking me. Just like that? You opened the box."

"Yeah. Exactly." Kyle said this sincerely. "There were two boxes. One of them had a picture of Abraham Lincoln."

"Didn't the boxes have my name on them?"

"No. I mean, I don't know."

"Where are they, the boxes?" Charlie asked.

"I put them in the basement. The guy left them outside and they said it was going to rain."

Charlie nodded, then turned his attention to the tall boy. He had a prominent chin and large, curious eyes that reminded Charlie of Ned Meyer. Charlie took an immediate disliking to him. "Give me the cape. Now."

The boy quickly took it off and handed it to Charlie.

"Thank you." Charlie returned his gaze to Kyle. "You really shouldn't touch my things."

Kyle stared at the ground. "Matt wanted to see your cape."

"Did Brett Favre wear that cape?" Matt asked.

"Yes." Charlie carefully folded the cape like a Marine color guard would fold an American flag, and tucked it under one arm. With his free hand, he picked up the telescope. "What were you guys looking at?" he asked, although he suspected he knew. Gloria Wilcott, an attractive, middle-age divorcée who lived behind them, occasionally forgot to close her shades while getting undressed. Charlie had experienced this event himself once, months before. He glanced out the window now and saw, through the swaying trees, that her house was dark and that there would be no show this night.

"The planets," Matt said.

"Yeah, we were looking at the planets," Kyle said. "We were looking for Jupiter. And Uranus."

"You mean her anus," Matt said. Kyle stifled a laugh.

"Excuse me?" Charlie asked.

Matt hung his head.

Charlie walked into the kitchen, clutching his things. "Is your mother at home?"

"She's upstairs."

"Did she see this stuff? The telescope?"

"No . . . I don't know. Maybe. I don't think so. She just got home."

"How's she doing?" Charlie asked this innocently, as if he were inquiring after an old friend.

"I don't know," Kyle said. "Okay."

"Did she say anything to you today?"

"About what?"

"I don't know. About anything? The boxes?"

"No."

"Where is she?"

"She's getting ready to leave," Kyle said.

Charlie jumped at this comment. "What do you mean, leave?"

"She's going to visit Uncle Aaron. She's packing. I think she said she's leaving tonight."

Charlie relaxed. "Oh, yeah. Aaron." Then he asked, "You mean, she's leaving tonight? Now?" He set the cape on the island with its large red B facing upward, and put the telescope on the floor next to it, making sure the spindly legs of its tripod were balanced and secure. "Don't touch my stuff again, okay?"

"Okay."

"How old are you?" Charlie asked him.

"Sixteen."

"When I was sixteen, I was working," Charlie said. "I had a job. I pumped gas at Gas City. My parents didn't have a lot of money. They were teachers. We lived in a bungalow. You know what a bungalow is?"

"A what?" Matt asked.

Charlie ignored this question and instead asked, "Do you have a job?"

"No," Matt said. He stopped laughing.

"Maybe you should."

"What's a bungalow?" Kyle said.

"It's a small, crappy house with one bathroom and a shower that leaked." Charlie studied them. Both looked floppy, their shorts long and hanging, their shoes untied. They seemed entirely too happy and carefree and he found all of this floppiness, this happiness, intolerable. "Kyle was thinking of getting a part-time job," he said.

"I was?"

"I think it would do you good. I think it's important to make some money, don't you?" Charlie asked.

Kyle put his hands in the front pockets of his jeans. "Yeah, I guess," he said. "Where would I work?"

Charlie thought about this. "Gas City."

"Gas City. You mean, like a gas station?"

"Yes. I worked there twenty hours a week when I was your age."

"What would I do there?"

"Pump gas."

"Gas is a subject Kyle is extremely well versed in," Matt said. He waved his hand in front of his nose. They both exploded into snickers and snorts.

Charlie watched them snicker and snort while the back of his neck grew warm. "I'm glad you guys are having a good time, I really am. It's important to have a good time when you're sixteen years old and you have absolutely no responsibilities and you completely rely on your parents for financial support and don't live in a bungalow in Mount Greenwood with one bathroom and work at Gas City with John Morrissey."

"Who's John Morrissey?" Kyle asked.

John Morrissey had been president of Charlie's high school class, a hardworking all-American boy. "A drug addict," Charlie said.

He stopped and waited for this to sink in. Both boys examined the floor.

"That's what my life was like," Charlie said. "Gas City and drug addicts. Plus, I had a hernia. When I was twelve."

"A what?" Kyle asked.

"Never mind. Forget it."

The two boys grew quiet again, then Kyle looked up. "Hey, Dad, I forgot to tell you. We tried out for basketball. We both did. I think we're going to make it."

"Yeah," Matt said. He stood up straighter. He had to be at least six-six.

"Congratulations." Charlie pointed at Kyle. "But I hope it doesn't interfere with your job. Because work is important." With that, he patted the cape once on the B and headed upstairs to see Donna.

He found her leaning over the bed, trying to cram a gray sweat-shirt into her already overflowing travel bag. Her concept of packing—stuff as many things as possible into suitcases with-out any sense of order—never failed to amaze and alarm Char-lie. Her packing skills had been a bone of contention for years. He watched her struggle with the sweatshirt before finally giv-ing up. She tossed it at a chair but missed.

He walked over, picked up the sweatshirt, and made a point of folding it neatly.

"Are you really leaving tonight?"

Donna was surprised to see him, her cheeks flushing. It took a moment for her to activate her protective, robotlike gaze.

"Yes." She brushed away some hair from her face, then went back to assaulting her bag.

"Are you going to wear those on the plane?" He pointed at her feet. She was wearing pink flip-flops, her usual footwear regardless of the season.

She looked down. "Yes, I am. Is that okay with you?"

"You shouldn't wear flip-flops on an airplane. It's almost October."

"My feet will be fine."

"Maybe you should wear some socks. It's cool out. There's a breeze."

"I'm not planning on sticking my feet out of the window of the plane, okay?"

"I'm just saying that maybe you should wear different shoes. You're going to Minneapolis."

Donna yanked on the zipper of the bag. "I know you hate flip-flops, I know you hate to look at people's feet. I know you think they're the ugliest part of the human body. But they're comfortable and I'm going to wear them, okay?"

"Fine. They're your feet. Go barefoot, I don't care." He re-folded the sweatshirt. "Why are you going to Minneapolis again? You were just there a month ago."

"I was there six months ago."

"Then why are you going so late? What's the big rush? Go tomorrow."

"It's not that late. And this is when the plane leaves. I don't make the flight times. If you have a problem, call United."

"I can't believe there aren't different flights to Minneapolis. They probably leave every hour. Do you want me to check?"

"Listen, I'm all set. I'm going tonight."

"Fine."

He walked aimlessly around the room and stopped by the window, fiddled with a shade, then walked over to the bed and fiddled with the Rain Forest humidifier. It looked clean and cheerful, eager for use. If it were a puppy, it would be wagging its tail. He turned it on, turned it off, resisting the urge to pet it.

"What time's your flight?" he asked.

"Nine. I called a cab."

"I'll take you."

"What?" She popped up on her feet and quickly shook her head. "I already called a cab. It's on the way. It'll be here soon." She seemed nervous, uncertain.

"What's wrong with you? Are you okay?" he asked.

"I'm fine. I just don't want to be late." She patted her hair once, her hands fluttering through her curls. Then, with one last violent tug, she finished zipping the bag and swung it off the bed with both her hands.

He reached over and took it from her. "If you really want to go tonight, fine. But I'm taking you to the airport."

Traffic was light and they made good time to O'Hare. He kept his eyes firmly on the road while Donna sat scrunched up in a ball by the window, quiet, and millions of miles away.

They were more than halfway to the airport when Charlie said, "I'm a little worried about Kyle." Donna's silent withdrawals were common occurrences and he knew that talking about their son sometimes brought her back.

As hoped, she sat up straight. "He's not sick, is he?"

"He's not sick. I mean his general attitude and approach to

things. I think he has it too easy. I think he should get a job. It would be good for him. He's clueless."

"About what?"

"About everything."

Donna contracted again, scrunching up and sliding over to the door. "He's fine."

Charlie switched lanes. "I don't know. We were watching *Jeopardy* and he didn't know who Fidel Castro was."

"Wow, that's a big concern. Maybe we can arrange a field trip to Cuba. They should really meet."

"I'm just saying that he doesn't seem very mature."

"He's doing fine. And if you're so concerned, maybe you could make one of his parent-teacher conferences. Maybe you could help him with his homework. Maybe you could talk to him once in a while. Be a father."

"Be a father," Charlie repeated. Despite a resolve to stay cool, he was growing angry. He slowed, then stopped to pay a toll. As he was pulling away from the booth, he asked, "When are you coming back again?"

"I'm not sure."

"What do you mean?"

"I said, I'm not sure."

"It might be helpful to know this."

"Why?"

"We should know when you're coming back. Kyle and I need to know."

"You always come and go. I never know where you are."

They drove for a good ten minutes in silence. When he turned off at the airport exit, she finally said, "I'll be back soon enough."

This last comment, said sharply and with intent, finally set him off. He turned toward her. "What is your deal lately, huh? What is this whole act? When are you going to get tired of it, huh? Why do you hate me so much? What have I done that's so bad? All of a sudden you stop talking to me."

"I don't want to talk about this right now," she said.

"You don't want to talk about it? Fine, don't talk about it."

She shook her head and gave him one of her incredulous I-can't-believe-this-guy, can-you-believe-this-guy? smiles. "I've been trying to talk to you for years. And now you decide to talk on a twenty-minute ride to the airport. That's when you decide to talk," she said. "That's how important I am. Squeeze me in. You know, Charlie, you've been squeezing me in for years, now. I'm an inconvenience to you now. Always a second priority. Not even second. Third. Fourth. Last. You're never at home, don't even know Kyle anymore. And he's going to be gone soon, gone!" She stopped yelling and Charlie heard a muffled sob.

"Relax." They were approaching the terminal and he drove as slowly as he could. "Everything is going to be all right. Try to breathe. Take deep breaths."

She pounded the side of her seat with her fist. "Don't tell me when to breathe! You tell me everything else, but do not tell me when to breathe."

"Fine, don't breathe. Hold your breath."

"I'm sick of you always telling me what to do. Sick of you always correcting me when you're around. I'm not good enough for you anymore. I never went away to college, haven't been to Singapore, or wherever else you always go. Argentina or . . . or Texas. I'm just dumb old Donna, wearing my flip-flops. Dumb Donna from the South Side. Dumb Donna who can't decorate her new, big, stupid, dumb house, who can't talk to any of her stupid neighbors. I'm just someone to come back to when you have nowhere else to go."

"That's not true. That's not true at all."

They were at the terminal now, so he stopped. A policeman immediately pointed at them and began blowing his whistle, motioning for them to move on. Donna quickly wiped her eyes with her sleeve and unbuckled her seat belt.

"Wait, I have to move," he said. "I can't park here." Behind them, a car honked.

"I'll get out here," she said.

"You can't go now. Not like this." He tried for her hand, but she pulled it away, opened the door, and jumped out. "Come on. Get back in the car, please." He tried to sound calm, but his voice was rising.

She didn't respond. Instead, she opened the back door and reached for her bag. It was jammed between the floor and the seats, though, and she had trouble getting it out.

"Donna, you shouldn't go off like this, leave like this."

She yanked on the bag. The policeman blew his whistle again and headed toward the car. Behind him, Charlie heard more honking.

He turned, and at the exact moment that she pulled her bag free, he yelled, "I got fired. They fired me. Helmut fired me."

Donna had no response to this either. Charlie wasn't sure she'd heard him, "Donna! Come on, get back in. I said, I got fired. You can't go now."

She slammed the rear door and stood one last time by the passenger window, peering back at him. It was only then that Charlie realized she wasn't going to visit her brother Aaron in Minneapolis.

"Where are you going?" His question scared him. She stared at Charlie, her hard jaw retreating, her mouth trembling. She turned and rushed off through the revolving doors and into the airport, which was ablaze with lights.

A clear sky at night is a strange place. Mysterious. Peaceful. Perspective can be found in the distance and space. Looking up into the darkness at the stars, a man is reminded of his station, his overall state of helplessness.

Charlie used to like looking at the stars when he was a boy. He found them reassuring. He believed they had a purpose, and he sensed an order, a connection to God. Perspective shifts with age, though, and now he saw them differently, now he recognized their frailty and saw them for what they were: random pinpricks of light and nothing more.

"I'm fifty years old," he said out loud, his face turned up to the sky. "Fifty years old."

It was late and the night had grown windy and cool. Despite the fact that he had made a serious dent in a new bottle of bourbon and was wearing his Bagel Man cape, the cold was bracing and he knew he should go inside. It was after midnight and he had been in the backyard for hours, gazing up at the sky, his telescope at his side, sifting through things.

As he lay on the ground, he tried to trace the roots of his situation, tried to identify when things had gone south between Donna and him. Several moments, fights, incidents, came to mind, but one stood out. It had happened about three or four years ago. Kyle had gotten a small part in the school play and Charlie had promised to leave work early so he could be there to cheer him on. He had recently made the move over to the new agency and had missed a string of family functions: Donna's father's eightieth and, it turned out, last birthday; Kyle's Little League All-Star game; a block party in the old neighborhood. His absences had resulted in loud rows with Donna that lasted well into the night, concluding only with his sworn pledge that he would change.

On the afternoon of Kyle's big play, the expected happened and he was called into an emergency meeting and wasn't able to make it. When he came home late that night, he was fully prepared for a major scourging, but instead was greeted with indifference. No outburst, no dramatics, no silent treatment. Merely a shrug and a quick summary of the play and Kyle's performance when he asked how things had gone. At the time, he was relieved by this reaction. But it was at that moment, he now realized, that Donna had started her retreat; it was at that moment when things had begun to die.

He considered this until the skies clouded and the stars disappeared. Then he headed back to the house, leaving the telescope and bottle of Jim Beam to mark his spot. His cape, however, was firmly clasped around his neck and fluttered royally behind him in the breeze. As he walked, he felt like a defeated king leaving a battlefield.

He drank two glasses of water at the kitchen sink, shut off all the lights, then trudged on upstairs. In the dark hallway, he saw a bar of light coming from under Kyle's door. He knocked.

"What?"

"It's me. Your father. Can I come in?"

"Yeah."

Charlie opened the door and found Kyle lying on the bed, reading a book.

"It's late," Charlie said. "What are you doing?"

"Nothing." He sat up, brushed the hair out of his eyes, and gave Charlie a strange, worried look.

"You're not doing nothing. You're reading." He reached over and turned the book around so he could see its cover. It was Thomas Pynchon's *V.*

"I read this in college. I remember thinking it was complicated and long. What's it about? I never understood it."

"I don't know yet. It's kind of confusing. That's why it's so cool."

Charlie let go of the book and glanced around the room. He couldn't remember the last time he had been in here and was surprised at its order and neatness. The top of Kyle's desk was clear and his bookcase, with shelves of paperbacks, relatively organized. On his walls were the obligatory posters of basketball players with their mouths open, all in various stages of dunking the ball over shocked and helpless opponents.

"Hey," he said. "When are you going to hear about the basketball team?"

"Soon."

"Hope you make it."

"Yeah."

Charlie looked around his son's room again. "How many books do you have?"

"I don't know."

"Seems like you have a lot." He walked over to the bookcase. It had six deep shelves, was made of oak, and had cost $25.95 in 1979. Donna and he had bought it soon after they were married, at a furniture warehouse sale. Charlie lightly ran his hand over the top of it, stopping at a nick at the corner. He remembered banging the bookcase against the front door while they were moving it into the old house. Donna had to call Sean and Mike, two of her brothers, to help them get it upstairs.

"This is really old," he said, tapping the top of the bookcase. "We bought this before you were born."

Kyle looked at the bookcase. "Yeah." He nodded. "It's pretty old. I've always had it."

"Yep, it is." He picked at the nick with his index finger like he was trying to extract something. "Hey," he said. "I've been meaning to tell you, you don't have to pump gas."

Charlie turned to face him. Kyle looked confused, his eyebrows forming a tight, straight line. Then his face relaxed and he nodded again. "Oh, yeah. Pumping gas. I don't think, you know, there are any jobs like that anymore. People pump their own gas, don't they?"

Charlie reached out for the bookcase again, this time to steady himself. He had drunk a fair amount and was just then feeling its impact. "I guess you're right. When I was young, people used to pump gas for you. Sometimes they even wore uniforms."

Kyle was amazed at this. "What kind of uniforms?"

"I don't know. White ones. We used to wear them at Gas City."

"You and that drug addict?"

"What? Oh. He wasn't a drug addict. He was just a kid. A regular kid." Charlie pushed off from the bookcase and headed toward the door.

"Dad, are you all right?"

Charlie stopped. "I'm perfect, why?"

Kyle motioned with his book. "Why do you have that on?"

Charlie had forgotten about the cape. He stood up as straight as he could and adjusted it, trying to look dignified. "I was cold." He noticed the grass all over the front of his shirt and pants and made an attempt to brush it off. "I was outside. I fell asleep in the yard."

Kyle studied him, his mouth half open. He had something stuck in his braces on one side of his mouth, possibly a lima bean. Charlie was going to tell him to brush his teeth, but decided not to. Instead he said, "It's really late. Go to sleep."

"Hey, Dad, sorry to hear about your job."

Charlie stiffened. "What do you mean?"

"About getting fired."

Charlie's head, which had been comfortably warm and muddled, instantly cleared. "Did you read the paper?" he asked.

"No. Was it in the paper?"

"How did you find out, then?"

"Mom told me."

"What? Your mom? Mom told you? Did she just call?"

"No."

"When did she tell you, then?"

"I don't know. She told me not to talk about it. She said you felt, you know, bad, and not to talk about it."

"But when did she tell you? Yesterday? Day before? When?"

He shrugged again. "I don't know. She first told me a while ago. Right after it happened, I guess."

Chapter Eleven

The next day, Robert, a tall man with news anchor looks who sat back in the cubicles, got a job. He brought a box of doughnuts to the office to help celebrate his return to the working world. All of the refugees stood quietly in the kitchen area and pretended to be happy for him, as they ate the glazed doughnuts and sipped lukewarm orange juice from oversized Styrofoam cups, while listening to him talk about his new position as the head of marketing for a pesticide company.

"He was only out three months," Bradley said, after the little party was over. "That's not very long."

"Well, good for him," Charlie said. This development depressed him. Robert's leaving meant one less job out there.

"Yeah, good for him," Bradley said. He leaned his back against the sink and took a sip of his orange juice. "Ever notice that guy's face?"

"Who?"

"That Robert guy. Ever notice how he looks?"

"No. What do you mean?" Charlie asked.

"Looks like he's had some work done. A little nip and tuck."

"Hadn't noticed," Charlie said.

"Around his eyes and mouth. He's older than you think. Probably mid-fifties. I think he's gay too."

"How do you know that?"

Bradley shrugged. "I just got that vibe. Not that it matters."

"No, it doesn't."

"Gays need to work too," Bradley said. He sipped some juice. "I wonder if that's the reason he got the job, though."

"What?"

"I wonder if the reason he got the job was because he's gay," Bradley said.

Charlie was having a hard time following this train of thought. "I think sometimes that might work against you."

"Not if the person hiring you is gay. Then it would work for you. Don't you think?"

"I don't know, maybe."

"I mean, if I were gay, I would probably hire another gay, wouldn't you?"

"I honestly never thought about it."

Bradley was quiet. Then he said, "I'm probably thinking too much."

Charlie strode over to the coffeemaker and poured himself a cup. The coffee at Rogers & Challenger was brutally weak, but he was committed to drinking it. Avoiding Starbucks was an essential, albeit small, part of The New Frugality. He estimated that he could save close to $40 a month by drinking the office coffee; $500 a year, God forbid, if it came to that.

"I was watching TV the other night," Bradley said. "They had a guy on in New York who was walking around Manhattan wearing one of those advertising sandwich boards. The board said I NEED A JOB. He was walking around like a clown, passing out résumés. Jesus Christ, have some damn pride."

"Maybe he was desperate."

"No one's that desperate. That's pathetic."

"Things are bad," Charlie said. He blew on his coffee. "Hey, how did your dinner go the other night? Your interview?"

Bradley stared into his Styrofoam cup. "You mean my lunch? Got stood up."

"What?"

"Never showed."

"Did you call?"

"Only three times. Waited in the bar for an hour."

"Three times! And they never called back?"

"Nope."

"That's unacceptable, unbelievable!"

Bradley gave Charlie a Texas-sized smirk. "What's unbelievable is that it's the second time that's happened to me. Second time I've been stood up," he said. "*That's* unbelievable."

"You're kidding, right? I'd call them again or write a letter to the HR department. That's really unprofessional! You shouldn't take that shit. No one should. I wouldn't take that shit. I would have ordered lunch and sent them the fucking bill, at the very least."

Bradley didn't seem to hear Charlie. He was suddenly far away. "You know, I once played in the Cotton Bowl," he said softly, more really to himself than to Charlie. He looked very sad in his blue suit and red tie with the tight, perfect Windsor knot.

Charlie wasn't sure he'd heard him right. "What?"

"For Texas. I was a starter. For the fucking Texas Longhorns," Bradley said. Then, without warning, he threw his cup against the wall, orange juice spraying everywhere.

"Jesus!" Charlie jumped back.

Bradley didn't say anything. He just walked away.

Since he had run four miles on the treadmill that morning, the first time in weeks, he had gotten in late, and consequently was forced to sit in one of the cubicles at the far end of the hall. The day before, a large sales promotion firm, a client of Rogers & Challenger, had laid off a dozen workers and the office was flooded with fresh, mostly thirtysomething refugees, all looking dazed and confused.

He had planned to confront his résumé again, but as soon

as he unpacked his briefcase and got situated, he started obsessing about Donna. He had slept little the night before, berating himself for not following her into the airport and forcing a Bogart-Bergman-type scene on the tarmac. Calls to all the major airlines in the middle of the night had confirmed his fears; there were no late flights out to Minneapolis on United. He considered calling Donna's brother Aaron in Minneapolis, as well as the FBI, but decided to wait for her to contact him. She had never done this before and he was hopeful that she would come to her senses.

He made a halfhearted attempt to realign the margins of his résumé, before heading down the hall for some water. On his way back to his cube, he glanced sideways into an office and saw Karen Brisco sitting at her desk, her hands cupped over her face. He thought she was about to sneeze, then realized, by the way her head was shaking, that she was crying. He paused, continued on, paused again, and then returned to her doorway and popped his head into her office.

"Everything okay in here?" he asked.

She scooted her hands down and peered over her fingertips with red eyes. Even though she had her arms in front of her chest, he could see the top three buttons on her sleeveless blouse were undone, he assumed, unintentionally.

"The door keeps swinging open. This is a shitty office," she said, sniffling.

"Are you okay?"

She shrugged. "Yeah." She reached down for her purse and pulled out a tissue. "I'm great."

"You look it."

She blew her nose. "I ate an entire pint of chocolate mint ice cream this morning. An entire pint. What's wrong with me? I'm disgusting."

"No, you're not."

"I've gained five pounds since I lost my job. Five pounds. Who eats ice cream in the morning?"

"Lots of people do. I do."

She stopped blowing her nose and looked up him. "You do not."

"I have a banana split every morning. With bran flakes."

"You're a liar." She dabbed at her nose with the tissue.

He watched her dab for a few seconds. "Can I get you something?"

"A job."

"I'll get right on that."

"Thanks."

"How about a milkshake?"

She looked at him.

"A frosty?"

"Very funny. I'm okay. I'm just having a bad day."

"Tomorrow will be better."

"It probably won't be." She crumpled up the tissue but kept it in her hand. "Can you try to shut my door? You have to fiddle with the doorknob after you close it."

"Sure you're okay?"

"Yes." She then covered her eyes again and resumed silently crying.

"Hey, come on, now. It's not that bad."

"It's bad."

Charlie, unaccustomed to the cheerleading role, felt helpless. He considered making a quiet exit, but instead blurted out, "It's always darkest before the dawn."

Karen uncovered her eyes and sniffled. "I can't believe you said that."

"It's the best I can do."

"Will you please shut the door?"

"Failure is the path of least persistence," Charlie said.

She looked at him again but said nothing.

"Rise above the storm and you will find sunshine."

She started to laugh a little.

"Failure never comes to any man unless he admits it."

She sniffled again and shook her head. "Get out and shut the door, please."

"I've memorized every stupid poster in this place and will recite each one unless you promise to stop crying."

"I'm impressed. Now leave."

"Courage is being afraid but going on anyhow—"

"Okay, okay, I promise." She blew her nose in the tissue. "Hey, how are you doing?" she asked.

Charlie's smile vanished. He thought of Donna and the whole mess and shook his head. "Fine," he said.

"You sure?"

He paused. "Yeah. I'm okay." He then made a quick exit, closing the door behind him.

Back in his small cube, bare with the exception of a phone and an old Apple computer, he felt the high over helping Karen seeping away. He looked around the room, saw other refugees silently hunched over their screens, heard the faint hush of the air vents, smelled the stale air of the office. Then he saw Karen crying again and closed his eyes. A bad dream, he thought. This is all a bad dream. He would wake up in the St. Regis in D.C. or the Peabody in Orlando or the Brown in Denver, then go to a meeting, go to a lunch. I'm going to wake up soon, he thought, I'm going to wake up soon.

When he opened his eyes, he called the Wizard. He was put on hold for close to five minutes before he heard Preston's breathy voice.

"Charlie, what's the problem?"

"No problem. Thought I'd check in."

There was a pause. Charlie envisioned Preston's ghostlike form, a head only, swirling in the air, surrounded by clouds of fire. "But we just talked," he said.

"Well, I know, but I just thought you might have something."

"I don't even have your résumé."

"Come on, you don't need one of those things. Come on, Preston. They're a pain in the ass to do."

Preston didn't say anything, so Charlie said, "Okay, I'll get you one. But is there anything out there right now? I just want to start the process. Getting a little antsy."

"You have to be realistic."

Charlie snapped at this. "Realistic? You know, Preston, I threw you a lot of work, I mean a lot of work, over the years. I could have worked with any headhunter. Any headhunter. They called us every day." Charlie said this loudly and two refugees, sitting nearby, glanced over at him. He pressed closer into the cube. "Listen, I'm sorry, but I'd like to get moving on things." His hands were sweating and his heart suddenly racing. He had scant experience asking people for favors.

Preston was quiet again.

"Listen, I got to go," Charlie softly said. He realized calling was a mistake and felt ashamed. "I'm sorry I called. Just let me know when you have a minute."

"Hold on there, boss," Preston said. "There is something that just popped open. I don't know if you would be right for it, though."

Charlie's heart leaped. "Really? Well, what is it?"

"This is all on the hush-hush, now."

He inched even closer into his cube and whispered loudly, "I know, what?"

"Xanon International."

"What's that? You mean the drug company?"

"Pharmaceuticals. Big-time company. Fortune 500. They canned the CMO a while ago and they're looking for a replacement. They're pretty far along in the search, so it's a long shot, but who knows? They haven't fallen in love yet. Based here in Chicago too."

"Well, that could be interesting. What do they do, exactly?"

"Drugs for animals."

"Drugs for animals," Charlie repeated.

"Try to sound excited, chief."

"What kind of animals?"

"Cattle, mostly."

Charlie had to think about this. "Do cattle need drugs?"

"Everyone needs drugs."

"How much does this pay?" Charlie asked.

"It pays. It pays fine. Listen, I have to run. I'll poke around, see what's what. I'll call."

"When?"

"Soon," the Wizard said, hanging up.

After the call, Charlie felt a brief blip of optimism and allowed himself to hope. Even though it didn't quite fit his definition of a dream job, the fact that it was a huge company and the fact that it paid were definite pluses. Also, he knew that just having something, anything, going on this early in his search was a major coup. Sensing a shift in momentum, he picked up his cell phone with the intention of calling his brother-in-law Aaron and tracking down Donna. As soon as he flipped it open, however, he heard Donna's voice.

"When were you going to tell me you were fired?" she asked.

"What? Donna?" His phone hadn't rung. He pulled it away, looked at it, then tentatively put it back to his ear. "Did you just call? My phone didn't even ring."

She had no interest in this phenomenon. "When were you going to tell me you were fired?" she asked again.

He glanced nervously around the room. "Where are you?"

"When were you going to tell me you were fired?"

"Can you stop asking me that?"

"When?"

"I told you in the car when you were leaving. Now, I'm not going to answer any questions until you tell me where you are."

"In a restaurant."

"What restaurant? Where?"

"I'm in a place. I don't know. Cook's."

"Cook's. Where's that? I never heard of it."

"It's on an island. Bailey Island. It hasn't opened yet. I'm in the parking lot. It's in Maine."

"What? What do you mean, Maine? You mean the state?"

"Yes."

"What?" He could not comprehend this. Maine was incredibly far away and, he thought, dangerous. It was one of the few places he had never been. In an instant, he envisioned oceans and rocky cliffs, fog, black bears. "I don't understand. What are you talking about? What are you doing in Maine?"

"I wanted to come here."

"Why?"

"Because."

They stopped talking and he listened to Donna breathe. From across the room, Walter stared at him with one glassy carp eye, his lips slighting parted. Charlie turned his back to him and leaned forward into the cube

"Apparently I didn't have to tell you anything. Apparently you knew all along," he said.

"Why didn't you tell me yourself? I was waiting for you to tell me."

"I was going to."

"When? A year from now? Ten years? I'm your wife. Your wife. We're married."

"When did you know?" Charlie asked. "I mean specifically."

"Why does that matter?"

"I want to know. It's important."

"Why?"

"It just is."

"When you were holding the can of lima beans in the kitchen. After you went shopping."

He shook his head in disgust. "I never should have bought those stupid lima beans! I knew it! Why didn't you say something then?"

"What was your plan, then, never to tell me?"

"I was going to tell you."

"Why didn't you, then?"

"I don't know. I was going to, though."

"I know why you didn't tell me. Because I'm not important enough to tell, because I don't matter anymore."

"Oh, come on! That's ridiculous. Completely ridiculous."

"Why, then?"

"Because I was embarrassed. Why do you think?"

"You were embarrassed? That's it? That's why you didn't tell me? You were *embarrassed*?"

"Yeah, okay, I was. Because you told me not to take the job. You never wanted to move. All that."

"So you were afraid I was going to say I told you so? That's what you think of me?"

"Jesus." His face was hot. He switched the phone to his other ear. "Is that why you're in Maine? Because I didn't tell you right away?"

"No. I'm in Maine for lots of reasons."

"Like what?"

"I don't have three hours, Charlie."

"Well, how long are you going to be gone?"

"I don't know."

"You don't know? What about our son? If you could stop thinking about yourself for a minute, maybe you should think about him."

"Stop thinking about myself? Myself? I've never thought about myself. Ever. I've never had time to. I'm always thinking about you. What mood you're going to be in when you come home. *If* you come home. *If* you're going to get that big account. *If* you're going to win that big award. *If* you're going to get promoted. *If* you're going to be in Paris for a month. You're the only person who matters in our house."

"Listen, just settle down."

"Don't you dare tell me to breathe. I know that's what you're about to tell me to do, so do not do it. Do *not*."

"I'm not going to tell you to do anything." He said this very calmly, even though he had been about to tell her to breathe. "Listen, you have to come home now. This is ridiculous. Do you want me to come out there and bring you back?"

"I can get back on my own, thank you very much. I'm very capable of doing that."

"You've never traveled by yourself before. What happens if you have one of your sleeping things and . . . and walk into the ocean? Maine is a very dangerous place. Stephen King lives in Maine."

"I'm not going to walk into the ocean," she said. "Unless I want to." She hung up.

. . .

When he got home, he went upstairs and immediately began a search for Bailey Island, Maine. He needed information.

He didn't find much other than an odd photo gallery featuring artsy and, he thought, menacing Bergman-like black-and-white pictures of weather-beaten homes and rocky windswept shorelines. This did little to comfort him. He imagined Donna walking in her sleep over the rocks, her arms out in front of her and in a trance as she stumbled around in her pink flip-flops, while nearby, black bears raised their noses to the wind and picked up her scent.

Exactly what Donna was doing there, he didn't know. The fact that she could do something so drastic as to leave him, then head across the country to a remote and possibly hostile place, was dumbfounding. He had known this woman for his entire adult life and if someone had asked him if she was capable of such a stunt, he would certainly have said no.

He went downstairs in search of the mail and then bourbon but instead found Kyle sitting at the baby grand, softly plunking at the keys. He looked up quickly when his father entered the room.

"You going to play something?" Charlie asked. A few years back, Kyle had taken lessons, though Charlie had never once heard him play.

"No," Kyle said. "Do we have anything to eat?"

Charlie's body sagged. He had planned on being alone and indulging himself with his worries, but now he had to deal with the task of feeding his son. "Isn't there anything in the refrigerator?" he asked.

"I didn't look there."

"Where did you look, then?"

"Nowhere." Kyle pushed the hair out of his eyes with a slow, sweeping motion of his hand, a gesture Charlie had seen Donna make a hundred, a thousand, a million times with her own explosion of hair. "What's wrong?" he asked. Charlie was staring at him.

"Nothing," Charlie quietly said. "Come on. Let's go get some dinner."

A half hour later, while Kyle was pouring syrup out of a small stainless-steel pitcher onto a high stack of pancakes, Charlie asked if he had ever heard of Bailey Island.

"Bailey Island," he repeated. "Is that near Cuba?" He stopped pouring and licked some fingers.

"It's out East. In Maine, or by Maine." Charlie paused. "You've heard of Maine, right?"

Kyle's eyes were blank.

"Have you ever heard Mom mention it? Did she ever say she wanted to go there, or had friends there, something like that? Did it ever come up in conversation?"

Kyle finally responded. "Maine," he said, thinking. He started in on his pancakes.

Charlie sipped his coffee and watched him eat. They were sitting in a booth by a window at Will's, the very coffee shop Charlie had spied Donna in. While Kyle ate, Charlie searched the room for clues that might tell him how often she frequented the place, but all he saw was the old man wiping down the counter.

"Is that where Mom is?" Kyle asked. "In Maine?"

"Yes. She called me from there today."

Kyle had no reaction. He methodically ate his pancakes, pausing only to stuff some bacon into a side of his mouth. Charlie sipped more coffee.

"How come you're not eating anything?" Kyle asked.

Charlie shrugged and put down his cup. Outside, a young couple walked by, hand in hand. They wore matching Burberry raincoats and were carrying brown weatherworn leather briefcases. The woman, a short, Nordic-looking blonde, swung hers energetically at her side. When they passed the window, she glanced Charlie's way and smiled, a perky little corporate smile. Up until recently, Charlie's life had been full of perky little, briefcase-swinging women and suddenly he missed each and every one of them.

Kyle stopped eating. "You can have some of my pancakes, if you want," he said.

"No, I'm all right."

"You want some of my bacon? We can split it." He pushed a side plate forward. Charlie picked up a piece, and took a small bite. It was hard and overcooked. He put it back.

"So," he said. "How's school?"

"Okay. I'm in a play."

"A play? A school play? I thought you were going out for basketball."

Kyle drank his milk. "I am. I can do both."

"Do you have time to do both?"

"Sure."

"Does your mother know you're doing both?"

"Yeah, she knows."

"Okay. Well, we'll have to make sure we come see the play. What's the name of it?"

"Mr. Vengeance."

"Mr. Vengeance? I never heard of it. What's it about?"

"It's about a guy who kind of flips out and kills a bunch of people in a high school."

Charlie absorbed this description before asking, "What kind of play is that? Who wrote it?"

"Matt."

"Matt? Matt who? You mean your friend Matt?"

"Yeah. Matt."

"The tall guy? He wrote a play?"

"Yeah. It's a student production. He writes a lot of plays."

"Jesus, that guy's a playwright? What kind of part do you have?"

"It's pretty small."

"How small? Do you have any lines?"

"Not, like, officially."

"What do you mean, not officially?"

"I kind of scream."

"You scream? That's it?"

"Yeah."

"You don't do anything else?"

"No." Kyle ate a piece of bacon. "I play a dead body."

"A what? A dead body? The whole time?"

"Yeah. Except when I scream. I'm still alive then. But then I get shot, so the rest of the time I lie there dead."

"How long are you dead?"

"About two hours. I'm the first one shot."

"Two hours. You mean the whole time you're onstage, you're dead?"

"Yeah. Pretty much."

Charlie stared out the window. He was becoming concerned. "Is this Matt a good friend of yours?"

"Yeah, I guess."

"Does he have other friends, or are you his only one?"

"I don't know. He has other friends."

"Matt doesn't do drugs or anything, does he?"

"What?"

"I mean, as far as you know."

"No."

"You probably wouldn't tell me if he did, would you?"

"No."

Charlie drank more coffee. "Why would you want to play a dead body for two hours?"

Kyle shrugged. "I only have to go to one rehearsal." He cut into a pancake with the side of his fork. "Did you get a new job yet?"

"What?" Charlie was trying to determine what his son's desire to play a dead body in public said about his parenting abilities.

"Did you get a new job yet?"

"I just started looking. It takes time. Sometimes a long time."

"Do we have any money left?"

"We'll be okay. We have to economize a little. Just to play it safe."

"Be frugal?"

"Yeah. You know what that means?"

"Yeah." Kyle stopped eating again and stared at his food.

"Maybe we shouldn't go out to eat so much. Mom and I go out to eat a lot. That's not being frugal."

"I can afford pancakes."

He went back to his food, but with less gusto than before. "I was thinking that maybe I should get a job like you said."

"You don't have to get a job. I'll be working again soon."

"Maybe we shouldn't have moved here. Maybe we should move back home."

His comment, which Charlie knew was an unspoken sentiment in their house, shook him and he couldn't immediately respond. "We are home," he finally said. "This is our home." He picked at some of the bacon. "Why? Do you miss the old neighborhood?"

Kyle shrugged. "I don't know. Sometimes."

"Don't you like it here? We've been here awhile."

He shrugged again. "It's okay."

"What don't you like about it?"

"I don't know. It's real quiet all the time. I kind of feel like I'm in outer space. I can hear myself breathing, like an astronaut." He drank his orange juice and finished a last corner of toast. "How come you got fired from your job?"

"I don't know. Lots of reasons."

"How did they do it? Did some guy come into your office and say you're fired?"

"Actually, I went into his office. You got the rest of it right, though."

Kyle looked out the window and nodded. "That's pretty harsh."

"It wasn't that bad. It happens. If you work for a big company, you can't count on anything. Sooner or later, they're going to get you. It was my turn, that's all. Pretty much everyone gets fired eventually. It's like dying."

"Do you think they might call you and give you your job back?"

"No." Charlie saw his own reflection in the window. He was smiling, for some reason. "That's over. I never had a chance there. Let's just say it was a bad marriage."

Kyle looked out the window and Charlie's and his eyes locked for a moment in the reflection. Then he turned his head back down toward his plate. "Are you and Mom getting divorced?" he asked.

Charlie froze. He was still looking at his own smiling reflection. "What? Did Mom say something about that?"

"No."

He looked at Kyle. "Then why would you ask that?"

"I wondered, that's all." Kyle's face reddened. He kept his head low over his plate, but Charlie could feel his knees pumping nervously under the table.

"No. We're not getting a divorce. Everything's going to be fine. It's a tough time right now for us. We're all stressed. Everything's going to be all right, though."

"Mom cries a lot," Kyle said.

"She does? When? What do you mean?"

"When I come home from school. I see her crying. Ever since Bill Morgan left."

Charlie swallowed. "Who's Bill Morgan?"

"He's from Bright Day," Kyle said. "He worked there with her, I think. He lives in a lighthouse or something. He showed me pictures."

"Lighthouse? What are you talking about?"

Kyle pushed the remains of his pancakes off to the side of his plate with a knife. "He used to come to the house a lot," he said. "For like coffee and stuff. He was there a lot."

"At our house? How old is he?"

"I don't know. About your age," Kyle said. His eyes were still down on his plate. "He went back home, though, a few weeks ago."

"Back home? Where does he live?"

"Maine," Kyle said. "He went back to Maine."

Chapter Twelve

Charlie never had time for epiphanies, one of those life-changing moments of clarity and self-realization that happen regularly in movies or in contemporary fiction. Epiphanies happened to other people, people who had time for introspection, and a natural inclination for reflection. Up until the moment Kyle told him about Donna and Bill Morgan and Maine, he had never seen the need for one.

After they returned from dinner, he sat in his office and tried to conjure one up. He figured that, all things considered—finding out that his wife was in another state, with (possibly) another man—an epiphany was in order. He spent a good part of the evening sitting alone in the dark, breathing deeply, waiting for understanding, and clarity, to find him.

The fact that he had taken his first-ever Valium before his epiphany search definitely played a role in the Zen-like way he approached matters. An ER doctor had prescribed the Valium months before to help settle him down after the loss of the Southwest Airlines business, but Charlie had been hesitant to indulge, turning instead to bourbon. Tonight, though, he had taken two, along with a large glass of white wine.

The medication was helping. As he sat in his office, staring at a photo of a lighthouse he had found online (he had Googled "Lighthouses," then "Lighthouses in Maine," then "Lighthouses in Maine+sex"), he felt weightless, airborne. And while clarity and understanding continued to elude him, he didn't feel entirely unpleasant.

Around midnight, he tried Donna's cell phone again, then made his way up to Kyle's room. He found him sleeping fully clothed on top of his blankets. Charlie turned his desk light on and stared down at him. His mouth was slightly open, and his hair was pushed back to reveal a light patch of pimples. As he watched him lie there with his arms tucked under him in such a way that only his hands were visible, like cupped paws, Charlie's mind flashed back to his days at the zoo. Kyle looked like a peaceful, slumbering animal. A big puppy dog.

He sat on the edge of the bed and looked at his man-puppy son.

"How you doing?" He asked this loudly, like a deaf person might. He had no control over the volume of his voice.

Kyle's eyes shot open. "What?" He looked confused, but remained perfectly still.

"What's up?" Charlie asked.

"What?"

"Were you sleeping?"

Kyle had tiny headphones plugged into his ears and stared at Charlie with wide eyes.

"You were sleeping, weren't you? Sorry. I'll go now. I didn't mean to wake you. I thought maybe you were just lying there."

Kyle blinked. "What?"

The Valium and wine were really kicking in. Charlie felt the room spin, then tilt to the left, then right. He wiped some drool off his chin and looked at Kyle: his son, his child, his *legacy*. When Charlie was dead and gone, Kyle, not the Bagel Man commercials, not the commercials with the parachuting kitten wearing tiny red galoshes, would be the only proof that he had ever existed. This thought struck him as profound. If he weren't so highly medicated and if his tear ducts were able to function, he certainly would have wept.

He said, "Good night, son," deeply, hoping to sound like Atticus Finch.

Kyle closed his eyes. Charlie could hear tinny music coming from the headphones. "Everything is going to be okay," he said, even though he knew Kyle was asleep. Charlie tried to pat him on the head, but missed and instead affectionately patted the side of the pillow.

He stood, shut the light, and walked unsteadily toward the door and out into the hall. At the top of the stairs, he decided that he might need a drink or something to eat. He wasn't sure what time it was, what day, or even his last name, but he had a sense of being hungry, very hungry. He put his hand on the banister and stared down the stairs. Everything tilted again and he gripped the banister tighter. The floor below seemed far away, very far away.

A light. A voice. Things in and out of focus.

"Dad? Are you all right?"

Charlie followed the voice, and gradually Kyle came into view. He was staring down at him, his eyes wide with concern. "I'm fine, why?"

"Are you sure?" Kyle asked.

"Yes."

"Why are you lying there?"

"What?" Charlie tried to move and managed to lift his head an inch or so.

"Why are you on the floor?"

It was only after he asked that question that Charlie felt the pain in his face. It was intense and searing and he considered screaming.

Kyle put his hands under Charlie's shoulders and pulled him to a sitting position. "Did you fall down the stairs or something?"

"Fall?" Charlie was trying to move his mouth back and forth.

"I think you fell down the stairs last night."

Charlie stopped working his jaw and considered this theory. He moved his head slowly from one side to the next. He was seated at the bottom of the stairs and his face was throbbing.

"I might have," he said. His teeth hurt.

"Your face is all weird."

"What do you mean?"

"Like, puffy. And you got a lump or something on the side of your forehead. Right there." He pointed and then helped Charlie to his feet.

"Is there any blood?" Charlie asked. He lightly touched his forehead.

"Yeah. A little on the floor and a little on your face."

Under normal circumstances, the prospect of blood, particularly his own, would have catapulted him into a hysterical search for the nearest ER. But since he was so dazed, he decided to table his panic until he could think clearly. Besides, he still had a fair amount of Valium cruising through his system and the parts of his brain that housed the hysterical neurons weren't quite operational.

"I'm okay," he said. "I must have slipped. But I'm okay. What time is it?"

"It's about seven-thirty."

"In the morning?"

"Yeah. Should I call someone? Like a doctor?"

"No. I think I'm okay." He walked stiffly into the kitchen, purposefully keeping his back to Kyle, embarrassed and disgusted with himself. He didn't want Kyle seeing his face any more than necessary.

"Do you want some breakfast?"

"I have to go now," Kyle said.

"Go where?"

"School."

"Oh, that's right. School. You go to school. That's right."

"Are you going to be home when I get back?"

"Sure." Charlie opened the refrigerator, leaned down into it, and took out a jar of mayonnaise, which was the first thing he could put his hands on. He was doing his best to pretend that falling face-first down a flight of stairs after taking drugs was not in any way, shape, or form a cause for alarm, or even interest.

"Are you sure you're not hungry? How about some eggs?" He held the jar of mayonnaise up high over his head, his face still buried in the refrigerator. "I can make them fast. Whip them right up."

"I gotta go," Kyle said.

"You sure?" Charlie held the jar up even higher. "I make great eggs."

"I don't want any."

"Okay, well, see you soon, then."

After Kyle left, he took stock in the hallway mirror: he had the beginnings of a black eye, a heavy and drooping eyelid, and rough scratches on one cheek, which was at least twice its normal size. From the looks of things, it appeared that he had fallen on just the left side of his face. He turned his head one way, and then the other: one side was normal, the other, Elephant Man. Normal. Elephant Man. Normal. Elephant Man. He kept turning his head, both amazed and horrified at the difference. As Kyle had pointed out, there was also a Milk Dud–sized bump on his forehead. He gingerly touched it and moaned. Then he stepped closer to the mirror and probed his mouth. His lips had a film of dried blood on them and he carefully peeled it off with his thumb and index finger. It was while he was doing this that he discovered that one of his upper front teeth was loose. He touched the tooth with his pinkie finger; it wiggled.

"Oh, my God," he said. He stepped close to the mirror and touched his tooth again. It was now crooked.

"Please, God, no," he said.

When he touched it a third time, it completely gave way, falling out of his mouth and onto the floor, where it bounced crazily.

"Oh, my God," Charlie said again. "Oh. My. God."

On his way downtown to the dentist, he wondered if he could be unconscious and not know it. His head ached terribly and he felt out of focus, disoriented. He wasn't sure if it was because of his head injury or the Valium, but either way, he knew he was in no condition to drive. He hugged the shoulder of the right lane as he drove, hunched forward over the steering wheel, a wad of blood-soaked toilet paper stuck in the tiny hole in his upper gum. When he entered the Loop, he adjusted the wad, pressing it in tight, and called Donna. He got her voice mail.

"It's me. Listen, I don't want to interrupt your little vacation or whatever it is you're doing, but I was in a serious accident. I think I'm okay. I'm in stable condition. I'm on my way to the dentist right now. I lost a lot of blood. A few pints, maybe. I don't know how much, but I'm a little dizzy. Call me ASAP. And you should come home ASAP. This is ridiculous." Then for effect he added, "We have no food in the house and Kyle is hungry."

Since he had called ahead to the dentist, they were waiting for him. As soon as he got there, a hygienist rushed him into an office and began rinsing out his mouth with warm water. He closed his eyes and tried to remain calm as she worked in silence. Her focused urgency alarmed him and when he could, he took extra-deep breaths. In his right hand, he clutched a bloodied napkin that held the remains of his severed tooth.

When the hygienist was finished, he asked where Dr. Ronin, his dentist, was.

"He'll be right in." She was a small, pretty Hispanic woman whose brown eyes worriedly searched the Elephant Man part of his face. "Were you in an accident?"

"No, I woke up like this. Now, where is he? Dr. Ronin. I need him now! Pronto! I lost a lot of blood."

"You're fine," she said.

"I am *not* fine. Do not say I'm fine. Where is he?"

A moment later, Dr. Ronin walked in and, after inspecting the inside of his mouth, quickly assessed the damage.

"I'm afraid you're going to need a prosthesis," he said.

"Prosthesis? What do you mean? Like a fake leg?"

"Yes."

"I don't understand. What do you mean, yes?"

"I mean, yes, you need a prosthesis."

This diagnosis and, he thought, the overly direct way it was communicated, shook him. "I can't believe this. You mean you can't use the old one?" Charlie presented him with the bloody napkin.

Dr. Ronin backed away. "What's that?"

"Unwrap it."

The dentist carefully took and unfolded the napkin, then picked up the tooth.

"See, it's in perfect shape," Charlie said. "Can't you just insert it back into place? Just pop it in?"

Dr. Ronin examined the tooth. He was a small, shy man with white hair and bushy Einstein eyebrows. Charlie had been his patient for more than twenty-five years and, despite the fact that he had moved his offices three times and never once sent him a change-of-address notification, Charlie still believed he cared for him. "No," he said. "It wasn't a clean break. There's still some tooth fragments in your gum. You need a prosthesis, Charlie."

"For the rest of my life?"

"Yes."

"Jesus. Well, how will this work? Will I be able to eat regular food?"

"You'll be able to eat anything you want."

"Really? What about apples, then? Can I eat apples?"

Dr. Ronin put the bloody napkin with the tooth on the counter behind him. "You probably shouldn't eat apples," he said. "At least not for a while."

Despite the fact that Charlie hadn't held, much less eaten, an apple since the fifth grade, this news stunned him. "You mean to tell me I can never eat an apple again? Is that what you're telling me? For the rest of my life? Come on, you're kidding me, right? I mean, you're kidding."

Dr. Ronin turned his back to Charlie and started washing his hands in a sink. "Charlie, please, you'll be fine."

"What about other things? Other foods?"

"Like what?"

"I don't know, like . . . like taffy? What about taffy?"

"Taffy?"

"Yeah, taffy!" Charlie yelled this.

Dr. Ronin turned and leaned against the sink while he methodically dried his hands. "Do you eat a lot of taffy?"

"Sometimes," Charlie said. He put a hand up to his mouth and then pulled it away with a snapping motion, like he was eating taffy. "I eat it sometimes."

"I would probably advise against eating a lot of that."

"Advise against . . . ?" Charlie stopped, not able to complete the sentence. The news kept getting worse. He started breathing deeply again.

"Charlie, please. You're overreacting. I need you to stop this right now."

"Overreacting? I can't eat apples, I can't eat taffy. I bet I can't eat corn on the cob. Am I right? Can I eat corn on the cob? Tell me the truth! I want everything on the table. Everything."

Dr. Ronin was silent.

"Tell me! I have a right to know the truth about the corn!"

"You can eat creamed corn."

"Creamed corn? *Creamed* corn! That's just perfect. So, for the rest of my life, I basically have to take my meals intravenously and you're telling me to relax. Come on, Jim. This is big news. I don't think I'm overreacting. I don't think I'm overreacting at all. This is life-changing. I'm . . . I'm handicapped now. I'm disabled. This will impact my life expectancy!"

"You'll be fine. We'll fit you for a permanent one today. You'll be as good as new."

"Good as new," Charlie repeated. He shut his eyes and sucked in air.

"Charlie, are you all right?"

His chest tightened. Sitting in the dentist chair, he felt, truly felt, the full scope of his situation. Up until that point he had been in a hazy denial, if not shock. But now, at this moment, he saw things clearly: He had lost a job, a wife, and now a tooth.

He was figuratively and literally falling apart. And there was nothing, it seemed, that he could do about it.

"Charlie, are you all right?" Dr. Ronin asked again.

But Charlie didn't hear him. He just sat there, eyes closed, hands folded on his lap, taking very deep breaths.

When he got home, he wandered the empty house, his mouth and head aching. The hysteria, anger, and fear had since drained away, replaced by a now-all-too-common sense of melancholy. He sat in the reading nook for a while, his feet up on the ottoman, and watched the afternoon sunlight fade in the backyard. Another day almost gone, he thought. One more down the drain. He considered calling Donna, then decided against it. He wasn't in the mood to talk to her or anyone, for that matter, right now. He needed, he thought, to be alone. He got up, checked the answering machine, heard Kyle's voice say he would be eating dinner at Matt's, then drifted over to the front hallway and stared at his face. He didn't recognize himself.

He smiled and looked at his teeth, delicately touching the prosthesis with his pinkie finger.

He eventually settled on the bench in front of the baby grand. The house was silent and the overhead recessed lighting fell weakly on the piano keys. He studied them, admiring their simplicity, their elegance. He should have led a different life, he concluded. Been a pianist. Developed a talent, a passion. He placed his hands over the keys, his fingertips gently, imperceptibly touching them. He held them there, hoping that some divine, creative surge would pass through him so he could play. He sat in that pensive position for a few seconds before slowly lowering his hands and putting them in his pockets. He felt foolish, and for the first time in his life, he suspected he might be a fraud.

He went to bed early that night and didn't even bother to put the humidifier on.

Chapter Thirteen

The next night, as soon as he finished hanging the Cuckoo for Cocoa Puffs picture next to the Abraham Lincoln portrait in his home office, Donna called.

"Charlie?"

"Oh, hello." He put the hammer down on the desk and waited for what he thought would be an outpouring of concern over his condition. None came, however. Instead, she was quiet.

"Where are you?" Charlie finally asked.

"I'm still in Maine."

"On that island place?"

"Yes."

"Why are you still there?"

"I don't know."

"You don't know?"

She didn't say anything.

"Hello, are you there? Donna?"

"I'm here," she said.

"Well, can you at least tell me where you're staying?"

"In a motel. The Bailey Island Motel on Bailey Island."

"The Bailey Island Motel on Bailey Island. Very catchy."

"It's nice."

"I'm glad it's nice." He began pacing. "Did you get my messages? I've been trying to reach you. You should leave your phone on. Especially when you're on the road. I always leave my phone on when I'm on the road in case of emergencies."

She was quiet again.

"Did you hear about my accident?"

"Yes."

"But you never called. You could have called and asked me how I was." He stopped here because he thought his next sentence deserved its own space. "You know," he said, "I have a prosthesis. I have it in my mouth right now. They put it in yesterday. I can't eat taffy for the rest of my life. You know what a prosthesis is?"

"A fake tooth. I know all about it."

"How did you know that?"

"Kyle told me. I talked with him this morning. We talk every day."

"You and Kyle talk?" He felt a jolt of betrayal; Kyle had not mentioned this. "When are you coming home?" he asked.

"In a few days, I'm not sure yet."

He stopped pacing by the window. He knew what he wanted to ask, needed to ask, and had a right to ask, but hesitated. He pulled back the curtain and gazed out at the dark backyard, then decided to plunge in after all. "Are you . . ." he began. "Are you with someone out there?"

"What do you mean?"

"You know what I mean. Are you *with* someone? Another person? Specifically, a man."

She paused. "We'll talk about this when I get home."

"Are you with this Bill Morgan guy? This lighthouse person? I know all about him, Donna. Kyle told me. We talk too. Just tell me, are you with him? I think I have a right to know."

"I said we'll talk about it when I get home."

"I don't think this can wait."

"We'll talk when I get home."

"Listen," he yelled. "Tell me the truth! I deserve to know."

"I have to go now," she said.

"Okay, okay. Don't go, don't go. Let's talk, then."

"I think I want a divorce."

His body shook at this announcement. The utterance of that sentence, the communication of that desire, officially signified his bottoming out. After weeks of free fall, he had ripped through the atmosphere and finally hit earth. He thought the afternoon before in the dentist chair was his low point. But he was wrong. He was very wrong. He reached for the ledge of the window and steadied himself.

"We'll talk when you get home," he said quietly.

"I don't think I can live with you anymore. It's too hard. You're compulsive, passive-aggressive, a hypochondriac, controlling, self-centered, an egomaniac."

He made his way back over to the desk, in shock. "I can't believe we're even talking about this. I can't believe you would even think about this. Especially now, with what happened to me."

"You mean because of your tooth?"

"Because of my job. I can't believe this. How can you even think about doing this, especially now? You must know what I'm going through."

He looked down at a calendar on his desk. October 3. He wondered if this date would be forever burned in his memory: October 3, the date Donna said she wanted a divorce. October 3, the day everything ended.

"Charlie? Are you still there?"

He sat down and said and felt nothing. Finally, he managed to again ask, "Are you with someone? Please tell me."

"I'm by myself. I'm alone out on the beach. The road just ends here at the beach. It's a small beach. They call it Land's End. There's a sign. You can't go any farther."

"Donna, you shouldn't be out there alone at night. Go back to your room and call me from there."

"I'm okay. It's nice out here. There's a breeze. It's so dark.

You can't see the ocean, but you can hear it, you know it's here. You and I never went to the ocean together, did we?"

"No. But we will. When you get back. Listen, go to your room. Crazy people comb the beaches at night. That's what they do. It's their job."

"I was thinking you and I should have traveled more."

This was an old subject, a familiar battleground. "I asked you to come with me on lots of trips. Many times. Especially when I went overseas. You remember how I wanted you to go to Cannes with me? You know that's true."

"I know, I remember. That would have been good for us. I realize that now. To do things together. To get away. That was my fault. I never wanted to go anywhere. I think I was afraid."

"What were you afraid of?"

"I don't know. I think I was afraid of changing and I don't think I wanted to change. I just wanted things to be the way they used to be. But everything's changed anyway." Charlie heard her sniffling.

"Everything's going to be fine."

"I'm sorry about your job," she said. "I've been meaning to tell you that. I can't believe they did that. Who did it? Was it Helmut?"

"Yes. He did it."

"He's a jerk."

"It's not his fault. I was wrong for that job. You were right. I never should have gone there."

"Well, I'm sorry. No one worked harder than you did, that's for sure. What are you going to do now?"

Charlie didn't like the way she said "you" instead of "we." "We'll figure something out," he said. "Anyway, you should go to your motel now. And lock the door in case you start sleep-walking. How close are you to the ocean? Is there a fence?"

Donna didn't seem to hear him. "I had a dream last night," she began, her voice halting. "That we, you and me, were in a room. It was a strange room, all white with no windows. We had two chairs. We were sitting next to each other, waiting for something. I don't know what we were waiting for, but we were waiting for something. I couldn't look right at you, directly at you. I could only look at you out of the corner of my eye. If I looked right at you, you would disappear. I could only see you out of the corner of my eye."

"Maybe it wasn't me, then."

She sniffled. "It was you. The room had a humidifier."

Charlie didn't say anything.

"How do you know if a marriage is over?" she asked. "How do you know for sure? Do you have to decide, does something have to happen, or do you just know?"

"Our marriage isn't over," he said.

"I've known you since I was a teenager, do you know that, Charlie? I was just a girl."

"Go back to your room now, please. It's late, it's really late."

"I know. Don't hang up yet. Can you not hang up yet? I don't want to sleep. I want to sit here and be out here. Can you do that for me?"

"Donna."

"Please?"

He took a breath and let the air seep out of him. "Okay," he softy said. "Sure." He switched the phone over to his other ear, closed his eyes, and listened to his wife cry, a thousand miles away.

Four days later, with the swelling in his face gone, the bump on his forehead shrinking, and his prosthesis fairly well broken in, he returned to Rogers & Newman. When Ned saw him in the hallway, he reacted as if Charlie were a just-released prisoner of war.

"Charlie! Charlie!" He bounded toward Charlie, his tongue hanging out of his mouth, Lassie-like. Charlie backed away, fearing he might try to lick his face. "How are you?" he asked. Ned was clutching a huge hardcover book.

"Fine." Charlie made a deliberate effort to keep his mouth closed. He didn't have much confidence in the prosthesis, which still felt very foreign.

"You don't look well. Your face is all red." Ned pointed. "This side. And your eye. Do you have a black eye?"

"I'm fine." Charlie headed down the hallway in search of an available office.

Ned followed. "Do you have a minute?"

Charlie found an office across from the copy room and dropped his briefcase onto the desk. Ned slipped in behind him.

"First, and most importantly, are you *really* all right? Really, now?" Ned asked. He placed the book down on the desk: *A History of the English-Speaking Peoples*, by Winston Churchill.

"I'm super."

"Super." Ned winked and pointed. "You're being sarcastic now, aren't you?"

"Yes." Charlie sat down behind the desk.

Ned winked and pointed again. "See, I'm getting good at detecting that."

"Then I've done my job." Despite himself, Charlie was almost happy to see Ned. Over the past few days, he hadn't seen or talked to anyone but Kyle, and then it was only snatches of conversation. "What's with the book?" he asked.

"Oh, this." Ned picked it up. "It's for my book club. It was my turn, so I decided on a selection."

"So you picked Churchill's latest?"

"Right. I think most Americans are very ignorant about European history, so I thought it a good choice. I am distantly related to him, you know." He raised his chin high and looked very British when he said this.

"Really."

"Yes. Very, very distantly. But I am. I mean, I can verify it."

"You don't have to do that."

Ned lowered his chin and became Ned again. "Anyway, how are things on the home front? I know it's none of my business, but in regards to your spouse, how are things holding up? I know I shouldn't pry, and I really don't mean to, but I feel involved now."

Charlie had a sudden impulse to tell Ned everything about

Donna and her leaving. But he fought back the urge. He barely knew the man. "Everything's fine," he said.

"Really?"

"Yes."

"Are you sure? This can be a very stressful time for families. If you would like, I would be happy to meet with you and your wife. I do that sometimes. I can discuss the job-search process, offer some tips on getting by on a budget, things like that." He squinted at Charlie. "Do you have a bump over your eyebrow?" He stepped forward and pointed. "Right there."

Charlie ducked his head, opened his briefcase, and began to empty it. "We'll be okay," he said. "But thanks for the offer." The office had a faint odor of cold cuts, salami in particular. He sniffed. "This place smells," he said.

"It's from the deli downstairs. We have an air vent problem. They can never get it right. Some days it's fine, others, it's horrible. This office seems to get it the worst."

"We're fifty floors up from that deli."

"That's just the way it is. It shoots straight up here, it seems. Anyway, I want to tell you about a conference I think you should attend. It's opening this afternoon over at McCormick Place. It's a job fair. I'm encouraging all my clients to go. It's really excellent. I go every year."

"I don't think today is a good day." Charlie turned on his computer.

"It's not your typical job fair. It's for entrepreneurs. It's called Living the Dream."

He waited for a reaction from Charlie. Charlie had none.

"Yes, well. It's designed for people who want to own their own businesses. Franchises, hotels, Internet companies, convenience stores. There are all sorts of business opportunities out there, all sorts of them. Many people in your situation, former executives, realize that they don't want to go back to corporations. What they really want is their independence. I know of one client, a former banking executive, who ended up buying a quick-oil-change shop. Can you imagine that? He's doing really quite well at it. I had my oil changed there not too long ago and he seemed extremely happy. He changed my oil personally."

"Living the dream."

"You never know. It's certainly worth some investigation. There are all sorts of advantages to being your own boss."

"Thank you, but I have no interest in changing oil for a living, okay? I'm in advertising. That's what I do."

"I wish you would consider it. You, Walter, and I can head over there this afternoon. I'll even drive. We'll leave after lunch. Maybe we'll get Bradley to come. The four amigos."

"Fine. I'll think about it," Charlie said, though he had no intention of going or being part of the four amigos.

"Excellent!" Ned smiled, snapped his fingers. "And how's that résumé coming along?"

"Fine."

"Really?"

"Yes."

"May I see it?"

"No."

This disappointed Ned. "Well, maybe later, then. And how is your networking tree?"

Charlie stared at his still-blank computer screen. His initial happiness over seeing Ned was disintegrating. He did not appreciate being pestered by a man who today, he just now noticed, was wearing white socks with his Hush Puppies. "That's fine too," he said.

Ned suspiciously considered this response. He cocked his head to the side and studied Charlie with one knowing eye. "Is it really, now?"

"Yes, it is." Charlie entered his password and logged on. "Now, if you don't mind."

Ned sighed and bowed. "Of course. Of course."

Rather than work on his résumé, Charlie actually did decide to construct his version of a networking tree—a list of people he knew in advertising or related marketing fields. He included everyone—account people, secretaries, former clients, former vendors—whom he thought he could call for help. He then placed an asterisk before those with whom he had a good relationship; two asterisks before the names of people with whom he thought he had an excellent relationship; and three after people with whom he felt he had a "super" relationship. In the end, his tree listed a hundred and eight people: sixty-three with one asterisk, twenty with two, and twenty-five with three.

He decided to focus his primary efforts on the super-relationship people, those he believed genuinely liked him and would help at all costs. He reviewed this list carefully, and made more changes, demoting nine people from the super list to semi-super status. He then studied this newly created "Super Sixteen":

*** Susan Goldman
*** Gayle Ziolkowski
*** Jon Asperger
*** Steve Larson
*** Susan McDonnell
*** Sally Hart
*** Vicki Foreman
*** Laura Dihel
*** Sue Powers
*** Scottie Frandsen
*** Leslie Kenter
*** Lisa Tentinger
*** Ellen Ryan
*** Victoria McHugh
*** Joe Nora
*** Vicki Hill

He rearranged the asterisks, moving them one space closer to the names, then read the list one last time with a growing sense of confidence. While it bothered him that no member of the Super Sixteen had, as of yet, made any attempt to contact him since he'd been fired, he still believed that these super people would remember his friendship and come through.

Inspired, he immediately went to work on the inaugural issue of *The Charlie Update!* On the ride in that morning, he came up with the idea of creating a newsletter that would update his networking tree on his situation and progress. He thought such a creative vehicle would play to his strengths as a former copywriter. He had already decided on a light, breezy tone. He didn't want *The C.U.!* to be a downer of any kind.

𝕿𝖍𝖊 𝕮𝖍𝖆𝖗𝖑𝖎𝖊 𝖀𝖕𝖉𝖆𝖙𝖊!
Charlie B. Out on the Street

As many of you may know, Charlie Baker, former Ad Man of the Year (1998), has been hitting the pavement, looking for work and fielding dozens of inquiries. While interest has been high—he's had several "feelers"—he's still very much a free agent and eager to explore, network, and buy lunch/ dinner/drinks for anyone who thinks he knows someone who knows someone who knows someone who might be willing to employ the man *Brandweek* once hailed as "brilliant." (Actually, they called me clever. But clever in 1998 is now considered brilliant once you factor in inflation.)

Anyone willing to share information will receive a free subscription to *The Charlie Update!*

He added a critique of two new ads, one for Odor Eaters and the other for Apple, then formatted the newsletter the best he could to make it look like the front page of a newspaper. Despite its somewhat primitive look—the margins were uneven— he was still proud of his effort and, even though a tiny and apparently uninfluential part of his brain suspected the whole thing might be a tad sophomoric, he e-mailed it out. Satisfied that he was making progress, he headed downstairs to lunch.

At the deli, he unfortunately bumped into Walter, the annoying fish-eyed man. He was seated at a table near the front and when their gazes locked, there was no escaping him.

"Walter," Charlie said. He pulled out a chair and placed his salad on the table.

Walter hitched his shoulder in that strange way that made Charlie think he knew him, then ripped into his pastrami sandwich with his carp teeth. His face looked pasty and deep circles hung from his eyes. Charlie wondered again how long he had been out.

"Were you in the Ad Club?" he asked.

Walter swallowed. "No."

"I thought you might be. You seem familiar. I think we know each other."

He gave Charlie a super-sized smirk.

"Did you ever work at Southwest Airlines?"

Another smirk. "No."

"How about Ford?"

"No."

Charlie nodded and began tearing open the little plastic packet of fat-free Italian dressing. "So," he asked, "how are things?"

"Things suck."

"They'll get better."

Walter went back to his food. "I made thirty-six calls this morning. That's a new record. Didn't get a single person. All voice mail. That's also a new record. Caller ID is killing me. They see Rogers & Newman and don't pick up."

"Who are you calling? People you know?"

He chewed and swallowed. "I'm way past that. These are cold calls. HR people, mostly. Responding to ads online. Are you working with a recruiter?"

Charlie decided not to mention the Wizard. The less Walter or anyone who was looking for a job knew about his efforts, the better, he thought. "Not yet. I probably should be calling them, I guess."

"Don't bother. Recruiters are great if you've got a job and they're trying to get you to leave, but if you're already out, you're damaged goods. Just ask Bradley. They won't touch him."

"Seems like he's had it rough."

"Yeah, well, that guy is crazy."

"What do you mean?"

"Let's just say he's had a violent past. Played football, was in Vietnam. Went after his boss with a hammer or something. Smashed his car windows."

Charlie vaguely remembered Ned mentioning such an incident. "I think I heard about it. I didn't know it was Bradley."

"The guy is at the end. Been out too long." Rather than seem worried, Walter looked amused.

Charlie finally managed to open the dressing package and spread some over his salad. He attempted to eat, but felt his appetite waning in the warmth of Walter's sunny presence.

"Do you have any leads? Anything going on?" Walter asked. He was chewing his food desperately and gulping it down like he hadn't eaten in weeks.

"No. But I'm still new at this."

"It'll get old fast. It's a wasteland out there. Nothing moving." He quickly finished one half of his sandwich and began to wrap the other in a napkin. "I did get one lead yesterday, though."

"Yeah? Where?"

"The Gap."

"Really? Hey, great. They're based in San Francisco, right?"

"I'd be working here in Chicago. Right here in sweet home Chicago."

"That's even better. What, regional marketing?"

"Nope." Walter smiled. "I would work at their Michigan Ave store."

Charlie looked up from his salad. "What would you be doing there?"

"I would be in charge of men's sweaters," he said. "Shirts too."

Charlie stared at him, trying to understand. Then, all at once, he did. "You mean you're working at the store? The Gap?"

"Pretty exciting, huh? My boss just turned twenty. She's thinking of going to community college. Thinking about it. Hey, you don't need any sweaters, do you? I'd get an employee discount after three months. Just in time for the holidays."

Charlie decided not to comment. He suspected Walter was saying this, in part, to demoralize him and reduce him to his own beaten-down state. He wanted to fight back, let Walter know that he was nothing like him, but before he could think of a proper Rogers & Newman uplifting-poster counterpoint, Walter stood to leave.

"I can see if they have any more openings," he said. "Interested?"

"I think I'm doing fine," Charlie said.

"You do, do you?" He winked and left, the top of his uneaten sandwich sticking out of the side pocket of his shabby sports coat.

As soon as he got back to the salami office, Charlie closed the door, did twenty jumping jacks, then did twenty deep knee bends, then sat down, breathing heavily. He needed to be proactive and aggressive, accomplish something. He knew he couldn't stay here with people like Walter and Ned and Bradley. It was time to get going, time to take charge. He grabbed his cell phone.

He resisted calling the Wizard, and instead started in on his Super Sixteen list. He began at the top with Susan Goldman, leaving her a friendly voice mail. Then he called numbers two, three, four, five, and six, and left them equally upbeat messages. He repeated this process with the others, and in less than ten minutes had made his way through the entire Super Sixteen without talking to a single person. No one, apparently, was in. Or no one was taking his call. He tried not to think about that, then did. Was he that disliked? Didn't he have any friends?

He stood and did ten more jumping jacks, then ten deep knee bends, then sat back down.

Of course he was liked, of course he had friends. He made four more calls, this time using the office phone and this time to people on his semi-super list. No one answered, though, and he left no messages.

He sat back, took several deep breaths, felt the room getting smaller. He wished he had the Lincoln portrait with him. He wanted to stare at Abe's dark, soulful, wise eyes. He needed inspiration. Needed something, someone, to lean on, to draw strength from. He picked up the phone, hung up. He wasn't sure who he should call, then, of course, he was.

Donna answered on the first ring.

"Oh, hello there," he said.

"Hi."

"Where are you? Are you still there, in Maine? At that place?"

"Yes. Why are you breathing so hard? Were you on the treadmill?"

"I thought you said you were coming home."

"I'm still here. I need some time. I need some time away."

Charlie squeezed the phone and closed his eyes. Just hearing her voice calmed him. "Can I ask you a question? One quick question?"

"What?"

"Do you hate me?"

There was a distinct pause. "No."

"I think everyone else does. I can't get anyone to take my call. It's like I don't exist. Am I so evil? When did this happen? Why didn't you tell me I was evil? I had a right to know. Someone should have told me."

Donna sounded tired, her voice flat and dull. "You're not evil. You're a lot of things, but you're not evil."

"What am I?"

"You're crazy."

"Crazy. Then why did you marry me?"

"Because you weren't always crazy."

"What was I before?"

"I don't want to get into this now. I have to go."

"Please, tell me what I was like before. Please."

He heard her sigh. "I don't know. Okay, you were funny and . . . and interesting, I don't know, interested in other things, other people."

"And I'm not that way anymore?"

"No, you're not."

"I'm not?"

"No. I have to go."

"You have to go? You always have to go. Where you going? You're in Maine. How many times can you stare at the ocean? Just tell me what's wrong with me again. You said some things the last time. What were they? It was like you were reading off a list."

"You're going to be fine. Go put your humidifier on and take a nap."

"Don't patronize me," Charlie said, though the notion of his humidifier and a nap was very appealing to him. "Please come home, Donna. Please."

"I'm going now," she said.

"I'm going to come out to see you, then."

"Don't even think about that. I'm going now."

"Wait!" he said, but she was gone.

Chapter Fourteen

The next day at the morning networking meeting, Charlie began to detect some not-so-subtle physical changes in Bradley Smith. While he was dressed in his usual 1980s standard-issue dark blue suit and statement-making tie, this time an eye-popping bright gold, he looked different. His face, usually ruddy and rough, had a pronounced orange tint, as if someone had applied a thin coat of paint to it but had run out around the ears. His hair also seemed to be transitioning from silver to an odd reddish brown and looked, very much, like a squirrel's fur in autumn. His eyes too were different. While Charlie had never noticed their color before, he was almost positive they had never been emerald green.

"Morning, there, Charlie!" Bradley said when the meeting broke up. His voice was miraculously the same, deep with the hint of a West-Texas-oil-fields twang.

"Morning, Bradley." Charlie gathered his things, not sure if he should comment on this new look.

"I'd say it was a pretty good morning."

"Why would you say that?" Charlie asked. They walked

down the hallway to the kitchen, where Charlie poured himself a cup of terrible coffee.

"Got something cooking. Think it's hot," Bradley said.

Charlie deliberately trained his eyes on Bradley's gold tie, which featured a series of tiny brown stains at the bottom, near the tip. He could not bring himself to look at his face. "Something cooking? Where?"

"Confidential. Don't want to jinx it."

"How did you get the lead?"

"Believe it or not, a recruiter set me up. First time he's come through."

"Good luck. I'm happy for you," Charlie said, surprised that he meant it. Based on how he was disfiguring himself, Bradley, he deemed, had suffered long enough. He poured Bradley some coffee, then watched as he mixed in powdered creamer.

"You know, I have a good feeling about this one. I can feel this one, *feel* it," Bradley said. "It feels right."

"That's great. Think you can feel me up a lead too?"

"Ha! You just got here. Let me go first."

"Hey, when you get back to the real world, don't forget your old buddies in the jungle."

Rather than laugh, Bradley fell wistful. "Don't worry. I won't forget anyone," he said quietly. "Or anything."

Charlie studied him and noticed that the collar of his starched shirt was beginning to fray. "It's been a long road, I bet, huh?"

"You have no idea. There've been times . . ." Bradley stopped and looked down at his coffee. "This is the one. It has to be. This one is mine. I'm going to get this no matter what. No matter what." He broke out of his trance, smiled, and slapped Charlie on the back. "Maybe we'll do lunch later," he said.

"At the deli."

"The deli is for losers," Bradley said. "Someplace else."

"Someplace else, then."

Motivated by Bradley's news, Charlie impulsively decided to relocate from the small salami office to the nicest office at Rogers & Newman, Office A. Charlie had had his eye on it for some time. It was large and airy, with a parquet floor, a leather couch, and an immense and gleaming old-fashioned mahogany desk. He felt his spirits lift as he unpacked his briefcase, inspired by the partially obscured view of the lake and the powder-puff clouds that seemed within reach. This office was always occupied and he thought it a portent of good things that it was empty this morning.

He went right to work on his résumé, slashing and rearranging things with a vengeance. Five pages became three and then three, somehow, became three and a half again. Still, he was making progress. He was just about to make another run at it when Ned glided past his office door. He then reappeared and walked inside.

"Charlie?"

"Yes?"

"What are you doing here?" He looked concerned.

"Working. I'm almost done with my résumé. Can you take a look, or is that enabling me?"

He ignored this request. "This is Office A." He said this in a quiet, reverential tone. "You can't work in Office A."

"Why not?"

"You're not a Category A client."

"What do you mean? What's that?"

Small red splotches began forming on Ned's cheeks. "Our agreement with your employer, former employer, categorized you a certain level." He glanced around Office A. "I'm sorry, but you're at a level B and can't work here."

"Level B?"

"Well, B-*plus*, which means you work in different office spaces."

"Oh, you mean smaller, shittier offices."

"Yes. Well, not exactly, but different offices, yes."

"I see." Charlie thought about this. "So I'm a B-plus, huh? Not an A?"

"No. Everyone has different classes—I mean, levels."

Charlie continued to digest this information, his indignation rising. "What level is Walter, then?"

"Who? Oh, I can't tell you that."

"Just tell me."

"I can't. That's sealed information. Absolutely confidential. Absolutely."

"Tell me."

"He's a C." Ned lowered his voice. "Don't tell him that, though. He thinks he's a B-minus, though we don't really categorize people as pluses and minuses. I just say that to make people feel better." He splotched red again. "Oh," he said. "Sorry."

"What about Bradley?"

"He came in an A, but he worked his way down and, well, really doesn't have a category anymore. We let him stay on. He's like an institution. Besides, he helps write the Rogers newsletter. It's a bartering arrangement." Ned glanced over his shoulder. "I'm sorry, but it's nothing personal. I don't make up these categories. It all depends on our arrangement with your former employer. Whoever pays the most, gets the most."

"I don't know why I'm not an A. I headed an office."

"I'm sorry, Charlie, that's just the way it is."

Charlie shook his head, thought of Helmut and Marken, the twin devils. "So those bastards screwed me over again."

"Level B is really a very good level, really it is."

"Why? What's so great about it?"

"Well, you get private office access and other benefits."

"Such as?"

"More of my time."

"Ah," Charlie said. "Priceless." He leaned forward and began working on his résumé again. "I'll leave after lunch, maybe."

"I don't think that's possible. Someone's moving in here this morning," Ned said. He stepped over to the desk and started gathering up Charlie's things.

"What are you doing?"

"I'm helping you pack up. There's one open office left, down the hall. If we hurry, we can still get it."

"You mean the one by the copy room?"

"Yes."

"That's the salami office. I just left that room. It doesn't have any windows. I can't work in there." Charlie took a deep breath as if he were inhaling an ocean breeze. "I like the air in here."

Ned worked faster, his splotches creeping down his neck. "Please, come now. We have to move along. Please!"

"I said I'll move after lunch. What's the rush?"

"You would be doing me a great favor if you packed up now. This office has been promised to someone else. He could arrive early."

"Who?"

"I have a new client. An important client. I've just been assigned him. Very high-profile."

"I don't give a shit," Charlie said. "I got here first and I'm pretty high-profile."

"I've explained the process."

"Who is this guy?"

"I'm not at liberty to tell you just now."

Charlie folded his arms across his chest. "I'm not leaving until you tell me. I have a legal right to know."

"You have no legal right to know."

"I'm going to find out anyway."

"Tom Tamales."

"Who?"

Ned lowered his voice. "It's Tom Tamales." He sounded secretive.

"You mean the Hot Tamales? The short guy? He got fired again?"

"Yes. Him."

"Wow." Tamales had a significant and controversial reputation in the ad business. A chronic job-hopper, he was adept at generating publicity for himself at every stop in a career that, despite numerous failures, seemed to lead consistently upward. He had held a number of big-time, heavy-coin positions and his name was feared and loathed by many an agency. He was a difficult, if not impossible, client.

"He's on his way in." Ned looked both nervous and proud. "He's been assigned to me," he said.

"Oh. Big-time guy."

"Very."

"Congratulations."

"Thank you."

"Category A, right?"

"Yes."

"A-plus?"

"Ha, ha. Very good."

"Working with him must be quite a coup for you."

"It will be interesting."

"You know, he's supposed to be an asshole," Charlie said. "A major pain in the ass."

Ned started to clear the desk again, bundling Charlie's *Business Week, Advertising Age*, and *Brandweek* together. "I'm sure the reports are exaggerated. Would you mind, now?" He handed the magazines to Charlie.

He took them. "I hope you won't forget about us Category B types."

"I'll make an effort to stay in touch," Ned said.

Being back in the salami office, with its hokey posters (MAKE A DIFFERENCE–TODAY; GREAT THINGS START WITH LITTLE ACTIONS), took the life out of Charlie and he found work impossible. Learning that he was a Category B, a mere level above short-sleeve-shirt-wearing, soon-to-be-Gap-working Walter, was a blow to his motivation, to say nothing of his self-esteem. Apparently there were different levels of hell.

He grabbed his coffee mug, got up, and strolled down the hall past Office A, hoping for a glimpse of the Great One, Mr. Category A, Tamales himself. Unfortunately, the door was closed. He paused in front of it, then doubled back and headed to the kitchen. While he was rooting around the refrigerator for a pint of skim milk, someone poked him in the ribs. He jumped and turned around to find Karen Brisco standing there, smiling, her ski-slope nose all pointy and cute and perfect.

"Hello." He stared at her, and felt the heat roll up his neck and flood his face. She looked sternly erotic in a black suit and dark hose, offset with a low-cut starched white blouse. Her shiny black pumps completed her businesswoman/dominatrix look.

"Sorry, I shouldn't have done that," she said.

"You look great today."

"I feel great," she said. "Are you ready for this? I think I have something good going with Coke. In Atlanta."

Charlie said, "Oh." Then he said, "Oh," again, but much louder.

She bounced up and down on her high heels and held up crossed fingers. "I think I have a good shot. A real good shot."

"Wow. That's great. Congrats."

"I don't know yet. But it looks good. I have a contact, a guy I used to date who works there. He said it looks good."

"When did all this happen? I didn't know you were even talking with them."

"I wasn't. It came out of the blue. I had talked with them a while ago but nothing happened. Now, suddenly they're interested. I just had a two-hour phone interview with them."

"Great."

"Sorry if I acted crazy. But I had to tell someone."

"That's great," Charlie said again. He gazed at her and felt a strong longing. It had been months since he had so much as even hugged Donna.

"Once you get the offer, we have to celebrate," he said. His eyes settled on her cleavage, which was picture-perfect.

"I'm ready to celebrate right now," she said. She wiggled her hips. "I'm going to go dancing tonight. You want to come?"

"Dancing? No. I'm a middle-aged white man. There are laws that keep us from doing that."

She gave Charlie a look that he could have interpreted any number of ways. "Thanks for being nice to me the other day," she said. "In my office."

"I didn't do anything. Anyway, when you get the news, I'll come out and watch you dance. We all will."

She winked and did another little twist. She then touched Charlie's nose once with her finger and walked out, her high heels clicking happily on the tiled floor.

177

As soon as she left, Charlie's lust dissipated like steam and he reluctantly returned to the salami office, weak coffee in hand. Rather than feeling encouraged, he felt himself falling. Everyone, it seemed, was getting good news that day but him. He shut the door, stared at a wall poster—GREAT THINGS START WITH LITTLE ACTIONS—sat down, and, rather than call someone from one of his lists, quickly called directory information for the phone number of Bill Morgan of Bailey Island, Maine, instead.

Karen's touch had activated a serious Donna longing. He desperately needed to get her back. Calling this Morgan person, confronting him, was a critical step.

He jotted the number down and dialed. Up until now, Bill Morgan had been only a name. Now he was a phone number. Soon he would be a voice.

He answered on the third ring. "Hello?"

"Is this Bill Morgan?"

"Yes," a raspy voice said. "Who is this?"

"Is this the Bill Morgan who owns a lighthouse? Or lives in one or something?"

"Yes, it is. Who's this, now?"

"This is Charlie Baker. I'm Donna Baker's husband. I just want you to know that Donna and I have every intention of staying married and working this out. Okay? So stay away from her."

There was a pause and then the voice said, "You must want my son, Billy. I'm his father."

"Oh." Then Charlie said, "How old is Billy?" He feared he had the wrong number and that the Billy in question was eight.

"I'm not sure. Do you want me to ask him?"

"Is he middle-aged? Is he a man?"

"Who is this again?"

"How tall is he?"

"You're asking a lot of tricky questions. Why don't I go get him? He's up in the lighthouse right now, down the way. There's a lot of stairs so it might take me a while before I can get up to see him, so you'll have to sit tight. If I hurry, I can be back in an hour or so. Just hold on."

"Doesn't the lighthouse have a phone?"

"A phone? Funny you ask. We were just thinking we might put one in. Say, how about I try to yell up to him? That might save some time."

"Don't yell up to him."

"Are you sure? Sounds like you have important business. If he's by a window, it might just work."

"Don't yell up to him."

"If you leave your number, I'd be happy to have him call you back when he comes down. I can try to find a pencil. I know we have one. My wife had one just the other day. It's probably still lying around here somewhere."

"I'll try him later," Charlie said.

"Are you sure? Billy hates missing phone calls. We don't get many."

"Good-bye, Mr. Morgan."

Just then a woman's voice came on the line. "Who's this?" she said in a rough New England accent, each word partially strangled. "Who you talking to now?"

"I'm talking on the phone!" Mr. Morgan yelled. "We're having a nice conversation. He's a friend of Billy's."

"I'm not a friend of Billy's."

"Where's that pencil I saw you with yesterday?" Mr. Morgan asked. "You had it behind your ear, showing off, all fancy-like."

"Pencil?" the woman asked. "Now, what do you need a pencil for?"

"Here it is!"

"That's a fork."

"It's not a fork."

"It's a fork. I put the pencil in a safe place. I'm tired of you losing my pencils all the time! Listen, Billy isn't here," she said.

"I know."

"He's in Chicago."

"Where? Chicago?"

"Chicago?" Billy Morgan's father asked. "I thought he was up in the lighthouse. I just saw him."

179

"Who'd you see? You haven't been out of this house in a month," the woman said. "Anyway, Billy's been gone a week. He'll be back in a few days. Do you want me to give him a message?"

Charlie was confused and tried to think things through. "No," he said. "No message."

"Good-bye, then."

"Good-bye," Charlie quietly said.

Later that afternoon, when he arrived home, he trudged upstairs, turned the Rain Forest humidifier on high, then flopped face-first down on the bed. He wasn't sure what was going on. If Bill Morgan wasn't even in Maine, what exactly was Donna doing there? Was the woman on the phone, presumably Bill Morgan's mother, lying? Or was Donna lying? Was she even in Maine? For all he knew, she might be in downtown Chicago, shacked up with the guy in some hotel.

He rolled onto his back and listened to the soft hum of the humidifier, the invisible moisture a godsend for his throbbing sinuses. Finally, when the afternoon shadows reached his bed, he dragged himself downstairs for what he suspected would be the first of many bourbon-and-waters. His plans changed however, when he encountered Kyle and his immense friend Matt, the playwright, in the kitchen trying to make bacon and eggs. Matt was sliding a frying pan with several raw egg yolks inside the oven, while Kyle surgically separated strips of still-frozen bacon with a scissors.

"What are you doing?" Charlie directed this first question to Matt because he was so tall.

"What? Oh, hi, Mr. Baker."

"What are you doing?"

"I was trying to make basted eggs."

"I told him I know how to make scrambled eggs, but he wanted these other kind," Kyle said.

Charlie took the frying pan from Matt and placed it in the sink. "Don't touch that again," He glanced sideways at Kyle, who was licking his fingers. "Is your mother home?"

"No."

"Did she call?"

"No."

"Fine." He opened the freezer and discovered a package of hamburger patties. His stomach growled. He couldn't remember the last time he had eaten anything other than a salad or soup. "Why don't you guys go to the store and get some buns? Get some cheese too. And an onion. Get a yellow onion. And some other stuff too. Potato chips."

"Why?" Kyle asked.

"Because I'm going to make dinner. I'm going to make cheeseburgers."

"You're going to make cheeseburgers?" Kyle asked. He stopped licking his fingers and looked at his father, confused.

Charlie closed the refrigerator door. "Yes, I'll grill them outside. We still have a grill, right?"

"Yeah, we have one. We never used it, though."

"Well, we're going to use it tonight."

Kyle nodded. "Okay, we'll go get that stuff. Can I have some money?"

"Oh, yeah, here." Charlie handed him two twenties. "But I want change," he said.

It took him a while to find the gas grill. Donna had it covered up and tucked away in a narrow walkway by the side of the garage. After he wheeled it out onto the deck and pulled off the cover, he was surprised by its size. It was a relic from the old house and he had forgotten how small it was. He had been meaning to buy a new one, but since they never grilled, he had never gotten around to it. He opened the gas valve and clicked down hard on the ignition button. Despite its size and age, it started right up.

Standing on their deck, grilling the meat, drinking a bourbon, he wondered how much longer he could continue to do what he was doing with his life, which was essentially nothing. He had been out of work for more than a month and other than a half-finished résumé and *The Charlie Update!*, which still hadn't elicited any responses, he didn't have much to show by way of efforts. To be sure, there were extenuating circumstances that were hurting his focus—he had lost a wife and a body part—but still his lack of progress puzzled him. Clearly, something was missing: direction, a sense of urgency, if not panic. He had a long history of throwing himself into projects, but he seemed unable to get moving now. Everything was an effort. The résumé, the phone calls, walking, breathing. He wondered if he was simply burned out, then wondered exactly what that meant.

He flipped the burgers, and considered options. There were alternatives to getting another high-paying job. For example, he could get a low-paying job. They could truly embrace The New Frugality and downsize, sell the house, sell one of the cars, cancel the membership at the country club, which they never went to anyway, and eat all their meals at home.

He flipped the burgers again.

They could embrace a simple life. They could move to the country near a resort town with some culture, decent restaurants, a Starbucks, but cheap housing. They could start a vegetable garden, drink tap water, and buy a hen for eggs. Donna always loved the country. He had no idea how he could make a living in the country—maybe own the Starbucks—but the idea, inspired in part by the quiet of the cool fall night and his bourbon, appealed to him. He should keep his options open, not rush headlong back into the rat race. He sipped his drink and inhaled the smoke of the cooking meat. He should take his time with things.

The idea that they would soon be homeless and living above a heating grate was a concern, however. He had run the numbers several times and knew that things soon would be coming to a head. Still, standing outside, drink in hand, cooking meat, he felt a calmness, which he found refreshing. It had been a long time since he had had a peaceful moment like this, and he enjoyed it. He made a private vow to be more reflective in the future; ponder things. He took another swallow of bourbon. He had never been much of a ponderer, but suspected he might be good at it.

When Kyle returned with the cheese, Charlie immediately placed a slice on each burger. Then they both silently watched in awe as it melted over the meat.

"Pretty amazing," Charlie said.

Kyle agreed. "Yeah."

"Want to flip one?" Charlie held out the spatula.

"No."

"Have you ever grilled before?"

"Yeah. At the old house. We used to do it sometimes when I was little."

Charlie paused, remembering: Kyle, a little boy, waving smoke away from his face, laughing and coughing on the patio. Kyle, a little boy, in his white underpants and a cowboy hat, shooting the smoke with a six-shooter.

Charlie finished his bourbon. "That doesn't seem that long ago," he said. "Man, it goes fast, it goes fast."

"What does?"

"Everything." Charlie inched a burger over a flame, then held out the spatula again. "Sure you don't want to try? Re-create the magic?"

"No, it's all right. I don't want to smear the cheese on top. We probably shouldn't flip them anymore. I don't know what I was thinking."

Charlie looked at his son with renewed respect. "You're right, Kyle," he said. "You're absolutely right."

When they returned to the kitchen, they found Matt standing by the island, holding an immense pineapple and an even larger butcher knife. Charlie had more or less forgotten about him.

"What's he doing?" he asked Kyle.

"He's cutting up a pineapple."

"Why did you let him buy a pineapple?"

"You said buy something else," Kyle said.

"I was thinking more along the lines of potato chips or french fries."

Matt decided to interrupt. "Pineapples are great," he said. "Can I cut it?"

Charlie considered Matt, wondering if he could trust him with a butcher's knife. "How tall are you?" he asked. "I've been meaning to ask you this."

"I'm six-seven."

"Jesus, six-seven," Charlie said. "Okay." He pointed at the knife. "Do you know what you're doing with that thing?"

"Absolutely. I'm very adept with knives, Mr. Baker."

Charlie motioned for him to proceed, then took a step back and watched as Matt placed the pineapple on a cutting board and expertly sliced into it, bringing the knife down hard right through the middle. Juice sputtered and dripped out. Charlie stepped closer to inspect the cut.

"Good work," he said.

Matt nodded. "This is an excellent knife."

Since it was so nice outside, they decided to eat on the deck, something Charlie had never done during his time in Wilton. The night had turned still and breezeless: a few surviving crickets serenaded and a blurry hook of a moon hung low over the hedges of the yard.

They ate in silence, absorbed in their food. Charlie had made six burgers and within minutes they were gone, along with a jar of pickles he had found in the back of the refrigerator. After they were done with the meat, Matt went inside and returned with the cut-up pineapple. He carried it on a tray, which he held out carefully in front of him, like a birthday cake lit with candles.

He placed the tray on the table. "Here it is," he said.

They ate chunks of pineapple with fingers that were soon sticky and sweet. Both boys stuffed several ragged pieces in their mouths, their eyes wide with effort.

"Good pineapple," Kyle said, swallowing.

"Yeah, it's pretty good." Charlie chewed carefully, not wanting to put too much strain on his prosthesis. While he ate, he stared over Kyle's shoulder, into the house. Even though it was after eight, he still held out hope that Donna would walk in and witness this scene of family togetherness: father, son, and some tall guy whose last name he didn't know.

"Hey, Matt. What's your last name?"

"Parker."

"Matt Parker. Do you live around here?"

"Yeah. I live next door." Matt shot Kyle a sideways glance.

"That's right." Charlie reached over and took another chunk of pineapple. "So, how's the basketball team doing?"

"I quit the team," Matt said.

"What? Why'd you do that? You're huge."

"I'm trying to defy stereotypes. Just because I'm big doesn't mean I should play basketball."

Charlie nodded and tried to determine if he was serious.

"Plus," Matt said, "my dad won't let me because of my grades."

"Oh."

"I'll be back next year, though, for sure. But things are going great for Kyle."

"Shut up," Kyle said.

"What?" Charlie asked. "What's going so great for Kyle?"

"Nothing," Matt said. He turned to Kyle. "I don't know why you're so weird about it."

"What's he weird about?"

"Nothing," Kyle said. He tried to kick Matt but missed and instead hit his knee on the underside of the table.

"What's he so weird about?" Charlie asked again.

"Kyle won the Pat Bogi Award this week. It's for the guy who hustles the most in practice."

"Wait! You guys made the team?" Charlie turned toward Kyle. "You made the team?"

"Yeah." He kept his eyes on his empty plate.

"Well, that's great. And you already won an award?"

"Yeah," Kyle said. He didn't look that happy.

"Well, that's good, isn't it?"

"I don't know," Kyle said.

"Yeah, it is," Matt said. "It's a pretty big deal. Pat Bogi is a legend."

"That's great, Kyle. Why is that weird?"

He shrugged and rubbed his knee. "It's a stupid award," he mumbled.

"He's afraid everyone is going to think he's a hustle dork," Matt said. "Pat Bogi was this little guy, but he ran all over the place and dove for loose balls and stuff. He was kind of like a crazy little person."

"He bit a guy once during a game," Kyle said.

"Yeah, he was pretty psycho," Matt said.

"I don't think you have to worry about biting anyone," Charlie said. "Anyway, I think it's great. Awards are important in life. I won a lot of awards for my work. They helped me in my career."

"What kind of awards did you win, Mr. Baker?"

"Oh, I don't know. Some Clios in the old days, an Effie. I won this award at Cannes. Well, almost won. Should have won. No big deal. Never won the Pat Bogi Award, though."

"Did you make that commercial with that talking rat?"

"You mean the one with the hamster? No." Charlie reached for his drink, then remembered that his glass was empty.

Kyle picked up his plate and headed into the kitchen. "I think there's some Cokes in the garage," he said. "You want one?"

"Yeah," Matt said.

"Dad?"

"No, I'm okay. But hustle back, Kyle," Charlie said.

Matt laughed and hunched forward, his shoulders shaking. "Excellent, Mr. Baker, really rich."

"Thank you, Matt."

They sat in silence, the sound of the crickets now gone. Matt stretched his legs out under the table. "Which way do you live?" Charlie asked. "Which house?"

He pointed. "That house."

Charlie stared over the hedge but couldn't see the house, just its dark shape. They owned three lots and there was quite a bit of space between the homes. "How long have you lived here?"

"My whole life." Matt started bopping his head up and down as if he were listening to music.

Charlie glanced to the garage to see where Kyle was. "Can I ask you a question?"

Matt stopped bopping. "Me? Absolutely."

"Why can't you give Kyle some lines for that play you wrote?"

"What play?"

"The play you wrote. The one with the dead people."

"Oh, you mean *Mr. Vengeance*?"

"You've written other plays?"

"Yeah. I wrote forty-five different plays last year. I type really fast."

Charlie studied Matt. This kid was very difficult to figure out. "Getting back to Kyle for a second. Why does he have to be the first guy killed?"

At this question, Matt sat up, attentive and thoughtful, like he was responding to a caller on *Larry King Live.* "First off, Mr. Baker, I've decided not to go ahead with the production for now."

"Why not?"

"Because Principal Delleman won't let me do it."

"Oh. Well, it sounded pretty violent. I didn't like all those kids getting killed."

"Technically, Kyle was going to be the only person killed."

"I thought other people were killed too."

"No. Kyle's the only one killed. He wanted the part. I wanted to give him the part of the nice gym teacher. He has a lot of lines. But Kyle wanted to play the dead guy."

"Why?"

"I think you'd have to ask him that."

"But what do you think? He's your friend."

Matt put his index finger up to his mouth and tapped his lips, thinking. "He's a pretty laid-back dude. Stardom doesn't appeal to him. You got to respect that."

"Yeah, I guess." Charlie crossed his legs and gazed up at the sky. He had spent most of his life seeking attention. How had he produced a son like this?

"I remember when he won the three-point contest," Matt said. "He didn't even want to go onstage and get the trophy. We had to make him do it."

"Three-point contest? You mean for basketball? When did he win that?"

"Last year."

"I didn't know anything about that. He won the contest? I mean, the whole thing?" Charlie glanced back to the garage again. "Jesus, he doesn't tell me anything. That's great."

"Yeah. He won that and the free-throw-shooting contest."

"Both of them? Where was this contest? At school, before a game or something?"

"No, it was at the father-and-son tournament."

Charlie swallowed. "Really. When was that? The father-and-son thing?"

"At school. They have it every year on Dad's Day. You know, all the fathers and sons compete in a two-on-two thing."

"I must have been out of town," Charlie said. He pretended to brush something off of his shoe. Then he asked, "Who did Kyle play with? At that tournament?"

"Mrs. Baker."

"His *mom*?"

"Yeah, they let her play. She was great. She can shoot. They lost early on, but she can shoot and so can Kyle."

"He played with his mother?"

"Yeah, she's good."

Charlie sat there motionless and wondered what meeting, what trip had been so important that he couldn't make that tournament. Then he wondered how embarrassed Kyle must have felt to have to play with his mother. He shook his head.

"That must have been strange. Him playing with his mom."

Matt shrugged. "I don't think so. She was good. A couple of other guys played with like their brothers and stuff because their parents are divorced. Um, Mr. Baker?"

"What?"

"Can I use the bathroom?"

"What? Yeah, sure. You know, it's inside." He pointed vaguely toward the house.

"Right."

Charlie was still sitting there contemplating things when Kyle returned with two cans of Coke and two glasses filled to the top with ice. When he sat down, Charlie felt like he should say something to him, apologize for things, but he couldn't and didn't. Instead, he patted him once on the knee, stood up, and quietly began clearing the table.

Much later that night, after another bourbon and a listless mole check, Charlie wandered down to the office and searched for the family photo albums, big red books, that Donna used to meticulously maintain. He found them on a shelf in the closet packed away in a plastic bin.

He sat cross-legged in the middle of the floor, pried off the lid of the bin, and slowly flipped the plastic pages. There were five albums and he carefully studied each one.

Since he wanted his presentation to be honest and simple, he eventually decided on just four photos. One was of Donna and him slow-dancing at her father's bar before they were married. Donna looked surprised and wildly happy, her mouth partially open, her eyes bright and intense as she peered over his shoulder.

The second photo was of Kyle tenuously riding a rocking horse in his white underpants. His posture was ramrod-straight as he sat on the horse, his red cowboy hat pushed high on his forehead to reveal an apprehensive, worried look.

The third was of Kyle and Charlie standing in front of the swing set in their old backyard. Charlie was holding Kyle and proudly grinning, his eyebrows arched in a very self-satisfied manner.

The final photo included all three of them. They were sitting at a round table in a restaurant in downtown Chicago. Kyle was wearing a blue-and-white-striped suit and bow tie. Donna was in a short dress he no longer recognized and Charlie was wearing a dark blazer. It was the Christmas season and they had spent the day shopping and looking at window displays. Kyle had seen Santa.

Charlie had chosen this picture, and had in fact been specifically searching for it, because he remembered it being a good day, the kind of day that does not leave you. Their expressions, their faces, radiated a shared happiness. If he ever needed proof that they had been a family, this photo, taken some twelve years ago at the Walnut Room in Marshall Field's, was it.

He examined the pictures one last time, then took them out of their plastic coverings and placed them all into a Federal Express envelope along with a note: *This Was Our Life. This Can Still Be Our Life.* He then sealed the envelope up and addressed it to Donna Baker, c/o The Bailey Island Motel, Bailey Island, Maine.

Chapter Fifteen

The next morning, refreshed from two hours of teeth-grinding, jaw-clenching sleep, Charlie awoke before five and dropped off the FedEx package at a delivery box by the train station. Then he bought a dozen glazed doughnuts, which he left on the kitchen island, along with two twenty-dollar bills and a note:

> Kyle: The money is for lunch. I will be home early for dinner. In regards to that issue, do you want to eat Thai? That's one option. I am open to your input, though. Let's discuss.   –~~Charlie B.~~ Dad.

Even though he got to the office very early, he already had three e-mails waiting for him. The first one was from the Wizard, a cryptic, *Call me.* The second was from Jason, the head partner at Rogers & Newman, reminding everyone to attend an exciting new seminar on the *importance of being bilingual in the global workplace.* The final one was from Ned asking him to call his mobile ASAP because he was quitting and joining the seminary.

He called Preston back first, but got his assistant's voice mail. After leaving a message, he next called Ned, who immediately answered.

"I think I was meant to be a holy person," he said.

"Where are you? What are you talking about?"

"I've had an epiphany," Ned said. "Do you know what an epiphany is?"

Charlie was silent.

"I had it last night when Tamales was trying to force me to move his desk."

"What?"

"He, Tamales, demanded that it face the window, so he tried to get me to move it."

"Move his desk? What a shit."

"I agree. That's why I'm quitting. It's too much. I can't work with him. He's an arrogant, terrible, just truly horrible person. He really is. I'm personally telling all of my clients that I'm leaving. You're my first call."

"You're not quitting, so just relax."

"That's not possible if I'm working with Tamales. He is arguably the rudest person I have ever encountered in my years as a transition consultant. He uses very coarse language, vulgar. Then, if you can believe, around seven, as I was leaving—I had some comic-book buyers coming over to my apartment, some very big buyers—"

Charlie interrupted him. "Comic-book buyers?"

"Yes, I'm a collector, a very serious one. I have a significant collection and I'm selling off the *Spider-Man* series. The entire series, so it is very important to me. Anyway, as I was leaving, he asked me, Tamales did, commanded me, really, to move the desk. When I balked, explaining that it wasn't allowed because it wasn't really his office, he turned hostile. He called me an idiot, among other things, and threatened to tell Jason."

"Unbelievable. Did you move the desk?"

"No. I refused. Actually, I couldn't. That desk is very large. He wasn't about to help me, I can assure you."

"What a prick." Charlie had to admit, despite his disgust

with Tamales, he was fascinated by Ned's tale. He had heard stories about Tamales for years, but this one was firsthand and came from a very credible source. He couldn't wait to repeat it to the next person he ran into.

"Did he say anything else, do anything else?"

"That's enough."

"I told you, I told you."

"Taking him on wasn't my idea."

"Can't you ask to have him reassigned?"

"It would be too embarrassing. It would be easier if I just quit. I've about had it here anyway. I'm tired and need to do something else, I'm afraid. Go back to law, maybe. In the public defender's office. They're always looking."

Charlie glanced up at an oversized poster on the office wall, this one depicting a gray-haired old man lifting an impossible-looking amount of weights over his head. His face was contorted in pain and determination, his back arched, his neck a web of thick blue and red veins: FAILURE NEVER COMES TO ANY MAN UNLESS HE ADMITS IT.

"Unless you admit failure, it never comes," Charlie heard himself say.

"What?"

Charlie began again. "Failure never . . ." He stopped. "Listen, just fuck him, fuck him, okay? You can't just quit because you got roughed up by some asshole. That's ridiculous. Listen, you're good at what you do."

"I am?"

"Yes, you are."

"Are you being sarcastic? I can't see your face. Are your eyes slinking sideways? They have a tendency to do that when you're being facetious."

"Everyone thinks you do a good job."

"Everyone? Really? Who, specifically?"

"I don't know, Bradley. Walter."

"Ah, the two amigos. What about Karen? What does she think of me?"

"Karen? Karen Brisco?"

"Yes, her."

"Well, she thinks you're very good at what you do." Charlie tried to sound sincere and convincing despite the fact that he was making all of this up.

"That's very kind of her. Does she say anything else about me?"

"No. But I don't talk to her that much."

"What about you, Charlie? Do you think I'm good at what I do? Please be honest here. I sense, at times, that I irritate you. Do I irritate you?"

Charlie took his time before answering. "No."

"So, overall, do you think I do a good job?"

"Yes, yes, I do. You're professional and determined and involved. Very involved."

"Then why did you ask to be reassigned? Apparently you talked to Jason."

Charlie grimaced. Early on, he had briefly discussed switching consultants with Jason, but had never followed up.

"I made a casual comment. Listen, you're my consultant, end of story."

"Well, thank you. That means a lot, you saying these things. You're a kind person, Charlie, you really are."

It had been years since anyone had called Charlie kind. He was surprised by it. "Thanks," he said. He was breathing hard and wasn't sure why. "Just remember you're good and you shouldn't let some jerk who just got fired, some idiot who everyone hates, run you out of town. If you leave, leave on your own terms, okay?" He looked over at the wall again. "Remember, failure never comes to any man unless he admits it."

"Well, you've given me something to think about, you really have. Thank you, Charlie. You've been inspiring."

"Okay, then!" Charlie said loudly. He had gotten himself all pumped up.

Ned countered just as loudly. "Okay, then! I might come in today after all. We have a special bilingual seminar. Maybe I'll see you there!"

"Maybe you will!"

"And maybe you'll take that evaluation test again!"

"Maybe I won't!"

"Ha, ha! Charlie, very good."

Inspired by his own inspiring speech, Charlie left another message for the Wizard, then checked his e-mail again and received a jolt of hope. Susan Goldman, a key member of the Super Sixteen, had responded to *The Charlie Update!* He eagerly clicked open the note:

> Take me off this list.
> SG

He read the note over several times, not sure that he understood. He had worked with Susan at the old agency. He had hired her straight out of Northwestern and although he had once denied her a promotion (she hadn't been ready), he still regarded her as a friend. They had, he thought, an excellent working relationship. For a number of years they had performed a funny hand-puppet show at the agency's annual breakfast, a show that mocked their clients as well as themselves. Her curt response forced him to question if their puppet show partnership had been a lie.

He spent the next few minutes staring at the e-mail, lost in thought, trying to remember the agency puppet shows, wondering if he had somehow upstaged or offended her. He considered calling her, then decided against it. Instead, he reluctantly called up the Super Sixteen list and deleted her name. Then he left the office for some coffee.

The hallways were, as always, quiet, deathlike. As he walked past the dying plants and upbeat posters, all he could hear was the soft hum of forced air coming from the overhead vents, a monotonous, suffocating sound. He glanced into a few offices, looking for Bradley or Karen, even Walter, but saw no one he recognized. Just strangers, all staring blankly at the computers, their faces tired and grim.

On his way back from the coffee room, he noticed that the door to Office A was open and impulsively popped his head in, hoping, once again, to get a mere glimpse of the Hot Tamales. He was surprised to find him sitting behind the huge desk, still facing the wall, absorbed in *The Wall Street Journal.* He turned and watched as Charlie approached.

"Welcome," Charlie said, probably too cheerfully.

"Do you work here?" Tamales asked.

"No one works here." Charlie took a sip of his coffee.

Tamales didn't smile, but chose that moment instead to sneeze violently into a handkerchief. "Are you here to move my desk?" he asked.

Charlie chuckled at the mere notion of this. "No. I don't move desks." He extended his hand. "I'm Charlie Baker. I'm sure our paths have crossed over the years."

Tamales folded the handkerchief up, put it in his back pocket, and appraised Charlie with hooded eyes. He was a severe-looking man, with pale, slightly pockmarked skin and a thin, angular face. His hair was more white than gray and he wore it short, almost buzzed. After considering Charlie's hand, he reluctantly shook it, his grip loose and fleshy. He didn't bother to say anything.

"I heard you speak at the Economic Club. Last year, I think," Charlie said.

The Hot Tamales continued to stare at him.

"I was over at DiSanto & Herr. Before that, I was at Collins & Park. I was there for about twenty years."

Tamales remained silent throughout Charlie's biography, briefly glancing over at his paper, then back up at him. Charlie thought he might be smirking, but he couldn't be sure. He considered making one more attempt at conversation, but decided to cut his losses. "Nice meeting you," he said. He retreated to the doorway.

"I know who you are."

Charlie turned.

"Excuse me?"

"I know all about you," Tamales said.

"What do you mean?"

Tamales now fully revealed his smirk and it rode high up on his face. "Charlie Baker," he said.

"That's right."

"Charlie Baker." With that, the Hot Tamales shook his head and swiveled around in his chair.

Back in his office, Charlie brooded. Tamales's behavior, particularly his insulting comment, "I know all about you," ate at him. After almost thirty years in the business, Charlie was concerned that, like Tamales, he had developed something of a reputation.

Exactly how big his reputation was, he wasn't sure. While he was well known in the industry, he hardly felt he was infamous. Advertising, as a rule, attracts a certain type of person— egotistical, insecure, and insane—and while he had spent some time straddling the lunatic fringe, he didn't think he ever crossed the line into the Tamales zone. For example, he had never called a woman a "whore" in a meeting, never demanded his staff adopt a six-day work week, hadn't been fired six times, once for screwing the daughter of the chairman, and hadn't plagiarized George Will in a guest column in *Advertising Age*— all crimes Tamales had allegedly committed. And while Charlie once did make his team come in on Easter Sunday (just a half day), and once called a young copywriter an idiot in front of a (small) group of people, and had recently thrown a gumball machine at a bald man (he was provoked), compared to Tamales, Charlie was Gandhi.

He spent the rest of the morning alternately plotting his revenge and fretting about his standing in the ad community. Around lunchtime, just as he was developing message points for his next encounter with Tamales (1. Fuck you; 2. Fuck off; 3. Fuck yourself), Ned walked in wearing a straw sombrero and a black and red corduroy vest.

"*Hola,*" he said.

Charlie looked at the vest. The buttons had gold glitter on them and they sparkled.

"*Dónde está Charlie?*"

"*Dónde*, what?"

Ned wet his lips and spoke slowly. "Where. Is. Charlie?"

"I. Am. Here."

"I mean for our bilingual meeting. We're discussing how a second language can boost your career."

"I. Am. Not. Going."

"*Por qué?*"

"I. Am. Busy."

Ned glanced around his office, saw that Charlie's desk was reasonably clear and that his computer wasn't even on. "I can see that," he said. He stepped closer. "Why don't you sit in on the meeting? It will be fun and educational. I hung a piñata. Monster.com sent it over. It's full of Hershey's Kisses."

"I'd love to come to your bilingual jamboree, but I can't. I have to wrap things up and leave early today. I'm going home to have dinner with my son."

"But Charlie, in a global economy the more languages you know, the more marketable you become. For example, I speak three languages."

"Congratulations."

"*Gracias. Merci. Danke.*"

"Can you get out now?"

Ned took a deep breath, set his jaw, and ripped off a few sentences in rapid-fire Spanish. "You're probably wondering what I just said," he said when he was finished.

"I don't care what you just said."

Ned said something else very quickly in Spanish, his face serious, his head shaking with the intensity of the words and the effort.

Charlie had endured enough. "Get out of my office right now. Pronto. Get out. Now! Now! Now!"

At that precise moment, Tamales walked in, a look of extreme annoyance on his face. He immediately pointed at Ned. "Where were you this morning? I was looking for you."

"I just got in," Ned said.

"I thought I asked you for the conference room. I told you

yesterday that I needed the conference room for a meeting, and there are people in there wearing costumes."

Ned slowly took off the sombrero and began pulling on some of the straw. "Yes, well, we have a meeting scheduled. The other conference room is available, down by the cubicles."

"I'm not having a meeting in that shit hole. I need the big room with the windows. I have some people waiting here. I can't take them back there." He glanced at Charlie, then back at Ned. "There's a damn piñata hanging in the big conference room right now. A piñata. I need that room and you're holding some kind of party. What kind of place is this? This is ridiculous. I want those people out of that room now."

Ned stopped playing with his sombrero. Red splotches were rapidly materializing on his cheeks and neck.

"There's a meeting going on in there, Tom," Charlie said. "So you're out of luck, pal."

Tamales ignored Charlie and turned on Ned one last time.

"And move my desk over to where it should be." His voice had shifted and he said this evenly. "All right? I'm not going to ask again."

"Hey, Tom," Charlie said.

Tamales glared at Charlie and then walked off without a word.

"He's impossible," Ned said after they were alone. "I feel like he's purposely baiting me, purposely trying to do me in. I don't know what to do." He had placed his sombrero back on and looked both ridiculous and miserable.

"Hey," Charlie said. "Don't let him get to you. He's a bully. You have to stand up to him. That's how you treat bullies. I know. I used to be one."

"Well, I'm apparently not very good at that. I don't know what to do."

Charlie chewed on his lip, thinking. "I do," he finally said.

"You do?"

"*Sí,*" Charlie said softly. "*Sí.*"

. . .

"I think we're making a big mistake," Ned said.

"Do you hate him?"

"Yes."

"Do you think he deserves this?"

"If not worse."

"Then lift. On three. One . . ."

"It's too heavy, Charlie. I need a second to stretch out some. I have to be limber to do this." Ned did a couple of toe touches, bending forward in a slow manner, his face flushed.

Charlie watched him stretch and then grew impatient. They had already managed to push Tamales's desk over to a corner in Office A, as far away from the window as possible. Now they were going to flip it over, no easy task since, as Ned repeatedly pointed out, it was very heavy. "Ready? Come on. We can do this," Charlie said.

Ned continued to stretch, dangling his arms in front of him. "Just give me another moment. I don't have the best back."

After Ned's seminar on second languages, during which Bradley had broken the piñata using two staplers, one in each hand, Charlie had lured Ned downstairs to the deli for coffee. It was there that he convinced him that turning a man's desk upside down was a natural and even professional response to rude behavior. After some thought, Ned hesitantly agreed, though he was now reconsidering this strategy.

"I'm not so sure about this," he said.

Charlie played his trump card. "Aren't you related to Churchill? Didn't you tell me that?"

Ned's back visibly stiffened at the mention of his warrior ancestor. He lifted his chin defiantly and in his eyes Charlie thought he saw the resolve of the Blitz. This transformation was fleeting, however. As soon as Charlie thought he had him, Ned wilted and became Ned again, all asthma and anxiety.

"I could lose my job for this," he said.

"Come on, lift." Charlie grabbed hold of his end of the desk. Perspiration was streaming down the sides of his face. He had long passed the point of no return and was willing to die to get this done. Tamales was evil, he had insulted Ned, and, much,

much worse, he had insulted Charlie. He had to be stopped. "Let's get this over with. One, two, three. Now lift and turn. Turn! Turn! Jesus! Turn it over!"

The desk weighed as much as a not-so-small boat. Ned's face flashed an alarming beet-red, all his splotches connecting, as he struggled to lift it.

"Come on!" Charlie yelled.

They were turning the desk sideways when Charlie began to lose his grip. He panicked, thinking they were going to drop it on his feet. "Put it down, put it down!" He gasped for breath. "Okay, leave it like that for a second."

The desk was now on its side, its legs shooting out like a dead horse. Charlie mopped at his forehead while Ned paced around the room, hands clasped behind his head.

"You doing all right? How's the asthma?" Charlie asked.

"I'm fine."

"You use a humidifier?"

"They don't help."

Charlie thought of his beloved Rain Forest waiting patiently for him bedside, like a loyal hound dog. "Then you're not using the right one," he said. "Come on, now. Let's finish this." He grabbed the desk again. "It's late. I was supposed to have dinner with my kid."

"I don't know about this, Charlie."

"Come on. We're defeating evil here. Standing up to him. Like your uncle Churchill did to Hitler."

Ned returned to the desk, his English jaw rigid. "He wasn't exactly my uncle," he said. But he took hold of his end of the desk and began to lift.

Chapter Sixteen

After some thought, Charlie decided it might be best to avoid the office the next day. Instead, he woke early, bought Kyle more glazed doughnuts, went to the Wilton Memorial Library, and camped out in a secluded cubicle in the corner. Between doing research on cattle for his possible interview with Xanon and reading *Beloved*, he alternately called the Wizard, Donna, and Ned but talked to no one.

He returned home around six with the intention of spending some quality time with Kyle—doing what, he didn't know—but instead collapsed on his bed and dreamed that he was talking to a mole. The mole was circular and brown and had a bushy Groucho Marx mustache and eyebrows. It was sitting in a chair in the reading nook, its hairy, thin spider legs crossed, casually smoking a cigar, and holding a BlackBerry.

Charlie addressed the mole. "You have to go away," he said. "I can't take any more bad news right now."

The mole cast him a sideways glance, raised his eyebrows up and down, Groucho Marx–style, but didn't utter a sound.

"I don't care who it is, but the next bad thing has to happen to someone else. I'm at my limit."

The mole shrugged and flicked some ashes off his hairy little legs, checked his BlackBerry.

"Please," Charlie said. "You have to go away."

The mole took a deep, contemplative puff of his cigar and motioned for Charlie to lean in and listen to what he had to say. "Dad," the mole said in Kyle's voice. "The toilets are backing up."

"What?"

"There's something wrong with the toilets."

"What?" Charlie opened his eyes and found Kyle standing at the foot of his bed clutching a toilet plunger.

"Something's wrong with the toilets," he said. "Water is, like, coming out of them."

Charlie cleared his throat. He was still in a fog. "What do you mean? Coming out of what? Where? What are you talking about?"

"All of the toilets are backing up. All of them."

Charlie sat up and surveyed the room in the fading light. While there was no trace of his cigar-smoking mole, there was a sizable pool of water forming by the bathroom door.

"Jesus Christ! What do we do now?"

"I don't know."

Charlie jumped out of bed. "Give me the plunger. Just give it to me. Now!"

When he reached the bathroom, he found water already an inch deep on the floor.

"Are all of them like this?"

"This one is the worst."

"Has this happened before?"

"A few times. But this is really bad."

"What have you've done? How do you fix it?"

"Mom calls Tony DeAngelo Plumbing."

"We're not calling them. We've got to fix this ourselves. All right?" Charlie looked unconvincingly at Kyle. This was not the kind of father-and-son activity he'd had in mind.

"Okay." Kyle swallowed, his Adam's apple bouncing.

"All right." Charlie hoisted the plunger up like it was a loaded M1 rifle. "Stay here."

With that, he entered the bathroom and peered into the toilet. The water was swirling and spinning madly like a whirlpool. Without thinking, he thrust the plunger into the epicenter of the vortex and began pushing down.

"I tried that already," Kyle yelled.

Charlie ignored him and continued to thrust. Rather than help, his efforts seemed to infuriate the toilet. The water was literally gushing out now. He backed away, breathing heavily.

"This is serious," he said.

"There's something wrong with our pipes," Kyle said. "The plumbers are always here."

"Screw the plumbers. They're ripping us off!" Charlie raised the plunger and thrust it hard into heart of the beast. Toilet water splashed everywhere. He did this again and again and again while simultaneously yelling, "Goddamn it! Goddamn it! Goddamn it!" as loudly as he had ever yelled anything in his life.

God must have heard him, because the noise, the water, everything, suddenly ceased. He stood there drenched from head to toe in toilet water, amazed and dazed, still clutching the plunger. He slowly peered into the toilet, and saw calm waters, then felt something shift, sensed a new presence in the bathroom. He turned toward the doorway and saw Donna standing there, arms folded across her chest.

"Hey, Mom," Kyle said. "When did you get back?"

After she hugged and kissed Kyle, and after she led the cleanup efforts in all of the bathrooms, and after she had asked Kyle to go return the borrowed plunger to Matt's house, Donna called Tony DeAngelo, the rip-off artist/plumber. Charlie leaned against the island in the kitchen in his wet clothes and watched her, still shocked at her sudden presence.

She looked thinner and prettier, her curly hair captured tight in a bun, her face drawn and serious and a little wind-burned. As she waited on the phone, Charlie considered his next steps. While he had imagined her return many times, he had failed to map out a clear response strategy. By default, he decided to play it by ear and follow his mood. Unfortunately, his mood at that moment wasn't particularly good.

"So, how was your trip?" he began. She was wearing a baggy kelly-green sweatshirt he had never seen before, and had the sleeves rolled up high, past her elbows. She seemed lost in it.

"It was okay." She had her back to him, and was on hold.

"Well, that's good." He wondered if she had received his package of photos, and if they had played any role in her return. "Well, that's nice." He walked over to the refrigerator, opened it, closed it. He was a bag of emotions. He knew he had to stay calm, though, knew he had to proceed carefully.

"We're glad you're home," he said in what he thought was a casual voice. "Kyle missed you. I cooked dinner for him and Matt, his friend."

He waited for her to comment, but she didn't.

"So, how was your flight?"

"It was fine."

"Well, that's nice." He paused here, thinking. He had quite a few questions, but wasn't sure if this was the right time to ask them. He decided to regroup. "I'm going to check the pipes," he said. He disappeared downstairs to the basement, ostensibly to inspect the main water valve that Donna had turned off. He found the valve in the furnace room under a washtub. He bent down and double-checked to make sure it was closed tight, then slowly went back upstairs. His anger was rising. He had assumed an apology would have been the centerpiece of her return, though none seemed imminent.

He entered the kitchen, and listened to Donna say good-bye on the phone. "Thank you so much, Mr. DeAngelo. We appreciate it so much."

"Mr. DeAngelo," Charlie said.

"He's a nice man." She hung up the phone.

Charlie swallowed. "Nice man."

"He's coming out himself. He'll be here in a few minutes. He was finishing another job close by. He's just two blocks away. We're lucky. You know how hard it is to get a plumber to come out?"

Charlie made one more attempt to control himself. He swallowed again. He couldn't believe they were talking about a plumber. "We're blessed," he said.

Donna gave Charlie a look, then brushed some hair out of her face. Finally, she asked, "Has Kyle eaten dinner?" She picked up a dishrag and ran it under the faucet, then slowly began to wipe down the counters.

"Kyle? No. I was going to cook dinner, again, then this toilet thing happened."

"How's your tooth?"

"It's okay. It's fine," Charlie answered. Then he couldn't resist. "Listen," he said. "Can we cease with the chitchat charade? I need to know about this guy. Tell me everything right now. I need to know this, I have a right to know this. Let's get it out in the open, then we can get back to talking about dinner and Kyle and my teeth. I need to know about this guy."

Donna continued to wipe down the counter, her face impassive. "He has nothing to do with us," she quietly said.

This was too much. Charlie finally exploded. "*Nothing* to do with us? You're kidding, right? He has everything to do with us. Everything!"

Donna covered her face with her hand. "I knew it was going to be like this," she said. She was trying not to cry, but not doing a good job of it; her voice was jittery and her bottom lip trembled. "I knew it. I knew you would start."

"I'm just asking a question, that's all. I'm not starting anything. I've been very calm, considering you're screwing some guy!"

"I'm not screwing anyone!"

With that, Donna threw the dishrag at Charlie. It hit him square on the forehead, then fell on the floor. "I don't know why I even came back," she said. "I don't know! I don't know why I did." She covered her face again, her fingertips poking through her sleeves, which had now slid down her arms.

"Okay," Charlie said. "Let's just settle down. Everything's going to be okay. We just have to talk this through." He was picking up the dishrag when the doorbell rang. "It's probably Kyle," he said. "So let's both calm down."

She wiped her eyes with her sleeve. "It's not Kyle. He's not going to ring the doorbell." She sniffled. "It's Mr. DeAngelo."

"Oh, Jesus, him. I'm surprised he doesn't have his own key. Let me get rid of him."

Charlie stormed toward the front hallway, prepared to rip open the door, but found Mr. DeAngelo already standing in the foyer.

"The door was open," he said. He was a small, older man, with puffy white hair, a matching white beard, and a slightly hunched back. He looked a cross between a mad scientist and Santa Claus.

"This isn't a good time right now," Charlie said.

Mr. DeAngelo peered over his shoulder toward the kitchen, pushing wire-rimmed spectacles up his nose with a long, delicate finger. "Not a good time for what?"

"For you to be here. We're busy right now. So please leave."

"I'd like to see your wife. She called me."

"She's busy. Now, if you don't mind."

Mr. DeAngelo cupped his hands against the sides of his mouth. "Mrs. Baker," he yelled. "Mrs. Baker!"

Donna immediately emerged from the kitchen wiping some tears from her face. She meekly smiled at him. "Hi," she said.

Mr. DeAngelo looked at Charlie and back at her. "Are you all right?"

She nodded, sniffled.

"See, she's perfect. So can you leave now?" Charlie said.

"I came to do some work."

"You're not doing any more work here, so just leave. Leave now. You've ripped us off long enough."

"I beg your pardon? What did you just say?"

"Oh, come off it. I've seen the bills. Ongoing water flow problems, bullshit."

At that comment, Mr. DeAngelo puffed out his chest. When

207

he did this, the hump on his back seemed to move down lower. "What are you insinuating?"

"I'm not insinuating anything. I'm just telling you to stop coming here and stealing my money."

Mr. DeAngelo's face, now red, remained composed. "I think I resent that comment."

"I'm sorry if I hurt your feelings. I really am. I know plumbers are very sensitive, very delicate people. I wouldn't want to upset you."

"You owe me some money," Tony DeAngelo said. Up until this point, he had come across as well spoken, articulate even, but he said "owe me some money," in a threatening, Tony Soprano way. "Before I leave, I wanna get paid. You owe me fifteen thousand dollars."

Charlie was momentarily blinded by this, the room actually going dark. He reached out to steady himself against the wall. "What? Fifteen *what*?" He looked at Donna, who was still standing in the dining room.

"I thought I paid you, Mr. DeAngelo," she said.

Charlie couldn't believe what he was hearing. "You thought you paid him fifteen thousand dollars? *Thought?* You don't remember paying someone fifteen thousand dollars? It slipped your mind?"

"I thought I paid you a few weeks ago," Donna said. "I'm sorry if I didn't."

"Paid him for what?" Charlie yelled.

"You had roots in the pipes, so we had to dig them out and get rid of them. Tree roots," Mr. DeAngelo said. "We did it right around Labor Day. It was a big job. We had to dig them all up, dig up a lot of your lawn."

"You dug up our lawn? It cost fifteen thousand dollars to dig up our lawn? *Shoveling* cost fifteen thousand dollars?"

"We got rid of the roots and replaced some piping."

"Obviously, you didn't do a good job. We still have problems."

"We did the best we could."

"'The best we could'? Are you kidding me? Fifteen thousand dollars and you did the best you could? What is this, second grade? I'm supposed to give you an A for effort? A gold star and fifteen grand? Tell me you're kidding me. Tell me so I can laugh." Charlie folded his arms across his chest and waited. "I need a good laugh. Come on, tell me. Tell me this is a joke."

Mr. DeAngelo turned his attention back to Donna. "The check you gave me bounced, Mrs. Baker."

Donna was visibly horrified. She put her hands up to her mouth in shock. "It bounced?"

"Yes, ma'am. I tried to cash it and it bounced. I'm sure it's some mistake," he said.

"I'm so sorry, Mr. DeAngelo. I had no idea. I don't know why it bounced."

Charlie wasn't sure which was worse: the fact that Donna paid a plumber $15,000 or that the check had bounced. He decided to combine the two outrages.

"You gave him a fifteen-thousand-dollar check and it bounced?" he yelled. "Didn't you check the balance? Always check the balance before writing a check for that amount. Always."

"Are you still getting paid?" she asked. She turned to Mr. DeAngelo. "My husband was fired a few weeks ago. That might be the problem with the check."

Charlie shot Donna a heated look. He couldn't believe she had just told a stranger, a *plumber*, about his situation. He was going to mount a protest, clarify that he had resigned to pursue other interests, when he felt the pain in his chest. It was sharp and long, like someone was digging a knife deep into him, rooting around for his heart. He reached over again to prop himself against the wall and started gulping air.

"What's wrong with him?" Mr. DeAngelo asked.

"He's fine. Mr. DeAngelo, I am so sorry about the check," Donna said. "Let me write you another one."

"Don't!" Charlie croaked. Things were going dark again. He pointed at Donna. "Do not give this man a check!" he gasped. "Do not!"

"Are you sure he's okay?" Mr. DeAngelo asked. "Why is he all wet?"

Donna ignored his questions. "I'm going to get my check-book. I'll be right back."

Charlie stayed there, holding on to the wall and taking deep breaths, while Donna raced upstairs. Between gulps of air he said, "This is consumer fraud. I'm calling the Illinois attorney general."

"Give him my best."

When Donna returned, she handed Mr. DeAngelo a new check. Charlie pushed off from the wall and pointed at the white-haired plumber when she did this. "I don't know how you sleep at night. You're a damn thief!"

"And you have a very big mouth," Mr. DeAngelo said. He folded up the check and slipped it into the front pocket of his shirt. Charlie then thought he winked at him, but wasn't sure.

"I saw that!"

"Saw what?"

"Fuck you!" Charlie yelled. "Fuck you, you slimy crook!"

Charlie thought he had gotten the last word in and was proudly turning, chin up, toward Donna to gauge her reaction when he felt the wind kick out of him. Apparently, Mr. DeAngelo had punched him in the stomach. Charlie instantly crum-pled to the floor, unable to breathe.

Donna deftly jumped in front of Charlie's writhing body and yanked the door open wide. "Get out of our house," she said to Mr. DeAngelo.

"I'm sorry, Mrs. Baker. I just don't appreciate being called—"

"You have no right to punch my husband. Now get out, please. If you don't go now, I'm calling the police." She said all of this in an even, matter-of-fact manner that made her threat seem all the more real.

"You're right," Mr. DeAngelo said, "I'm sorry. I probably shouldn't have done that." He looked down at Charlie, then ex-tended his hand in an attempt to pull him up off the ground. Donna seized his arm, though, and said, "Don't touch him. Just leave. Leave right now."

Mr. DeAngelo looked at Charlie one last time and said, "I apologize for any inconvenience I may have caused," then shuffled out, his head down. Donna waited until he was in his car before closing the door and sitting down on the floor next to Charlie's head.

"He's gone?" Charlie asked. The chest pains had disappeared, but his stomach ached.

"Yes."

"You sure?"

"Yes."

They were both quiet, then Charlie said, "You think I'm pathetic, don't you?"

"A little." She was staring straight ahead at the door.

"You think I'm obnoxious too?"

Donna didn't say anything.

"And I'm selfish and self-centered and all those other things."

She remained quiet.

He reached over and took one of her hands. "I'm going to change," he said. "I promise, I'm going to change back to the person you married. But you have to help me. I don't know how to do it. All I know is that I can't do it alone. So can you help me? Can you? Can you try?"

Donna held on to Charlie's hand, but continued to stare blankly at the front door.

"Donna?"

"I don't know," she said.

"Donna, please. Can you try?"

"I don't know," she softly repeated. "I've been trying for a long time now."

Chapter Seventeen

Over the next week or so, things at home remained Scotch-taped together, Donna and Charlie tiptoeing around each other like polite strangers, saying please and thank you, commenting about the weather, Kyle, and the state of the toilets, which were once again, inexplicably, running fine. It wasn't clear what their next steps would be; they each seemed to be waiting for the other to make the first move and present the blueprint of the future of their marriage.

For his part, Charlie proceeded carefully, walking around on eggshells, afraid he might do or say something that might send her fleeing. He decided to push questions about Mr. Lighthouse aside for the time being and instead busied himself with research on marriage-saving, reading the only book the Wilton Memorial Library had in on the subject, *Road to Recovery* (1977) by Dr. David J. Prioletti, "a.k.a. The Father of Love." Dr. Prioletti's central message was to communicate, communicate, and communicate, then make "vigorous" love. This advice was obvious but worrisome because other than the occasional polite comment, Donna and he were hardly speaking, and sleeping in separate bedrooms.

They were doing a very good job of getting in each other's way, however. With both of them home now, the house was suddenly crowded. Despite being married close to thirty years, they had no domestic rhythm, no routine to fall back on, no defined division of labor. Donna had spent decades running the household, doing the wash, the shopping, paying the bills, and raising Kyle, while he was away. Now he was back and neither one of them knew what to do with him.

His attempts at helping with the housework were futile and counterproductive. If he wiped down the counters, she would quietly wipe them again. If he swept the floor, he would find her sweeping it soon afterward. Before he emptied the garbage, she would check the garbage can and remove any recyclable items.

He tried his hand at rearranging furniture. He hoped this would underscore his willingness to change, as well as his re-newed commitment to his family and home. It started in the reading nook, where he impulsively moved a leather chair from the window over to a bookcase. This switch allowed for a better view of the yard, he reasoned. After he was done, he sat in the chair and stared out the window, pleased with himself. He thought Donna would appreciate his initiative. If she did, however, she kept it to herself, never commenting.

At night, he would lie awake in the guest room and try to read Lincoln biographies. He took some comfort in the fact that Lincoln too had a troubled marriage. His wife, Mary, was a lunatic, prone to tantrums, depressions, and wild spending sprees. Abe persevered, however, and Charlie initially drew strength from this until he realized that, if anything, in his own marriage, he was the Mary, and Donna the Abe. This con-clusion did little to help him sleep.

Still, he knew he had to earn his way back into the family, so he did try. He packed a lunch once for Kyle, offered to help Donna write the annual report for Bright Day (she said she could handle it), and raked the leaves in the backyard.

He thought he was making progress until the day he tried to move their bed. It was a huge king-sized bed and it was too close to a window. After analyzing the layout, he decided that it needed to be repositioned by an interior wall. With winter coming, he thought it made sense to be as far away as possible from the window and stiff neck–producing drafts. Unfortunately, as he was moving it, he broke off the brass headboard. It fell off its hinges and lay crookedly half on and half off the bed frame. When Donna returned from the grocery store about half an hour later, she found him trying to jam it back into place. She watched him do this for a few minutes before quietly reattaching the headboard and then helping him move the bed back near the window.

"Thanks," he said when they were finished. He hoped that the fact they had accomplished something together was a step in the right direction.

Donna busied herself with straightening the bedsheets.

"We probably couldn't function here without you, you know," he said.

Donna managed a tight smile and puffed up the pillows. She looked worn and tired and for the first time Charlie realized that he wasn't the only one not sleeping at night.

"Glad to have you back," he said, trying to sound cheerful.

Donna said nothing. Instead, she shook her head.

"What's wrong?"

Donna tossed a pillow off to the other side of the bed.

"What did I say now?"

"I wish you wouldn't say things like that."

"What? That we're glad to have you back?"

Donna smoothed a pillowcase. "The only reason you want me back is because you lost your job," she said. "That's the only reason you're glad to have me back."

"That's not true," he said. "That's not true at all. How can you even think that?"

Donna shook her head. "Once you get a new job, you'll vanish again."

"No, I won't."

"Yes, you will. You'll go."

"Don't talk to me about going anywhere, okay? You're the one who took off to Maine to screw another man!"

The last sentence just came out and he immediately regretted saying it. But it was too late. Donna threw a pillow against the headboard and left the room.

The next day, he decided it might be best to return to Rogers & Newman. He didn't like leaving home, he was worried Donna might disappear again, but he felt it a necessary move. His severance pay was ending soon and he urgently needed to get the job search in motion. Besides, his marriage-saving efforts were obviously leaving something to be desired and he thought it might be wise to lay low for a few days and regroup.

His first morning back, he set up shop in the salami office and placed a call to the Wizard, leaving a voice mail and apologizing for not sending in his résumé. He then fell to work developing the second issue of *The Charlie Update!* Undaunted by the response the inaugural issue had received—other than Susan Goldman's rude message, it had been virtually ignored— he wanted to give it at least one more shot.

The Charlie Update!
Charlie B. Still Out on the Street

Just a quick update to let you know that Charlie Baker is alive and well and still out on the street. Although he has seriously considered a number of options, he is holding out for the job that will combine his creative and administrative talents with his penchant for picking the perfect place for lunch. He knows you're all busily employed, but he's still hoping you'll have a minute to respond to an old— and growing older—friend. While he is enjoying his temporary hiatus from the rat race, he's eager to share his considerable experience and skills with a new company.

He looks forward to hearing from you!

He added his perspective on some industry news gleaned from *Advertising Age*, as well as a critique of the new Bud Light campaign, which he thought weak. In an attempt to upgrade the look of *The C.U.!* he then spent close to two hours wrestling with the font and format. He wanted it to look as much like the front page of *The New York Times* as possible. Eventually he gave up on this, though, and sent it off looking more like a church bulletin than a newspaper.

This completed, he finally confronted his résumé. It was still too long and, he feared, confusing. After reviewing it, he deleted a small section pertaining to his awards, then decided to put the section right back in. Awards were important, he thought. They validated a person's work, gave it weight.

He continued to fiddle with the document for a while, growing increasingly frustrated. He thought it a belittling task, having to sell himself like this, like everyone else. He still didn't think a résumé was necessary. He had close to thirty years in the business, thirty years, and he was well known and respected. His work spoke for him, not two pieces of paper.

He eventually clicked off the résumé and checked his e-mail, hoping for some response to the latest *Charlie Updates*. He had but one message, from Scottie Frandsen, a member of the Super Sixteen list. They had worked together for years and Charlie knew him as a man with a sense of humor. If anyone appreciated the spirit and tongue-in-cheek nature of *The C. U.!*, he would. He quickly opened the message:

> Charlie—you're kidding me, right?
> I mean, you're kidding me!

Charlie's cheeks burned with embarrassment. He could not believe this indignity, this insult! He had been Scottie's manager for three years, they had worked together on the toilet paper account, a very high-profile piece of business. While Charlie had always treated him fairly, during his last year at the old agency he had sensed a growing resentment from Scottie over the attention the campaign—and Charlie—had received. He wondered if this note was a way of evening the score.

The more he thought about it, the more he believed it was. He never liked Scottie. Scottie was an ad agency stereotype: he wore wrinkled black clothes, had a goatee, and kept a bottle of Grey Goose vodka in his freezer. He fought back the urge to send this poseur an appropriate response (*I was the toilet paper account. Don't ever forget that. And Grey Goose sucks*) but opted instead to merely delete his name from the Super Sixteen list. Afterward, he reflected on his shrinking list.

He couldn't understand why Victoria McHugh, someone who had worked with him for years, whose wedding he had attended, hadn't bothered to respond. Ditto for Steve Larson, a research geek from the Ad Club, who once listed Charlie as a reference when he was applying for a job at Leo Burnett; and Sally Hart, a media buyer he had hired; or Ellen Ryan, or Susan McDonnell, or Vicki Foreman, or Laura Dihel. None of them had written so much as a word acknowledging his situation. None. He felt abandoned. Had he no friends at all? What had happened to them? In the old days, people were always calling him, always asking him to lunch or coffee. One year, the last year at the old agency, he was invited to *four* different Christmas parties on the same night. Four!

As he was drowning in a wave of self-pity, Ned walked in wearing a sharp blue blazer and a well-pressed pink shirt. He looked sternly at Charlie before speaking.

"Well, well, well, look what the cat dragged in," he finally said. His voice had an edge to it.

"Hi," Charlie said.

"Well, well, well," Ned repeated.

"What's wrong?" Charlie asked.

Ned shut the door. "Don't what's-wrong me."

"What are you doing? I'm in the middle of something here."

"Where have you been? You've been gone for more than a week."

"I've been at home. Why? What's wrong?"

Ned glanced back at the door and put a hand in the side pocket of his nifty blazer. "You know what's wrong!" His voice was a loud whisper. "You've left me here all alone to . . . to . . . deal with the fallout."

"Fallout?" It was only then that it occurred to Charlie what Ned was talking about. "You mean that desk thing? Tamales's desk?"

"Yes, that desk thing."

Charlie sat up, concerned. "I hope you didn't tell anyone about that, did you? That was really stupid. I don't know what I was thinking. I was nuts."

"Of course I didn't tell anyone! Our little secret is still safe. But it's been hard around here. Very hard. That whole escapade caused quite a stir. Tamales went on a witch hunt. He wanted someone's head."

"Don't worry about that midget."

"Easy for you to say. Jason called me and asked me quite a few pointed questions. He was very suspicious. Do you know that we broke the desk? The top was cracked. We cracked it. That was a very expensive desk. They were considering filing a police report. A police report, Charlie!"

Charlie swallowed. Being arrested for flipping a desk over would add new meaning to the word frenetic. He couldn't believe this. "You didn't bring my name up, did you? Please tell me you didn't mention my name."

"It was your idea! You practically forced me to do it."

"I didn't force you—" He stopped here. "Listen, I'm sorry. It was stupid. The whole thing."

Ned appraised Charlie for a moment. "Anyway, you're safe. We're safe. No one saw anything. Let's just keep mum about it. It's in the process of blowing over."

Charlie relaxed. "Tamales deserved it and more. Much more." He sat back in his chair. "What was his reaction? What did he do? Was he pissed?"

Ned spoke petulantly. "I really don't remember."

"Please tell me. I need to hear some good news today. Tell me he was outraged. Tell me he screamed."

Ned straightened his pink shirt collar and avoided Charlie's eyes. "I don't recall."

"Please tell me."

"Well," Ned said. He stepped closer to the desk. "If you really must know, he actually did scream."

"You're kidding! He did?"

"Like a woman in labor. And then he ranted and raved." Ned paused. "And then he began throwing his arms about . . . like a complete idiot."

This news was a tonic to Charlie. "Ha!" He clapped. "That's great."

Ned smiled, his whole face transforming. His next words came out in a gush. "It really was, I must admit, it really was. You should have seen him. His face was all red and his eyes bulged out like an insect's. I wish I had a camera. He kept repeating, 'This is my office, my office!' in his annoying, fascist voice. He had to sit in a cubicle all day. A *cubicle*!"

Charlie clapped again, loving every second of this account. "A cubicle! Ha! Perfect! Perfect!"

"Next to Walter!"

"No way! Unbelievable! That's like sitting next to a Porta-Potty." Charlie pumped his fists, this time in triumph. "It gets no better!"

"It was a special moment, it really was." They both laughed insanely.

"I wish I had been there," Charlie said. He laughed some more and pounded the desk, very glad now that Ned had come into his office; very glad to just have Ned around.

He eventually calmed down and shook his head, then took in Ned's blazer. It was a radical departure from his usual Mr. Rogers attire. He glanced down at Ned's shoes and noticed he was wearing new black wingtips. "Are you going to a funeral or something?"

"Oh, this." Ned tugged on the ends of the coat. "It's nothing.

I just thought it was time for a change. Jason always dresses stylishly. He's always on me about my clothes. He gets his suits from London, supposedly."

"Well, you look good."

"Thank you. I had a very good salesperson. She picked everything out. Matched things up. You think the pink is all right? You don't think it feminine?"

"It's fine."

"Good. I wanted to look nice today for our networking meeting. We're going to hear about some good news, I think."

"What good news?"

"We're getting close on some searches. Bradley is actually making some progress on a job."

"You mean a boob job? He's had everything else."

"Ha! I don't believe he's doing that, no. But he is getting close on a real job. As is someone else."

"Who?"

Ned tilted his chin up. "Karen." He said her name softly. "She's getting very close. I shouldn't be speaking out of school, but I believe today she'll be announcing that she's leaving us. She accepted a position in Atlanta."

"With Coke?"

"You knew about that?"

"She mentioned something."

"Well, we're bringing a cake in. Do you think carrot cake is appropriate?"

"I don't like it."

"Neither do I. But I think she does, and she deserves a real send-off. She's a very special person. I've asked Tina, the receptionist, to bring it in during the networking meeting. So act surprised."

"I'll scream."

"You don't have to do that." Ned turned pensive, almost wistful. "I've gotten to know her fairly well, you know," he said.

"Who? Karen?"

"Yes. Did you know she writes short stories?"

"I didn't know that."

"Yes. She's been published. In literary journals, small publications. She showed me one once. It was very good, though I didn't entirely understand it. It was about a neighborhood being overrun with rabbits. I think the rabbits were a metaphor for something. I'm not sure what. I've never been good with metaphors. I'm a very literal person." He was quiet, then said, "I'll miss her, I think."

Charlie considered the office without Karen. It was already a stark and lifeless place. Without her, it would be even more so. He fought back yet another sinking feeling and opened his briefcase.

"It's very difficult sometimes," Ned said. "This job. You get close to people and then they leave."

"That's pretty much true in any job."

"It's different here, in this business," Ned said. "We have different relationships. We get involved with people in different ways. I'm dealing with people at probably the lowest points in their lives. I work side by side with them, see them every day for months, and sometimes longer, and then one day they're just gone. They go away. They say that they'll stay in touch, but they never do. They don't have time for me anymore. They don't want to remember where they were, that they spent time here. They have a job."

"I bet she stays in touch."

"No one does. And I suspect she won't be any different." His voice trailed off and he glanced at his watch. "Anyway, we should go now, we're running late." With that, he buttoned his blazer and walked out.

The networking meetings were held in the windowless conference room, back by the cubicles where all the Category C's sat. The size of the group varied; this particular morning it was only a handful: Bradley, Karen, Walter, and three bored-looking young men from the recently imploded sales promotion firm. Another middle-aged woman began the meeting with them, but abruptly left when her cell started playing "London Bridge Is Falling Down."

Once everyone was seated, Ned said, "Good morning. And how are we all doing today?"

Everyone was quiet and fiddled with their phones and BlackBerrys. Bradley finally broke the silence.

"Are you going to a funeral?" he asked Ned.

"No." Ned shifted uncomfortably on his feet and brushed something off his lapel. "I just threw a jacket on, that's all. It was hanging there in my closet and I put it on."

"You look nice," Karen said.

Ned beamed. "Thank you, Karen. Thank you." He glanced down at a notepad. "Anyway, let's get started." He held up a copy of *The Wall Street Journal.* "You've probably all seen this. It just came out. Close to fifty thousand jobs created last month. Things are finally opening up a bit! It's been a long time since we've had any good news on the economic front."

"I don't believe that. Things are bad as ever. Did you see the market yesterday? Let me see that paper," Bradley said. The orange in his face had dulled considerably, but his hair was still late-autumn squirrel.

"Actually, it's not in here," Ned said. He folded the paper in half and put it behind his back. "This is yesterday's paper. I forgot today's paper on the bus. I just brought this in for effect."

"I saw the story," one of the sales promotion guys said from off in the corner. He had long, stringy hair and was wearing a black turtleneck. "I think you got it wrong. It said fifty thousand more jobs lost."

"Oh," Ned said. "Well, I read it quickly." He put the paper down on the table. "But I do know things are opening up a bit here in Chicago. I sense a shifting of momentum right here in the office." He winked in the direction of Bradley and Karen, who were sitting next to each other. Bradley nodded back, but Karen glanced away. "Anything anyone would like to share this morning? Any progress or . . . or news they would like to share?"

No one said anything.

Ned looked expectantly at Karen but, when he failed to get a response, turned to Bradley. "Bradley? How about you?"

"Things are proceeding nicely," he said with a smile. "I have a second interview lined up."

Everyone murmured their congratulations and tried not to look shocked.

Ned actually clapped. "Excellent! Anything you can share?"

"Nope," Bradley said. He was still smiling, his cheeks puffy and proud. "Nothing right now. I've had one interview and I'm scheduled for another one. Don't want to jinx it. Not this one."

"Have a good feeling about this one, do you?" Ned asked.

"No comment."

"Corporate side?"

"No comment."

"Chicago?"

"No comment."

"Well, that's an exciting update, it really is," Ned said, meaning it. He folded his arms and smiled. "Anything anyone else would like to share?" He once again glanced Karen's way, but she kept her eyes on her BlackBerry. "How about you, Charlie?"

He shook his head. "Nothing, really."

"Nothing at all?"

"No. Well, maybe something. I talked with the recruiter. That's about it."

"That sounds promising," Ned said. "Very promising." He turned once again to Karen. "Anyone else? Any news anyone has to share? Any *good* news?"

Karen continued to avoid Ned's eyes.

Ned paused and dipped both hands into his blazer's side pockets. Finally, unable to contain himself, he asked, "Anything you'd like to share with us, Karen? Anything at all?"

"No," she said.

Ned looked surprised. "Really? Nothing?"

"Oh, yeah. Coke took a pass on me, I guess." She didn't look up when she said this.

Ned's jaw dropped. "But I don't understand. I thought you had an offer."

"I never got it. They said they were putting one together, but they changed their minds. Must have, at least."

Ned teetered and reached for the edge of the table. "That's just . . . just terrible. Did they give a reason?"

"Budget. They can't hire anyone right now. They just called. They were nice about it, I guess. They could have just sent an e-mail, like everyone else."

"Big mistake on their part," Charlie blurted this out, feigning outrage. He tried hard to ignore his sense of relief. He didn't want Karen to leave. At least not before he did.

Karen looked up from her BlackBerry. "Can I ask a question?" she asked.

No one responded. Ned was still in shock. Finally, Charlie said, "Sure."

"Is there something wrong with me? Am I doing something wrong? Is there some big flaw I have that I'm missing? Am I saying the wrong thing, or dressing the wrong way?"

"No," Charlie said.

"Then *what is it*?" she said, her voice rising. "This is the fourth time I've gotten to the final stages, four times I've been cut. I'm doing something wrong. I must be. I want to know what it is so I can fix it. I'm tired of this. I don't deserve this. I was a hard worker. I *am* a hard worker." She covered her face with her hands. "I just want a job. That's all I want. Just a job! I just want to work. I don't want anyone to give me anything. . . ." Her voice trailed off.

"Karen, everything will be all right," Ned said. "You have to believe in yourself. Besides, you still have a home here." He smiled. "Isn't that right, fellows?" He looked hopefully around the room. "Isn't that right?"

"This isn't a joke, Ned!" Karen said. "I don't want to stay here. I'm not a loser. I don't want to end up like . . . like . . . Bradley walking around with an orange face!"

With that, the entire room fell into a deep, embarrassed silence. Charlie glanced furtively at Bradley and saw him smile, a thin, heart-rending smile.

"I'm sorry, Bradley," Karen said. She reached for his hand,

but he pulled it away. Still smiling, he rose from his chair and left the room.

After he was gone, Karen put her head on the table, covered her face with her arms, and cried. "God," she said, her voice muffled. "I think I'm losing it."

"You're under a lot of stress," Ned said. "You didn't mean that."

She lifted her head and started to wipe away tears with her fingers. "Oh, God," she said.

"How old are you?" Walter suddenly asked. He had been quiet and detached throughout the meeting, but was now staring at Karen.

"What?"

"How old are you? What, are you about twenty-nine, thirty, maybe?"

Karen sniffled. "I'm thirty-two. What does that have to do with anything?"

"You're thirty-two. And you don't have anyone to support, no kids, right?"

"I'm not married," Karen said. "You know that."

"And you think you're losing it?" He smiled his smirk smile. "Try being fifty-five, try being fifty-five like me or sixty like Bradley and being out of work. Then you can be dramatic. Then you can"—he made quote marks in the air with his fingers—"lose it."

Karen stared at him in disbelief, her tear-streaked face turning redder.

"Walter, please," Ned said.

"I may never work again," Walter said. He spoke quietly, his smirk fully intact. "Never. Never. Do you know that? So spare me all the dramatics."

Karen slowly stood, sniffling. She pointed at Walter. "I've always been nice to you, always," she said in a sad little-girl voice. "Always been nice." She put her hand over her mouth and quickly walked out.

Charlie watched her leave, then turned on Walter. He tried to remain calm. "You were out of line."

Walter was unfazed. "Just because she has big tits, everyone cuts her slack."

This got Charlie going. "You know something," he began, "we're all sick of your act. Sick of it. You walk around here feeling sorry for yourself, rude to everyone. I've got news for you, pal, you're not the only one who has it tough. I do too, we all do. We all have it tough. Everyone here has it tough."

Walter's eyebrows arched in apparent amusement. "You don't know what tough is," he said. "You don't know anything. You're some crazy creative guy who thinks his shit doesn't smell, who thinks he's too cute, too smart, too . . . too clever, for words. I've seen hundreds of guys like you. Hundreds. Empty suits who spend all their time taking credit and giving blame. No one can work for you. Everyone in the business knows that. You and your stupid shticky commercials with hamsters and kittens and capes. You're old news."

Charlie's neck burned, but he remained silent.

Walter leaned over the table and hitched his shoulder. "You don't even remember me, do you? I've been waiting for you to remember me, but you haven't and you probably never will."

"What are you talking about?"

Walter looked at Charlie with amazement. "I don't believe you," he said. He hitched his shoulder one last time, then snapped up his cell phone from the table and left.

A few minutes after the meeting, Ned walked into Charlie's office holding an enormous slice of carrot cake on a paper plate.

"We have a lot of this," he said.

"I don't like carrot cake."

"Oh, that's right." He held it awkwardly while searching for a place to put it. Finally, he shoved the plate onto the desk and sat down. "Well, that was a soap opera. Karen went home and I can't find either Bradley or Walter."

"Walter is an asshole."

"He's under an enormous amount of stress."

"We're all under stress here."

"He has more than most, I think."

226

Charlie wasn't having any of this. "You know something? You're too nice to people. You let people push you around. Tamales. Walter. You have to stand up to these people."

Ned crossed his legs and folded his hands in his lap. "There's nothing wrong with being sympathetic."

"Sympathetic? He's not worthy of anyone's sympathy. He's a loser. I know a million guys like him, bitter short-sleeved middle managers who can't cut it. They blame everyone but themselves." He waved his hand in disgust. He was still worked up.

"Walter is feeling extremely frustrated right now," Ned said. "He doesn't want to be here."

"Oh, he doesn't, does he? You're kidding me, right? Like I want to be here? I got news for you, Mr. Sympathy. Despite all your hospitality, despite all the great coffee and all the love and encouragement, none of us wants to be here. Especially me. I'm dealing with it, and he should too."

"You haven't been out of work as long as he has."

"That's no excuse."

"And your wife doesn't have cervical cancer."

"What?"

"And your insurance hasn't run out. And you haven't drained your 401(k) and can't take out another mortgage on your house because you did that four months ago. They may foreclose."

Charlie fell quiet.

"Sometimes the only way we can help people is to put up with them. Simply let them be. Sometimes that's all we can do, Charlie, sometimes that's all we can do."

Charlie took his time processing this information before asking, "Is all that true?"

"Of course it is."

"How bad is his wife?"

"It's quite serious, I'm afraid."

Charlie nodded. "I didn't know that. I didn't know any of that about him."

Ned raised an eyebrow. "One more thing you apparently don't know about Walter."

"What?"

"He used to work for you."

Charlie was confused. "Wait, what? What are you talking about?"

Ned adjusted his glasses. "Years ago. He was there at your old agency. He was a copywriter. On your first day here, he told me he knew you."

"That's ridiculous," Charlie said but then, of course, all at once he finally placed Walter: a plodding, not particularly imaginative copywriter who worked on a number of consumer accounts at Collins and Park, the old agency. He was heavier then and had more hair. "I guess I do remember him." He swallowed. "I don't think we worked together very long, though. Why didn't he say something to me?"

"I thought he had, actually. I can't believe you didn't remember him."

"I've worked with a lot of people. Do you have any idea how many people come and go at agencies? It's a transient business, full of gypsies. I can't remember everyone. I've worked with hundreds of people, maybe thousands."

Ned shifted uneasily in his chair. "I would think Walter would be one you remembered."

"Why?"

Ned grimaced and looked down at his hands.

"Why?"

"Well," Ned finally said, "according to Walter, you fired him."

Chapter Eighteen

The next morning, Charlie sat in the salami office and tried to recall Walter. Sketchy images came to mind, flashbacks of an overweight man with black, horn-rimmed glasses sitting against the wall in the back of conference rooms, doodling. He remembered nothing specific about him other than a concept he'd had for the Midas account, something about a talking car. Joan Rivers would do the voice-over for the car and insult the Midas mechanics, who would remain cheerful throughout. He remembered thinking the idea ridiculous and Walter not bright.

He had no memory about firing him, however. He concluded that it must have been during the recession of the nineties, a bad time for agencies and business in general. With billings in a tailspin, he was ordered to lay off about half his team. He did this on a Friday afternoon in a short memo, drawing from an initial list of names his directors had compiled. After submitting the list to human resources, he remembered beating a fast retreat to the bar at the 410 Club. Walter's name, he concluded, must have been on that list.

He was trying to decide the best way to deal with Walter,

acknowledge their shared past, or just ignore it, when the Wizard called. He sounded unusually animated, his voice warm and gooey.

"Charlie Baker. Got something for you," he said.

"The Xanon thing?"

"I floated your name out there, and they liked it. Liked it a lot."

Charlie felt a burst of elation. "What's not to like?"

"They want to chat. And soon. How are you this Friday?"

"This Friday works."

"Terrific. Why don't you shoot me your résumé and we can get going on this."

Charlie paused. "When do you need that?"

"As soon as you can."

"How about tomorrow?"

"Fine. Once I get it, I'll give you a call with the details. Got to run now."

"Wait. This is the CMO job, right?"

"Right. Top dog. Bark, bark."

"What else can you tell me about it?"

"I'll call back. In the meantime, you might want to bone up on cattle."

"Cattle."

"Hogs too, chief, hogs too."

Charlie spent the rest of the afternoon with his sleeves literally rolled up, working on his résumé. Faced with a deadline, he finally found the clarity and courage to cut and reorganize his life. He reduced his awards mentions, dropped three campaigns from the eighties, and cut back on his work on the Ad Council, a nonprofit organization he once chaired. When he finished, he meticulously proofread everything, searching then correcting grammar and typographical errors. At five o'clock, he took one last look at it and let out a deep breath. He had actually finished it. He had a résumé just like everyone else. In the end, he was no different than the next guy. This realization briefly saddened him, but he quickly brushed the thought away and e-mailed it off to Preston and left for the day.

In the train station and later on the train ride home, he boned up on Xanon. He checked their Web site on his laptop, read recent press releases, studied last year's annual report. They were big, a $50 billion company and profitable. Unfortunately, they weren't spending much of those profits on marketing. According to the annual report, their ad budget was a relatively small $50 million. He wasn't sure he liked that.

He also wasn't so sure he liked the field. Animal pharmaceuticals. Drugs for cattle. Though he had worked with kittens and hamsters, cows were uncharted waters. He was used to fun, if not downright wacky, creative campaigns with big budgets, celebrities. He liked hoopla and he thought there was little of that in promoting cures and chemicals for mad cow, bovine foot disease, cow tuberculosis, and, shockingly, the pinkeye cattle virus. This last disease shook him. According to the Xanon Web site, it was a worldwide problem. And while he sympathized, he had zero desire to work on campaigns featuring a cow wearing a black eye patch.

Still, he needed a job, and this was a good one. He thought that Xanon's hugeness would anchor him, and the inevitable pressure to conform would keep him grounded, focused.

Most importantly, he suspected it would make him rich, or at least close to it. Based on the company's size, he figured it had to pay north of $300,000, plus bonus. And, while he suspected he would be traveling frequently to their regional offices in Omaha and Tulsa, as well as two cities he had never heard of in Chile and Australia, it was headquartered in Chicago. He would be a fool not to pursue this with everything he had.

He was so lost in Xanon thoughts that it wasn't until he was halfway up the front walk that he noticed the police car parked in the driveway. He stopped dead in his tracks, considered the car, took another step, reconsidered it, then warily continued up the steps. When he got to the front door, he took a deep breath and opened it, half expecting to see the chalk outline of his family on the foyer floor.

Instead, he found Donna and Kyle alive and well, sitting across from each other at the kitchen island. Donna was staring at Kyle, who was staring at nothing.

Charlie swallowed, and even though he wasn't all that keen on a response, he asked, "Why is there a police car in our driveway?"

"Because the police came to visit Kyle," Donna said.

Charlie looked around the kitchen. "Where are they?"

"Next door at Matt's house talking to the Parkers."

"What happened?"

"Ask your son," Donna said. Her hair was tied back to reveal the tired, worried face of a mother.

"What happened?"

"Nothing," Kyle said.

"Tell him, Kyle," Donna said.

Kyle coughed. He was wearing a Wilton Lions T-shirt and red basketball shoes that looked enormous and clownlike. His eyes were large and sad.

"What happened?" Charlie asked.

"Matt and I did something."

"Tell me it was something heroic," Charlie said.

"Tell him what happened," Donna said.

"It was no big deal."

"Tell him," Donna repeated.

"We just changed some signs. We wrote on some signs."

"What signs? What did you write?" Charlie glanced at Donna.

Donna briefly closed her eyes and shook her head. "The high school Art Fair is next week," she began.

"And?"

"And there are signs up and down the streets that say, ART FAIR, with an arrow telling people where to park."

"Yes. And?" He was doing his best to be patient. Donna could be a maddeningly slow speaker, each word an eternity apart.

"And Kyle and Matt wrote graffiti on the signs. All of them. They changed them to say something else."

"What did they change them to say?"

"You tell him, Kyle," Donna said.

"What did you change the Art Fair signs to read?"

Kyle mumbled something.

"What? I can't hear you. Say it louder!"

"Fart Fair," Kyle said.

Charlie paused. "What?"

"Fart Fair," he said.

"Fart Fair," Donna repeated.

Charlie looked at her. "Well, that's kind of funny."

"What?" Donna's voice rose.

"I mean, that's unbelievable!" Charlie turned back to Kyle. "Jesus, what the hell is wrong with you? Was this Matt's idea?"

"No."

"I don't want you hanging around that kid anymore."

"It wasn't Matt's idea."

"Then whose idea was it?"

Kyle shrugged. "I don't know."

"You don't know? You don't know? Listen, kiddo, you can't do things like this. You're . . . you're practically an adult now. You . . . you're sixteen, you're tall. I mean, Jesus Christ!" He once again glanced at Donna to see if he was being sufficiently angry. She nodded approvingly, her chin thrust out.

Charlie took a couple of steps closer to the island. Even though he was secretly relieved it wasn't anything more serious, he recognized an opportunity to be a parent in front of Donna and decided to play his role to the hilt.

"Are you on drugs?" he asked.

"What?" Kyle looked shocked, as did Donna.

"You heard me!" He wanted to pound the top of the island, but was too far away, so instead he slapped his hands together like Richard Simmons leading an exercise class. "Answer the question. Are. You. On. Drugs?"

"No."

"Is Matt on drugs?"

"No."

Charlie shook his head. "Well, I'm very disappointed," he said. "Very."

"That we're not on drugs?" Kyle asked.

"That you're . . . you're . . ." he looked at Donna again. Her eyes were wide with anticipation. She was waiting for what came next. "I'm disappointed that you're a . . ."

"A graffiti-person," Donna said.

He looked at her, then waved his hand at her like they were playing charades.

"A vandal," she said.

Charlie snapped his fingers, then pointed at her. "Yes! A vandal!"

"We didn't break anything," Kyle said. "It was just a joke."

"Just a joke. I bet the cops were laughing their asses off. What did they want? Tickets to your next comedy act?" Donna nodded at this last salvo and Charlie knew parent points were rapidly accumulating.

"Did we get a ticket or what?" Charlie asked.

"They said it's a misdemeanor crime." Donna closed her eyes when she said the word crime and her bottom lip began to protrude. "A crime," she said softly.

This word shook Charlie as well. First Tamales's desk, and now this. Another Baker flirting with jail time. "Damn it, Kyle! A crime. A *crime*! You have a record. This is going to follow you around the rest of your life. Forget about college. You're through! *Through!* You're going to end up in the army or . . . or working at Gas City."

"They're not going to charge him," Donna said. "They gave him a warning."

Charlie settle down a bit. "Well, that's good."

"But we have to pay a fine. Five hundred dollars."

"Five hundred dollars!"

"Plus we have to go out and change every sign tonight."

"What do you mean? What are you talking about?"

"We have to change every sign back. From Fart to Art," she said.

"How are we going to do that?"

She held up two black Magic Markers. "With these."

Charlie looked at the markers, then at Kyle, then at Donna, then at the markers again. "How many signs are there?"

"Thirty-four," she said.

Donna and Charlie used to sit in parked cars before they were married. The cars were their oasis, their hideout. He was living at home with his parents while attending grad school, and she was living with her father and brothers, and cars were the only place they could be alone. They used to cruise the South Side looking for empty parking lots and quiet side streets where they could take up temporary residence and have sex. Looking back on it, Charlie thought they were too old for that kind of behavior, but they didn't have much choice. Money was tight and apartments or motels were not an option.

Parked under a streetlight in front of the closed Starbucks in downtown Wilton, waiting for Kyle to change the signs, Charlie's mind flashed back to those times: how they would climb into the backseat and wrap their legs and arms around each other, how the windows would sometimes steam up in the fall and winter, how they lived in fear of a tap on the window. Donna had owned a number of used cars, rusted hand-me-downs from her brothers, and for a short time they served their purpose. Eventually, though, Charlie bought a new car, an accommodating Chevy Caprice, aka the Love Mobile. It was wide and comfortable and Donna cried when he finally sold it for the red BMW. He glanced over at her now, sitting silently next to him, and recognized the irony of the situation. The hope of having sex with her in a bed, much less a car, presently did not exist. He decided not to think about that and instead searched the street for Kyle.

"I wish he could work faster," he said.

"He does everything slow. That's the way he is."

"He's really slow. Is that normal, to be that slow?"

Donna didn't respond. Charlie spotted Kyle about half a block up on Main Street and started up the Navigator to follow him.

They had been driving around the neighborhood, restoring the Fart Fair signs to their original, true meaning, for more than an hour. When they located a sign, Kyle would jump out of the backseat and blot out the F with a black marker, while they followed him. It was, Charlie realized, their first real family outing in years.

"Thank God it's dark," he said. He stopped on Ellenby Avenue, adjacent to Main Street, and watched Kyle perform his penance on another sign, this one attached to the front door of a bank. "Do they really need all these signs?" he asked.

"Everything in this town is overblown."

"Why doesn't everyone just park in the high school? Do they really need thirty-four signs to tell people where to park for an art fair?"

"The fair is in the art center, not the high school," Donna said. She glanced over at Charlie, who was slouched all the way down in his seat. "You don't have to sit like that," she said. "It's not like the paparazzi are after us."

"Hey, I'm embarrassed by this," Charlie said. He sank lower in his seat.

"It's late. No one's out," Donna said.

They watched Kyle scurry across the street to another sign, this one on a streetlight pole.

"How come Matt doesn't have to do this?" he asked.

"He has to do something else. Work at the art fair."

Charlie lowered the window a crack and watched as Kyle reached another streetlight. It was close to ten o'clock and, other than Will's, all the other businesses, the overpriced antique shops and clothes boutiques, were long closed, their lights out. Rather than appearing abandoned, Wilton looked never-lived-in.

"This is a weird town," he said.

"You're just figuring that out?"

"Maybe we were wrong in moving here." He made this comment without thinking, and Donna looked at him.

"Little late for that," she said.

"Maybe it's not."

"What are you saying?"

"We can move anytime we want. We can do anything we want. As soon as I get situated."

Donna looked out her window. "I've been meaning to ask . . . how's that going?"

"Okay. I have an interview coming up with Xanon. It's a good job."

"Is that an agency?"

"No, it's a drug company. Pharmaceuticals."

"Is it in Chicago?"

"Yeah. Downtown."

"Xanon," Donna repeated. "I never heard of it."

"Drugs for animals. Cattle, mostly. Hogs too."

"What?"

Charlie shrugged. "Hey, it's not perfect, but I think it pays. I tell you, I'm lucky. I haven't been out that long. Things are still pretty bad out there. There aren't a lot of jobs for people like me. I know guys who've been out for years. And it's a good company."

"What about the old place, the old agency? Can you go back there?" Donna asked.

"They're laying people off."

Donna studied her fingernails while he turned down the heat.

"Did you pay that bill for the plumber?" he asked.

"Yes. You saw me do it."

He sighed. "I wished you hadn't. Did you transfer funds over from the money market?"

"Yes."

"Did we have enough in there?"

"Yes. For now."

"I called the office and they told me they were late with paychecks, that's why it bounced. Business must be really bad there. I mean *really* bad. I never heard of something like that happening."

"How long are you getting paid?"

"Another month."

"That's it?"

"That's it."

"That's why Xanon is a good company."

"That's why Xanon is a great company," Charlie said.

He kept his eyes on Kyle as he crossed back over to their side of the street. He was stooping over, trying to make himself seem smaller, if not invisible.

"What's his punishment going to be?" Donna asked.

"Punishment? What do you mean? Isn't this enough?"

"No. This wasn't our punishment."

Charlie caught himself shrugging and stopped. He couldn't remember the last time he'd punished Kyle, and wasn't up on current options. "I don't know. Maybe we should ground him or something."

"Maybe we should make him quit the basketball team."

"What? Oh, no. That's too harsh. Way too harsh. It's not like he robbed a bank. Come on. It's a prank. Jesus. He's a good kid. He's not on drugs."

"How do you know he's not on drugs?"

"He told us."

"Charlie."

"He's not on drugs."

"Not yet," Donna said. "But we have to watch him."

"Yeah, well, Kyle would never do that. He's a good kid."

"He's no angel," Donna said. "He's gotten in trouble before."

"What do you mean, trouble? Like what?"

"Cutting classes. Not doing homework."

"When did all that start happening?"

"Last year."

"How come I didn't know about this?"

Donna didn't say anything, and she didn't have to.

"Well, I'm going to be around more," Charlie said. "Even if I get a job at Xanon or wherever, I'll be home more. And I'll talk with him about this stunt. I'll deal with it."

Donna didn't respond to this either. She went back to looking out the window.

Charlie continued. "Anyway," he said, "in the grand scheme of things, it really isn't so bad." He started the Navigator and moved up a few parking spaces while Kyle half jogged down the street toward the historic square.

"Yes, it is."

"It's not that bad. I mean, when I was his age I did some dumb things. I was thrown out of our Christmas dance my senior year in high school. My date and I were caught drinking in the parking lot. I was suspended for a week. I should have been expelled."

Donna seemed interested in this. She turned and looked at him. "I never heard that. Who did you go with?"

"To the dance? I went with Mary Anne Sullivan. Why?"

"I didn't know you went out with her."

"I did."

"I didn't know that," Donna said again.

"Why are you so interested?"

"She was very pretty."

Charlie nodded proudly. "Yes, she was." Then he said, "I went out with her a few times," which wasn't true at all.

"I can't believe she went out with you."

"What is that supposed to mean?"

"She was a cheerleader."

"So? What's your point?"

"I mean, you had braces and everything. You were so skinny."

"I was a teenager. Everyone had braces." He pretended to sound annoyed, but wasn't. Though they were only discussing Mary Anne Sullivan and his Christmas dance more than thirty years prior, this was the most Donna and he had talked in months and he wanted to keep the dialogue going (communicate! *Road to Recovery*). Only after diplomatic relations had been officially restored could he inquire about other critical family issues, such as the long-term future of their toilets, her feelings about them being evicted from their home, and the particulars of her relationship with Mr. Lighthouse. The last issue was understandably gnawing at him.

"Mary Anne Sullivan was pretty stupid," Donna said. "If I remember correctly."

"Hey. She was smart in the right places."

"Ha! Right. Like you knew what to do with those places."

"What's that supposed to mean?"

"I don't think you had even kissed a girl before me."

"That's where you're wrong. I was a man of the world when I met you."

"Yeah, right." She shook her head when she said this, but was smiling a little.

He turned the radio on, fiddled with the dial, then turned it off. Kyle had momentarily disappeared around the corner in the square.

"How long did it take them to do all these signs? When did they do this?" he asked.

"I don't know. I think they did it two days ago."

"I can't believe they did all of them."

"I'm sure there were other boys involved. Matt and Kyle won't say who. Probably boys on the basketball team."

"Who saw them?"

"I don't know, someone."

Charlie shook his head. "I bet Matt was the brains behind this. Kyle isn't that creative."

"Kyle is creative."

"I bet it was Matt's idea. He writes those plays."

"Wow, I'm glad you're so impressed with him. Changing Art to Fart isn't the mark of a genius, you know."

"Kyle isn't assertive enough to do something like this. He's too laid back. Did you know that he's playing a dead guy in a play? Or was going to play. A *dead* guy? He wasn't going to have any lines. He was just going to lie there. Don't you think that's strange?"

"Not everyone can be the star."

"I think that says something about him." He checked his cell phone, then put it back in his coat pocket. "I had the lead parts in plays in high school. *Music Man.* Do you remember that?"

Donna fell quiet. He glanced over at her leaning against the door, her face tight in thought, then turned and watched Kyle emerge from around the corner. He headed down the block, taking loping strides as he walked. In the streetlights he looked like a lonely, lost giraffe.

"Do you remember *Music Man*? Professor Harold Hill? I sang, I danced?" Charlie snapped his fingers. "My senior year. Come on, you had to remember that. It was a big deal."

"No."

"You don't? I thought you were there."

"No. Sorry, hard to believe, but I guess I missed the big show." She unbuckled her seat belt and zipped up her jacket.

"Where are you going?"

"I'm going to help him." Donna retrieved an extra marker from her purse.

"I thought you said he had to do this himself."

"It's taking too long and it's cold. He's going to be there all night and he has school tomorrow." She opened the door.

"Wait," Charlie said.

"What?" Donna had one foot outside.

"Just wait." Charlie sighed. The absolute last thing in the world he wanted to do was go out there and change those signs, which was exactly why, he knew, it was the one thing he had to do. "Get back in the car and give me the marker," he heard himself say.

"What?"

"I'll help him. You go home."

"What?"

"Give me the marker. Give it to me."

"You're going to walk home?"

"It's a few blocks." Charlie opened his door and immediately felt cold air fill the car. "Go on, now, go home. It's late. You're tired. I got this covered. Go on. It's my turn."

Donna hesitated before finally leaning over and handing him the marker. Then Charlie got out of the car, zipped up his jacket, and set off in search of his son.

Chapter Nineteen

On Friday, about two hours before his interview with Xanon International, Charlie told Ned about his dental prosthesis. He was feeling insecure about things and needed assurances on all levels. They were sitting in the nice conference room, the one with the large windows that overlooked Lake Michigan, reviewing interview techniques, when Charlie let him in on his deep, dark secret.

"A fake tooth?" Ned asked.

"A prosthesis. Can you tell? I'm worried people can tell."

Ned leaned forward and stared at Charlie's mouth. "Which one is it?"

Charlie grinned and pointed.

Ned leaned even closer, his face contorted into a grimace as he squinted. "Well, now that you mention it, I guess I can tell."

Charlie stopped grinning. "What do you mean, you can tell?"

Ned sat back. "It's a little off-color." He gestured at his own mouth. "It's different from the other teeth. Whiter. But just a touch."

"Whiter? So you mean my other teeth are yellow?"

"Not yellow. But they're not as white as the imposter."

"The prosthesis."

"Right. The imposter is almost too white. How long have you had it?" He peered at Charlie's mouth again.

"A few weeks."

Ned nodded in wonderment and in a soft, amazed voice said, "All this time and I had no idea. None whatsoever."

"Do you think they'll notice?"

Ned gave Charlie's mouth one last squint. "No. I think it blends right in with your other teeth. It matches quite well. I think you'll be fine. I don't think that will be an issue at all." He went back to the Rogers & Newman *Guide to Interviews*.

"Anyway," he said, "I assume you've researched this company? You've done your homework, I assume?"

"I'm set. I did some reading and the recruiter sent over some stuff. I know that company."

"Excellent! When were they founded, then? What year?"

"What?"

"When were they founded? What year?"

"I don't know that."

Ned looked up from the book, concerned. "I thought you did your homework."

"I didn't memorize every factoid. It's not a test."

"That's where you're wrong, Charlie! That's where you're *very* wrong. It is a test. It is *very* much a test and I highly recommend that you start treating it like one."

Ned abruptly stood and began pacing, his hands clasped behind his back, his face grim. Churchill in the war room. "Charlie . . ." he began. "Charlie, walking into a job interview is like walking into the great unknown. Do you know why that is?" He stopped pacing and looked at Charlie, eyes burning. His head was amazingly square that morning, like a portable television set.

"Because you don't know what to expect," Charlie said.

"Because you don't know what to expect," Ned repeated.

"I read your manual."

243

"You did? Excellent!" He pumped a fist, then resumed pacing. "You should know all about energy and passion, then. Energy and passion."

"I didn't read that far."

Ned stopped. "That was Chapter Two."

Charlie said nothing. His head was developing a small, dull ache, and he was tired. He had spent another near-sleepless night in the guest room, staring at the ceiling, thinking and worrying about everything: Donna, the interview, their finances, now Kyle. It was just all too much. He checked his watch, then massaged his temples with his fingertips.

Ned, unaware of Charlie's precarious state, forged ahead. "You should have at least read that chapter, you really should have," he said. "Energy and passion are essential during an interview. You have to show, you have to communicate, that you *want* the job." With that, he whirled around and dramatically pointed at Charlie like a prosecuting attorney might during a climactic point in a trial. "Do you *want* this job?"

Charlie paused. "Maybe."

"Maybe?"

"Possibly," Charlie said calmly. His headache was growing.

"Possibly?" Ned clenched his hands into a fist. "Not good enough! Not good enough at all, mister! It can't be *possibly*, it can't be *maybe*. You must want it. Want it!"

"Okay, I *want* it."

"You don't sound very convincing."

"I'll be more convincing in the interview, okay? Besides, I really don't know if I want it yet. I haven't even talked to them."

Ned conceded this point. "Fair enough, I suppose. But regardless, you must convey great interest and enthusiasm. Convince them you're interested. Very interested." He began walking again. "If you didn't get past Chapter Two, then I suspect you don't know anything about the Big C."

"The Big C."

"Chapter Three. The Big C is essential. You must have it if you have any hope of succeeding in an interview. Do you know what the Big C is, what I'm referring to?"

Charlie continued to rub his temples. "I don't know."

"Take a guess."

"I don't know."

"Guess."

"Cancer."

"Charisma!"

"Oh."

"Yes, charisma is important. It's essential that you're as charismatic as possible in an interview. May I make a very basic suggestion when it comes to enhancing your charisma? A small, simple trick?" Ned once again pointed at Charlie.

"What?"

Ned thrust his extended index finger at Charlie. "Point."

"Point?"

Ned jabbed at the air with his finger. "Yes, point when you're talking. It's very effective. There's been studies. Charismatic people point. Now, may I offer another suggestion when it comes to the Big C?"

Charlie remained silent. On one hand, he appreciated what Ned was trying to do; on the other, he had a sudden desire to push him out the window.

"Wink," Ned said.

Charlie's head throbbed harder. He glanced at the windows. He would probably have to break them first with a chair, then throw Ned out.

"Yes, winking implies a certain playful confidence, a can-do, cocksure spirit. Combined with pointing, it can be extremely effective." Ned winked and pointed at Charlie. "See how easy it is? Wink and point, wink and point. After a while, it will seem like second nature. Come, now, let's practice. You can wink first, then point, if you'd like. You might find that easier."

"That's it, that's enough. I can't do this right now. I just can't. *Please!*" He shouted this last word.

Charlie's outburst caught Ned in mid-wink. His one open eye bulged with surprise. He slowly put his finger away. "I'm just trying to help."

"I know you are, but I'm not in the mood for this right now."

Ned gave Charlie a searching look.

"Can you please open up your other eye?" Charlie asked.

"Oh. Sorry. Let's move on, then, try something else. Let's do some role-playing."

"Not that again."

"Now, I'm going to ask you some potential questions. Questions you might expect in the interview."

"I don't have time. I don't have time for any of this."

"Yes, you do."

Charlie glanced at his watch. "Hurry."

Ned quickly walked back over to Charlie and sat down across the table from him. He put a finger up to his lips.

"Charles," he said. "What would you say is your greatest weakness?"

"Charles?"

Ned nodded. "Yes, Charles. I was thinking you might want to start going by Charles, rather than Charlie. Charles is more dignified. Charlie, well, Good Time Charlie or Choo-Choo Charlie come to mind."

"You're kidding, right?"

"It's just a thought. A new job, a new beginning, a new name."

Charlie glared at him.

"I would consider it," Ned said.

Charlie continued to glare.

"Right, anyway. Char*lie*, what do you think you can bring to this organization?"

"Experience," Charlie said immediately.

"Excellent. In what area?"

"In every area."

"Can you be more specific?"

"How specific do you want me to be?"

It was now Ned's turn to be exasperated. "Well, very!"

"Fine." Charlie swallowed and his mind instantly went blank. Ned's square head zoomed in on him, a box of worry and concern.

"Can you stop looking at me like that?"

"Like what?"

"Like that. With your big square head."

"My big square what?" Ned touched the side of his face.

"You're overdoing this." Charlie knew that he should be focusing on the interview, but his mind was on Donna. She had risen early that morning and had left the house before he had, which was very unusual. He had no idea where she was, or, more importantly, who she was with. His arms tingled and he took a couple of deep breaths.

"Charlie, are you all right?"

"I'm fine."

Ned stepped closer and examined Charlie's face. "You look tired."

"I didn't get much sleep last night."

Ned nodded. "Well, that's only natural. You're nervous over this interview. It's a big opportunity."

Charlie swallowed. "It's not just that."

"Oh," Ned said. "It's something else?"

Charlie paused. "Yes. I don't know. I don't know."

"You don't know what? Oh, is it your family, may I ask? Your wife?"

Charlie paused again, then said, "Yes."

"I see. I see. Things aren't going well?"

"Not really, no."

"I see." Ned tapped the tip of his nose with a long, skinny finger. "This is common, you know. The strain when one spouse—"

"Can I ask you a question? Am I a bad person? I mean, from what you know of me?"

Ned was taken aback by this question. His eyes grew worried. "Why would you ask such a question?"

"From what you know of me. Am I obnoxious? Really obnoxious?"

Ned grimaced again and he began slowly, "Well, to be frank, you do have a temper. I've noticed that. I think you have to work on that."

"Temper?"

"Nothing major, but you have one and I think it gets in the way of things. Anyway, we're getting sidetracked here. I think you should really knock them dead in the interview and then go out with some friends tonight and just, you know, relax, have a good time." Ned punched the air when he said this. "You need to take a break from things, I think."

Charlie sadly nodded his head. "Friends. I don't have any friends."

"Oh, now, that's ridiculous. Of course you do. Everyone has friends. Even I have friends."

"Sorry, not me. I thought I did, but I don't. No one cares what happens to me, no one has offered to help."

"Now I think you're feeling sorry for yourself."

"No. I'm being honest. I'm like Tamales. Maybe worse, I'm a phony. I bought all these stupid books on Lincoln and leadership and I've never read any of them. I only read the ads in *The New Yorker*. I have a piano I can't play. I'm a fake, a phony. Like my tooth." Charlie said all this very softly while looking down at the table.

"I assure you, you are nothing like Tamales."

"I don't know. It's like I woke up and I don't know anything anymore. I used to think I knew things, like how to be a husband, a father, a . . . a friend. But I don't know how to do any of that anymore."

"That feeling isn't that uncommon," Ned quietly said. "Life can be confusing at times."

Charlie continued, "You get caught up in all the daily shit and you don't think. Can't think. Where did it all get me? All the hours, all the sacrifice? Look at me. Look at me now. I'm nothing. I would have been better off working at Gas City."

"Where? Is that a town?"

"Nothing. Never mind."

Ned studied Charlie with his intense eyes. Finally, he said, "Would you like to hear my theory?"

Charlie shrugged. "What's your theory?"

"Well," Ned started, "I've always suspected that work gives

you an excuse not to think. I've always thought that work is sort of a distraction. For most of my clients, at least at the executive level, work is just a game. They rationalize what they're doing is important. The activity, the motion, helps them avoid certain truths, keeps them from admitting certain things to themselves."

"Like?"

"That maybe it's sometimes easier to jump on a plane or go to a meeting than it is to be at home. Sometimes work is the easier way out. Work is an excuse."

Charlie considered what Ned said. "I don't know about that. Maybe. I don't know though."

They both fell quiet, then Ned said, "We should really get back to—"

Charlie cut him off. "Let me ask you another question here. Something else that has been on my mind."

"All right. Fire away."

"What would you do . . . what would you do if, say, your wife slept with another man?"

Ned's eyes widened. "Excuse me?"

"Let me clarify that: You *think* she's slept with another man. Or is sleeping with. I don't have proof. I haven't had confirmation on that. She won't discuss it."

"If your wife is sleeping with another man," Ned said.

"Yes. What would you do?"

Ned looked very uncomfortable. His face began to splotch. "To start, I guess I would ask her to immediately stop. I would insist."

"Thanks." Charlie let out a terrific sigh. "Good idea. Do you have a pen? Let me write that down." He slunk down in his chair. "The problem is that I still think I love her."

"Why is that a problem?"

"Because if she's had an affair, I'm not sure I can get past that."

"Even though you still love her?"

"Yes."

"I imagine that would be difficult," Ned said.

"I'm not sure what to do. How to handle this. I mean, she should be apologizing to me, making things right, but I'm the one making all the effort here. I'm the one still trying."

"Sounds like she's given up," Ned said.

Ned's comment shook Charlie. "Given up. Wow."

"I shouldn't have said that. I really shouldn't have. I don't even know her."

"Given up," Charlie said again. "Maybe she has. I don't know. Man, I hope not. Of course, most of this is probably my fault."

Ned stood and walked over to the large windows, his hands clasped behind his back. He cleared his throat, then spoke. "Love, relationships, they're all a mystery to me. I'm afraid I can't help you much in this regard. I have little wisdom on matters of that sort. I've never been very successful with women. So, I guess, my only piece of advice is to keep trying. If you want something, just keep going. If you love her, I mean. The heart has a way of prevailing."

Charlie didn't say anything.

Ned stepped away from the window and turned to face him. "You're not a bad person, Charlie. You have a temper, and you're self-focused, which means you're like ninety percent of the executives I deal with. The fact that you're asking questions like this, being introspective like this, is proof to me that you'll be all right, though. Most of my clients would never ask those types of questions. They go through life unaware of anything but their own careers. That's all that matters to them. They care about nothing else. I can tell you care about other things, or at least you're trying to."

Charlie shrugged and managed to say, "I think it's too late."

"It's not too late. It's never too late."

Charlie shrugged again. "Maybe you're right. I don't know."

"I'm sure I am. Anyway!" Ned clapped his hands. "I'm afraid we have to switch gears now. My job is to prepare you for this interview. So let's fight the battle at hand. Let's go do this interview, let's really knock their socks off, really give it a go, and then sort out the other issues. Are you ready for this now? Time to spark up!"

"Spark up?"

Ned shook his fist. "Right. Energy and passion! Are you ready, Charlie Baker!"

"I guess so."

"I can't hear you!"

"I said I'm ready."

Ned cupped a hand to his ear. "I still can't hear you!"

When Ned pumped his fist again, Charlie couldn't help himself. He smiled. "I'm ready," he loudly said. Then, because he knew Ned wanted him to, and because he was beginning to appreciate how much Ned seemed to care, Charlie slowly pointed and winked.

"Are you being sarcastic?" Ned asked.

"Just a little."

Ned's square face glowed. "Good luck, Charlie!" he said, and winked back.

Xanon was headquartered in downtown Chicago, not too far from the Board of Trade, near the south end of the Loop. Its location was something of an anomaly; most major corporations in Chicago had long fled to the northern or western suburbs. Xanon, however, once known as Watson Cattle & Feed, founded on May 4, 1898 (Charlie looked it up right before he left), was a traditional company that was skeptical of, if not resistant to, change. While the Watson family was still the majority shareholder, and Miss Cindy Watson, the seventy-one-year-old veterinarian and matriarch, still had a seat on the board of directors, their day-to-day involvement was minimal. For the most part, they left the company in the hands of Kevin F. Woods, the Harvard-educated, Proctor & Gamble-trained CEO. Kevin F. had been with the company for close to two years, and according to Ted Greene, the company's human resources director, he was gradually molding it in his image.

"And what image is that?" Charlie asked.

"A dynamic one."

They were having coffee in the company cafeteria on the third floor, a dark and silent place that smelled more of cleaning fluid than food. Ted was something out of human resources central casting: part psychiatrist, part Gestapo. A cautious man with inquisitive eyes and a white starched shirt, he gave the impression that he would eagerly give his life for his corporation, if only given the chance.

Their conversation had been going along well enough. They spent a good twenty minutes chitchatting about their histories, where they went to school (they both graduated from Northwestern), and where they had lived.

"I like Chicago so much more than New York," Ted said. "I lived in New York for five years and never adjusted. I never could get in the rhythm."

"That's because it has no rhythm. It lurches from note to note," Charlie said. "Chicago has a strong undercurrent to it. A consistent flow."

Ted nodded. Charlie suspected that underneath his shiny corporate veneer Ted was gay, so he was trying, subtly, to act gaylike.

"So, what kind of books do you read?" Ted asked.

"Oh, fiction." Then Charlie said, "Poetry."

Ted was impressed. "Oh, really? I enjoy poetry. Who do you read?"

Charlie waved dismissively. "No one specifically. Whoever's in *The New Yorker.*"

"Do you write any?"

Once again Charlie waved the question away. "Occasionally," he said. He quickly picked up his coffee cup, desperate, suddenly, to change the subject. The conversation had veered ridiculously off track. He had never written so much as a limerick before, much less a poem. "When are you looking to fill the spot?" he asked.

Ted sized him up, his eyes narrowing. Charlie knew every question, every word, every gesture, was being filed away to be measured, weighed, dissected in a human resources laboratory at a later time. One wrong move and he was gone. This was what his life had come down to: one wrong move.

"Soon," he said. "We're going to move fast on this. But to be fair to ourselves, it's a difficult fit. We're an evolving company. It was a family business for more than a century. We're trying to change, trying to shake things up, but we need someone to help us do that."

Charlie nodded. "I've worked for family businesses before. The transitions can be a challenge. The culture is ingrained, even if the family isn't that involved anymore. I think it has to be done in stages, phases. Pick your battles. Keep your priorities. Don't try to do too much too soon."

Even though Ted didn't respond, Charlie thought he was scoring points. "How long have you been here?" he asked.

"Two years. I've enjoyed it. We're building something here. Going in a new direction. It's been exciting."

"I can imagine," Charlie said.

Ted glanced down at a notepad. "So, tell me a little bit about what happened at D&H. I know things didn't work out."

Charlie steadied himself before jumping in. "Well, I was hired in by Bob O'Malley and then . . ." He paused and dropped his voice. "I'm sorry, but do you know what happened to him?"

Ted nodded "Tragic."

"I know." Charlie tried to look very sad before continuing. "I never really recovered from it. I was out of sync, I think. I never wanted to get the position under those circumstances. It was hard. I was trying to heal an agency, heal myself, while running a business." He paused again before saying, "He and I were close." He folded his hands on the table and stared down at them, as if in prayer.

Charlie felt Ted watching him. When he said, "That must have been difficult," Charlie sensed a light shifting of the wind. He was afraid Ted wasn't buying the O'Malley-as-second-father bit. He quickly hit the brakes and spun the steering wheel in another direction.

"And I never saw eye to eye with management," he added. "Never. It was difficult working with them. They were new to the region, new to the country, really, didn't understand our clients. They're a holding company. Bottom-line-focused. It wasn't a good situation for me."

Ted nodded. "You do good work. We've seen some of it. The toilet tissue commercials were especially memorable."

"Thank you. I enjoy what I do." Charlie sipped his coffee. It was every bit as weak and tasteless as the Rogers's brew. "Tell me about your new direction."

"It's a work in progress, really. But for the first time ever, we're thinking of doing some TV commercials. Sunday-morning-type things. More corporate profiles. We need people to know and understand that Xanon is about more than just cattle."

"What else are you about?"

"We're about hogs too."

Charlie swallowed. "Of course."

"The new products we have in the pipeline are going to change hog breeding forever."

Charlie's left arm began to tingle. Hog breeding. Hog *sex.* "Exciting," he said. Then he said, "Amazing."

Ted sipped his coffee. "So, tell me about your style. How do you like to work?"

"Oh. I'm Type A, I guess. Fortunately and unfortunately."

"Why unfortunately?"

Charlie lightly rubbed a hand over his chin and did his best to look introspective. Even though he had anticipated a question like this and even had rehearsed an answer, he wanted to appear as if he were thoughtfully searching for words. "I suppose I expect too much from other people. I want people to work as hard as I do. Stay up all night, come in on weekends. It's a weakness, but I'm working on it."

Charlie thought he detected the faintest trace, the vaguest outline, of a smile. His answer had been transparent, clichéd.

Ted said, "Kevin F. is Type A. Do you think two Type A's can work together?"

Another introspective gaze, another chin rub. "I think so, I really do. For years I worked with a client, Bagelman Delis."

"I eat there all the time. There's one right by my place."

Charlie nodded. "And Jacob, Mr. Bagelman, is Type A. Very involved. I made an effort to work with him, sought his input. All that matters are the results, not the process. You have to submerge your ego in this business. The brands are the stars."

Ted smiled. "I have to say, I enjoyed those Bagel Man commercials. This is silly and a little off subject, but did you ever meet Elton John?"

"Oh, yes, several times."

Ted's corporate shield vanished and his smile was large and genuine when he said, "I used to love Elton John. I still play some of his music. What was he like?"

Charlie recognized the opening and he scurried, ratlike, through it. Even though he had met Sir Elton just once, and even then only briefly in front of a men's room, Elton was now Charlie's twin brother. "He's fabulous. Wonderful to work with. Funny, nice. He brought a certain energy and passion to his work. We stay in touch."

"You do?"

"Yes. We e-mail each other."

"Well, that's fun," Ted said. He was still smiling.

"Yes, it is," Charlie said. Then he winked and pointed.

During the drive home, he dissected the interview. Overall, it had gone very well. After the magical Elton John connection, Ted had warmed to him considerably, opening up about the company (old-fashioned but with a real soul), why the search had taken so long (their number one candidate had dragged his feet before saying no because he didn't want to relocate from San Francisco), and Kevin F. (he was tough but fair, but mostly tough). Afterward, he went so far as to lead Charlie through a brief meet-and-greet of the marketing department. Then, even though they weren't on his schedule, Ted impulsively took him by to shake Kevin F.'s hand. Unfortunately, Kevin F.'s door was closed and his assistant said he was in conference.

On the way to the elevators, they walked past the empty chief marketing officer's office. It was late afternoon and pink sunlight was leaking through the half-open window blinds, giving the expansive room an ethereal look. As Charlie passed, he peeked in and confirmed it had more than enough space for a telescope and a new gumball machine.

He was replaying his parting with Ted—they had patted each other on the back, always a good sign—when the Wizard called.

"Hi, chief. Heard it went well." His voice sounded particularly Lauren Bacall-ish.

"Where did you hear that?"

"A little Elton John–loving bird. Say, I'd like to read one of your poems one day. Could you send me one?"

"What's the next step?"

"Before we get to that, what did you think? Are you interested? It's not an agency. It's old-line and it's animals. And remember, you'll be a manager, not creative director. Lots of administration, lots of H.R. bullshit. So before we go much further, I need to know you're serious."

"What does it pay?"

"Four and a quarter, plus bonus."

"I'm serious."

"That's my boy." Preston's voice changed, his cadence quickening. "They're going to move fast on this," he said. "They've lost so much time. I think they're going to bring you in for an all-day thing, meet the team, bond a little."

"Fine."

"So, we're proceeding?"

"Yes, absolutely."

"Okay, some advice. This is our little secret. Don't tell anyone you're talking to them. It's best to keep things quiet when you're in discussions."

"My lips are sealed."

"That's good. Up, up, and away, then, chief."

"Yep. Up, up."

The Wizard's call gave him a jolt of optimism. He turned the radio on, then turned it up high. Beach Boys. "Good Vibrations." A sign. A good sign. Things would turn out okay, he thought. He would get a job, jump-start the cash flow, and then fix things at home.

As he fought his way through traffic, however, his good mood slowly, inexplicably began to dissipate. The doubts, which, he knew, were always there, finally began to reveal themselves. Exactly what was he doing? Was this the right move for him? Did he even want this job? He had been out less than two months and was already getting a serious look. Maybe he was going too fast and settling too early. Maybe the phone would start ringing, connecting him to his dream job. He wasn't exactly sure what his dream job was anymore, but he was pretty sure hog breeding wasn't involved.

He turned off the radio and put both hands on the steering wheel.

While he was never a subscriber to the bird-in-the-hand philosophy, he was fifty years old and had to avoid Bradley's situation at all costs. He could not survive long financially without a mature money tree in his backyard. Despite a lifetime of large earnings, he had little to show for it other than a heavily mortgaged house with bad pipes and mounting bills. Plus, his severance package was ending soon and the economy was hardly robust. He mulled these factors over and, by the time he pulled off the expressway, concluded that his decision, in effect, was already made. He needed this job, therefore he wanted it. And he was prepared do to everything he could to get it.

At home, he found things empty and dark. He called out to Donna and Kyle, but got no answer. A quick search of the first floor confirmed that he was alone.

Fighting back a sense of gloom, he poured himself a glass of pinot, then headed upstairs to the office to send off an e-mail, to Ted Greene:

> Ted:
> Just a note to say it was terrific meeting you! The more I learn about Xanon, the more excited I become. It's a dynamic company with a clear vision of where it wants to go. That's not only refreshing, it's rare.
> My best,
> Charlie Baker

P.S. So funny! I just got an e-mail from Elton. He's alive and well and loving life—as always! I told him I met you—his biggest fan. He was amused.

Afterward, he checked his Rogers & Newman e-mail to see if anyone had responded to the second edition of *The Charlie Update!* He had but one message, from Terry Pocius, a midlevel member of his B-list, someone he hadn't seen or heard from in at least three years.

Charlie: Been out for 16 months. If you know of something at the director level, give me a call. I'll take anything, go anywhere. Thanks. TP

This note quickened his descent. Terry was a bright, hardworking woman with solid credentials. The fact that she had been out so long didn't make sense. There was no reason for people like her, like Bradley, like Karen, or Charlie, not to be working. Her message confirmed what he suspected: Xanon was a gift, if not a miracle. He could not end up like Terry. Sixteen months.

He was in the process of logging off, but changed his mind, and impulsively wrote a response:

Terry:
Good to hear from you. I will let you know if I hear of anything. Hang in there. I know things are rough right now, but they'll get better.

Then,

I'm getting close to something. If I get it, I'll try to set up an interview for you, maybe bring you in if I can.

He reread his message, added, *Stay in touch!*—then sent it off and went back downstairs to the kitchen, where he called

Donna. She didn't pick up and this worried him. Though she was probably running an errand, an image of her boarding a Maine-bound United Airlines flight came to mind and hovered. He poured himself another glass of the pinot and sat at the island.

He was halfway through the wine when he heard the music. It was soft and gentle, like rain at night. He started, popping off his stool, a hand to his chest, heart racing. Someone was playing the piano, his piano, the Great Unused. He stood by the refrigerator and listened to this foreign sound, both an intrusion and a delight, trying to process things. It was either Kyle, he concluded, or a very talented burglar.

He carefully made his way into the living room, approaching the piano from behind. He stopped when he confirmed that it was indeed Kyle playing, though it easily could have been a stranger, from the way he looked. His posture was perfect, his shoulders unaccustomedly square and balanced, his head bent down in concentration. The song was the standard Gershwin's "Rhapsody in Blue," but Kyle played it with great life and feeling.

Charlie close his eyes and listened, recognizing the moment for what it was. His son playing the piano, his son making beautiful music in the dark. He drank in the moment, letting the requisite lump form in his throat, and clapped loudly when Kyle finished.

Kyle turned so quickly he almost fell off the bench. He had to steady himself with a hand.

"I didn't know you could do that," Charlie said.

"I didn't know you were home."

"I didn't know *you* were home."

"I just got here," Kyle said.

Charlie pushed off from the wall and flipped on the light switch. Kyle's backpack and coat were lying in a heap on the floor. "You could probably play even better if you could see."

"I can see okay," he mumbled.

"Who taught you that song? Your piano teacher?"

259

He shrugged. "I don't know. I just know how to play it," he said.

"Do you know other songs?"

"Yeah, a few."

"Can I hear some more? Play anything, I don't care."

Kyle hesitated and Charlie realized that he had walked in on a secret, interrupted something private. He was not supposed to share in this moment. "I got to do some homework," Kyle said. "I got to finish an English paper."

"Oh. All right. I'd like to hear you play some other time, though. You're good."

"Yeah, okay." Kyle started to gather up the sheet music. "Where's Mom?" he asked over his shoulder.

"I don't know. I was hoping you did."

He glanced back at Charlie. "She's usually here when I get home."

"Well, she's out, that's all."

"Yeah, but she's usually here when I get back from practice."

"She's out shopping, then. Or at that community place."

Kyle turned away and faced the piano. His posture was eroding, his shoulders sagging. "You think she left again?"

"What do you mean?"

"You know, do you think she left again?"

His question, asked simply and with sadness, shook Charlie. All he could think to say was, "She'll never leave us. Especially you."

Kyle sat in the shadows, looking very much like the young boy he still was, a boy in the middle of things. He deserved better than this, deserved better than to be playing the piano alone in the dark worrying if his parents were getting divorced. Charlie felt a flash of anger toward Donna, but was mostly angry at himself. He hadn't given any thought to how his and Donna's situation was affecting Kyle.

"She'll be back," Charlie said. "She's just out. She'll be back."

Just then, as if on cue, the headlights of Donna's car splashed and slid sideways across the wall. A second later, they both heard the garage door opening. Kyle glanced again at Charlie.

"See? She's back," Charlie said, trying hard not to look as relieved as he felt.

Chapter Twenty

The next day, Charlie ran into Karen Brisco in the coffee room. She was wearing a short skirt that barely covered her thighs, shiny black spiked heels, and a definitely too-tight white blouse that lovingly gift-wrapped her breasts in a way that made him feel like the fraternity man he had once been. She smiled at him as he reached for the coffeepot.

"You look nice today," he said.

"Thanks. I have an interview later."

"Hey, that's great." He wondered if it was with an escort service.

"How are things going with you? Got anything going on?"

He poured a short cup of coffee and sniffed it critically, hoping that for once it was fresh. "Yes, actually. I had a good meeting yesterday."

Karen smiled. She had been ambitious with the makeup this morning, her lips a glossy red. "Really? Great. Who with?"

Charlie hesitated. While talking about Xanon would give him the opportunity to examine her a bit longer, he remembered the Wizard's words of caution. "Top secret."

She stamped her high-heeled foot. "Give me a clue. Come on. Who am I going to tell? No one ever tells anyone anything here. Drives me nuts."

"I'll tell you later."

She shook her head and he took a sip of his coffee and deemed it drinkable. "How about you? Anyplace I might know?"

"Yeah, and I'm not afraid to talk about it. Be Sport. A sporting goods company. It's Australian-based. They're opening a regional office here in Chicago. It's a long shot and I'm not really that interested because I think it's more promotional work than public relations."

"Can't hurt to go check it out."

"That's my attitude."

He was trying not to stare at Karen's wonderfully firm thighs as she bent down to retrieve some juice from the refrigerator when the Great Pockmarked One, Tamales himself, strutted into the room. He had kept a low profile since the desk caper, and Charlie was surprised to see him out and about. He looked hawkish this morning, his nose hooked and sharp, his hair buzzed shorter than usual. He dismissed Charlie with a beady-eyed glance and headed over to the water cooler.

"Hello, Tom," Karen said. She shook a carton of orange juice.

Tamales drank some water. When his eyes found Karen, they wouldn't let go. After he finished, he crumpled up his Dixie cup and tried to toss it into the wastebasket. He missed, though, and it bounced off the rim, landing on the floor. He made no effort to pick it up. That was someone else's job.

"Congratulations on your news," Karen said.

"What news?" Charlie asked.

"Thanks," Tamales said. He was blatantly staring at her, an incredulous smile creeping over his creepy face. "Why don't you stop by later? There's something I'd like to discuss with you."

"Oh. Okay," Karen said.

"Give me a few minutes," he said. He gave her one last look before he strutted away.

After he was gone, Charlie asked, "He didn't get a job, did he? He didn't!"

"Honda," she said.

"Come on! No way. He's only been here about, what, a few weeks? That's impossible."

"It's possible. He was talking with them before he got fired."

"What?" Charlie was floored by this. "I can't believe that. That guy gets fired every year. Why do people keep hiring him?"

"Certain people always get jobs." She straightened her blouse and ran a hand through her hair. It was then that Charlie realized who she was really dressing for that day.

"I got to go," she said. "Wish me luck."

"Yeah. Good luck."

She picked up Tamales's crumpled cup and dropped it into the wastebasket. "Thanks," she said.

A little more than a week later, he had his second, and two days after that, his third interview with Xanon. Each time, Ted Greene greeted him in the reception area with a warm handshake and the now-expected pat on the back. Throughout Charlie's visits, Ted was an amiable host and tour guide, introducing Charlie to everyone and anyone who crossed their path. Charlie officially met with half a dozen people: four very polite but cautious directors in the marketing department (cautious because they would report to Charlie), the chief financial officer, and the head of research and development. All told, he spent two six-hour days in the somber, thick-carpeted halls of Xanon, grinning, shaking hands, asking questions, and listening. By the time he made it down to the parking garage after the second day, he was physically and emotionally drained.

The moment he got inside the Navigator, the Wizard called.

"How goes it, chief?"

"I'm exhausted. If I have to use my personality one more time, I'll die."

"Long day, I know. But whatever you're doing, keep doing it. All the reports are thumbs-up."

"Well, that's good." He started up the Navigator and headed toward the exit.

"So you're still on board?"

"Holding on with both hands," Charlie said.

"I want to give you a heads-up about something, then. I don't think it's a big deal, but that frenetic thing came up, apparently."

Frenetic. Charlie hit the brakes when he heard that word. Behind him, someone honked. He scowled in the rearview mirror. "What do you mean? What did they ask?"

"They asked if there was any validity to it."

"So they basically asked if I was insane."

"That's not what they asked."

"What did you say?"

"I said I wouldn't be working with you if there was."

"Why do you think they asked about that now?"

"Because you're getting close."

Charlie frantically retraced the events of the afternoon, wondering if he had, in any way, shape, or form, acted insanely. (Why did he order cappuccino instead of coffee at lunch?) Finally, he yelled, "I knew I should have sued someone! Goddamn it! Goddamn it!"

"I wouldn't worry about it too much."

"Too much? But I *should* worry about it? Is that what you're saying?"

"I just wanted you to be aware of it, that's all, in case they ask. Don't bring it up, though."

"This just pisses me off!" He turned onto lower Wacker Drive and, for no reason, honked. "How bad is this going to hurt me? Are they talking to someone else?"

"Maybe one other candidate, I'm not sure. Listen, I have to run."

"Have to run? You always have to run. You're supposed to be helping me. Not running off every second! I'm not some stupid brand manager, some director of marketing!"

"Calm down, Charlie. I'm on your side, remember?"

"Don't tell me to—" Charlie caught himself. "All right. Okay."

He paused again and tried to compose himself. He took a deep breath.

"I have to go now," the Wizard said, his voice now stiff and formal. "I'll call."

"Hey, wait, Preston, wait," Charlie began. He took a breath. "Listen, I'm sorry I went off like that. It's—I'm . . . everything is just so messed up—"

"Got to run, chief. We'll talk."

"All right. Yeah, okay." Charlie slowly laid the phone onto the passenger seat, took one last deep breath, and drove on in silence, both hands on the wheel.

Before he got home, he impulsively stopped off and picked up dinner at Paulie's, a small Italian place that radiated garlic and Chianti. He had been meaning to stage a family dinner for weeks, but Donna or Kyle's schedule had never allowed it. This time, he was just going to bring home some food and force the issue.

Paulie's was located one suburb over in a nondescript strip mall and, having developed something of a cult following with commuters, was usually crowded. Tonight was no exception. He had to stand in line for fifteen minutes to place his order— three lasagnas, a large Italian salad, a loaf of garlic bread— then, rather than hover by the door and wait for his food, he walked back out to the Navigator to review the Bright Day annual report.

He was supposed to have worked on this for Donna months ago, but hadn't gotten around to it. Seeing it on the kitchen counter that morning, he had made a copy and taken it to the office, where he spent a good two hours reviewing, then editing it before his interview. It was still in draft form, but Donna had done a good job; her writing was, for the most part, strong and clear. Still, he thought it needed some work, especially in terms of tone.

Sitting in the Navigator, he quickly reassessed his notes in the margins, hoping he hadn't overstepped his bounds. He had been particularly aggressive in his comments on the ending, rewriting the last two paragraphs to reflect a more hopeful view: *Everyone has potential, everyone has a future. By working together, there's no telling what we can achieve.*

He now thought the closing predictable. He probably should have researched the organization—he was embarrassed how little he knew about it or what Donna even did there—before jumping in and writing. Donna had no idea he was working on this and he wanted to surprise her with a good effort. He berated himself for being lazy, then went back inside to pick up the food.

When he got home, he found the house (as always, it seemed) dark and empty. Moving quickly, he heated up the lasagna and bread in the oven, tossed up the salad, then set three places at the kitchen table. A few minutes later, while he was pulling the food out of the oven, Donna and Kyle arrived home together.

"Where were you guys?" Charlie asked.

"I picked him up from practice," Donna said. She scanned the table. "What's this?"

Charlie proudly laid the tray of lasagna on the table. "I got something from Paulie's, that place we like. I just heated it up. You're supposed to heat it up. Thought we could all eat together, for once." He made his way over to the wine refrigerator. "You want some wine?"

"We just ate," Kyle said. "At McDonald's."

Charlie stopped dead in his tracks, his hand on the refrigerator handle. "Oh," he said.

"We ate a lot," Kyle said.

They were all quiet.

"Well," Charlie said, letting go of the handle. "I guess I should have called."

"You can eat," Donna finally said.

"I'm not really hungry."

"Why did you buy all this food, then?" Kyle asked.

"I don't know. I thought you would be hungry."

They all looked again at the food. Charlie was beginning to feel foolish.

"I got to go," Kyle said. He vanished around the corner without even taking off his jacket.

"I guess I can put this in the fridge," Charlie said. "Maybe we can eat it tomorrow."

"Yeah, maybe," Donna said. She walked into the mudroom and took off her coat. "His first game is tomorrow, though."

"We can eat it after the game, maybe."

She walked back through the kitchen, passing him on her way to the family room. "I might have a meeting," she said over her shoulder.

"Oh, okay. Well . . ."

He slowly wrapped up the food and put everything away on the bottom shelf of the refrigerator. Then he unset the table, quietly putting the plates back in the cabinet, and swept the floor, though it didn't really need sweeping. When he was done, he retrieved his briefcase from the front hall and pulled out the copy of the Bright Day annual report. He had planned on reviewing his comments with Donna after dinner, maybe over a second glass of wine, and explaining his changes, but no longer felt the time or his mood were right. So instead he laid it on the now-cleared kitchen table where she would find it and wearily trudged upstairs.

He spent the evening alone in his office under the watchful gaze of Abe Lincoln and the Cuckoo for Cocoa Puffs Bird, half-heartedly searching job Web sites, and checking their finances. Around ten o'clock, rather than head down to the guest room where he had been spending his nights, he stretched out on the floor and thought about things.

Mostly, he thought about Donna. Despite his efforts, she had given him little encouragement. Since her return, she had remained, for the most part, distant and removed. Lying on the floor, he began to fear that she had only come back because of Kyle. How long she would stay, he couldn't be sure.

Sounds like she's given up.

He slung an arm over his face and, not for the first time in the past few months, marveled at his plight, amazed at the depth and speed of his descent and how someone could just stop loving you like that.

He eventually fell into a deep sleep full of short, disturbing dreams, dreams a psychiatrist would have a field day with: him running in an airport barefoot, leaving his BlackBerry on the train, being on an elevator that never stopped. When he finally jerked awake many hours later in the middle of the night, he found the room dark and it took a moment for him to get his bearings: he was still on the office floor, but covered with a blanket. He pulled it up tight to his chin, took deep breaths to calm himself, then fell back asleep while listening to the gentle hum of what he believed to be the ceiling fan. It wasn't until morning, however, while he was stretching his stiff body awake, that he realized that that gentle noise was, in fact, his humidifier, which had been quietly set up in a far corner of the room.

Chapter Twenty-one

A few days later, Ned entered Charlie's office after lunch and confessed that he was obsessed with Karen Brisco.

"I find myself aroused whenever I'm around her," he said. "It's very distracting. This has never happened to me before. I think about her often. For no special reason. Every time I see a woman, I think she looks like Karen. I think, oh, if her hair were a little longer, or if she were a little shorter, she would be Karen. Just this morning on the bus, I saw someone who was her identical twin. I couldn't believe the resemblance. I kept staring at her, I couldn't help myself. Well, finally the woman looks over at me and it turns out it *was* Karen. She was only sitting one seat away. I'm completely losing perspective."

"I'm in the middle of something right now," Charlie said. He had been researching the pinkeye cattle virus in an attempt to determine if humans, particularly middle-aged chief marketing officers, could contract it from cows. "I want to finish a few things."

Ned didn't seem to hear him. He plunked down in a chair and continued to talk about Karen. "I've given this quite a bit of thought," he said. "On the one hand, I want to pursue things with her, since we're both unattached, and in the same age bracket—we're ten years apart and I consider that the same age bracket—but on the other, I worry that it isn't professional. I'm afraid it will come to a bad end and somehow compromise my position here." He shifted his focus to Charlie. "This is all very confidential, of course. I hope you will be discreet with what I'm telling you."

"Of course."

"What do you think?" Ned asked.

"About what?"

"About her. Karen and me."

"I'm not sure."

"Have you ever had a romance with someone you worked with?"

"No."

"Neither have I. But I'm forty-two years old. I feel I shouldn't pass things up. I haven't had sex in three years," Ned said. "Well, four years, because that one time wasn't really sex, technically."

"Why are you telling me this?"

"Because Bradley isn't in yet."

Charlie considered sharing his suspicions regarding Karen and Tamales, but decided against it. Though it was an educated one, it was, after all, still just a hunch. He also didn't want to be the one to break Ned's horny heart. So instead he said, "I'm probably the last person you want to talk about love with."

"Oh, yes, of course, I'm sorry," Ned said. "How are things at home? Your suspicion about your wife . . . have you . . . had any confirmation on that?"

"No."

"I see. Well, are things any better with her, then?"

Charlie thought about the humidifier and the blanket from the night before. "I might be making some headway. A little, maybe. I don't know. I'm trying. She's hard to read, though. I'm not sure what she wants me to say or do."

"Just keep trying. I'm sure things will work out. Just keep at it. Speak from the heart. Don't tell her what you think she wants to hear, just tell her the truth. Women can detect insincerity, I suspect. At least, that's what I've heard or read."

Charlie took this in. "Thanks. Thank you. I'll do that."

Ned sat back in his chair and crossed his legs. Long white socks shot out from under his pants leg. "And how are things proceeding with the animal company, the cattle place?"

"Fine. I'm meeting with them again in a few days. I think something might happen there."

Ned's eyes grew large. He sat back up. "What do you mean? They're going to make you an offer? In a few days? This week?"

"Maybe. I'm not sure. But maybe, yeah."

This news threw Ned into a tizzy. He started splotching and sputtering. "Charlie, that's . . . that's . . . why, that's terrific news!"

"Yes, it is."

"But you don't sound very excited."

"Oh, I am. I am."

"But you don't sound it."

"I am," Charlie said.

"But?"

"But? There is no but."

Ned gave Charlie a knowing look. "I believe there is a but."

Charlie paused. "Okay, maybe the field isn't that exciting," he decided to say. "And I think I'll be gone a lot again. A lot of travel. And I'll be managing again, not really doing the creative work, not that there's much creative to be done there." He caught himself. "But it's still a good job. I'd be lucky to have it. It fell in my lap. Things are terrible out there."

Ned didn't say anything. Instead, he examined Charlie's face.

"What now?" Charlie asked.

"May I speak honestly?"

"What?"

"I think you're conflicted."

"Conflicted?"

"Down deep, I think you suspect this job might not be right for you. There will be lots of stress."

"I didn't say it was a perfect job. There's stress in every job."

"It varies. The stress in some jobs consumes you. In others, it doesn't. In this one it sounds like it might."

Charlie paused again. He was becoming irritated with Ned. "I thought your job was to help me get a job."

"My job is to help you get the right job."

"This job pays four hundred thousand. Maybe more. It's the right job, trust me."

"Is it?"

"Yes, it is. I don't want to work in some piece-of-shit job. Sit in some cubicle."

"It doesn't have to be a piece of..." Ned shook his head. "Fine. Whatever. I didn't mean to get you worked up."

"I'm not worked up."

"All I'm saying is maybe you shouldn't rush things. Maybe you should consider options, take a step back and reevaluate. Consider a job that maybe offers some balance, a chance to be home more. It may pay less, but it might be worth it. Remember our discussion about work being a game? Ask yourself, are you just trying to get ahead in the game, or are you trying to get ahead in your life?"

Charlie swallowed hard. He looked past Ned at the wall, then back at him. "I'm busy, so are we done here?" he said.

Ned gave Charlie one final, searching look. "Apparently we are," he said.

After Ned left, he stared at a poster of a silver-haired construction worker with oversized biceps operating a forklift on a loading dock (IT CAN BE DONE...AND NOW) and mulled things over. Ned's points had, of course, echoed some of Charlie's own private doubts about the job at Xanon, which was why, he knew, he had grown so short with him.

He eventually began searching Web sites for jobs that might minimize stress. He searched for more than an hour, but the only thing he found that even remotely fit his qualifications was a position for senior marketing director for a nonprofit group called the Midwest Parks and Recreation Association. It was a decent-sized group, probably paid a quarter of what he had made, but was located in a suburb only fifteen minutes from his house.

Could he be happy in a job like this? Could he spend the last third of his career promoting parks and recreation? Swing sets and monkey bars? Midwest summers? Brown-bagging his lunch, overseeing a small staff of two or three recent college graduates, being home for dinner every night at six P.M. in time to watch the evening news? Little or no travel?

He thought about this and wondered what he would do with all that extra time. For years he had filled every available minute with work. He had become addicted. Consumed.

He hadn't always been this way. When he was just starting out, he had some balance. He recalled family dinners, neighborhood barbecues, school plays. He remembered once even calling in sick to go to a White Sox game with Donna. Calling in sick! He must have been a different person back then. What happened? Why had he changed? To be sure, he had become more materialistic, and more competitive, but there had to be other reasons. Those were too easy, too obvious.

He then thought about something Ned had said: work is an excuse. He began to suspect that there might be some truth to that. Maybe, just maybe, as he got older and being a parent and a husband got tougher, he took the easier way out. Maybe, just maybe, rather than going to work all these years, allegedly for Donna and Kyle, he actually had been running away from them. To pursue his own interests, he thought.

He sat back in his chair, considered, but did not completely concede this point. Then he got up for some water.

In the kitchen area, he ran into Bradley, who was once again wearing his blue suit. Charlie now suspected that this was the only suit he owned.

"Hey, there, partner," Bradley said. He blew into a gray Rogers & Newman coffee cup and smiled.

"What's going on, there, Bradley?" Charlie made his way over to the refrigerator.

"Going good, going good."

"Things still moving along with that job?"

"Things are proceeding nicely. All systems go." Bradley winked. "That's all I'm going to say about that, though, buddy, right now. Don't want to disturb the karma."

"Karma is key." Charlie searched for a bottle of water in the refrigerator, but didn't find one. Instead, he poured himself a short cup of coffee, even though he knew the afternoon coffee was especially rancid, since it had been sitting there for hours. He was leaning back on the counter when he noticed something sticking out of the side pocket of Bradley's jacket. He was about to comment when he realized what it was: several packages of coffee and creamer that Bradley was obviously smuggling home. He quickly looked away.

"Hey, I have Bulls tickets," Bradley said. He again blew into his coffee. "Got them from a friend. I'm not a big basketball fan, but I'm thinking of going—"

"Shit!"

"What's wrong?"

Charlie put his coffee down and pushed off from the counter. "I gotta go."

"Where? Everything okay?"

"My son's first game is tonight. It's at six. I almost forgot."

Bradley checked his watch. "It's just after four. You got time."

"Yeah, but I can't be late," Charlie said as he raced out. "I cannot be late."

He was late. Traffic was terrible, a flipped-over van had things backed up forever, and by the time he found Donna, sitting up high in the bleachers, third row from the back wall, his heart was pounding, his adrenaline in overdrive. As soon as he saw her, he immediately launched into his well-rehearsed apology.

"I'm really sorry," he said. "But traffic was unbelievable! I tried, but it wasn't moving. I left at four o'clock. I was sitting there for two hours. Two hours. I tried to call you. I called twice. Did you get my message? It was on the radio. The accident."

Donna surprised him by saying, almost cheerfully, "That's

okay, I just got here," and scooting over to make room for him on the bench. "Hurry up. It just started. There's no score."

"Oh." Charlie was confused and relieved. At the very least, he had expected the silent treatment. He glanced over his shoulder, down at the court, then sat. "Yeah, good, okay. I'm sorry, though. I left—"

"I said, okay. Relax."

The gym was hot and crowded with people crammed shoulder to shoulder. Off to one side, blue-and-gold-clad cheerleaders kicked their legs and yelled, "*Go Lions*," through cone-shaped megaphones. Up in the dark rafters, oversized banners celebrating past conference championships somberly hung. Charlie looked up at them, impressed. Apparently, the Lions were a powerhouse: he counted five straight titles.

As soon as Charlie got situated, he scanned the Wilton bench for Kyle. "Where is he?"

"He's playing," Donna said.

"What? He's playing? You mean in the game? You're kidding." He searched the floor and found Kyle standing out of bounds under the far basket, about to pass the ball in.

"What's he doing? He's got the ball in his hands," he said. This amazed him. Based on his role in *Mr. Vengeance*, he had assumed Kyle was a seldom-used reserve. "Does he start?"

"Yes," Donna said. "He's the starting point guard."

Charlie immediately sat taller, his chest inflating. "He starts," he said loudly to no one. "That's unbelievable. I didn't know he was a starting point guard. He's only a junior. He must be pretty good. I mean, look at all those banners. This is a good team. This is great." He was feeling an uncontrollable and completely unfamiliar rush of excitement and pride.

His pride exploded a few seconds later when Kyle took the ball deep in the corner and hit a three-point shot. Overwhelmed, Charlie leaped to his feet, pounded his chest, and let out a primal scream.

"Unbelievable! That was unbelievable." He looked down at Donna, who was frozen in embarrassment. "Did you see that shot? It was all net. All net!" His face was hot and he was breathing fast. Donna gently tapped the bench and he sat down.

He shot back up a moment later, though, when Kyle stole a pass at midcourt and went in uncontested for a layup. "Did you see that? That's amazing. How's he doing this? I mean, what is going on?" Several people turned to look at him.

"That's my son," Charlie said, pointing back down to the court. "Number thirty-three. Kyle Baker. I'm his biological father."

"Charlie, please!"

He sat back down. "I'm sorry. You know how I get. But are you seeing this, are you *seeing* this? That's Kyle out there," he said. "He's scoring baskets, everything. That's Kyle. Our son!" Without thinking, he grabbed Donna and planted a big, sloppy kiss on her cheek.

She was shocked by this, her face flushing red. She quickly pulled away from him. "I know who it is," she calmly said. But a second later, she briefly reached over, took his hand, and squeezed it.

Throughout the game, Kyle continued to score, it seemed, at will. Charlie watched in disbelief as he weaved, cut, passed, and dribbled his way around other players, his face uncommonly focused, his jaw set, his hair flopping. As the point guard, he handled the ball during nearly every Wilton possession, pointing to other players and barking out orders, directing their movement and flow. His transformation from Mr. Laid Back to confident field general was incomprehensible. If it weren't for his breathing techniques, Charlie would have certainly hyperventilated.

After the game, his exhilaration intensified. Kyle had scored twenty-six points and grabbed eight rebounds while leading the Lions to an impressive victory over archrival Hinsdale Central. He wanted to scream, dance, take off his shirt, and pound his chest again. More than anything, though, he wanted to get down on the floor and congratulate Kyle. Unfortunately, since they were so far up, all he could do was stand there, stuck in the bleachers, while the crowd slowly filed out below.

"I wish they'd hurry," Charlie said. "He's going to go in the locker room. We're going to miss him."

"Settle down," Donna said. "There's a pretty good chance we'll run into him at home tonight."

When he saw Kyle making his way across the court toward the locker room, he could wait no longer and began to force his way down to the floor, leaving Donna with a gaggle of well-wishers. He pushed through the crowd, wearing a new blue and gold Lions cap and sweatshirt he had bought at halftime. ("Make way for number thirty-three's dad. I'm his father, number thirty-three's father. Kyle Baker's dad. That's right, Kyle Baker's dad coming through. Make way, please.")

Kyle was about to enter the locker room but turned when Charlie yelled his name. A look of fear crept over his face as his father approach.

"What's wrong?" Kyle asked. He backed away from Charlie's extended hand.

"Nothing. I just wanted to personally congratulate you." Charlie jiggled his hand up and down. "Shake it," he said.

"Oh, yeah."

"Other hand."

"Oh, yeah." Kyle switched hands. "Where'd you get that stuff?" he motioned toward Charlie's new cap and sweatshirt.

"Where do you think? I bought it. Hey, you played very well. You played great. You had twenty-six points. Did you know that? The next-highest scorer had just fourteen. We're proud of you. Very proud."

"Oh, yeah. Thanks."

"Okay, well, let's go home and have dinner. Should we wait for you? What's the process here? What's next?" Charlie was talking fast and, he noticed, perspiring. He was very pumped up. He dabbed some sweat away from his forehead with the back of his hand.

"We're all going out," Kyle said.

"What do you mean? Who is? Who's we?"

"Guys on the team. Is it all right that I go?"

Charlie glanced past him to the locker room door. "Oh, you mean like a team dinner?"

"Yeah. Can I go?"

"Sure, yeah. Team dinners are important, I guess."

"You sure?"

"Yeah, why not?"

"Because I'm grounded, I thought."

"Oh, yeah. That. Yeah." Charlie had forgotten about Kyle's punishment for defacing the signs. He thought about this, actually rubbing his chin. "Well, just this once, since it's team-related."

"Is it okay with Mom?"

He paused. "I think so," he said slowly. "As long as this is officially team-related. I'll talk to her. Just don't stay out too late, okay? And no Coke. No caffeine. Zero. You need your sleep. Drink club soda. I always drink club soda at night when I'm on the road."

Kyle silently mouthed the words club soda.

"Okay." Charlie slapped him on the shoulder again. "Hey, you need some money? For the team dinner?"

"No, I'm okay. I have money."

"Let me give you some, just in case." Charlie whipped out his wallet and handed him five twenties. "Here."

"Dad, that's a hundred dollars. We're getting pizza. Only six of us are going."

"Get dessert," Charlie said.

"Dad."

"Don't worry about it, okay? Just don't worry about it." He pushed the money toward his son. "And remember, Kyle, club soda."

Later that night, after he ate some of the lasagna while standing over the kitchen sink (Donna had predictably run off to Bright Day), he went upstairs to the office and relived parts of the game: the back-to-back three-pointers late in the second half, the no-look pass to that big center for an easy layup, Kyle's spirited fist pump to the crowd after he blocked a shot. Soon he was online, researching basketball. Other than pickup games, Charlie had never played the sport in an organized fashion and he knew he would have to bone up on things if Kyle were to have a long and successful career in the NBA.

After some searching, he eventually discovered a treasure trove of material on a Web site dedicated to the philosophy of John Wooden, the legendary basketball coach at UCLA. Charlie pulled his chair close to the screen and took copious notes on strategy and conditioning on a legal pad.

It was close to eleven when he remembered to check for voice mails, and when he did he discovered that the Wizard had called during the game. Charlie considered calling back, but it was late, and besides, his mind was on other things.

On his way down the hallway, he stuck his head into the bedroom. Donna was in bed, propped up with pillows, reading.

"Is he back yet?" he asked.

"He's asleep." She didn't look up.

"Sleeping, already?"

"It's late. I think those games take a lot out of him."

"Boy, I didn't even hear him come in." He peered down the dark hallway.

"You shouldn't have let him go out for dinner," Donna said. "He's grounded, remember?"

"I told you, it was a team thing. He had a responsibility to go. He's the best player on the team."

Donna shook her head and kept her eyes down on her book.

"Think I can wake him?" Charlie asked.

"Wake him? Why?"

"I want to go over a few things with him."

This got Donna's attention. She looked up from her book. "What do you want to talk to him about?" She nodded at the notepad Charlie was holding. "What's that?"

"I want to talk about the game. I have some ideas for him, some plays I want to go over. I found all this great stuff online. Great plays and everything. Might help."

Donna gave one of her sideways glances to nobody.

"There are some things he could work on," Charlie continued. "He has to use his size more. He's big for a guard and I think he should post up. Take advantage of his size against smaller guards."

"Post up."

"Yeah, post up. You take the ball and, you know, you post up. You take the ball one-on-one—" Charlie stopped. "What's wrong?"

"Come in here and shut the door."

"Why?"

"Come in and please shut the door."

Charlie slowly walked into the room and obediently shut the door behind him, hugging his legal pad close to his chest.

"What's the matter now?" he asked.

"Don't overdo this, okay?"

"I just want to talk to him."

"I thought you already talked to him after the game."

"I want to talk to him some more."

"And I think you might want to leave him alone."

"Why? Is something wrong? Is he okay?"

"He's been playing basketball a long time."

"So?"

"So, don't do too much too soon. You can't make up all the lost time in one night, okay? He'll resent it."

"What do you mean? Why would he resent it?"

"Because he's been playing basketball since he was ten years old, by himself, out in the driveway while you were gone. He practiced for hours. Hours. He's been on teams before. He's been to camps. But you weren't there. You were never there. So I wouldn't try to be his best friend too fast when it comes to this, okay? That's my advice."

"I went to some of his games."

"The last game you went to, he was in sixth grade."

"No way, that's wrong, totally wrong." Charlie paused and thought about this. "Really? How do you know that?"

"He told me. He said the last time you saw him play, he was twelve years old. He remembers things like that."

"He said that?" Charlie felt all the energy seep out of him. He glanced at the diagrams on his pad, the post-up moves, his summary of the motion offense. "He told you that?"

"Yes."

Charlie shook his head, deflated. "All right. Okay. Maybe you're right." He was turning to leave, retreat to the guest room, when Donna said, "He was pretty good, though, huh?"

Charlie turned right back around. "He was amazing."

Donna finally smiled. "He really was."

"It's weird, but that's probably the proudest I've ever been of anything in my life," Charlie said. "That meant more than anything, anything. I never thought I could be proud of something that I didn't do or wasn't, you know, involved in. It's weird. I can't stop thinking about it. I'm, like, shaking."

Donna studied Charlie, her face blank. "Well, he's sleeping now, but you can talk to him tomorrow," she said. "I'm sure he'd like to hear that."

Charlie thought he detected a change in her voice, a softening, but it was fleeting, gone before it was really there. He offered up a small smile.

"All right, then. Good night, then," he said.

Donna held his gaze for a second longer, then slowly returned to her book. "Good night, Charlie."

Chapter Twenty-two

The next afternoon, slick-looking Jason, the managing director of the office, gave a talk about collecting unemployment pay. He walked through the procedure, then passed out a brochure offering information as well as a map identifying the various unemployment offices in the Chicago area. Charlie refused to take one of the brochures when they came his way.

"There's nothing embarrassing about collecting unemployment," Jason said. He was a thirtysomething man, tall and lean, with gelled-up jet-black hair and a permanent tan. "You've earned this, ladies and gentlemen. Earned this."

Charlie felt Jason's eyes on him. He looked down and checked his cell phone.

"It might not be much, but it helps," Jason said. "Now is not the time to be too proud."

Charlie looked up and saw Jason staring at him. He slipped his phone in his pocket, coughed once, then slowly reached across the table and took a brochure from the pile.

While he was reviewing the map—he noted that there wasn't

any unemployment office near Wilton—Jason launched into an overly rehearsed tale about an executive, a former senior financial officer and client of Rogers & Newman, who had been out of work for an extended period of time.

"How long is extended?" Bradley asked.

Jason sucked in his cheeks and thought about this. "Almost a year."

Bradley's face fell.

"Oh, longer than that, much longer," Ned said. He had been leaning against a wall in the back of the room, but jerked to attention at Bradley's question.

"How much longer?" Bradley asked.

"I'm not sure. But much longer than a year."

Bradley bravely nodded.

According to Jason, this nameless executive was rejected dozens of times over the course of his search, but stayed focused on a clear and specific vision. He wanted to work in mergers and acquisitions, he wanted to work in New York City, and he wanted to be the "main man." Jason didn't elaborate on exactly what being the "main man" was, and no one asked.

"And he made it," Jason said, pointing. "He became the main man. He used all the tools at his disposal, he used all his resources. He swallowed his pride, stood in line at the unemployment office, leveraged relationships. But most importantly . . ." He paused and took in the room with fierce green eyes. "Most importantly, he had a clearly defined image of who he was and where he wanted to be. In other words, he visualized his success. And now he's living it. As the head of M&A at an international bank."

"In New York?" Karen asked.

Jason glanced at Ned, who was still in the back, nodding inspirationally.

"Well, no, actually," Ned said. "He lives in Guam. But he travels to New York very frequently."

"Very frequently," Jason said. "Very frequently."

Jason and Ned fell silent so their words and nods could sink in.

"Does anyone have any reaction to that story?" Ned asked. "Anyone care to comment?"

"Where's Guam?" Karen asked.

"It's in the Pacific," Ned said. "Very nice. It's a U.S. protectorate, I think. Which is very nice."

No one else said anything. Charlie pretended to study the unemployment map again. Bradley sneezed and someone muttered, "Bless you." Jason pulled out his BlackBerry, peered at it, then immediately left the room without a word.

"Well," Ned said. "I think Jason's story underscores the importance of developing and maintaining a vision. It's essential that everyone here visualizes their success. It's critical, in fact. So critical that we're all going to spend a few minutes working on that right now."

"Oh, God," Walter mumbled. "Not this."

"I heard that, Walter," Ned said. He clapped his hands, smiling. "Now, for those of you who aren't familiar with this exercise, we call it Future Perfect, we want you to spend a few minutes envisioning, picturing, where you would like to be in five years. Now, don't be afraid to dream big. We want you to think of the perfect position for yourself. The absolute perfect position. Get wild and get creative. Provide details." He rubbed his hands together. "Give us the nitty-gritty. All of it. What's your office going to look like? Who will be working with you? What are your perks? Will you have an office with a window? A company car? What kind of company car? Does it have an FM radio?"

"A what?" Bradley asked.

"In a perfect, absolutely perfect future, what would you be doing?"

Ned passed out pencils and legal pads of paper. "You can add personal details too," he said. "Describe your family life. Paint an accurate and colorful picture. Hopefully, when you're done, a few of you can share your visions."

Everyone stared at the pads of paper, then shot embarrassed

glances at each other. There was a larger-than-usual group in the room, about fifteen people, and the lack of enthusiasm over Future Perfect was palpable. Ned smiled nervously. "Come on, now, this is fun. It's your chance to dream. No limits! Paint that picture so you can hang it over your mental mantel. It will serve as a goal, a reminder of where you want to be. Come on, now!" He punched the air with his fist and smiled harder, his square head radiating hope.

Karen started to write. Soon, pretty much everyone but Walter was doing the same. Charlie picked up his pen, stared at the blank page before him, then gently rubbed his tongue along the inside of his prosthesis. He was surprised how natural it now felt.

Ned circled around the room like a schoolteacher, hands behind his back, checking on everyone's progress. He naturally stopped behind Karen, glanced over her shoulder, and chuckled along with his prized student. "Excellent," he said. "Quite excellent." He next made his way over to Charlie at the very end of the table and hovered.

"Writer's block Charlie?"

Just to annoy him, Charlie quickly wrote, *I WANT TO WORK AT XANON AND MAKE FOUR HUNDRED THOUSAND.*

"But will you be happy?" Ned asked.

Charlie turned to a new page and wrote, *NED LOVES KAREN!!!*

Ned quickly walked on.

Rather than visualizing his perfect future, Charlie began to develop a list of questions he needed to ask Ted Greene. He wanted to discuss his compensation, specifically stock options. After his experience at D&H, he didn't want them to be a significant part of his pay or bonus structure. In addition, he wanted to know about a car allowance, something he should have had but was denied at D&H.

He worked on this until Ned said, "Pencils down." He was standing in front of the room in his sharp blue blazer, smiling excitedly, a game show host leading the bonus round. "Anyone want to share?" he asked.

No one said anything.

"Walter? How about you?"

Walter blankly stared at him.

"Right," Ned said. He turned to Bradley. "And how about you, Bradley? Do you mind sharing what you wrote?"

"I didn't write much."

"What do you have? Anything would help us get started."

Bradley shrugged. He readjusted some reading glasses and brought the pad up close to his face. "I want to head a department, a large marketing department. In an international company. I want to stay here, live in Chicago. I want to be involved in all marketing matters, from conception to execution."

"Very good," Ned said. "Anything else?"

Bradley put the pad down. "I want a big office and an even bigger salary."

"Can you be more specific? What does your office look like?"

"Office A," he said.

Everyone laughed at this. Ned clapped, obviously pleased. He pointed and winked. "Spot on, Bradley."

"Okay, I'll go," Karen said. She was sitting next to Bradley and had been exchanging whispers and giggles with him throughout the meeting. Apparently, Bradley had forgiven Karen for her crack about his orange face. "I will be vice president of communications for a large international company," she began.

Ned interrupted. "What company?"

"A large consumer company. Automotive, maybe."

"Au. To. Mo. Tive?" Ned asked.

"I will travel all over the world, overseeing communications for the company. The annual report, external and internal communications, special events, media relations." She stopped and glanced sideways at Ned. "You said make stuff up, right?"

"Yes," Ned said. "Well, visualize."

"I'll have a staff of between ten and fifteen people. I'll have my department divided into three groups so I can have just three direct reports. That's manageable, I think."

"I think that's the ideal structure," Ned said.

Karen paused. "You said do personal stuff too, right?"

Ned's eyes blazed with eagerness. "Oh, yes. Absolutely. By all means."

"I will also have an anthology of my short stories published and be married and have children," she said. "Two children. Two girls. Maybe twins."

Ned's eyes drifted. "Two girls," he said, his voice dreamlike.

"We'll have a house overlooking a lake, maybe."

"A lake, yes," Ned said.

"We'll face west, so we can watch the sunset together. And my husband will be a great cook."

"A great cook," Ned said. "Is that important to you? His being a great cook?"

"Not as important as what he looks like," she said.

Everyone laughed and a heavyset woman by the door applauded and said, "You go, girl." Ned smiled, but sadly. "I hope that dream comes true. All of it," he said.

"So do I," Karen said. "Believe me."

They were all still laughing a little when Walter said, "I want to matter again." Everyone turned toward him. He was sitting opposite Charlie, at the end of the long table, his hands clasped behind his head. "That's all I want," he said. "I want to matter." His eyes were closed and he was leaning back in his chair.

"Of course you do. Of course you do," Ned said quietly. "That's a fundamental need."

Walter continued. "I want to get up in the morning and have someplace to go. I want to feel like I'm doing something. And at the end of the day, I want to come home tired." He put his arms down and opened his eyes. His face was expressionless. "I want to matter," he said again.

The room was quiet. Ned cleared his throat. "But you matter now. Of course you do. We all matter."

Walter smirked, and slowly scanned the room, eventually stopping at Ned. "I'm not going to come back here," he said.

"This is my last day. You're not going to see me again." He waved a hand. "I have to go. This is my last day, forever. I can't stay here anymore and do this."

He stood and headed toward the door without glancing back.

"Walter, wait," Ned said. He moved toward Walter.

Walter brushed past him. "I have to go," he said. He hitched his shoulder one last time and left the room.

After the meeting, Bradley followed Charlie back to his office. Once they were inside, Bradley said, "That Walter is out of it."

"Yeah, he's in pretty bad shape." Charlie sat down, turned on his computer. Walter's farewell address had put him in a pensive, bordering-on-depressed mood and he wanted to be alone.

Bradley, oblivious, plopped down on a chair and put his size-fourteen wing tips up on Charlie's desk. "He's snapping," he said. "I've seen this before. He's going jungle. Been out in the bush too long. People disappear inside themselves. He's been out in the bush too long."

"Yeah, well." Charlie started to check for e-mails. One of Bradley's shoes, he noticed, had a small hole in it, near the toes.

"He hasn't even been out as long as I have," Bradley said. "Plus, I think he's got some health issues."

"I think it's his wife who has the issues."

"Oh, yeah, that's right." Bradley shook his head and wiggled his shoes. "Man, it's a long road. Long road."

"Tell me about it."

Bradley laughed. "Get off it. You've barely been out."

"Been out long enough."

"Yeah, it's a long road," Bradley said again. "But I think I'm finally close."

"Good for you." Charlie didn't bother to ask Bradley where he was getting close to. He knew. Earlier that morning, before the networking meeting, he had overheard Ned tell Jason in the kitchen that Bradley was in talks with a local hospital. The job was in marketing, sounded midlevel, might pay $85,000, tops, and had cubicle written all over it. He glanced again at the small hole in Bradley's shoe, repressed a shudder, then squinted at his computer screen. He once again had no e-mails.

"Do you have anything going on?" Bradley asked. "I thought you said you might."

"What? Yeah, I might. I do."

"Good for you too," Bradley said. "Where?"

"What?" he asked. He was distracted. The Wizard was supposed to have sent him some more background info on Xanon and he wondered why he hadn't. He was usually very good at follow-up.

"Where are you looking?" Bradley asked again. "Who you talking to?"

"Oh, ah, Xanon," he said absentmindedly, still thinking about the wizard.

"The drug company?"

Charlie clicked off his e-mail. "What? Yeah."

"Xanon? Really? How did you hear about that?" Bradley asked. He was sitting up now, shoes back on the floor.

"Recruiter."

Bradley sounded so surprised that Charlie realized what he had done. He shouldn't have told Bradley about Xanon. He had clearly one-upped him and his local hospital job. "That's a big company. What's the job for?" Bradley asked.

"Head of marketing," Charlie mumbled.

"CMO?"

"Yeah."

Bradley sat quietly for a few seconds, then said, "I heard it's kind of a strange place."

"What do you mean?"

"I hear strange things about it."

"What do you mean, strange?"

"Old-fashioned. Backwards. Very conservative place. You don't seem like a conservative kind of guy."

"They're changing. Besides, I can be conservative on what they're paying."

"They pay a lot?"

"So I'm told," Charlie said. He opened the side drawer of his desk and pretended to search for something. He was starting to feel embarrassed and wanted Bradley to leave.

"That Woods is the CEO there, isn't he?" Bradley asked. "Kevin F.?"

Charlie closed the drawer, then picked up his unemployment brochure, crumpled it up, and dropped it in the wastebasket under his desk. "Kevin F. Woods. Yeah."

"Supposed to be an asshole. I don't know, Charlie. You may want to think about that."

"Don't worry about me."

"You haven't even been out that long. You sure you want to take that job?"

"Absolutely, I'm sure. Wouldn't you?"

"I don't know."

Charlie looked hard at Bradley. "Come on, you wouldn't take that job?"

"I honestly don't know if I would."

Charlie had a hard time believing this. Bradley had a hole in his shoe and here he was claiming he wouldn't take a job that might pay close to half a million with bonus.

"You're serious?" he asked. "You wouldn't take the job?"

Before Bradley could answer, Ned raced in. "Have you seen Walter?"

"No," Charlie said. "Why?"

Ned's face was predictably red. "We need to help him," he said breathlessly. "I think he left. We need to reach out to him."

"Maybe it's time to leave him alone," Charlie said.

"He shouldn't be alone right now. His words, this is my last day, forever. I think he's in a bad place right now. A very bad place."

At this, Bradley exploded. "You know something, Ned? You worry too much. And you know something else? You drive everyone fucking nuts. You're like . . . like our mothers. Our goddamn mothers. And I already have a goddamn mother who's about to get kicked out of assisted living because I can't pay her fucking bill!" With that, he stood up and stormed out.

Ned looked at Charlie shaken, his eyes immense and hurt. "Now, what's wrong with him?"

Charlie shrugged.

Ned shook his head. "I'm afraid this isn't shaping up to be a very good day," he said. "I thought it might, but it's just not."

Charlie spent the rest of the afternoon idly surfing more job sites. He called home twice, but got no answer. He wondered where Donna was. When he tried her cell, his call went straight into voice mail. This naturally worried him. He considered going home, but instead pushed his concerns out of his mind and set about preparing a cover letter to the Midwest Parks and Recreation Association. When he was finished, he sent it off to them, along with his résumé.

The Wizard finally e-mailed the background on Xanon near the end of the day. Charlie's relief over getting the information quickly gave way to despair when he opened the document. He groaned. It was some type of position paper from the American Association of Swine Veterinarians. Charlie attempted to read it.

> *Last year, swine practitioners in the United States started to report increased numbers of cases of postweaning multisystemic wasting syndrome (or PMWS) in finisher pigs.*

Charlie read that sentence over twice, said, "Finisher pigs," out loud, then clicked out of the document. He then Googled Kevin F. Woods.

The Xanon Web site had the most information: fifty-two years old; a graduate of University of Oklahoma, where he starred as an All–Big Twelve offensive lineman; the obligatory

292

MBA from an Ivy League school, this one Penn; a thousand-acre cattle ranch outside of Tulsa. He was married, had two grown children, was an avid "outdoorsman" (i.e., hunter), and looked exactly like John Wayne.

Charlie scrutinized the photo and tried to imagine spending the rest of his career reporting to a man who, no doubt, would have bullied him in high school. Of course, Ted Greene seemed to be doing well enough there, and he hardly seemed the John Wayne type. He gazed at the photo a little longer—so much depends on this man, this stranger, he thought—then clicked off his computer and stared at the blank screen.

He left the office around six. It was raining and cold, and getting to the parking lot was an ordeal. The wind was howling and he had to walk straight into it, his shoulders low, his head thrust forward. He hadn't bothered to wear a raincoat, and by the time he made it to the Navigator, he was drenched. As he was reaching in his pocket for the keys, he spotted Walter in a nearby parking space peering into the open hood of a drab, olive-colored minivan. He had his back to Charlie.

Charlie slipped into the Navigator and slunk low in his seat and waited. To get to the exit, he would have to pass directly in front of Walter, who apparently was stranded. Charlie was trapped.

He remained in the slunk-down position in his soggy clothes for a short eternity, waiting for Walter to finally get the van started. After about ten minutes, he finally decided enough was enough and turned the key in the ignition. Then he switched it off, got out of the Navigator, and walked over to Walter.

He was now sitting inside the van, loudly grinding the engine, which refused to turn over. Charlie cupped his hands to the side of his mouth and yelled, "You're going to wreck your car," over the wind and noise.

Walter looked up, very unsurprised and unimpressed by Charlie's presence. He resumed the grinding with renewed vigor. Charlie knocked on his window.

"You want to use my phone and call a tow truck?"

Walter lowered his window. "What?"

Charlie held up his phone. "You want to call a tow truck?"

"No."

"You sure?"

"I'm fine."

"Fine." Charlie walked back to the Navigator and got inside.

It was beginning to sleet now, wet splats of snow and rain pelting the windshield, a Chicago specialty. Charlie turned on his wipers, sat there, then got out and walked back over to Walter's van.

He knocked hard on his window and when Walter lowered it, he said, "I'm sorry I fired you, okay? I don't even remember doing it, you were a name on a list, but I'm sorry I did. And I'm sorry about your wife. It's shitty. The whole thing is shitty, okay? But I don't hate you or . . . or hope bad things happen to you. I don't, okay? I'm just another idiot trying to get through another day."

Charlie stopped here, breathing heavily. He thought he was through with his little speech, but he wasn't. "Oh, wait, I almost forgot, wait. You'll love this. This is the best part." He pinched the prosthesis out of his mouth with his index finger and his thumb and held it out toward Walter. "Look at this." He smiled broadly to reveal his teeth.

Up until that point, Walter had been doing an admirable job of ignoring him, staring straight ahead with both hands on the wheel of his dead van. But the carnival-barker tone of Charlie's voice must have piqued some curiosity, because he slowly turned to look him fully in the face. That's when he gasped. It was the first time he had ever looked at Charlie with anything but contempt.

"Jesus Christ," he said.

Charlie smiled even wider. "Pretty neat, huh? I fell down the stairs after I took Valium. I bet the Gap wouldn't even hire me." He put the prosthesis back in his mouth. "Now, you want to call a tow truck or what?"

Walter turned away.

"Fine," he said. "I'm going." Out of tricks, Charlie once again trudged back to the Navigator.

"I called the towing service three hours ago," he heard Walter say.

Charlie stopped, turned. "What?" he yelled.

"Been sitting here three hours."

Charlie put his hands in his pants pocket and stamped his feet. The sleet was turning into full-fledged snow, thick and heavy, and it was clinging to his clothes. "Where do you live?" he asked.

"Beverly."

Charlie nodded. "I used to live there."

"You did?"

"I'll take you home. Come on."

"That's a pretty long way. I can take the train, maybe."

"Come on. I'll drive you home."

Walter didn't budge. He looked scared, his hands still gripping the steering wheel.

"Listen, it's snowing and everything, I'm wet, and I'm going. You're the one who's stuck here, not me." Charlie once again got back in the Navigator and flipped the heat on high. But when Walter opened his passenger door and asked if he could take along a few boxes of files, Charlie stepped back out into the snow and wind and helped him load up his things.

The next two hours were a case study in awkwardness. Walter conveniently spent most of the time on hold with various towing companies while Charlie pretended to focus on the traffic and weather. It wasn't until after Walter had finally gotten through to a service and made new arrangements that Charlie finally spoke. "Pretty bad out there," he said.

"Yeah. Pretty bad."

Walter sniffled and Charlie countered with a cough. He considered turning on the radio, until he realized it was on. He switched lanes, then switched back. Traffic was predictably a mess, every inch hard-fought.

"Man, it's bad out," Charlie said.

"Yeah, it's bad."

They drove on in silence, Charlie regretting his offer. If he had just kept his mouth shut or had parked on a different level in the garage, he would have been halfway home by now, not stuck on the Dan Ryan Expressway with a man who made no secret of loathing him.

Charlie tried again. "So," he said. "How's the search going?"

"What search?" Although he couldn't see Walter's face, Charlie assumed his question had prompted a smirk. "I have nothing going on. Nothing. I need a break from it. I think I need a break from everything."

"Yeah. I know what you mean."

Walter looked out the passenger window and said, "Did you hear about Citicorp? All those layoffs?"

"Yeah, I saw that."

"I know a guy there. I bet he's gone next week."

"Bet he's already gone." Charlie switched lanes again.

"Where the hell is everyone going to end up?"

"I don't know. Maybe nowhere."

They drove a little farther. After they had come to another stop, Walter said, "I'm looking at going into business for myself. I think that might be the only way to go."

"Really? What are you looking at?"

"An online thing. Sell pet clothes online. Kind of like Amazon, but for dogs and cats. It's a long shot." He turned to face Charlie. "What do you think about that?" he asked.

Charlie was surprised that his opinion was being solicited. He took his time answering. "Pet clothes," he said. "What kind of clothes?"

"I don't know. Sweaters, mostly. You know, booties for Snowball. Scarves."

It didn't sound promising, but Charlie held his tongue. "I don't know much about that category. Have you done any research? Are there other companies doing this?"

"Yeah, a few. But not many. And no one is really doing it

right. If we market it right, it could take off. The clothes are pretty nice. Good-quality stuff. A guy I know wants me to go in on it with him. He has a source, a company that makes these clothes. In Mexico. Small company. They don't know anything about distribution or marketing. He wants me to go down there and take a look at it, but I don't have time. I'm putting in long hours at the Gap and then I got my wife." He stopped speaking and looked back out his window.

"I was sorry to hear about her. Ned told me."

"What are you going to do?"

Mention of Walter's wife plunged them back into a long silence. Walter soon busied himself by inspecting the contents of his overflowing briefcase. Charlie checked his voice mail, which he knew had no messages, then turned the radio up higher.

As they were pulling off the expressway, Charlie asked, "What's your address?"

When Walter told him, Charlie was stunned. "That's a block from our house, from where we used to live, I mean. How long have you lived there?"

"I don't know. Twenty-five years."

Charlie's amazement grew. He did some figuring. "Then we must have lived a block from each other for about twenty years. Longer, even. We moved about three, four years ago."

They both let this register. "That's weird," Walter finally said.

"Yeah, it is. We're going to drive right by my old house."

"That's weird," Walter said again.

A few minutes later, they turned down Damen Avenue. "That's it. That's our house," he said. He slowed, then stopped, surprised at the emotions the brick colonial elicited.

"You lived there?" Walter asked.

"Yeah. I did. I lived here." He stared at the house. "We lived here," he said softly.

"That's really weird."

"Yeah, I know, we were so close."

"No. I mean, I was there, at your house."

"What do you mean?" Charlie turned to face him. He wasn't

sure he had heard Walter correctly. "What are you talking about?"

"Was your wife . . . is your wife's name Donna? Does she have black hair? Real"—he made a circular motion with his hand—"curly?"

"How do you know my wife?"

"Through school. PTA or something. I went there for meetings. I liked her. She was the only one who knew what was going on."

"Wait a minute, you were at my house? *Inside* my house?" Charlie pointed. "*That* house?"

"Yeah."

The image of Walter sitting in his house, standing in his house, breathing the air in his house, was inconceivable. "That's unbelievable," Charlie said.

"Yeah, I was there a few times."

"A *few* times? And you didn't know it was my house?"

"How would I know that? I never saw you there or anything. I might not have even known you."

"When was it?"

"I don't know. A while ago. Six, seven years ago, maybe longer. I don't remember exactly."

"Unbelievable."

Walter shook his head and actually laughed. "Donna Baker. I never made the connection." His voice sounded different—alive, excited.

"That's unbelievable," Charlie said again.

"Yeah, it is." Walter was actually smiling, not smirking. "Do me a favor. Tell her Walter Konkist says hello. Walter Konkist."

"I know your name, Walter." Charlie pulled away from the house and headed down the block. The snow had lightened, but the wind was still fierce. He could feel the Navigator straining as he drove into it.

"She's a nice woman," Walter said. "Good-looking too."

"Thank you."

"I said she was good-looking, not you."

"Anything close to a compliment, I'll take."

Walter pointed. "That's it. Over there. Third one from the end. Better not go in the driveway, you might get stuck."

Charlie pulled up in front of a tidy brick Georgian, its roof already submerged in snow. It was dark with the exception of a single porch light. Walter stared silently at the house before unbuckling his seat belt.

"You need any help with those boxes?" Charlie asked.

"No, I can get them. Just pop open the back."

"You sure?"

"Yeah. There's only three of them. They're light."

Charlie reached down and unlatched the rear door. "Hope your car is all right."

"Yeah, we'll see. They said they'd pick it up tomorrow." Walter opened the door and grimaced when the wind hit his face. Then he crouched down low and looked back inside. "Thanks, you know, for getting me home in this weather," he said. "You saved my ass. I appreciate it. I do." Walter awkwardly reached out his hand and when Charlie shook it, he knew this was the reason he had come all this way. Guilty men seek forgiveness anywhere they can.

"See you later," Charlie said.

"Yeah, maybe. And say hello to your wife Donna."

"I will."

"All right. I'll see you, maybe."

"All right," Charlie said.

He turned around in the middle of the street, then headed back down Damen Avenue, stopping in front of his old house again. He sensed an epiphany was approaching, heavy with purpose, and he was right. He threw the Navigator into park.

Seeing their old house in the snowfall, the glow of a bedroom light, the slight rise in the lawn by the front steps, the now-leafless but always messy birch tree by the street, he felt like he was looking at a photograph, something that should exist in memory only. He swallowed. After he died, on the application form to heaven, he would list this address, not their house in Wilton, not even the house he grew up in as a child, but this house as home.

He sat there in a half trance, the heat blowing high, his wet clothes sticking to his tired body. He turned his wipers off and watched the snow stick on his windshield, amazed at how fast it gathered. The house soon disappeared from view, then he too had a sense of disappearing.

There was a sudden knock on his window and this brought him back. He lowered it. A young boy of about ten holding a shovel looked in at him, cheeks red, jacket open to the wind, yellow-and-black-striped scarf loosely tied around his neck.

"You stuck?" the boy asked. He had a round face and curly black hair, flecked white with snow.

"No."

A man next appeared over the boy's shoulder. He also had a shovel, this one slung over his shoulder. He was bundled up in a large parka, a knit hat pulled down low over suspicious eyes.

"You okay?" he yelled.

"Yeah," Charlie said.

"You sure?"

"Yeah. I'm fine," Charlie said. "You should put a hat on," he told the boy. He smiled, turned the wipers back on, and drove off.

It took him more than three hours to get home and when he did, he walked straight upstairs to their bedroom, not bothering to take off his still damp clothes. He needed to talk to Donna, immediately and finally. He now knew what he had to say.

He opened the door, expecting to see her. Instead, he found an empty room.

He switched on a light, glanced at his watch. It was close to midnight. Fighting back panic, he glanced into her closet, not sure what he was looking for: a missing suitcase, a note, some signs of departure. He bounded downstairs, taking them two at a time. The house was dark and he could hear the wind, a thin, high cry.

He raced through the dining room, the kitchen, the family room, and finally found her standing in the reading nook, looking out the window. The lights from the deck illuminated the snow and it sparkled.

"Donna?"

She didn't respond. Instead, she turned from the window and softly made her way in bare feet to the kitchen, passing right by him with unseeing eyes, a worried, faraway look on her face. She was, as he suspected, asleep.

He followed her until she stopped by the island. It was only then that he approached her and carefully put his fingertips in the palm of one of her hands. He gently steered her upstairs to their bedroom.

After he had covered her with a blanket, he pulled up a chair to watch her sleep. Her eyes were closed and her breathing even and shallow.

His first experience with Donna's sleepwalking had been disturbing. They had been married only a few weeks when he awoke, late at night, to an empty bed. Searching frantically, he had found her in the backyard, sitting cross-legged on the grass. It was the first warm night of spring and the air was filled with the scent of lilacs. He remembered watching her as she gazed up at the moon, young and pretty and peaceful. He had no idea she was sleeping, and after he approached her and took her wrists in his hands, he asked for an explanation. Her face crumpled when he did this, fell into itself, confused and terrified. When she started to cry, he realized his response had been wrong. He should have let her be, should have let her gaze up at the moon in her dream.

As he watched her sleep now, he tried to control his emotions. Things were rumbling inside of him, though. Finding her gone like that had put a deep scare in him.

"Listen, Donna, listen," he said, even though he thought she was sleeping. "I want you to stay here with me, with us, forever. I don't want to lose you. I love you. I'll do whatever you want. I'll go to therapy, that counselor. And I don't care what happened in Maine or wherever. I don't care. The last few years have been terrible, I know. It was like I left you. I brought you out here, forced you out here, then I left you. I should have stayed home. I know that now. With you and with Kyle. I was wrong. I just got caught up in the game. It was just a stupid game." He paused, waiting for her to say something, but apparently she was still asleep.

"I was at our old house," he continued "I was just there. I had to drop this guy off, this guy Walter Konkist, he says he knows you, anyway I was sitting in the snow looking up at our bedroom window. The light was on. And I remember how I used to feel when I came home late, and saw that light on, and knew you were waiting for me. How good that felt." He stopped, ran a hand over his face, tried to regroup. "I was lying to myself, and lying to you and to Kyle. I used to think I was working so hard for our family, for us, but I know now that I was just working for me. Everything I did was because of me. I'm sorry. I want to get things right now, but I'm running out of time. I'm running out of time."

Other than the wind, the room was quiet. He hoped she would say something, but she didn't.

He finally gave up. "Well, good night, I guess."

He was leaning down, about to kiss her on the forehead, when she said, "I wanted to see the ocean."

He straightened. He thought she might be talking in her sleep, though she had never done this before.

"That's why I went there, to Maine." Her voice was just above a whisper. "I wanted to see the ocean. He wasn't there. I wanted to see everything that Bill talked about. He said it was beautiful and he was right, it was. I just wanted to see it and be alone for a while."

Charlie sat on the edge of the bed. "Are you awake?"

"He was a friend. A nice guy. I know you think I had an affair, but you're wrong. He might have wanted to have one, I don't know. But I'm not going to do that. And I'm not going back to Maine again. I know you think I am." Her eyes opened.

"Are you really awake?" He needed to confirm this before he allowed himself to feel any relief.

"What do you think?" she said.

"What's my name?"

"What?"

"If you're awake, what's my name?"

"Idiot," she said.

He relaxed. "Close enough."

They were quiet. The wind blew and when the windows rattled again, Donna said, "I know I'm not blameless in all this. I know I could have made more of an effort, tried to fit into your life. You asked me on trips, and I said no. You asked me a lot. Like I said, I guess I was scared or something. I didn't want things to change. I wanted everything to be the way it always was. But you have to change sometimes. I could have tried too, I guess."

"It's not your fault. None of this is."

Donna sniffled and Charlie took her hand. "I'm not going anywhere," she said.

Charlie just nodded.

"So it looks like you were wrong about me," she said.

"I'm glad I was wrong."

"And you were wrong about something else."

"What?"

"You said you were running out of time."

"I am."

She sat up, and when she did he could see she was about to cry. She blinked furiously and fought to control her voice. "No, you're not," she whispered. "You still have time, Charlie." She reached for him. "You still have lots of time. We both do."

Chapter Twenty-three

A few days later, Karen walked into the coffee room carrying a box of doughnuts. The box was huge and had grease stains spreading on the bottom.

"Oh, no," Ned whispered.

"I got a job," she announced. Ned and Charlie were the only ones in the room and they watched as she placed the box on the counter and triumphantly raised her arms over her head like a triathlete crossing the finishing line.

"Where?" Ned asked.

She dropped her arms. "Honda."

"Honda?" Ned asked. "You mean with Tom?"

Karen's cheeks flushed and she kept her eyes on the doughnut box. "Yep. He offered it to me over the phone last night."

"With Tom?" Ned repeated.

"Yep. In Torrance, California."

"I knew you were talking to him, but . . ." Ned didn't finish.

Karen avoided his eyes. She busied herself with opening the box, struggling with a thin white string that bound it. "Yeah, things moved pretty fast, I guess."

"Very fast, I would say," Ned said.

She finally undid the string and carefully opened the box. "I went to that bakery you like. The one we went to that time on Fullerton. You said they had the best éclairs."

Ned smiled, but his eyes were sad with the memory. "Yes, I like that bakery." He glanced over at Charlie. "We went there, you know, Karen and I," he explained.

Charlie smiled. He was beginning to feel like he was intruding.

"Here," Karen said. She handed Charlie a vanilla éclair and a small pink and yellow napkin.

"So this is official?" Charlie pretended to examine the éclair. "Yep."

"Congratulations, then. And good luck."

"And when do you leave?" Ned asked.

Karen went back to the box and began rearranging the éclairs. "They want me there Monday."

"Monday? You mean, *this* Monday? So soon?" Ned asked.

"I have to go on a trip to Asia with Tom the week after that. We're touring some new parts plants. He wants me along with him." She said all this while studying the éclairs.

"Asia," Ned said. "With Tom." He no longer even attempted to smile.

"Here." She handed Ned an éclair. "It's butterscotch. I remembered you liked them."

Ned quietly accepted the éclair. "Karen, I'd like a moment with you if I could."

Karen ignored him. "Hey, is Bradley around?"

"Karen?" Ned asked again.

Karen picked up the box of doughnuts. "I want to tell him," she said. "I want to tell him myself, before he hears it from someone else."

"I think he's in the back, by the cubes," Charlie said. "I saw him back there earlier."

She smiled at Charlie a little desperately. He gave her a weak smile back and bit into his éclair. "This is good."

Karen started for the hall, but stopped and walked back

toward Ned. Charlie thought she was going to say something, but she didn't. Instead, she kissed Ned once on the cheek, before hurrying out of the room, the sound of her high heels clicking in her wake.

After she was gone, Ned said, "That's interesting news, isn't it?"

Charlie patted him once on the shoulder and threw his éclair in the garbage.

He spent the rest of the day sequestered in an office back by the copy room, trying to read up on Xanon. His mind kept wandering, though, back to Karen and Tamales. Her decision to go work for that creep bothered him to no end, but it was none of his business. She was a grown woman, knew the risks. Still, he was disappointed in her decision. What people will do for a job, he thought.

He shook his head and started in on an article on swine breeding.

Around lunchtime, he avoided a brown-bag seminar on dressing for success, and slipped down to the deli to pick up a cup of low-fat chicken noodle soup. When he returned to his office, the phone on his desk was ringing.

He pried off the cover of his soup, then answered. It was, as he expected, Ned asking if he was coming to the seminar. They were waiting for him.

"I'm sorry, but I can't. I'm in the middle of something."

"We have a very interesting discussion planned."

"Sorry."

Ned asked, "Are you in for a while?" His voice was now low, hushed. "I wanted to talk to you about something."

"I'm here."

Charlie hung up. Almost immediately the phone rang again. He counted the rings, then, assuming it was Ned again—one else called him on the office phone—answered on the fifth one.

"Yes?"

"You there?"

"What? Who is this?"

An unfamiliar voice responded. "This is Kevin F. Woods."

This took a moment to register. Charlie stared down at the receiver in disbelief, John Wayne's head, wearing a Stetson, rising before his eyes. Finally he thought to say, "Why, hello, there."

"Is this Baker? Charlie Baker?"

"This is me. He." Charlie's mind started to race. "I'm sorry, there's been some problems with our phones."

There was a terrible pause. Finally, Kevin F. Woods said, "Just wanted to set up a time when we could meet." His voice was loud and to the point. Charlie thought he might be in an airport. There was some commotion in the background.

Charlie spoke louder himself. "Yes, of course. Yes. That would be terrific. I was waiting to hear from your human resources department on that."

"If I waited for them, it would never get done. Let's do next Tuesday in New York. I have to give a talk there. We can meet in the morning before my talk. Does that work?"

"Absolutely. That works fine. Where?"

"I'm not sure where it is. Someone will be in touch with you. All right? Let's meet in the health club, though. Let's make it early. All right? Seven. No, six. Make it six. I got a meeting at seven-thirty, I think."

"Yes, fine. I'll call Ted. Ted Greene from your HR department for the details."

"Don't call him. Call someone else." Kevin F. sounded put off by this suggestion.

"Okay. I'll call someone else."

"Good. Hey, I saw some of those commercials. They were pretty good."

"Thank you."

"Liked the one with that lady and the bank teller and that kid. That one was pretty good. Solid. That kid was great."

Charlie had no idea what he was talking about.

"Yes, thank you," he said.

There was a silence.

"Hello?" Charlie asked.

"I'm going through security at O'Hare. Taking off my shoes. I'll call you right back." The line went dead.

Charlie hung up, not sure what to make of all that. He considered calling the Wizard, to let him know about the meeting, but decided instead to wait for Woods to call back. He stood up and did ten jumping jacks. He sat back down and took a sip of his soup. Then he folded his arms across his chest and watched the phone.

He was still sitting there twenty minutes later when Ned walked in. He was wearing a loud electric-blue blazer with wide, pointy lapels. A puffy white handkerchief was blooming from his breast pocket. He looked like a comic-book gangster, or an evil character in a Batman movie.

"Are you in the middle of something?" he asked.

"Waiting for a call."

"Mind if I join you?"

"I'm waiting for a call."

Ned sat down and gave Charlie a meaningful look.

Charlie finally asked, "What are you wearing?"

"Oh, this." Ned tugged on his lapels. "It was Jason's idea. How *not* to dress in an interview. Jason thought it would be funny. To be honest, I'm getting a bit tired of being his prank monkey." He crossed his legs and continued to stare at Charlie, a thin, rueful smile spreading across his face. "So strange," he said.

"What, your jacket?"

Ned recrossed his legs. His black socks were too short and a patch of hairy white leg emerged. "Karen leaving. So strange."

"Oh, yeah. She's going to regret her decision."

Ned's delicate smile vanished. "I said that to her a week ago, when she first told me they were talking. I warned her, but she took the job anyway."

"Maybe I should talk to her."

"Don't bother. Her mind is made up. Very made up."

"That's a shame, then."

"I'm in love with her, you know."

Charlie picked up the receiver, checked for a dial tone. "Are our phones okay?"

"I said, I'm in love with her."

"What? With who? You mean Karen?" He hung up the phone.

"Yes."

"You're not in love with her."

"I am."

"You just think you're in love with her."

"What's the difference?"

"She's not for you."

"Now, why would you say something like that?"

"Because she took that job. I'm sorry, but that says a lot about the kind of person she might be. To go into a situation like that, that's just stupidity, pure and simple." Charlie picked up the phone one more time, heard the dial tone, then hung up.

"She thinks she can handle him," Ned said. "She wants a job. She needs a job. I guess I can't blame her for that. She knows what she's getting into."

"That just makes it worse, if you ask me." Charlie sighed and pushed the phone away. It was apparent that Kevin F. Woods wasn't calling him right back. "Does she know how you feel about her?"

"I'm fairly confident she does, yes."

"Why do you say that? How do you know?"

Ned cleared this throat. "I sent her an e-mail last night. Late last night."

"An e-mail? About what?"

"Oh, nothing, really. I merely informed her that I am in love with her and would like to marry her."

Charlie paused. "You. Did. Not."

"I'm sorry to say that I did. I regret doing that now. I had been drinking wine. I don't drink much and I don't think I shall again for a while."

"Did she respond?"

"Oh, yes. She's moving to Torrance, California."

He studied Ned's pale face and urgent, sad eyes. He was a

cloying middle manager, the exact type of person Charlie had built a career, if not a life, around avoiding. And at that moment, he realized that the beaten man sitting across the desk from him, looking for all the world like an ad for an asthma medication, had somehow become a friend.

"Hey, listen." Charlie searched for something inspirational to say. His eyes fell upon a poster on the wall of an elderly, gray-haired man rock-climbing. "Defeat never comes to any man until he admits it," he said.

"Please don't quote our posters to me. Please don't do that. I hate those posters. They're all of old people. Jason bought them from the AARP when they relocated out of this building. He is so cheap."

Charlie looked around the room for another prop. He picked up the phone receiver. "Come on, call her. Come on."

"Oh, no." Ned shook his head. "It's too late, she's gone. She already left. I said good-bye to her at the elevator. She said she didn't want to have an emotional scene with everyone. She's probably on a plane now, jetting toward a new life. She's going house-hunting. We're just a memory now. I'm just a memory. And probably an unpleasant one."

Charlie put the receiver back. "She's gone? Already? I didn't even get a chance to say good-bye."

Ned nodded. "You liked her too, Charlie, I can tell."

"Sure I liked her. She was like a ray of sunshine in this place."

"Sunshine, yes. Very good. Yes. That's exactly what she was. Sunshine."

They both were quiet. Overhead, air from the vents rushed into the room.

"And how are things with your wife?" Ned asked.

"Oh. Actually, I'm starting to think things are going to be okay. We cleared some things up, had a good talk. We have some things to work on, though, but I think we're going to be okay. At least, I hope so."

"That's wonderful news. It really is," Ned said. "You have a wife, a child, a family. I, on the other hand, have nothing. To-

night I'll go home and fix myself a can of soup and maybe indulge myself with a stale piece of cheese, then stare at my
comic books. *Spider-Man, Superman, Batman.* Someone should
write a comic book about me—*Pathetic Man, The Adventures
Of.*" He closed his eyes. "I've wasted my life. My entire life. Not
just part of it, all of it. I have no one to love. I have nothing."

Charlie wracked his brain for something to say that could
cheer Ned up, bring him around. "Hey," he finally said, pointing. "You love your job."

"My job, yes," Ned said. He stood. "But I think it would be
nice to love something that can love you back. Don't you?"

Chapter Twenty-four

On the Monday before Thanksgiving, Donna arose early and made Charlie an impressive country breakfast of eggs, hash browns, bacon, and toast, food he loved but never ate because of concerns over cholesterol. He heard her downstairs in the kitchen clanging away, while he showered and packed. He was leaving on a midmorning flight for New York to meet Kevin F. Woods at the Marriott Marquis in Times Square. The Wizard had coordinated the details over the weekend and said things looked so positive that an offer was imminent.

When he entered the kitchen, Donna was pirouetting between the stove and the island, a long, baggy light blue robe hanging like a cape over her thin body. They had had sex the night before, ending a record nine-month period of zero contact. He had been lying in bed, reading the special college basketball issue of *Sports Illustrated*, when she walked out of the bathroom wearing a short red negligee that he had not seen in a very long while. He'd been happy merely to be back in their bed, and sex had not been on his mind.

He put the magazine down when he saw her standing at the foot of the bed. "Oh," he said.

They held on to each other for a while before Charlie began kissing her, starting at her neck and making his way down. Before long they were all arms and legs. Midway through, things got a bit out of hand and Charlie, in an understandable state of frenzy, almost fell off the bed. After they were done, they dozed and, to their mutual surprise, did it again an hour later.

"Hi," she said when he sat down at the kitchen table. She plopped a brown coffee mug in front of him and he watched her fill it. She looked like she was blooming that morning, her hair wild and mussed, her freckles proudly out in force.

"Sleep okay?" she asked.

"I was kind of busy." He reached for the coffee.

"Oh, yeah, I forgot about that." She went over to the stove.

"Ha, ha. Ha." He took a sip of his coffee. "Is Kyle up?"

"He's gone. He wanted to get to school early so he could run on the school track. He wants to build up his endurance."

"Run? He's running?"

She handed him a plate already filled with food. He liked his bacon undercooked and, even though it had been years since Donna had made him any, she had remembered.

"We have a treadmill in the basement. He should just run here. It's a great treadmill. I never use it anymore, it's just sitting there."

"He wanted to run with a friend."

He picked up a piece of bacon. "Matt?"

"Wrong sex." She arched her eyebrows up and down.

He stopped chewing. "You mean a girl? Who?"

"Her name is Jessica Weston."

"Jessica Weston." Charlie picked up another piece of perfect bacon. "Where'd she come from? What's her story?"

"Oh, she's cute." Donna sat down across from him at the island, holding her coffee cup in both hands. "He could do worse."

"That's hardly a ringing endorsement."

"He's sixteen. I don't think they're getting married anytime soon."

"Well, I hope he doesn't get too wrapped up with her. He has a lot going on. Basketball, school. He has to prioritize."

"Relax, Charlie. We have other things to worry about."

Charlie sighed. "Yeah, I guess we do."

She drank her coffee but continued to hold her cup close to her face, her elbows on the table. "I made an appointment for that counselor," she said. Just the top of her eyes were visible over the cup and she was speaking softly.

"Counselor? Oh, that's right. Her." He picked up his fork, Donna's eyes still on him. "Absolutely. We're going. A deal is a deal."

"We have to work on some things."

"Okay. You're right. We'll go whenever you want." He started in on his scrambled eggs. "Whenever you want. I'm serious."

"Also, I want to go back to work. I'm sick of sitting here alone all the time. I'm going to start looking. I've already called a few hospitals."

Charlie stopped eating. "Really? You sure?"

"Yes, really. I've been thinking about this a long time." She finished her coffee, then stood and returned to the stove, where she began scraping the bottom of the frying pan with a plastic spatula.

"Think you'll get this job?" she asked. She scraped harder at the pan.

"I have a good shot. I'm meeting the head guy tomorrow morning. We're working out together, if you can believe, at the hotel health club."

"Kind of weird."

"Yeah, a little."

"What are you going to do, watch each other lift weights?"

"I have no idea. The more I think about it, it's really weird. I hope we don't have to shower together."

"Do you really want this job?"

"It's a good job."

"Is it really?"

"Yeah." Charlie put his fork down. He knew where this was heading. "It's not going to be like before, I promise. It's not, okay? It's just a job now, it won't be my life."

Donna kept her back to him. "You can't just come and go, you know."

Charlie swallowed. "I know."

"We're just starting to get used to having you around here. *I'm* starting to get used to having you around here, and now you're going to be gone. You're going to disappear again. I don't know if this is good for us. For Kyle."

"Honey, listen, I need a job. I can't just stay home and go to basketball games. It pays a lot."

"Is there going to be a lot of travel? Are you going to be gone?"

Charlie was quiet. "There's some travel," was all he said.

She kept scraping, though Charlie knew there couldn't be anything left on that pan. "You're going to start getting sick again and going to all those doctors and getting tested for everything."

"It's not going to be that way anymore. It's not. I'm done striving. Now I just want to hold on, make money. We need money. My deal ends soon. Then the money stops. This job just fell in my lap. I'm lucky. Really lucky. There's people at the outplacement place who've been out for years. One guy, Bradley, he's been out two years. Can you imagine that, two years? I haven't been out three months."

"I don't want it to be like it was before, that's all. I can't live like that. It doesn't make sense. We don't need to make that much money."

Charlie pushed his plate away, went over to the stove, and held Donna from behind. "Let me just give this a shot, check it out, and we'll take it from there. I have to check this out. I would be crazy not to. Everything's going to be fine."

"You really think so?"

"Everything's going to be all right," Charlie said again, as convincingly as he could.

315

On the cab ride to the airport, he called Ned. His conversation with Donna and the bleak, rainy November day had once again raised his doubts. He was just getting things right at home and now here he was heading off again to take a job that could put him right back to where he had been: traveling, working weekends, checking e-mail at midnight. *Consumed.* He decided that he needed a dose of Ned's sunshine to chase away the fast-forming clouds.

Ned picked up on the first ring. "Charlie?" He sounded shocked.

"Yeah, it's me. What's wrong?"

"I wasn't expecting you. I thought you were going to New York."

"I'm on my way to the airport. Just thought I'd call for some last-minute advice. Thought maybe we could role-play."

Ned was quiet.

"Hello? Are you there?"

"I can't talk right now. I'm busy. I need to finish something for Jason."

"Forget him. You know, I was looking at his suit the other day. He's totally off-the-rack."

"I really have to run."

"Hey! I'm still a Category B. B-plus. You're required to talk to me. You're legally bound. I need a charisma jump-start. How many times do you think I should wink tomorrow?"

"I have to go now. Good luck, though, really good luck."

Charlie was disappointed. He had assumed that Ned would prattle on until he at least got to the airport. "All right, I'll call you later, I guess."

"Charlie?"

"Yeah?"

Ned paused. "I just want to say that I regard you as my friend. And I hope that you do too. I've always tried to treat you fairly. I try to treat everyone fairly."

Charlie waited for Ned to say something else, but he didn't. He just hung up.

When he reached O'Hare, he had an immediate sense of disorientation, if not an official out-of-body experience. He hadn't stepped foot in an airport in more than two months and was overwhelmed by the noise and rush, the controlled chaos that greeted him. Mondays and Fridays are always the worst times to travel, and this particular Monday, thanks in part to the rain and approaching Thanksgiving holiday, things were crazier than usual. The lines at the ticket counter, newsstands, and security stretched endlessly and the undercurrent of impatience and frustration was palpable.

After nearly thirty years of travel, Charlie had grown oblivious to airports: LAX, LaGuardia, Reagan, Dallas/Fort Worth, Heathrow, were all indistinguishable backgrounds, white noise. If he wasn't checking his BlackBerry or cradling his cell phone to his ear, he was lost in conversation with a client or colleague. With those buffers gone, he was left naked to the environment.

As he made his way to the gate, he took the scene in with the eyes and ears of a newly arriving immigrant. It might very well have been just his mood, but everyone seemed stressed and exhausted as they made their way through the terminals, dragging their luggage on wheels behind them, their faces stoic, their eyes either flat or on fire. Occasionally he would see small children with parents, explosions of color and energy, walking excitedly past. But everything else was muted, gray.

He was officially light-headed as he slowly made his way through the terminal, his head down. When he got to his gate, he found it crowded; all the seats were taken and more than a few people were standing, waiting for the flight to be called. Most of the travelers seemed downright depressed, while others looked like hostile schoolyard bullies, their eyes narrow, their jaws clenched, as they circled the area searching for precious electrical outlets for their laptops. Charlie stood off in the corner and leaned against a wall and waited.

His flight was more than an hour late and by the time he boarded he was feeling decidedly tense. He had traveled first-class for years, so it was a shock to find himself back in coach. Xanon had made the arrangements and apparently they worked on a budget. Had Charlie known this, he would have used his own miles to upgrade. He hadn't bothered to check his ticket, so he was stuck.

He took his seat on the aisle and settled in next to a diminutive older man wearing a brown sports coat and matching tie with a knot the size of a fist. He smiled eagerly at Charlie when the plane took off.

"Boy, isn't flying something?" he asked when they were airborne.

Charlie was trying to find a comfortable position in his cheap seat when the man nudged him with an elbow.

"Going or coming?" he asked.

"Going."

"I'm coming home," he said.

Charlie nodded. Being back on an airplane, his second home for years, had an unexpected settling effect. His head cleared. He took out the current annual report from Xanon, as well as an old copy of *The New Yorker* from his briefcase. He considered the annual report, then put it down—he simply could not read anything more about this company—and began to skim the magazine.

After a few minutes, the man turned and asked, "Do you like that magazine?"

"Excuse me? What?"

"I've never read that magazine," the man said. "You would think I might, because I'm from New York, but I never do."

Since he did not want to encourage conversation, Charlie said nothing to this. He stared blankly at the man, then returned to his magazine.

"This is only the second time I've ever flown. Do you fly often?"

"Yes."

"What line of work are you in? Sales? People in sales seem to fly a lot."

Charlie kept his eyes on the magazine. "Advertising."

"My, that must be interesting."

"It's very interesting." Charlie flipped through the pages of *The New Yorker*. He stopped when he came across a small ad near the back: *The Incredible Swedish Smart Chair*.

They flew for a while. Charlie began to think that he was in the clear when the man said, "I'm a fireman from Queens. Used to be one, I should say. I'm retired. I was visiting my daughter in Chicago. I liked Chicago."

Charlie's heart sank. There was a code of silence in first-class that apparently did not apply in coach. Since he didn't want to be overtly rude—the man seemed nice enough—Charlie said, "I'm glad you liked it."

"Say, do you think they'll feed us on this flight?"

Charlie glanced up and down the aisle and saw the drink cart approaching. "I don't think they feed us . . ." He paused and bitterly added, "Back here."

"That's too bad. I'm a little hungry. Say, do you make commercials?"

Charlie rubbed his sinuses. "Yes."

The man said, "You know what my favorite commercials were? The one with all the celebrities wearing the capes. They were flying around. They used to be on all the time. You know the ones? A few years back?"

Charlie ceased his massage in mid-rub and finally looked over at the man. "What are you talking about? You mean"—he stopped, then said, "the Bagel Man commercials?"

"Yes." The man snapped his finger and smiled. "They were about bagels, and those delis, yes. They were so funny. Did you like those commercials too?"

"I made them."

The man was astonished. His mouth dropped wide open. "You did not."

"I did so."

"Why, I feel like I'm sitting next to a celebrity!"

"I wouldn't go that far." Charlie closed the magazine. He noticed that the drink cart was upon them.

"Hey," he said. "Can I buy you a drink?"

It turned out that Rob Rosenfeld, the intelligent, insightful retired fireman from Queens in New York, was a fine seat com-
panion. He was sincere, quiet, and more than happy to hear
Charlie discuss his career and life. Rob seemed particularly
interested in Charlie's family and was suitably impressed by
Kyle's basketball exploits.

"Twenty-four points. You must be very proud," he said.

"Twenty-six," Charlie said. He finished his first drink. "And
yes, I am."

"Are you two very close?"

"A little. Somewhat. He's a teenager now, so, you know, it's
tough."

Rob smiled wistfully. "I always wanted a son. But I have
three daughters."

"Daughters are nice too, I'm sure."

Charlie talked some more about Kyle and his chances of attending a major college on a basketball scholarship, then went
to the bathroom. When he returned, Rob was in the process of
buying two more bourbons on the rocks.

"My treat this time," he said, wagging a finger at Charlie.

"Well, then make it a double," Charlie said to the flight at-
tendant.

He reclined his seat. The cabin was relatively quiet, most
passengers either dozing or reading. The man across the aisle
stared transfixed at an Excel chart on his laptop. Charlie sipped
his drink and marveled again at that wonderful halting bite
bourbon makes in the back of your throat, before sliding down
to warm your innards.

"So," Rob said, "are you going to New York to make a new
commercial?" His face was flushed and his wispy gray hair
spread out in all directions.

Charlie hesitated. "Can you keep a secret, Bob?"

"Rob," he said. He smiled. "Sure I can. People say I'm good
at that."

"I'm going for a job interview. I'm ..." He hesitated again

because the next words still hurt. He whispered, "I'm, well, I'm unemployed."

"I'm sorry?" Rob leaned in closer, "I couldn't . . ."

Charlie leaned in close and whispered again in Rob's ear. "I'm out of work."

This confession took a minute to sink in. When it did, Rob looked very thoughtful. "You mean you don't have a job?" he asked.

"Yes." Charlie took a long swallow of his drink. "Rob," he said, "can you keep another secret?"

"Yes, I think so."

"I'm conflicted."

Rob looked confused. "Conflicted? Well, I get that way. Raisin Bran sometimes helps. Juice too."

"No. I mean, I'm not so sure I even want this job. I don't know if it's right for me."

"Oh. Well, why not?"

"I think it will be difficult. I think I'll be gone a lot too."

"Gone a lot? Where will you be? New York?"

"Omaha, and in Montana, and in Chile, maybe Australia. Oklahoma, maybe. That's where our customers are. They're ranchers and farmers. Plus, I have some concerns about my boss, the guy who would be my boss."

"Concerns? What kind of concerns?"

"He looks like John Wayne."

"John Wayne? The actor John Wayne?"

"Yes. Him."

"Why would that be so bad? I enjoyed his movies. John Wayne's not so bad."

"Would you want to work for John Wayne? Think about it. Would you? The Duke?"

"Work for the Duke." Rob stared at his drink. "He could be a pretty tough customer. I remember him in *The Green Berets*. And all those cowboy movies, those Westerns. He was tough. I remember thinking that."

"See what I'm saying?"

"Then why are you going?"

"I need a job. I need money. I may not get another offer. I know people who've been looking for work for two years. I'm fifty years old. This job pays a lot. I just need a job."

"Maybe you should think things over. Sleep on it. You might get other chances."

"Maybe I won't."

Rob fooled with his mouth, sucking on his lips. "Times are tough, that's all you read about. So I guess a man has to do what he has to do, then. A man has to feed his family," he said.

"That's what I'm thinking. Can I ask you a question? Did you like your job? Being a fireman, I mean?"

"I liked the people, the other firemen. I was the shortest one in our firehouse, so they always looked after me."

"But did you like the work?"

"You mean putting out the fires? Well," Rob said, his eyebrows knotted. "At first, oh, sure. But after a while, to be perfectly frank, I didn't. The smoke, the noise. I always came home wet. I can't say that I did, no." He picked up his drink. "Boy, and I spent forty years doing it. I regret that," he said wistfully.

Charlie looked down at his own drink, and jiggled the ice in his plastic cup. Why was he going to New York? John Wayne? Cattle? Hogs too? Exactly what was he doing? He glanced around the cabin. The plane seemed darker now and he thought he could hear every single passenger on board breathing.

When he got to the hotel, he took a hot shower, the first step in the sobering-up process. Drinking on the flight had been foolish, he knew, but it wasn't even four o'clock and he had plenty of time to clear his head and go to sleep unencumbered.

After his shower, he called home. That's when Donna told him that Kyle had broken his ankle in practice and would miss most of the season.

"Jesus Christ! What?"

This news, coupled with his raging indecision about the job

(and the three bourbons on the flight), proved too much. He lost it.

"Are you kidding me?" He was sitting naked on the edge of the bed when he yelled this.

"Settle down. He's okay. He's fine."

"Did you take him to the hospital?"

"Yes."

"What did they say?"

"It's the same one he broke last year. He shouldn't play for three months. But he might be able to make the state playoffs, if they make it that far."

"Three months. Jesus! What was he doing? Did someone push him or trip him? Is he there?"

"He's sitting right here."

"Put him on."

There was a rustling on the other end of the line, then Kyle said, "Dad?"

"Hey, buddy. God, I can't believe it. What happened? Did someone push you, or . . . or trip you, or what? Be honest. We can call your uncle Sean. He's a lawyer."

"No, I came down on it wrong. Why are you yelling?"

Charlie stood up and began pacing the room. "Are you hurt? Are you in pain?"

"No, I'm okay."

"When I get home, we'll go to a specialist. Where did you go? What hospital?"

"Um, we went to the one here."

"Wilton Memorial? Forget that place. Forget it. It's rinky-dink. We'll take you downtown to Northwestern. I'll set it up. I'll make a few calls."

"It was okay."

"Listen, don't worry about a thing. I'm going to come home as soon as I can, okay? Okay? I'm going to take care of every-thing. All right? Are you sure you're not in pain? I don't want you in pain, okay? You'd tell me if you're in pain, right? Noth-ing wrong with saying it hurts. I'm always telling people I hurt and half the time I'm fine."

"I'm not in pain."

Charlie was breathing too fast and felt dizzy. Kyle, his son who still had basketball posters on his wall, was hurt and he was in another goddamn hotel room. "Are you sure you're okay?"

"Yeah."

"Okay, because . . . because you know I love you. You know that, don't you? You know that, right? I love you more than anything else! You're my son and I love you!"

There was a long pause. "Yeah," he said.

Donna got back on the line. "Are you all right?"

Charlie's heart and mind raced. "Are you sure he's okay? Did they take X-rays? An MRI? What?"

"It's just a broken ankle. Just relax. He's going to be fine. What's wrong with you?"

"Who was the doctor? What's his name?"

"I don't know. He was in the emergency room. He was an ER doctor. Bill. His name was Bill Sarantos."

"Never heard of him. And I know all the ER doctors. Listen, is he on crutches?"

"Yes."

"Jesus! Crutches! Kyle is on crutches!"

"Calm down and stop yelling. Are you okay?"

Charlie caught a glimpse of himself in the mirror behind the desk. He was naked and deranged, never a good combination. He took a deep breath. "I'm all right. I'm fine. I'm just tense, that's all. I haven't traveled in a while. I'm sorry. I'm just . . . this job, everything. Is he okay, mood-wise? I mean, this has got to be a real bummer for him. It has to be. How is he taking it?"

"He's fine. I have to go. Jessica just came over with a pizza."

"Who? You mean that girl? What's she doing there? Keep an eye on her. What's her last name again? I want to Google her, check her out."

"Good luck tomorrow. Have a good workout or whatever."

"Are you sure he's okay?" Charlie asked, but she was gone.

After the call, he lay in bed, eyes on the ceiling, mind on fire: Kyle, the job, Donna. Then everything stopped and just like that clarity finally found him. In an instant, he knew what he had to do, was supposed to do, wanted to do.

IT CAN BE DONE . . . AND NOW!

He got dressed, packed his bag, and left the room. If he hurried, he might be able to catch the six o'clock from LaGuardia.

He was standing by the elevator doors, wondering if he had packed any aspirin, when he saw him, a ghost at first, tall and ambling in the shadows. Initially, he didn't recognize him; the hallway was dim, plus he was so out of context. But as he approached, Charlie saw who it was.

"Bradley?"

Bradley stopped about ten feet short of Charlie, then without saying a word turned on his heels and headed back down the hallway, walking fast.

Charlie followed. "Bradley? What are you doing here? Bradley?" Charlie caught him and put a hand on his shoulder. "Wait a minute! What the hell are you doing here?"

Bradley turned. "I can't believe they put us on the same floor." His face was expressionless.

"What are you talking about? What are you doing here?" But then, of course, Charlie knew. "Xanon," he said. "You're here for Xanon, aren't you? You're interviewing with them."

Bradley resumed walking and Charlie pursued him. His anger was rising. He found Bradley's presence a terrible betrayal. "You're interviewing for the same job I am, aren't you? You're meeting Woods. That's why Ned was acting so weird and everything. He knew about this."

Bradley kept walking.

"Answer me!" Charlie tried grabbing him by the shoulder again, but Bradley shrugged him off and continued again down the hall.

"At least say something!" Charlie said. He wasn't quite yelling, but he was talking loud. "You knew I was going for this job. And you just sat there and said nothing. You even tried to talk me out of it. You said it's a strange company. You said that!"

Bradley finally whirled around and faced him. Up until that moment, Charlie had not fully appreciated the fact that he was six-foot-four and once played in the Cotton Bowl for the Texas Longhorns. "You go to hell," Bradley said. "This is my job. *My* job, you understand? I've been talking to them for months. Now you come along at the last second and steal it from me. You have no right to do this, no right!"

"You should have at least told me! I told you," Charlie said. "You lied to me. You sat there and looked me right in the eye and lied to me. You're a damn liar!"

"And you're a goddamn asshole who never shuts up!" Bradley pushed Charlie against the wall. "I've been out of work two years! *Two* years! Do you have any idea what that's like? Any fucking idea at all?" Bradley yelled. "I'm eating canned food now. *Canned food!* I used to make three hundred grand a year and I'm eating goddamn fruit cocktail!"

"That's not the point. The point is that I thought we were friends. We saw each other every day! You could have told me after I told you. You just sat there."

He was inches from Bradley and when he wagged a finger in his face in an attempt to make a final point, he accidentally brushed his nose. This apparently infuriated Bradley and he responded by hitting Charlie square in the jaw. The blow knocked the prosthesis out of his mouth and it landed silently on the carpet like a dead moth.

Charlie initially didn't feel any pain, then all of a sudden he did. It was worse than the fall down the stairs, worse than the punch from the plumber. He yelled and closed his eyes. Then he instinctively lunged toward Bradley, grabbing hold of his throat. Bradley, in turn, grabbed Charlie's throat.

They tumbled to the floor, two middle-aged men in sports coats choking each other. Just as Charlie was beginning to think he might have the upper hand—Bradley's eyes were bulging—Bradley brought his head down onto Charlie's face. Things then went black.

When Charlie regained consciousness a few seconds later, he heard Bradley gasping for air. "I couldn't breathe. You were crushing my windpipe." He was sitting against the wall, rubbing his throat, his face red.

Charlie sat up. The pain in his jaw was still amazingly cold and intense. He let out a low moan and searched for his prosthesis, groping the floor with his hands. When he found it, he held it up to the light to check for damage.

"What the hell is that?" Bradley asked. "Your tooth?"

Charlie ignored him and tried to put it back in his mouth. It was bent and wouldn't fit.

A door opened down the hall and a middle-aged woman wearing a short white robe poked her head out and glowered at them.

"Get back in your room," Bradley said.

"What is going on out here?" she asked.

"Go on! Get back in your goddamn room," he yelled. She shut the door.

Bradley closed his eyes and massaged his throat. He looked old and shrunken, like a dying hound dog. Charlie attempted to stand, but felt the hallway spin and decided to stay on the floor.

They sat for a few minutes, until Bradley said, "I had a dream last night. I dreamt that I was back working. It was back in the old days. Ten, twenty years ago. Maggie was my secretary. Maggie. I was back at the bank. I remember typing something on a typewriter. Then I was going to a meeting and I was looking for my cell phone, and Maggie, she said, 'We don't have cell phones.' I woke up with a big-ass smile on my face. Remember how it used to be, Charlie? No cell phones, no computers, no e-mail? None of that? Your secretary handing you your messages? Food on the flight out? Food you didn't have to pay for? You did a good job and you kept your job? Jesus Christ, I don't know what happened."

"You got old," Charlie said. "We both did."

"All I wanted to do was keep my life. That's all I wanted. I just wanted to keep my life. Nothing more. They took it away. All the time you think you have control, but you don't have anything. You got nothing."

Charlie crawled over to the opposite wall and sat up against it. They were both still breathing hard.

"I know you think you have it tough, but you don't," Bradley continued. "You have no idea. I can't take out another mortgage on my house. I'm behind on my car lease. My wife left me last summer. You know what she said to me? You know what she said? She said, 'I didn't sign on for this.' Broad is twenty years younger than me. Never should have left Maureen, my first wife. Never."

Charlie carefully pushed himself up to a standing position. He no longer was all that interested in what Bradley had to say. He just wanted to call Donna and die peacefully with her on the other end of the line.

"I was afraid they might put us in the same hotel. I asked Preston to find out."

"The Wizard? He was recruiting you?"

"Yeah. Yeah, why?"

Charlie actually laughed, shook his head. "Preston. Unbelievable. Jesus, everyone was in on it."

"I should have checked out and gone home," Bradley said. "But they were paying for another night, the room, and, hell, I didn't want to go home. Why would I want to go home? I don't even have cable anymore."

"It's not easy for me either," Charlie said.

Bradley waved this away. "You're going to be okay and you know it. You're smart, creative, funny. Quick on your feet. You've barely been out and you're already getting close. You're going to be fine. People like you are always fine. I'm a big old dumb-ass. I'm fifty-eight. This is my last chance."

Charlie didn't say anything. He ran a finger over the front gums of his mouth.

Bradley continued, "My interview was this afternoon. It went all right. He's an intense son of a bitch."

Charlie now felt steady enough to walk. He started slowly down the hall, one foot after the other.

"Hey, Charlie, you all right?"

"Yeah."

"You sure? Where are you going? Maybe we should get a drink and talk about it."

"I'm done with drinks. I'm done with everything. I'm going home. The job is yours. I don't want it. Good luck."

"What?"

"I don't want it," Charlie said again. He kept walking. "I don't want that anymore."

When he got home, he had to ring the bell, because he had forgotten his key and the front door, for some reason, was locked. He had to ring it twice before a pretty teenage girl answered. When she saw him, she gasped and put her hand up to her mouth. By then Charlie was used to, if not expecting, this reaction. He had gotten so many stares and double-takes at the airport and during the flight home that they no longer had any impact. He nodded hello, smiled evilly to reveal his teeth, and said, "Trick or treat."

"What?" The girl looked terrified.

"I'm sorry. I'm Mr. Baker." He walked inside. "I bet you're Jessica. I bet you're here to see Kyle."

"Yes."

Charlie nodded and looked around the hallway. "Where's my wife? Mrs. Baker."

"She's at the grocery store. We were going to make brownies, so she had to get some stuff."

"Brownies? Now? What time is it?"

"About nine-thirty."

Charlie nodded. "Where's Kyle?"

"He's upstairs sleeping. Were you in an accident?"

"Not really." He walked into the kitchen and Jessica followed. There was some coffee in the pot and he swirled it and, even though it was cold, he poured himself a cup and took a sip. He wanted to go up and see Kyle, but didn't want to wake him.

"Do you know when Mrs. Baker will be home?" he asked.

"Pretty soon, I think." Jessica was a doll, with large blue eyes and a sweet, whispery voice. Charlie stared at her and, for the hell of it, smiled again. She backed away. "I think I'm going to go wait for Mrs. Baker outside," she said.

"Tell you what, why don't I go outside and wait for her and you stay inside?"

"Oh, okay," she said. He put the coffee cup on the counter and headed toward the back door. It was then that he noticed his telescope. It was set up in the reading nook, overlooking the yard.

"What's that doing out?" he asked Jessica.

"Kyle and I were going to look at the stars."

He walked over, picked up the telescope, and went outside.

The air was cold, but he refused to feel it. He turned his face up to the sky and let the November wind blow full against his beaten face. His head ached some, but not nearly as badly as before. He was mostly exhausted.

He dragged a deck chair to the middle of the yard and set up the telescope. Then he sat and took in the night. The trees were barren now, their branches lonely and twisted, but the sky had a sprinkling of stars. He slid down low and studied them.

"Charlie?" Donna was standing on the deck by the back door, her arms folded in front of her. She was wearing an oversized winter coat and had it zipped all the way up.

"Are those brownies done yet?" Charlie asked. He turned around and faced her.

"They're for tomorrow," she said. She made her way over to Charlie, and gasped like Jessica when she got close. "Oh, my God! What happened?"

"Grab a chair," Charlie said.

Donna listened quietly as he filled her in on his great adventure. She was especially sympathetic when he got to the part about Bradley smashing his head onto Charlie's face.

"Head-butts are the worst," she said. "I used to hate when my brothers did that to me."

"That was my very first one," he said. "You know, between falling, the plumber, and now this, I'm beginning to feel like a stuntman."

She laughed and they listened to the wind. Donna zipped

the parka all the way up to her chin and stuffed her hands into the pockets.

"Aren't you cold?" she asked.

"No. The wind is numbing my body."

"Do you want to go to the hospital?"

"I'm fine. I took about twelve aspirin. I'll start screaming when they wear off."

"Maybe we should go."

"I'm okay."

"You sure?"

"I'm tired of hospitals. I'm tired of doctors. I'm never seeing another doctor. Ever. I'm throwing my stupid humidifier out too. I want everything gone. Everything. And start calling me Charles from now on. No more Charlie, I'm Charles Baker. Or Chuck. I'm starting over. I'm Chuck. I'm Chuck Baker. That's all I will answer to."

"Okay. Chuck."

He leaned forward and tried to look through the telescope, but it was out of focus and he didn't have the knowledge or energy to adjust it. He sat back again.

"So, what's going to happen now?" Donna asked. "With the job, I mean?"

"I don't want that job. I don't want to do that anymore. I don't know what I want to do. But I know I don't want to live in airports and hotels and go to Omaha and Chile and stare at my goddamn BlackBerry all day and talk about cows and hog sex. And I don't want to work for a big company anymore either."

Donna sighed, relieved. She slipped her hand into his. "I think that's a good decision."

"We'll see." Charlie took a deep breath. "How's Kyle?"

"How do you think he's doing?"

He glanced back at the house. "Yeah, she's pretty cute. Is she still here?"

"She just left."

He looked back up at the sky. "Good for him. Maybe they'll get married and support us."

Donna leaned over and peered into the telescope. "Do you ever use this?" She sat back.

"Nope. I don't know how. I have all these things I can't use. I'm worthless."

They sat there, hand in hand in the cold night, husband and wife. The stars started to slip away, obscured by clouds. There were only a handful now, straight overhead.

"Hey, did you ever get those pictures I sent you? Of us? I sent them to you in the motel in Maine. You never said anything."

"I got them, all right," she said. "Very effective. You should be in advertising."

"You hiring?" He carefully touched the bump on his forehead. "I don't know what I'm going to do," he said again.

"We'll be okay."

"You really think so?"

"Yes." She squeezed his hand. "Hey, come on, cheer up, you're the famous Charlie Baker. Everyone loves you. Everyone knows you. You're famous. You've won awards. You met Elton John, Madonna, Bob Dole."

"The talking hamster."

"The talking hamster."

"I've got to figure something out soon."

"So what's the worst that can happen to us?" Donna asked. "We have to quit the stupid country club? We have to get a smaller TV? We're going to starve? We're going to be homeless? Come on. We're going to be okay. Just relax, it's almost Thanksgiving."

"Thanksgiving."

She squeezed his hand tighter and peered up at the sky. "You're a star, Charlie," she said. "I knew that when I first saw you onstage in *Music Man*. When you sang 'Marian the Librarian.' I knew I was going to meet you and marry you. I set my sights on you. You were wearing the white suit and that hat, that goofy straw hat. The way you danced and sang like that. My brothers thought you were crazy. But not me, I was sixteen years old and I knew back then that Charlie Baker was the guy for me."

He turned to face her. Her hair was flying all over the place and he watched as she tried to catch it and bunch it up. "You saw that play? You were there?" he asked. "I thought you said you weren't."

"I was there," she said. She let her hair blow free and squeezed his hand one more time. "I was always there."

Chapter Twenty-five

A Final Update:
A man's life, I believe, I have concluded, is really a simple process. Do the best you can. Be nice. Be fair. Be
honest. Love and be loved. Most times, though, we
manage to muck it up. We get off course, lose perspective, get greedy, make poor choices. Along the way, we
blame other people, our parents, our friends, our wives,
our bosses, our children, but in the end, disease notwithstanding, we usually get what we deserve.

   To all my friends and comrades in the business, I
promise not to bother you with any more e-mails or
inane updates. I will make my own way and prevail. I
just wanted to say that I am sorry if, over the course of
our careers, I was rude or mistreated you. It was never
my intention to be a lout. If I was, I apologize. I also
wish you all well and look forward to the next time our
paths cross.
Sincerely,
C. Baker

He sent out this last update on the Wednesday after Thanksgiving. He had slipped unnoticed into Rogers & Newman late in the afternoon and, finding Office A unoccupied, decided to write a final installment of his short-lived newsletter at the new desk by the window, while watching the lake fade to black. The sentiments he expressed were genuine, the result of a series of vivid epiphanies he had experienced over the long Thanksgiving weekend, a weekend he had spent convalescing with his son.

When he was finished with the installment, he had a sense of closure, if not peace. He still needed a job, but in order to find the right one, he knew he needed a fresh start.

He was about to check a new Web site for nonprofit jobs when Ned walked by. He stopped in the doorway.

"What?" He gazed at Charlie like he was Christ freshly risen.

"Hello, Ned."

Ned inched into the office, glancing over his shoulder as he approached. "Charlie?" His look of amazement grew, his eyes wide, his eyebrows pushing up against his bangs.

"I know. I'll move back to a cube." Charlie started to stand.

"No, no, no, please, sit. Please. I don't care. Sit. Absolutely."

Charlie sat back down, then allowed Ned to stare at him some more.

"Your face."

"I'm fine." He didn't elaborate and Ned surprisingly didn't ask any follow-up questions. He was visibly nervous.

"I'm so surprised to find you here. I wasn't expecting this." He continued to gawk.

"Can you quit with the staring?"

"I'm sorry. I don't mean to." He shut the door, stepped farther into the office, and swallowed. "We have to talk, I think."

Charlie politely folded his hands and placed them on top of the desk. He suspected an explanation, maybe an apology of sorts, was coming.

Ned cleared his throat and began talking, his words a torrent. "I know, or I should say I fear, what you must think about me, but on my word, I didn't know anything about Bradley and that job. I had no idea you two were going for the same position. Absolutely no idea whatsoever. He told me he was talking to some people at a local hospital. If I had known the truth, I would have persuaded Bradley to tell you. I think it would have been fair, since he apparently knew you were going for the position."

Charlie nodded. "Continue."

"He told me the truth on Sunday night, right before he left for New York. It put me in an awkward, very, very awkward position because of my friendship with you and my friendship with him. He swore me to secrecy. Professionally, I really couldn't have told you anyway, I suppose. I mean, that would have been overstepping my bounds. But I would have insisted he told you."

Charlie benevolently focused on his folded hands and remained silent. He was deriving a small amount of pleasure making Ned squirm. Finally, when Ned looked like he might fall to his knees, he said, "I absolve you."

Ned's face relaxed.

Charlie made the sign of the cross. "Say Three Hail Marys and buy me lunch."

"Really?"

"It's not your fault anyway. You're right, you probably couldn't tell me."

"Well, that's very generous of you. I haven't felt right since you left and I was sure you weren't going to come back. I was afraid you had enough of everything. I thought you would disappear like everyone else."

"You underestimated me."

"Yes, apparently I did." He stepped closer to the desk and squinted. "Your tooth? Did you lose another one?"

Charlie smiled. "Same one. I'm getting another imposter tomorrow. It's a long story. I'll tell you later."

"I see. Well, I'm sorry things didn't work out for you at Xanon. I really am. Though, on the other hand, I am happy for Bradley."

"Did he get the job?"

Ned looked crestfallen. "Oh, no, you didn't know?" He closed his eyes and shook his head. "My God, I can't do anything right."

"I figured he did. Good for him. Bradley's back out there."

"You're keeping a very good attitude."

"I'm on painkillers."

"I see. Oh, are you being facetious?"

"I am." Charlie drummed the top of the desk with his index fingers. "Anyway, it looks like I'm going to be here for a while. Do you want me to move or what? I can if you want, I don't care."

"No, no. Stay here. Stay here. This is your office, as far as I'm concerned, for as long as you want."

"Really?"

"Definitely. At least for the rest of the day."

Charlie glanced at his watch. "It's four o'clock."

"That's the best I can do."

"All right. Mine for a whole hour." Charlie swiveled all the way around in his chair, making a complete circle. When he finished, he drummed the desk again. "This is new," he said.

"Yes," Ned said. He whispered loudly, "I believe something happened to the old one."

Donna was in the kitchen watching TV when he got home. He could hear it blaring from the front foyer. He dropped his briefcase by the closet, shed his overcoat, and then stuck his head in to say hello.

"I'm here."

"Oh, hi." She was leaning against the counter, chewing on a fingernail, engrossed in something on the small flip-down screen. He scanned the kitchen and saw a pot of water on the stove.

"What are we having?"

"Spaghetti." She kept her back to him.

"What are you watching?"

"Nothing. Something about dreams. Interpreting them. It's stupid." She remained transfixed, though, still biting her nails. "You better hurry," she said over her shoulder. "He's been waiting. You better go."

"Where is he?"

"In the living room. We're going to eat soon, though, so learn fast."

"I'll try."

He found Kyle already seated at the piano, leafing through some sheet music. Matt was sprawled on the couch nearby, sleeping with one arm tossed over his face, his huge stocking feet hanging over the edge.

"What's he doing here?"

Kyle didn't even bother to look over at Matt. He continued to study the music. "Sleeping."

"Are you sure he's alive?"

"Oh, yeah. I'm positive he is." Kyle glanced up at Charlie. He had a baseball cap on backward and was wearing Charlie's blue and gold Wilton Lions sweatshirt. "You ready to do this?"

"Absolutely."

Kyle scooted over, making room for his father on the bench.

"How's the foot?" Charlie asked. "I mean ankle?"

"It's okay. Ready?"

"Wait, let me get loose." Charlie flexed his fingers a few times. "Okay. What do we do first?"

Kyle looked thoughtful "I don't know. I guess we'll start with some simple chords. You know, the basics."

"The basics." Charlie nodded. "Okay. Sounds like a good place to start." Then he raised his hands and held them gingerly over the keys, ready for whatever came next.

Acknowledgments

Many thanks to the following people who made this book possible: my agent, Lynn Franklin, for her always steady hand and vision, as well as her confidence in me; my editor, Nichole Argyres, for her wonderful talent and skill in taking this book where it needed to go; Gordon Mennenga, for reading through those always important first drafts; Sally Richardson and Matt Baldacci, for their terrific enthusiasm and belief in the book; Jonni Hegenderfer, who graciously allows her business partner to pursue other interests; Anne, my wife, for her love, support, and patience; and my boys—Johnny, Mikey, and Andrew—for making me laugh (almost) every day.